EVE BONHAM

Madness Lies
and other Stories

DRYAD BOOKS

© Eve Bonham 2008
Madness Lies and other Stories

ISBN : 978-0-9559315-0-5

First Published by Dryad Books in 2008
Rathmore House
Spring Road
Lymington
Hampshire SO41 3SQ

E-mail: dryadbooks@gmail.com

A CIP catalogue record of this book
can be obtained from the British Library.

Cover Photograph: Jess Bonham
Cover Design: Marcus Martell
Book Design and Typesetting: Michael Walsh

Printed and bound in Great Britain by
RPM Print & Design
2-3 Spur Road
Chichester
West Sussex
PO19 8PR

For Michael

Illustrations:

Illustrations on title pages of the stories
Ginkgo, Mirror Image, Requital, and Scars
by Joanna Barringer.
Illustrations on title pages of the other
stories by the author.

Acknowledgements:

I would like to thank my family: Michael, Julie and Jack for
their help, loving support and patience. My thanks also go
to Joanna Barringer, Jess Bonham, Glenda Goddard, Diane
Holt, Kaye Ivett and Richard Waterhouse.

CONTENTS

Madness Lies 1

Ginkgo 21

Hotei 33

Evanescence..51

Mirror Image..81

Fly Baby 97

Scars..117

Noise...129

Dragon's Mouth..153

Requital..165

Sauce 183

Blind Love 195

Poste Restante..225

Soul Trader 251

Poker Faces..265

Wet Floor 285

MADNESS LIES

Madness Lies

King Lear: "O! That way madness lies."

William Shakespeare

I was in a taxi the other day. The driver was the friendly talkative type, as opposed to the taciturn dour sort that I occasionally encounter. I always address questions to cab drivers – they are often bored and usually happy to chat with their passengers about the local area and in particular their own lives. They rarely show much interest in my life, and that suits me just fine.

I often enquire of a taxi driver as to whether he has always driven a taxi. The answer is always in the negative and usually elicits a catalogue of fascinating jobs that have preceded their current occupation. I have been driven by former army cooks, ships' stokers, nurses, waiters, failed entrepreneurs, retired civil servants and even an ex-accountant. One admitted cheerfully that he had been in prison; another lied outrageously that he had been a cat burglar. Not infrequently I discover that my driver is an immigrant who says he used to be a doctor, teacher or some other professional in his country of origin but is reduced to driving a taxi in his country of adoption. I don't mind whether this is all true or not, because the reasons why people do not tell the truth make for interesting conjectures, and often lies are more amusing and less mundane than facts. After all, one can create and embellish a lie but truthfulness produces only the plain unvarnished truth. The old adage of never spoiling a good story for the sake of truth is apposite. Though, to argue the other case, I know too that truth is often stranger than fiction.

On this particular occasion I was being driven across an English county and I was a willing taxi captive for about an hour. I usually sit in the front passenger seat as this makes for better communication – no one driving a car wants to address all his comments over his shoulder for the duration of a long taxi ride. It also allows me from time to time to look at the driver's face, even if it is only in profile. And it's more companionable.

This occasion was no exception, and after we had set off, I asked the usual question. He was happy to engage in conversation but, as usual, of the one-sided variety. He wanted to talk and I was content to listen. I learn more that way. I know myself quite well, and I do not seem to possess the inclination that other people have to tell total strangers intimate details about their lives.

My driver was originally from the Midlands and had moved to East Anglia some years earlier to work for the local authority inspecting the highways. I hadn't encountered a highway inspector before – so I was curious about what was involved. He explained that in some councils highway inspectors were called highway engineers or highway officers – I often find that people are unnecessarily precise about job titles. I learned that in all cases the job involved inspecting road surface condition, organising maintenance of drainage and gullies, dealing with subsidence and pot holes, arranging for pruning of overgrown trees and dealing with public complaints, reports of damage or problems. Their remit covered inspecting white markings on road (all those dotted lines.....) and also removing graffiti and discarded trash from the roadside. They often had to liase with the Local Authority's Legal Department if members of the public had infringed the law by obstructing or damaging a public highway. I was regaled with astonishing statistics about how many aluminium road signs get stolen each year and melted down for their scrap value.

I then asked my taxi driver what was the most unusual occurrence in his career with the local authority, and he embarked on the following story about a road that disappeared and farmer who went mad.

My ex-highway inspector had arrived at work one day a few years before, and on his desk was a message from the customer relations department, which had logged a telephone call from a woman who lived in a village some twenty miles away. She had been trying to find a small hamlet called Hay in another part of the county using an ordnance survey map, and could not locate a road. This was a small lane which was marked on the map and appeared not to exist. She had stopped about a mile short of a country village called Appleton at a place where the lane was shown on the map, and, whilst looking around, she had found lying in the ditch an old signpost which said "Hay". But there seemed to be no road to which it referred. In the end she had driven on and through the village and after about four miles she had taken another road to Hay – a detour of some six miles. She was puzzled and wondered if she ought to inform the Ordnance Survey of their error.

At this point, my taxi-driver broke off because he had to negotiate the passing of a tractor and large trailer on the road we were travelling along. "Bloody tractors," he muttered. Having successfully overtaken the obstacle, he continued his tale. I could see him frowning in concentration to remember the details, and realised that he was keen to be accurate.

"I telephoned her back during the morning, and assured her that the road did exist and that it was clearly marked on the detailed map in the Highways Department. She was adamant that such a road was not to be found at all. I privately thought she was mistaken. I don't have much admiration for the female ability in the sphere of map reading – my wife being absolutely chronically bad finding her way around without me in the car. This probably accounts for the fact that few women become taxi drivers," he concluded.

He paused waiting for my laugh, but when it did not materialise he sighed and went on with his story. He told me he was only slightly intrigued by the woman's report – but a few days later, his department had asked him to go over to a property which was only a few miles from Appleton where they had received complaints from some local residents about overhanging branches in a country road. He thought he might as well have a look for the lost lane. He felt sure he could locate it.

5

After his inspection of the obstructing trees, he had driven to the place on the secondary road from where the map indicated that the smaller road turned off. He had not been able to find it at all, nor had he noticed any signpost, so he had driven on through the village of Appleton and turned left to drive round to Hay by a more circuitous but wider road. After passing through the hamlet, which consisted of a small farm, a derelict chapel and about seven houses, he had tried to locate the missing road from that end. The minor country road on which he was driving and searching ran through the hamlet but there was no indication of the little lane which was shown on his map as clearly linking this road with the larger secondary road which ran parallel to it some one and a half miles away across the fields, and on which he had started his search.

"I was totally mystified," he said. "The road should have been in that position but there was just a grass verge and some fencing along what was the perimeter of a field of overgrown unkempt grass. The hamlet was a few hundred yards up the road, so I drove back and knocked on the door of the first house on the right. A woman answered, and upon my asking if she remembered that there used to be a small road linking Hay with the B road to Appleton, she seemed a bit vague and said she could not remember.

"There was no reply from the next house, and then I noticed an elderly man and a dog emerging from one of the other houses. He was clearly going to take the animal out for a walk, and I thought that he would probably be a good person to ask. Surely he would know about the lane."

He had approached the man with the dog enquiring how long he had lived there and on learning that the chap had been a resident in Hay for over twenty-five years, he then asked where the lane was. The man had looked a bit shifty and muttered something about there being no lane now.

"Well, of course, I knew the lane had to exist – my map told me it did – so I asked the fellow to show me where it was or had been. He seemed to be a bit reluctant to do this, but when I told him I was from the Highways Department of the County Council, he decided to oblige. I left my car parked

6

in the hamlet and we walked down the road together. He explained to me that the local farmer had had permission to get rid of the road, and that he had dug it up three years back. Well, of course, I didn't take this seriously. No-one digs up a tarmac road!"

After a few minutes they had arrived at an innocuous spot on the country road, and his companion pointed at a hedge beside the fence and said that the lane had started from that point.

"Well, I was astonished," my taxi driver said feigning a note of genuine surprise, "There was no indication of any road, and I asked him if he was sure. 'Yup,' he said. 'That were where it was.' And without any further comment, he stomped off down the road with his mongrel on a piece of string for a lead. So I climbed over the fence and walked down the hedge that led northwards from there. It was a big straight hedge – very overgrown – and larger than one usually finds separating fields. I found a gap in it and pushed my way through. The ground here was very uneven, and although overgrown with long grass, there had clearly been some excavations a few years back. Could a farmer really have been mad enough to dig up a surfaced road? Why hadn't someone seen it and reported it? The field with its bumpy perimeter stretched suspiciously across some fields in the direction which the old road would have taken."

The highway inspector – my taxi driver – had returned to his car and driven the six miles round to Appleton, which was near the other end of the missing road. The village had a small church and a tiny shop but there was no pub – the usual source of local news and gossip – so he had tried the shop. The elderly woman who worked there was rather vague and did not seem to have any recollection of a lane which might have once existed. She suggested that I speak to a Mr Carew who lived three doors along. Unfortunately he was not at home, but the woman in the shop gave me his telephone number, so I could ring him when he got home from work.

"By now, I was feeling rather like an amateur sleuth," the taxi driver said. "I was determined to get to the bottom of the mystery. My final effort on that first day was to drive slowly back down the road leading out of the village. After a mile and a quarter, I stopped. There was a grass verge and some trees on the side where the lane ought to have been, and a deep overgrown ditch on the other side with a ploughed field beyond. I walked along the ditch and eventually I found what I was looking for – the signpost – which the telephone caller had also located. It was old, dirty with green slime but its one arm clearly read 'Hay'. I then crossed the road, and peered over a relatively new barbed wire fence down what seemed to be an avenue of alders and birch trees. The lane had clearly passed down between the trees, but there was no sign of any road surface. Just tangled grass and cow parsley and some brambles. I ducked in between the top and middle strands of the wire and pushed my way through the tall grass – it was July and nothing had been cut. After about a hundred yards, the trees came to an end, and there was a field in front of me in which was growing some rather poor quality grass, well overdue for cutting and making hay. There was a further field beyond in which there were some sheep. All was peaceful in the afternoon sunshine, and there was no road!"

At this point, the taxi driver explained, he began to think that the error was probably in the local department, and that there had been a road, which had been de-registered and removed. So he returned to his office and checked the records. The land on either side of the missing lane belonged to a person called Bullivant and his farm and land stretched between the secondary road which led to the village and the minor road which passed through the hamlet. There was no record of any application being granted to close the lane. Because it was a little used thoroughfare and no one had reported anything amiss, such as fallen trees or other obstruction to its use, it had not been inspected for some years. It should still have been there and yet it wasn't. It had disappeared.

At this point, I asked my taxi driver a question: "But surely, someone would have complained if a lane had been closed."

"It hadn't just been shut off," he responded. "It had been totally obliterated. It was extraordinary." He told me that during his time with the Highways Department he had heard of the occasional green lane – an old un-surfaced roadway – which had been fenced off illegally, and the person responsible had been ordered to remove the obstruction. He had never heard of anyone digging up a registered road. The labour and cost of doing this to a mile and a half of tarmac must have been considerable, and could not have passed unnoticed by local people.

"What I wanted to know was who had done it and why had all the locals kept quiet about it," said the highway inspector and investigator. "That evening, I telephoned Mr Carew, explained who I was, and put the question to him. At first he pretended not to know what I was talking about, but I then pressed him further and invoked my authority with some firmness. He decided to co-operate, but only after eliciting my promise that I would not divulge who had given me the information.

"The farmer, Mr Bullivant, who owned all the surrounding land, had for a number of years been acquiring land from smallholders in the area. He had bought the fields to the west of the lane to add to those on the other side which is where his farm, barns and main outbuildings were situated. Mr Carew explained that Farmer Bullivant was a bad-tempered and difficult man who liked his privacy and who jealously guarded his land from all intruders. He had already fallen foul of the Ramblers Association because he had obstructed a little used footpath on another part of his land. That matter was still unresolved because of his inflexibility. According to Mr Carew, the farmer had resented the fact that the lane, which was rarely used, split his farm in two, so he had decided to remove it. He had hired a JCB and together with two farm hands, they had spent one November three years back digging it up. Of course this was noticed by the residents of both Hay and Appleton most of whom were under the impression that the landowner had gained permission to dig up the road. Mr Carew finished by saying that Bullivant was not an easy man to argue with and he had some unorthodox methods of persuasion which he used on the few villagers who dared to voice an objection. When I asked Mr Carew about this, he refused to elaborate further, and the telephone call ended."

"So what did you do next?" I asked, intrigued.

He told me that the next thing was clearly to visit the said farmer, and he tried to telephone the man to make an appointment, but there was always an answering machine and no response was ever made to his various calls and messages. A few weeks went by and, exasperated by the lack of progress, he decided to call on the man without prior warning. One Tuesday afternoon he made the long drive to Appleton – and located the entrance to Bullivant's Farm off the minor road that led to Hay. The metal gate was closed so he opened it and closed it carefully behind his car.

"I tell you, I drove up the track with some trepidation – I knew I had a tricky customer to deal with. There were some barns and a yard to the left and further outbuildings opposite, and a large sprawling farmhouse up ahead. I pulled up outside the yard, and got out of the car. The door of one of the store sheds opened and a tall young man with closely cropped hair emerged and stood leaning against the door with his arms folded. I called across to him that I wanted to see Farmer Bullivant. No reply. I asked him where I could find the farmer. Again no reply – just a slow grin. I started to walk towards the farmhouse, and the young man turned and went in to the shed, from which emerged a few seconds later three large dogs – I think two of them were Rottweilers – who started barking and running towards me. Well, I pretty quickly changed my mind about calling on the farmer and beat it back to my car. One of the dogs caught up with me and tried to bite my leg but I kicked at him and he snarled and got hold of one trouser leg in his teeth. As I leapt into the driving seat of the car, ripping my trousers in the process, another dog lunged at my arm and savaged my jacket, but amazingly he did not get his teeth in my skin. I managed to get the door shut and I drove off fast down the track with two of the dogs chasing the car and barking crazily until I gathered speed and left them behind. Luckily I lost them before I got to the end of the drive and had to open that gate again. I was shaken, I can tell you. I could have been badly bitten." The taxi driver shook his shoulders, as if agitated by the memory.

"What a dreadful experience," I murmured, amused by his dramatisation of the event.

My taxi driver was warming to his story and, as he accelerated down a long straight road, he continued: " I was furious at being attacked. I drove to Hay, and knocked on the door of the cottage from which my first informant had emerged some weeks before. The old man opened the door and pretended not to recognise me. I refreshed his memory and reluctantly he invited me in. I told him I had visited Bullivant's farm, and he looked my torn trousers and jacket and said knowingly: 'Set his dogs on yer, did he? He don't like visiters.' I discovered that this was the hostile farmer's usual way of repelling outsiders who invaded his land. No one dared to trespass on his territory. Bullivant clearly did what he liked and he had successfully instilled fear into his neighbours so that nobody had the guts to stand up to him. I assured him that the heavy hand of the law was about to fall on Mr Bullivant's shoulders. The old man laughed harshly and croaked: 'It'll most likely get bitten orf.' I said that I needed proof that the farmer had been the one who dug up the road – and he told me –'Fer yore ears only, mind you' – that all the asphalt and hard core was piled in and behind a large barn which could be seen from where the old lane had been, if I dared to go and have a look. 'Yer wouldn't catch me trying to snoop,' he sniffed warningly. I thanked him and left, determined to ignore his advice."

"That was brave of you," I prompted. He deserved some applause at this juncture.

He grinned in a jaunty way and went on to say that he had calculated that the barn must be some way from the main buildings and so decided to risk another sortie onto Bullivant's land. He parked his car on the road past the end of the missing lane, and climbed over the fence again, and walked along the hedge. After about ten minutes he found a gap and went through to the bumpy rough ground that had been the lane. He caught sight of what seemed to be an old rusty corrugated iron roof between two groups of trees a couple of hundred yards to the east, and he cautiously advanced across the field until he was close to the rear of the barn. It was a cheaply constructed building which had been allowed to decay and become overgrown. He crept round one end of it through some nettles and long grass. The barn had three sides and was open to the east so when he turned the corner he could see inside the length of it. Quite clearly it was full of rubble and broken up tarmac. This was the evidence he was looking for.

With some relish he said, "Well, as you can imagine, I was very pleased with my discovery. I thought about the bullying farmer and said to myself, 'I've got you nailed, you nasty piece of work'."

The ex-highway inspector driver broke off at this point – he was slowing down for a crossroads, where he came to a halt. He seemed to hesitate as if he was unsure of the way. I glanced out of my window at the country signpost, and noticed the figure of a man receding down the lane to the right. The taxi driver looked at me, as if assessing what my reaction might be, and said that, if he took a left turn here, it might be a slightly longer route to my destination but it would avoid a town and therefore be quicker. He added brightly that it would be more scenic as well. As I murmured my acquiescence, he turned left and set off along a narrow road which began to descend towards a wood. Looking back afterwards, I realize that it was at this point that my storyteller started to depart from the truth. Or perhaps the truth walked away from him. It soon became apparent to me that the circumstantial details, which had given the first part of his story its veracity, were being abandoned for a more lurid and imaginative style.

"Do go on," I encouraged him, giving the impression of being the perfect captivated listener.

"Well, I was elated because I now had the proof I wanted," repeated my taxi driver, continuing with his tale. "But then I heard a slight click and looked up." His voice took on a theatrical note. " Imagine my surprise and horror when I saw a large and angry man standing some thirty yards away, holding

12

a shotgun which was aimed directly at me. 'Get off my land, NOW', shouted this threatening figure, and I did not wait to argue but I turned and ran. He fired the gun as I tripped on some stones, and fell sprawling. He missed me – whether by luck or design I shall never know. He was mad enough to fire at me, but I suppose he might just have been trying to frighten me. He succeeded! I scrambled to my feet and set off across the field stumbling in my haste. There was no further shot and when I took a quick look over my shoulder, there was no one pursuing me. I arrived back at my car, choking with terror and breathless with exertion. I drove shakily into the nearest town – some 15 miles away – and went straight to the police station."

Apparently the police knew all about Farmer Bullivant – they had had complaints from some of the villagers in both Hay and Appleton about his bully tactics and his nasty dogs. But there had been no actual grounds for prosecution, and it seemed that there was some reluctance on the part of the locals to press charges – they were probably too frightened. This time a civil servant from outside the area had been attacked by the farmer's dogs and had also been threatened with a loaded gun and then shot at – probably by the farmer himself. The police were also informed that the fellow had illegally dug up a registered road. At last they had something to go on.

The taxi driver admitted that he had been a bit reluctant to return to the scene of the confrontation, but agreed to accompany the police so that he could positively identify the man who had taken a pot shot at him. "Well, it was a fiasco! We drove up to the farm, and stopped. There was no sign of anyone but the three large and ferocious dogs appeared from nowhere and ran barking round the white police car like red Indians howling around captives at the stake. Needless to say, the two policemen decided against getting out of the car, and retreated to review their options. I was happy to go along with that decision. As we accelerated down the drive, there was the sound of mocking laughter from one of the barns.

"By now the police were angry, and they decided to get reinforcements and return the next day. The Highways

Department, who were angry that one of their inspectors had been mistreated, gave permission for me to accompany the police. This time there were three police vehicles – two of them Land rovers – and nine police officers, some of whom were armed. The convoy proceeded up the drive, and arrived in the farmyard."

My taxi driver gave a laugh as he told me: "What we encountered was not an embattled madmen, defending his house and land, but a rural idyll. There was a pen of sheep which were baa-ing noisily, and two men in overalls and wellies were sheep-dipping. One of them was wearing a green hat and the other I recognised from the day before as the one who had refused to reply and had set the Rottweilers onto me. They both waved cheerily to us as they went on with their task. There was no sign of the dogs. The front door of the farmhouse opened and out stepped the portly figure of Farmer Bullivant."

Here the taxi driver looked at me – perhaps to gauge my level of credulity – and having satisfied himself that he still had my rapt attention, he continued. "I recognised him as the angry person with the gun from the day before. He emerged from the porch, stood on his doorstep and surveyed the situation. The words he uttered with a smile were inevitably: 'Can I help you, gentlemen?' What a smooth bastard!"

From this point, the story began to get convoluted and the surfeit of details started to strike a wrong note. I guessed that the taxi driver had travelled from fact to fiction some while back and was enjoying himself by inventing and embellishing. I began to wonder if he would finish the tale before we arrived. At this point we were driving through a small village, so to put a slight brake on his loquacity, I interrupted his flow and asked: "What's this place called?"

A look of irritation crossed his face, but he replied telling me the name of the place and adding, "Not long now. Just five minutes or so." I was a little unsure whether he was referring to our destination or the end of his story. But I tactfully avoided asking, and I urged him to tell me what happened in the end.

14

"Where was I?" he mused as we left the village. "Ah yes, Farmer Bullivant on his doorstep playing a game of bluff. At first I thought the police were flummoxed. They seemed to be outgunned by his change of tactics. He had almost made them feel that they had overreacted and had brought a sledgehammer to crack a nail.

"The senior officer and one other walked slowly to a spot a few yards in front of him, and said they wished to talk with him. The other policemen remained near the cars and a couple of them casually wandered over to watch the sheep-dipping and to keep an eye on the two hands. The farmer smiled again, showing large uneven teeth, and asked courteously what the problem was. The officer beckoned to me and I approached somewhat warily. Farmer Bullivant was unruffled and gave no indication that he had ever set eyes on me before. The officer explained that he had received two very serious complaints – one was an allegation of a criminal nature and the other was a civil matter. The farmer raised his eyebrows enquiringly, but I detected an underlying menace. When the officer elaborated, Bullivant slowly turned his pale eyes on me but with no flicker of recognition. I can tell you, I felt quite intimidated by his cold stare. I was asked if the farmer was the person who had aimed his gun at me and fired it the day before, and I had no trouble at all in saying quite emphatically that indeed he was the person. Bullivant's face registered tolerant disbelief and innocence whilst saying, 'But that's preposterous. I've never set eyes on this man before.' Upon being told that his dogs had tried to savage me prior to the incident with the gun, he coolly said that his dogs were there to guard against trespassers, that he was not expecting anyone to call that day and that he had been absent from the farm. He could not be held responsible if his dogs warned off a prowler.

"This bare-faced denial and distortion of the facts did not discompose the police officer, who calmly said that a visitor to the farm arriving by the main drive in a car could hardly be termed a 'prowler'. The farmer said nothing but there was a nasty glint in his eyes. The policemen then mentioned the matter of the illegal removal of a public highway. At this point, Bullivant lost his calm demeanour, and angrily said that he didn't know what they were talking about – and that they could leave NOW and stop wasting his time. The policemen stood impassively in the yard and the officer said quietly but firmly that he would like Mr Bullivant to accompany them to the police station." The taxi driver said this in the solemn tone of a policeman in a television drama arresting a suspect.

"We all waited for his reaction. 'I shall do no such thing,' shouted the farmer and swiftly stepping back inside the porch and the open front door, he slammed it in our faces."

My taxi driver paused. We drew up outside a large building, which proved to be the hotel and I realised we had arrived. He switched off the engine, and I thanked him very much.

"And then what happened?" I asked, wanting to know the outcome but also hoping he would be brief.

The taxi driver, leaned back in his seat and appeared to be studying the windscreen, or perhaps summoning up further powers of invention, before continuing. "The police officer calmly stepped forward and rang the bell. After a minute with no response, an upstairs window was thrown open and Bullivant's angry face appeared in it briefly and the twin barrels of a gun were seen to protrude from it."

"Well, I was stunned, I can tell you," said the taxi driver. "But before I could do anything the other policeman had grabbed me by the arm and pulled me round to the side of the house. From there I could see that the scene had changed completely. The two farm hands were running for a barn closely pursued by two policemen, and the other police were crouching down behind their cars. One of them had a gun in his hand. The senior officer was not in my line of vision but he seemed to be in the porch from where he shouted up to Bullivant. The policeman beside me told me not to move as the farmer was clearly a dangerous madman and might do anything."

My taxi driver was obviously enjoying his action-packed reconstruction of a story, which had started to become rather melodramatic for my taste. I had long suspected that he was fabricating a better ending than the one that had actually taken place. Perhaps he had described the incident before and felt the need to make it more interesting and dramatic. I looked at my watch surreptitiously, but he noticed and his expansive mood instantly evaporated. I regretted the lapse, and asked him if he had time to finish the story. But he realised he had gone too far. He knew he has lost me – I no longer found him credible.

"They captured him in the end," he said dully, giving no details. I no longer deserved his creativity.

"What happened to him?" I asked, trying to make amends.

"He was locked away in an asylum kind of prison," he stated flatly and stopped. I had clearly destroyed his enjoyment by curtailing his tall story. I may have been irritated by his verbosity before, but now I would be punished by his reluctance to give me any further details.

"But what about the road?" I asked, humbly – almost pleadingly. I found I really did want to know the ending – even if it was not the real one. I lingered even though I wished to get out of the car and into my hotel.

In a dead pan tone, looking out of his door window and half turned away from me, the taxi driver concluded his story: "His son, who was a nice quiet young man, came back from living in Spain, and took over the farm with his mother. She had left Bullivant a couple of years before and had been living with relatives in Wales. They were obliged to re-instate the lane – and I think some land was sold to pay for it. There were lots of debts. The locals weren't sorry to see Bullivant put away. Neither was I," he added.

"So he was mad," I said. The taxi driver shrugged.

"How much do I owe you?" I asked, and when he told me the figure, I added a generous tip to assuage my guilt and paid him. "Thanks you so much – and well, what an fascinating story!" I said enthusiastically trying to give the impression of the whole-hearted sincerity he obviously wanted to hear. Rather oddly he made no move to get out of the taxi and open the door for me. With chagrin, I realised that he had detected the note of artificiality and was offended. I was no better a liar than he was. I opened the passenger door and climbed out

17

with my small bag. He gave me a weak smile and started up the engine.

"It was good to have an ex-highway inspector as my taxi driver," I said genuinely as I leaned down to wave at him through the open passenger window.

"Yeah, well, they are both pretty boring jobs," he muttered moodily. He then said, "Cheerio then," in a false hearty voice, and put the car into gear and drove off. I mentally wished him better luck with a more gullible passenger for his next yarn, and went into the hotel.

Later that day, after my business meeting, I was sitting in my room, and I thought again of the taxi ride and the story of the lost lane and the mad farmer. The taxi driver was a more sensitive fellow that I had originally given him credit for, and without doubt I had hurt his feelings. Perhaps I had misjudged him. To be fair, it was a good story. I came to the conclusion that most of it was probably the truth and I wondered idly how much he had embellished or invented. After he became irritated with me, he probably reverted to the truth. No gun battle took place, and doubtless Farmer Bullivant had been incarcerated in a mental institution. Or maybe he wasn't. Had he managed to wriggle his way out of prosecution? Or had he paid a hefty fine and was he still living there? I'd probably never know.

* * * * *

Some months later I found myself back in the same part of the country at the offices of some solicitors in the county town. Afterward a long afternoon of negotiations, I went to the pub to have a drink with one of the partners of the firm. He was a dry sort of fellow with a pedantic manner. We talked about the meeting and then I asked where he lived. He told me that he have been living for some years in a small village called Appleton. The name sounded familiar, and after a few minutes I recalled the connection and remembered the story of the mad farmer. I asked him if he had ever encountered a local landowner or farmer called Bullivant. I added that he was probably no longer living there.

"No, indeed", said my colleague. "He's been dead for some years."

"Really," I said in surprise. "I thought he was insane and had been put away in an institution."

"Oh no. I don't know where you heard that from. His death happened a couple of years or so before my wife and I moved into the village, but my neighbour soon regaled me with the story. Apparently, Mr Bullivant was a kind unassuming man who had been accused of attempted murder by some vindictive person who was trespassing on his property. The police turned up in force at the farm, and the unfortunate farmer happened to have his rifle with him – probably for disposing of rabbits or something. Jumping to the wrong conclusion that he was threatening them, one of the policemen shot him dead. It was a terrible mistake and his wife was distraught. Afterwards, she went to live with relatives in Wales, and the son took over. He was a horrible fellow by all accounts, and soon got into debt and had to sell the farm. The villagers were fond of old Bullivant – he had been a generous benefactor of local charities – and they were all very sorry about the tragedy. But I never heard anyone say he was insane. The chap who concocted the crazy story of being threatened with a gun by the farmer was probably the madman. Perhaps he had some grudge?" My informant smiled. "Who knows?"

I asked him whether he knew the story about Bullivant digging up a tarmac road, which ran through his land, and he replied that he had never heard that, and it sounded a bit far-fetched. I let the subject drop, and finished my drink.

I could not reconcile this account with the story told to me by the taxi-driver. One is pre-disposed to believe lawyers. If what the solicitor had told me was true – that Bullivant was dead – then the question arose as to whether he had been given the correct version of the facts by his neighbour. What would the latter's motives have been in protecting the reputation of someone that apparently all the locals had hated? Had the neighbour been Bullivant's only ally in the village – or had he misinterpreted the police version of the accident? Perhaps the farmer had been universally liked by the villagers.

If Bullivant had been shot and killed, whether by accident or design, what puzzled me was why my storyteller, ex-highway inspector, taxi driver had lied about the end. He had opted for a less dramatic conclusion – and departed from the truth when the truth would have made a better tale. Was he trying to punish me for my lapse in courtesy by denying me the sensational death of the protagonist, or did he feel guilty that he had indirectly caused the farmer's death? Maybe it was simpler than that – and he was bored with driving his taxi and so he told stories to amuse himself and fascinate his clients, who might give him a larger tip as I had done. I didn't know.

* * * * *

Now, looking back after some years, I choose to opt for the taxi driver's version of events even though it might have been a pack of lies. I liked him better than the solicitor. He had amused me more, and I feel I owe him my allegiance. Perhaps he had never been a highway inspector at all and had merely repeated a story that he had heard from someone who was. In stories a villain is better value than a hero and his 'Bullivant' is the more memorable. A good story is worth hearing whether it is the truth or not. The different mouths that tell it add to the flavour, and amendments add richness and colour.

I am reminded of the game of Chinese whispers – which I used to enjoy at parties in my childhood. One child invents a sentence, and as it is passed on in whispers around the circle it is misheard or misinterpreted and becomes distorted by each participant. At the end it is often unrecognisable but it still amuses and entertains. There is another game too called Truth or Lies. One has to guess whether a statement by another is fact or fiction, and the inventions for the lies always seem to be more entertaining than the statements that are true. Stories often blur the lines between the two and I accept both as integral parts of the storyteller's art.

I dearly love a story and I do not demand veracity. I am a good listener.

GINKGO

Ginkgo

"In my opinion," said Colonel Lune, who was in love with my mother. "Your Ginkgo Biloba is greatly superior to the ones in Kew Gardens".

He was sitting on our terrace, looking through his dark glasses with concentration at what appeared to me the least interesting tree in the garden – a thin spindly specimen with twig-like branches and tiny leaves. I was an avid and adventurous tree climber and this tree offered me nothing. Too frail to climb, there was no prospect of a god-like view from its upper branches. It was inoffensive – there was no danger in it – unlike the tall cedar whose summit I could conquer with a gut-churning sense of terror, or the copper beech with its seemingly insurmountable smooth high sleek trunk, or the hollow oak with its furrowed bark and secret hideout. This slender dull tree, thin as a silver birch but without even the interest of white bark which peeled off in ribbons, had no attraction for a ten-year old veteran like me.

My mother was more discerning. "I call it by its English name – the Maidenhair tree. I've always liked its delicate fan-shaped leaves and gentle colouring. It doesn't look strong, though, and every winter I think a hard frost might get it."

The Colonel remarked that the tree was more robust than it looked. He and my mother took a stroll down the lawn to examine it further. He was wearing a light-weight beige uniform and boots, whilst my mother was in her habitual summer garb – a loose dress of faded cotton and flat sandals. She was beautiful, willowy and needed no adornment. "Moon", for that is what we always called him, trod carefully with precision, whilst she walked with unselfconscious freedom. She talked and used her arms to supplement her speech and he listened intently, his body straight but his head slightly bent towards her. When they reached the Ginkgo, he took off his glasses and appeared to examine the tree closely, but did not seem to have much more to say about it. He found it easier to admire my mother and the tree from a distance. At close quarters, he became tongue-tied, retreating from communication as if embarrassed.

The Colonel, who was aide-de-camp to the Queen's consort in his own country, came to our part of England occasionally when the Prince visited the old manor up the road. This was owned by close friends of my parents and so naturally we met their guests from time to time, particularly as the husband quite enjoyed discreetly advertising the informality of his friendship, forged in war-time, with one of the more flamboyant of European royalty. The Prince probably enjoyed having a silent and serious companion, who offered no challenge to his extrovert personality, and his aide-de-camp wisely maintained a deferential dignity which came naturally to him.

Moon had met my mother at a dinner party, where she had been seated beside him, and during the meal she had tried to be nice to a shy awkward man. She had a light-hearted but confiding manner and a lack of artifice which captivated many men. The dour colonel was enchanted. They met from time to time over the years, and he developed a deep but controlled and courtly love for my mother. We were all aware of this, even my mother, and I'm sorry to say it was the source of endless jokes. But he really believed that no-one knew. Whether his dark private passion was a source of soulful pleasure or despairing pain, I cannot say.

He used obvious ruses to visit my mother in our house when he was in England – and in order to gain access to the object of his adoration, pretended interest in her children (we were not fooled), in my father's collection of paintings (he was not fooled), and in her garden (she was delighted when anyone took an interest in her abiding passion for plants). He was unable to be at ease with her, and good manners and etiquette prevented him from declaring his devotion. So in her presence his conversation was stilted and formal, whilst with my father he was able to converse as normally as his taciturn personality allowed.

Letters and postcards with exotic foreign stamps often arrived, sent from Moon whilst travelling with his Prince.

Artlessly addressed to both of my parents, he was less clipped and more relaxed when writing letters, and sometimes his epistolary eloquence positively bloomed. My mother would regale us with these letters at breakfast. "Here's another one from my 'lofer'," she would announce laughingly, mimicking his foreign accent.

My father would look up from his newspaper. "Where is Moon this time?" he would ask with a smile. Neither of my parents took Moon's devotion very seriously. My father was used to basking in the reflected shimmer of admiration that others bestowed on his wife, whilst she accepted it gently or ignored it altogether.

Over the next few years, we saw Moon less and less, for his Prince became unwell, and seldom travelled abroad. Undoubtedly the poor man could think of no excuses to visit the locality, not considering love to be a sufficient reason, and there being no deviousness in him. Only the odd letter reminded us of his existence, and our lives went on.

We lived in a modest late Georgian house, with numerous outbuildings and a few acres of garden. For us children it was a beloved haven of familiarity and mystery, reality and myth. My elder brother and I had lived there since I was one year old, and my younger brother had been born there. The house was called Goodways, and was and always will be an integral part of the fabric of my childhood. The house was solid and secure with green-painted corridors, a large cellar with huge coke-fed boiler, a warm kitchen, a large drawing room with piano, and front and back stairs.

But the garden was wonderful – rose beds in geometric shapes and bushes curiously clipped, stepping-stone paved paths to run along, rockeries to clamber over, and wide flower borders with shrubs behind which one could hide. There was a large and tempting kitchen garden with fruit cages and greenhouses patrolled and guarded by Minns, the gardener, who tried to foil our attempts to gorge ourselves amongst the ripe fruit, lob stones through the scum on the pond, or steal pea pods to strip out the tiny delicious peas. There was a grassy field in which we made "houses" by flattening the grass to

25

create rooms and doors, and a "wild" woodland area behind a trellis at the bottom of the lower lawn. And most importantly there were trees. The garden was my Eden.

The trees in the garden were my obsession – the scars on my knees are witness to my attempts to scale them. The huge chestnut – the "conker tree" – near the lane was difficult to get into from the ground, with wide trunk and nothing to grip onto for the first ten feet, but wonderfully concealing when aloft amid the sticky white flowers. The tall and rough cedar with its barrel-shaped cones overlooked the old overgrown tennis court which was now a sea of waving lupins and tall weeds. This giant was initially easy if one ascended by clambering up one of the large lower branches which swept down to within a couple of feet of the ground. But it became tricky when one neared the top, with a tangle of brittle twigs, sharp needles and fragile toeholds. But the view over the roofs of the house and the surrounding field was superb from either tree, and they were my favourites. They had the attraction of being ancient and majestic but conquerable.

* * * * *

The devastating blow that we had to move fell during the unsettled year that followed after leaving school. The house and land was compulsorily purchased by the Town Council for redevelopment. They planned to put twenty-eight "units" (houses) on our "plot" (garden). And it did seem to me, as I tried to come to terms and accept what was inevitable, that it was perhaps a little unfair that we should inhabit an area large enough for many families. So we were to be uprooted and transplanted. Like immature plants instead of seedlings, it was more disrupting than it would have been if we had been younger and less attached to the place. It was more distressing because it happened when I felt dislocated and insecure having left the safe familiar confines of school and being confronted with the heady but fearful prospect of college and the new freedoms of life as a student.

My elder brother had made a break already two years before. He had gone to Australia but had just returned home

26

burned by sun and adulation to spend a final summer at home. His twenty-first birthday was our last midsummer rite, and we moved at the end of September. My younger brother was still at school and, being consumed by misery at the move, I don't remember how he reacted. I think that he was at the age when he didn't discuss his feelings, but he may inwardly have felt as bruised I did, feeling hounded out of our home.

We tried to find a house that we could compare with what we were to lose. My parents and I had searched throughout the spring, and many unlovely dwellings we saw – I remember the relief when father rejected dreary "Hortons" and mother refused to move to ugly "Bulwell". With their children on the verge of leaving home, their aim was to get a smaller house, but in the end a much larger house was bought – a Queen Anne manor with numerous bedrooms, a panelled library, and a park for a garden. Superior in elegance and beauty, this handsome though dilapidated residence was the sugared pill used to woo us from our beloved home.

And so we went, lock, stock and barrel. Space was no problem in the Manor, and as Goodways was to be demolished, we took everything with us – all the friendly clutter of eighteen years accumulation. We left only the huge grand piano – a battered immoveable relic – sitting in solitary sadness in the deserted drawing room, looking out over the terrace across the lawns we used to play on. And of course, we left the trees.

Mother tried to console me by pointing out that the new garden contained some marvellous specimen trees. But by then, either the familiar childish pleasures of tree climbing were waning, or the unknown terrors of embarking on a University career were looming, and my passion for trees declined. Interest in people had rightly reasserted itself as a more enthralling preoccupation. The study of humans – minds and bodies – and to a lesser extent books, became far more fascinating subjects than the outdoor games and challenges that had once occupied my time.

My father enjoyed the new house as much as mother and I had loved the old. He hired William – a handy man –to help with maintenance jobs. For my father, the quality of life had

27

improved. For my mother the activity of life had increased ten-fold. The house and garden were huge, and required long hours of work. The previous owner had kept five gardeners employed; we had one. Always an enthusiastic gardener, my mother combined perseverance with practicality. Some of the formal gardens were allowed to lapse into a pleasing riot of untended flowers and weeds. Others were carefully maintained. My father acquired a huge tank-like mower upon which he could sit whilst vanquishing the uprising army of grass. This sedentary mowing was his sole contribution to the upkeep of his new "estate". Apart from working to pay the bills, of course.

On the verge of adulthood we children flew back to the enlarged nest at weekends or holidays. But the manor never had the same attraction for me as the earlier house, though it did become home. It was in mid December, a few days after returning from my first university term that my mother received a rare letter from Colonel Moon. She read it aloud, and it proved to be a wail of lament at the transportation of his favourite English family from the fine Goodways to another place that could never rival it in his estimation. And it was so sad that the lovely house and garden were being annihilated. Moon's distress at the destruction was as unmilitary as it was passionate.

Following too closely after the disruption and disorientation of the big move, this letter was taken to heart by my mother, who decided to return to Goodways, now in the hands of a band of demolition men, and plunder some shrubs. They were after all her children; she had lovingly planted many of them and watched them grow to maturity, only to abandon them, she guiltily felt. Many of the smaller ones could be uplifted and found new homes under her protection. If we deserted them they would be uprooted and left to die or chopped down by the uncaring contractors.

An early evening raid a couple of days later, after the men had left work, reprieved some of the condemned, and the next day saw a further transmigration of refugees in my mother's battered car. Many of those moved survived in their new terrain, but many more had already been victims to the demolition squad and its weapons of destruction. My mother and I will never be able to forget the numbingly sad sight of our house in ruins, with no roof at one end, and no first floor at the other. Where her bedroom had been was a gaping hole, and the piano, that had been too old and heavy to move from the room below looked incongruous and dusty as it faced the sky. They had not yet started on the trees, but we knew that most of them would be felled, with the exception of the copper beech which the Council had promised would remain.

My mother gazed down the lawn at the doomed landscape, looking miserable and forlorn, her back to the semi-dismembered house that had once been a beloved home. Her eyes alighted on the Maidenhair tree, which we now called the Ginkgo, since Moon had ennobled it in our eyes by telling us that it was a fine example of the oldest species still extant from prehistoric times.

"We'll take the Ginkgo," said my mother decisively. "Moon says it's a living fossil and that ours is better than the ones at Kew. We must save it."

This noble aspiration caught our imaginations. The undertaking promised the challenge of adventure, difficulties to be surmounted and ultimate victory. It was a positive counterstroke and a way of striking back at the savage upheaval of all those special places and things which had had been so important to us during our life there.

"You will need permission to move a tree," said my father, who was always a pessimist and usually proved right.

"We'll get it," said my mother, always optimistic and invariably succeeding.

"We are prepared to let you remove this condemned tree at your own risk," said the Council.

"Help yourself," said the demolition squad.

This was not quite as easy as it sounded. There was no question of employing a professional to move it for us – that would be far too expensive. The tree was some thirty-five feet tall and, though narrow and with short branches, transporting it was undoubtedly going to be a problem since we would have to carry the ball of earth needed to surround its roots, if it were to

29

have a chance of survival. It would require a long and heavy vehicle. The farmer, who borrowed our field for his cows, agreed to lend us his tractor and trailer which William was able to drive. The problem of digging up the tree remained. It was the right time of the year from the Ginkgo's point of view, being dormant, and the ground in our old garden was muddy with rain, rutted by machine tracks and trampled by men's boots.

My mother put on some make-up – a rare occurrence – and a dress and went to charm the workmen. Of course she succeeded, and came away with the promise of the use of the mechanical digger for an hour during the following day. My mother rallied up the troops to help – friends and neighbours – to dig a hole for the new site of the tree. This was finished by dusk.

The next day was cold and windy as we set off the few miles back to Goodways. My mother had enlisted a local gardener called Charlie, a history student from Durham called Paul, whose utter devotion to my mother guaranteed his presence, in addition to William and me. We were too eager, too early. The men were pulling down an old outbuilding when we arrived and said that if we gave them a hand dismantling a brick wall, we could use the digger sooner. I will never forget the distasteful and bizarre situation in which I found myself – that of pulling down my own house. Unwillingly, criminally, I played a tiny part in its destruction.

The back yard was still familiar enough to hurt, but the garden when we walked through the flattened house was a strange moonscape of waste and wreckage amid a morass of clay. The condemned Ginkgo was near the rockery, and seemed to be waiting for us – and a reprieve My mother, who during the war had been in the army and, as she used to tell us, had driven tanks round the downs near Lulworth Cove, had undisputed claim to be the only one with enough experience to drive the digger. After a few words of instruction from its normal driver, no doubt charmed out of his wits by my mother's breathtaking practicality, she climbed into the cab of the digger and set off.

"You're going too fast," shouted Paul nervously, his concern for the woman rather than the threatened tree. But she mastered the lumbering monster quickly and began to dig round the base of the slender trunk. Charlie and William looked on enviously whilst my mother pulled levers and gleefully tossed mounds of earth around. Soon the tree began to totter, and we minions ran up to its roots and the earth clinging to them to wrap them up in sacking. Then my mother managed to get the ball of roots and earth into the scoop. Whilst we all steadied the tree the whole twiggy edifice was manoeuvred onto the trailer. I shall never be able to understand how and why my mother managed in the slippery mud so well – such inspirational adaptability was a part of her magic.

We all sat with the tree on the trailer for the slow drive back to our new home a few miles away. We were exultant in the pouring rain as we gazed down the length of the tree to its feathery tip which extending some yards beyond the end of the convoy. My mother wanted to drive the tractor too, but William was firm, and clung to the remnants of his manly dignity. The procession arrived in triumph at the manor house, and wobbled its muddy way down the lawn to the gaping hole awaiting the Ginkgo. Frail and drenched, our thin refugee was carefully rolled off the trailer by the muddy but gleeful rescuers, and erected with some ropes and many shouts. Charlie the gardener offered advice, but the system of law and order had broken down by this time, and we rollicked around the Ginkgo and its guy-ropes in a dance of celebration – of our endeavours rather than the its deliverance. In the wintry dusk, the slender tree looked forlorn amid the alien grass.

I think my mother must have mentioned the tree's move in a Christmas card to Colonel Moon, because early in the New Year we received his ecstatic response. He was so happy that we had cared enough to rescue this "slender leafy damsel in distress." The man was well able to manage flowery turns of phrase when talking about plants. The letter was passed at breakfast time to my father who, upon reading it, announced to his wife:

"There you are, Diana, he wasn't besotted by you at all. Its obvious that he was really in love with the tree." My mother smiled. My younger brother sniggered.

The Maidenhair tree has been known as HER tree ever since. Indeed we always considered the rambling manor

31

garden as hers, although the solid house was thought of as my father's possession. As an argumentative and egalitarian student, I did not care for this terminology. The concept of owning a house or its grounds I considered to be arrogant. How could the trees that had been there for years before our birth and that would remain long after our death belong to any one? Of course not! We simply shared the land they inhabited and the ambience they created for a brief period of time whilst on our way to mortality. Clearly, I was at that time enthralled by the stark power of Anglo Saxon texts and some of their bleak philosophy no doubt inspired my views.

My mother, removed from her adored first house and garden, began to put down roots in the new place, and gradually her influence and aura pervaded the terrain. The unkempt park-like garden developed and changed under her guidance and care. The walled kitchen garden and its produce kept her busy for hours. She made great efforts with the rose garden and herbaceous borders. So she found she had little time to spare for the trees.

The woods up near the road were left wild and the shrubs round the small lake had to fend for themselves. The willows wept unrestrainedly, the fruit trees were pruned, an elderly chestnut was propped up, and the paving round the sycamore tree was cleared of weeds. There was nothing she could actively do for the Maidenhair tree, but she cared about it. There were many other more beautiful more ancient trees in the park around that manor. But no one rivalled the Ginkgo's austere elegance. It was sickly for eighteen months, and we wondered whether it would survive, but after three or four years it settled in and no doubt stands there still.

We are gone, however. We merely borrowed the house and its trees for a few years before moving on. Humans are transient beings whilst firm buildings and mature trees remain rooted in one place. Unless, on rare and special occasion, through intervention of mobile man, a tree changes position. This happened the day we moved the Ginkgo.

HOTEI

Hotei

Maria has always been the breadwinner in our family. She goes out to work and I stay at home and look after the house and the children. She can earn more than me, and I really enjoy being a house husband and working part-time at home. I repair china and this work fits in easily with collecting children from school and doing the shopping, cleaning and cooking.

I love all children and our own in particular. They are infinitely precious to me – and as vulnerable as the most delicate and intricate porcelain figures that I work on. The fragility of our lives and our happiness is ever present in my mind – it is so easy to destroy confidence, calmness and harmony with discord and selfishness. As easy as accidentally dropping a Meissen figurine on the tiled floor.

I would never say this to my wife, but I really feel that I am better suited to looking after my children than she is. She often seems to lack sensitivity and consideration. Also she is a woman who is not demonstratively affectionate, though she loves our son and daughter as much as I do. She is often immersed in her work and she takes very seriously the responsibility that comes with her job. So she cannot give her family as much time as I can – and I really feel very privileged and fortunate that I do have the time to spend with our children when they are home from school or during the holidays. It also occurs to me that Maria might occasionally regret that her job gives her less leisure with her children than she would wish. She must realise that she is missing out on their childhood.

Of course, they are just normal children – not perfect – often noisy – and with the usual cargo of children's problems, worries and irritating habits. But I know that my presence in the house gives them security and confidence. Such peace of mind is sometimes lacking in households where the parents both go out to work. The most annoying time with children is when they are tired or hungry and start to whinge or argue.

The time I love the best is during the afternoon when they come home from school. I hear their clear high-pitched voices outside the door, and my son and daughter come tumbling into the house, shouting "Daddee". I carefully put down the piece I am working on or stop the household task that I am engaged in, and turn to welcome them. They fling themselves into my arms and I know a moment of such sweet happiness that I think myself truly blessed. I then make a cup of tea for me and give them a soft drink whilst I listen to their news and chatter about their school day, and I mind not at all that they never enquire about mine. That is how it is with children. Unselfishness and an interest in parents' activities come later.

After tea, they settle down to their homework at the kitchen table, and I usually join them, dealing with household accounts or answering letters, or just reading the newspaper, so that I can be there if they wish to ask me anything or show me what they are working on. I can also short-circuit any potential quarrels. Maria comes home usually about seven in the evening and often later than this. By this time the children are quieter – they are tired – and might be looking at television or playing a game before bed – they are still both under ten years old. They do not give her the welcome they give me. I am the recipient of their effusive greetings and their news about school and friends and their experiences, which they want to tell to their listening parent, who will react, confer praise or remove worry. I hear and absorb their joy and relief of being home after a day at that huge and often heartless school. Maria misses out – we both know it – but she pretends she does not mind, and bends down over their little shoulders as they sit on the sofa together and kisses them. They put up their thin arms round her neck and murmur "Hi, Mummy", while keeping their eyes on the screen.

We eat supper together after they have gone upstairs and are reading in bed or listening to music. I listen to Maria who unloads her day onto my shoulders – which are – I'm happy to say – broad enough to bear the emotional freight and confidences of my family. This is my role and I love it. It's not complicated, mainly requiring the ability to listen, care and

36

sympathise. This costs me nothing except the effort at the end of an active day, and I think they appreciate it.

I tend to take a back seat at weekends to give Maria the chance to interact and play with the children, and I am always surprised that she does not take more opportunity to do this – but perhaps they hold back a bit too. I'm the one who is always there for them, and she is the part-time parent. I now understand what some of my male friends and neighbours complain about – that they don't seem to be able to relate with their children as well as their wives do. Like these wives I know that it is all about putting in time and offering children a listening ear, and being the loving sponge which will absorb their communications and preoccupations. I am the lucky one, and I am also fortunate that I don't find housework or domestic chores any duller than sticking tiny pieces of broken porcelain together. I have a mind that continues to work, reflect and receive stimuli whilst doing these mundane tasks. If I organise my time well, there is usually a part of each day during term time when I can read a book, or hear the news or a programme on the radio, or chat to a shopkeeper or neighbour. I like people and I'm a good listener. I am content. There was a time some years ago when I was busy with my job but less satisfied with my life, and I compare and contrast how I was then and how I am now – and I know what I prefer.

On Thursday Lucy comes home from school and seems a bit upset. I can recognise the signs now. I can always tell when Robbie has been subjected to a bit of bullying – he goes very quiet and I have to coax it out of him. If it's serious I then have to contact his teacher but often he has exaggerated the problem because he craves for some extra portion of my sympathy and time. But on this occasion my son is breezy and carefree, and it is my little daughter's face that tells me that I have to give my attention to her.

I unravel it all in about half an hour – a storm in a teacup as is often the case with children. She has a friend in her class called Amy – they are as thick as thieves – and although I find Amy's mother a bit pushy, her child is delightful and often comes round to our house to play. But the girls have clearly fallen out today. At length, it all spills out – Lucy tells me that she has said something really unkind and untrue about her friend, and that Amy was very hurt and upset about this. I ask her why she did it, and she wails that she does not know but something nasty inside of her just made her say it. She tells me – and she is crying at this point whilst sitting on my lap – that she really regrets hurting her friend's feelings and she's desperate that Amy will never talk to her again. I smooth things over and say that this is certainly not going to wreck their friendship but that tomorrow she ought to go up to Amy and say that she is very sorry and never meant to be so unkind. I know this will be hard for Lucy – children always find it hard to admit they have been wrong. But she is a good kid and will do it. I reassure her that Amy will accept her apologies and all will be well.

Lucy stops crying, wipes her nose on her sleeve, and climbs off my lap to get a biscuit. All is well. I have again managed the magician's trick of converting a painful problem into a bright resolution. It is so easy – it is a recipe for success achieved with ingredients of patience, sympathy, sensitivity, advice and lots of love. In my life, you can have your cake and eat it, because the cake – like love – is self-renewing.

But Lucy is growing up a bit. This time she returns, clutching a couple of biscuits, to the sofa and to my knee and asks me a question. This is a rare event and it is my reward.

"Daddee," she says, "I am really sorry about what I did to Amy. Have you ever done something you were really sorry about? Something that made you feel really awful."

I cast my mind back and it fastens on an incident which took place before I met Maria, and I say to my daughter: "Well, yes, there is something, but it happened a long time ago, before you and Robbie were born. Would you like to hear about it, darling?"

Lucy looks up at me with round eyes. "Oh yes, Daddee," she says. This is clearly going to be a story and my little people love stories. "Come here, Rob," she calls out imperiously.

"Daddee is going to tell us a story about long ago." This sounds as if the tale might hark back to the Middle Ages, but that is probably where they think I spent my childhood.

"Well," I begin, as my son clambers on to the sofa beside us, "This is a story about something which I regret. And what is unusual is that I regretted something I did which was right but misguided. It is not about being sorry for doing something nasty and it all goes to show that you can feel sorry about lots of things and not just about being unkind to someone," I say, with a look at Lucy. Her face is serious and intent, and both of them are looking at my face. I know I have got their attention. This is parental power indeed!

I tell them that this story is not about when I was a child but about when I was in my first job. I had taken my degree in fine art and had been lucky enough to find a position in a local firm of auctioneers, who sold houses, chattels and, from time to time, antiques. I started out as a porter, which was a bit galling because I felt very important with my second-class honours degree, and I was slightly put out to find that I had to wear a green apron when at work. But it was a good way to learn about furniture and the auction business. I progressed up the ladder to junior cataloguer and after about three years I started to conduct auctions – not the important ones, just the low-key affairs. It was a bit frightening at first because I had to learn all the buyers' names, then sell the item, while being careful to remember the reserve price if there was one. Then I had to note down the price in the auctioneer's book, and ensure the clerk knew the buyer's name. But I soon got the hang of it, and rather enjoyed it. These sales were held only once a fortnight but it was the high spot of my work.

At this point, Robbie interrupts me to ask what I meant by a "reserve price". I tell him that this is the lowest amount that the person who is selling the item is prepared to accept, so the auctioneer must not sell it for less. Lucy then asks what a clerk is. I tell her that the clerk sits at a desk beside the auctioneer's rostrum, and records the price when the hammer falls, notes down the names of the buyers, and at the end of the sale takes the money in payment for the various lots. I inform my children that in an auction sale, the auctioneer holds what looks like a small hammer, which is called a gavel – sometimes this does not have a handle but it is a gavel just the same. When the auctioneer has achieved the highest bid for an item in the sale then he brings the gavel down sharply on the wooden top of his rostrum, a high desk at which he sits, and at that moment the item – known as a lot – is sold. No-one can bid after the hammer falls.

On the day in question, I tell my children, the auction sale included furniture, china, glass and some pictures. The furniture and pictures had come from the house of someone who had died, and were being sold without reserve. But the porcelain and glass belonged to a dealer who had an antique shop in the next town and who was selling some of his stock through the auction sale. I had catalogued all the furniture but I had not dealt with the rest of the items in the sale, and I had been so busy that week that I had not viewed everything. This was alright, because I knew that all the porcelain would have reserve prices placed on them by the vendor, so I would not have to decide at what figure I should start the bidding. I then explain to the children what happens at an auction sale and tell them about lots and bids.

The sale went well – the furniture first – and then the pictures and finally the porcelain and glass. There were quite a few people in the auction gallery, and some lots did not sell, because they failed to arouse any interest or because bids did not reach the reserve price. Then we came to Lot 342, and the porter held it up for me and for the buyers to see. This is normal so that people can check that what they are bidding for is what they want to buy. I read out the brief description and looked at the item. It was a highly glazed white pottery figurine of Hotei, but with a dark brown matt face, hands and belly. It was only about nine inches high but it was lovely.

"Who is Hotei?" chorus my little people.

"He is the Chinese god of happiness," I reply. "There is a superstition that if you rub his bald head and belly he will bring you good fortune. Hotei usually has a smile on his face, and this one was no exception. His mouth was extended wide with an impish grin."

I continue with my tale. I looked at this charming and charmed piece of pottery and I realised that I would like to own it and have it in the small flat where I lived. I really wanted it badly. I looked into the pale eyes in the dark face of the Hotei and he clearly demanded that I buy him. After a slight pause, I began the bidding. The reserve price was thirty pounds. I decided to bid for him myself and buy him if I could. Because I was the auctioneer conducting the sale, I would pretend to be a woman in a blue beret at the back of the auction gallery, who was chatting to a friend and not looking at me.

"What's a beret, Daddee?"

"A sort of round flat hat, often worn by the French," I reply, not too pleased to be interrupted in the middle of the bidding, so I continue.

I recall that there was only one other person in the room who seemed to want the Hotei – a man wearing a tweed jacket, leaning against the wall to the right. I usually started the bidding below the reserve price so as to conceal what the reserve was, but also to encourage bidding to start when the price was low – a normal procedure. So I began at about twenty pounds and the man in the tweed jacket nodded his head to bid, so I took my own bid of £22 off the beret at the back of the hall. Tweed Jacket then bid £24 by flicking the corner of his catalogue. People bid in different ways, I tell my listeners to try and forestall the inevitable question, and they often try to appear as if they are not bidding.

I looked at the back of the gallery and I pretended that Blue Beret bid £26. Tweed Jacket looked round to see who was bidding against him but could, of course, see nothing. His catalogue twitched and he bid £28. At this point, the woman in the beret looked up, so I could not pretend to be her, so I made my next bid of £30 pretending to be a tall man standing just behind Tweed Jacket. At this point, the children giggle. They are really enjoying this.

This was all happening quite quickly as is the way in auction sales. Tweed Jacket hesitated and, noting that the reserve price had now been reached, I was free to sell Lot 342 to myself pretending to be Tall Man. I glanced down at Hotei and his roguish smile encouraged me. I raised the gavel in my left hand, but decided that I should wait a few seconds to ensure that there was no further bidding.

Suddenly, Tweed Jacket shot up his hand and called out £32. I had to make a quick decision, and calculating that I could just afford to go another bid, I quickly responded with £34 from Blue Beret, who by this time was looking down at her catalogue. Tweed Jacket's shoulders slumped and he shook his head.

Carefully, raising my head and my gavel, I looked around the gallery and calmly asked if there were any further bids. I was far from calm inside – the Hotei figurine was almost mine, if only no one else put up a hand to bid. I brought the gavel firmly down with a large tap on the rostrum – the little god was mine. I leaned down to the clerk, who was new to the firm and rather nervous, and whispered my name. He looked a bit bewildered but wrote it down. The leering smile on the face of my little figurine seemed to congratulate me. I was delighted – £34 was a lot of money to me in those days, but I just had to have that Hotei. I smoothly went on with the next lot and to the end of the sale, with a warm glow of acquisition in my heart.

After the sale was over, I tell the children, the auctioneer and clerk had to balance the sale books.

"What's balancing the books?" asks Robbie puzzled by the vision of the auctioneer and clerk piling books high on top of each other.

Again I explain that this was a term used in accounting, and that what we had to do was to make sure that the total sums of money in his book and in mine were the same, to ensure that there were no errors. After that, the clerk would start to take the buyers' payments and issue clearing orders, so that the buyers could collect the correct items which they had bought and take them away.

By this time, the children are getting a little confused by all the auction terminology and Lucy, with a child's directness, decides to take things back to the reason for the story, and suddenly says: "But, Daddee, you were going to tell us about something which you were very sorry about. This story is

42

about you being very happy because you got your Hotei." She wrinkles her nose as she says this.

"But I didn't keep him," I say. "That's what I really regret."

"How did you lose him?" asks Robbie.

"I lost him by being too kind," and I go on to explain.

After all the buyers had paid and gone to collect the lots they had purchased, I handed my cheque to the clerk in payment for Lot 342. Then I collected my little god of happiness, and carried him to my office – a small room at the rear of the gallery which I shared with two others. I placed him carefully on my desk and bent down to rub his tummy and his head. His eyes looked straight at me, and I knew we'd get on just fine. He clearly needed a new home and I needed his smile and the good luck he might bring me.

Later on that afternoon, just before the end of the office day, Oliver, the clerk came into my office looking very upset, and he told me that he thought he might lose his job. Where we worked, the clerk had the responsibility of writing the reserves in the auctioneer's book. It was very important to get these right, because if reserves were wrong and if an item sold for less than the reserve, then the firm would have to pay the full amount of the reserve price to the vendor. Oliver explained that he had missed three reserves in the porcelain section of the sale, but luckily the price had exceeded the missed reserve prices so all was well. But, he had also failed to withdraw two lots from the sale on instructions from the vendor.

"What does withdraw mean?" asks Lucy.

"It means that you have changed your mind and do not wish to sell the item at all, so you ask the auctioneer to take it out of the sale."

There were two withdrawn lots that Oliver had missed. One lot had remained unsold so that could easily be returned to the vendor who was a dealer. He was called Mr Dean and he gave the firm a lot of business so it was therefore important to keep him happy. The other one, said Oliver, was Lot 342 – my Hotei. He pleaded with me to return the item and take back my cheque. The dealer, who had been telephoned after the sale, had been furious and insisted that the firm try to get the item back. This would normally be difficult to achieve because, once the hammer falls, the item is sold and no buyer would feel obliged to cancel his purchase and return the lot. If there has been a mistake then the firm of auctioneers has to take responsibility and recompense the vendor. But in this case, one of their own employees had bought Lot 342 and could be pressured to return it. I was told that I should be amenable, hand back my Hotei and save the firm from having a problem.

What could I do, other than agree? Oliver was so grateful, though I felt rather bitter about it. I was handed back my cheque for £34, and Hotei was taken from me and returned to Mr Dean. As he was placed in a box, I thought I detected a slight sneer in his wide smile as if he was disappointed in my feeble acquiescence. That evening, at home, without my little god of happiness, I really regretted my kind impulse to help Oliver and the firm. I was under no legal obligation to do so. Tweed Jacket would never have agreed to return the lot if he had bought it, and the firm would have paid out on their insurance. I could have kept my lovely Hotei.

For the rest of the week I felt cheated, so I resolved that on Saturday I would go into town to Mr Dean's antique shop to see if I could buy my Hotei from him direct.

I would have to pay more but it was worth a try. But when I went into Dean's Antiques, I saw my Hotei figurine reposing on a small bookcase at the back of the raised area in the window, priced up at £65, and my heart sank. I could not afford it. Even £34 had been at the limit of my resources. The smiling Hotei looked at me and his eyes seemed to urge me to try to raise the money. At this point the children laugh – they like the idea that Hotei was trying to communicate with me.

During the following week, I became obsessed with the little fat god and the need to buy him and own him, so I borrowed £10 off a friend, and took £20 out of my savings account. The following Saturday, I went back to the shop, but it was unaccountably closed, so Hotei and I stared at each other through the shop window. This time, I noticed that he had slightly raised eyebrows – as if he was asking whether my commitment was strong enough. I nodded at him – persistence would prevail!

As I could not take time off work, I had to wait until the following Saturday before I could go back. To my dismay, Hotei had been moved. Surely he could not have been sold? The shop seemed more dingy and less vibrant as I entered it. To my horror the shop assistant told me that Mr Dean had indeed sold the Hotei figurine the day before to a gentleman who lived in Scotland. I could almost hear the lingering echoes of mocking laughter from the little fellow as he departed for the cold north. He could probably visualise the chagrin on my face. Had I lost him or had he escaped me?

"I never saw my Hotei again," I tell my children. I was sad and sorry but decided to try to forget about my very brief ownership – only a few hours – of that lovely little pottery piece. But it was something that I always regretted, though it was probably selfish of me to want him so much.

"After that, the happiness went out of my life. During that year lots of things went wrong, and nothing seemed to go right until I met your mother. But I've never owned a Hotei and I probably never will." I say, concluding my story. Lucy and Robbie look suitably sad and then after a few seconds they change the subject, moving on to discuss a particularly revolting school meal they had not eaten for lunch that day, and then they run clattering out of the room.

What I omitted to tell my children is the odd fact that from the moment of my relinquishment of the Hotei, it was as though a jinx had been placed on my life. My wallet was stolen from my jacket the next week, and I lost a week's pay. The following month, I became ill and had to go into hospital. My parents decided to come and visit me but on the way they had a car accident, and Mum was killed. After my recovery, I had to go home to Leeds to look after Dad, who had been injured in the crash and was disabled. So I gave up my job at the auction house and the little flat where I lived in a nearby village. I also lost my girlfriend who did not want to move so

45

far away from her family. I had to live in the town instead of the country, and I could not find a job that enabled me to look after Dad as well as earn a living. So I became a carer and lived on benefit. On two evenings a weeks I went to china-mending classes held locally.

When Dad died three years later, I felt very sad and solitary. However, I regained my freedom of choice and I moved back to the country and did some gardening jobs, one of which was for Maria's parents. I was poor, lonely and demoralised. However, I grew to love gardening and found it very creative as well as very soothing.

When I had first met Maria, she was a student and had come home for the holidays. Then something miraculous happened – Maria and I fell in love. She had graduated in law, and was well on her way to becoming the energetic and successful lawyer that she now is. For some inexplicable reason my lack of worldliness seemed to appeal and, much to her parents' disappointment, we got married. She was then offered a good partnership in a law practice in the town we now live in and so we moved here. I gave up gardening and took up china mending and working in a local antique shop, and then along came the children.

Maria always worried about the time that she had to take off work with the birth of Lucy and then Robbie – she really likes her chosen profession, and slightly resented the intrusion of motherhood. So this was when I became a husband and a father who worked at home, ran the house and juggled all the domestic balls. The pattern of our lives soon established itself and it works well and we are happy. My career as a caring parent has been almost as successful as hers as a lawyer, though I doubt if the world sees it that way. The china mending is satisfying – putting together broken pieces of delicate porcelain to re-create a beautiful object is not dissimilar to pulling together the dislocated feelings and problems of my family to make it into a coherent and happy entity. It all seems positive and constructive.

I don't even mind if some of our more conventional acquaintance look down on me as an anomaly or a curiosity.

I have learnt much about women and the way they look at things. I learnt that people like to be needed – and they actually enjoy helping others who appear to be less fortunate than they are. Although privately I do not consider myself disadvantaged compared to them, I'm not proud and I don't mind accepting gratefully and gracefully advice about health problems and cooking meals. The Mums who collect their children from the local school used to cluck round me to see if I was managing alright but they have since got used to seeing a lone male in their midst and I'm now one of the gang. In fact I think I've become an honorary mother – the other day one of the women who collects her children started telling me about her husband and his seeming lack of interest in his family, and I found myself offering advice to her. It seems he wouldn't ever read stories to the children at bedtime whilst she prepared supper for the two of them. I suggested that perhaps he might prefer to do the cooking and then she could have the pleasure of reading to their children. She looked at me a little oddly. Some people are just not as emancipated as Maria and me.

I am clearly a successful parent because I manage to get the meal and tell the stories. It's all to do with timing – but I must be careful not to sound too efficient and organised. Some Mums are hopelessly chaotic and clearly know nothing about time and motion. It doesn't do to say too much on the subject – the inefficient ones might get resentful if they discover that you are managing better than a woman, who is, after all, a "natural" mother and carer. So from time to time I pretend to be a bit disorganised or tired, and then I'm acceptable again. My role is to cope – but not too conspicuously well. I must not be seen to be as competent as they are. I don't mind these games if it smoothes my path amongst my fellow Mums – in fact I find them quite enjoyable. I tell all this to Maria – when she's not too tired to take in the mundane subtlety of it all. We both know that it is to do with respecting other people's views and not criticising the way they run their own lives. With our maternal gang, I'm quite friendly and easy-going and don't have an axe to grind. In fact this probably contributes to the fact that I seem to be quite popular – I even get the occasional proposition from one or two of the Mums who are obviously eliciting little interest from their spouses.

I also tell Maria about this – and we laugh over it whilst I gently reassure her that I am not tempted. We have a good relationship. She is also aware of the times when I am tired and fraught – which does happen occasionally when the little monsters have been needling each other for hours and getting on my nerves. I dislike discord as much as anyone, even though my tolerance of it is usually higher than others. It is at these times that she makes an effort to give me some space and a respite from our offspring and takes them off to read to them or tell them a story. Even though her powers of invention are rarely as exalted as mine, at least she does it – even after a long days work with legal documents.

Sometimes, when you tell children a story, it stays with them and they ask to hear it again and again. But as they grow older books and television take over, and the memory and magic of the story fades with the passing of time. So I am surprised when, on my birthday, I unwrap a small present from Lucy to find a diminutive ivory-coloured figure of Hotei. This is nearly a year after I had told my children the story about him. I am always amazed at children and their ability to retain details of a picture, conversation or story from some months or years before. Lucy clearly remembers more than I realise.

"Now, Daddee," she says, seriously. "Hotei will bring Happiness back into your life." I do not tell her that I have been happy since I fell in love with Maria and even happier since I became a father. My daughter has clearly had the delightful notion that I have been gloomy and sad but will now be joyous and light-hearted, and that it is she who has flicked the switch.

Lucy then explains that she saw the Hotei in "Yin Yang", which is a small shop in town which sells earrings, lucky charms and other pretty items of decorative junk. I have often received gifts bought by the children in this delectable treasure house. I had, as usual, given them some money with which to purchase my present (something which the primary wage-earner of the household often forgets to do) and last week, when Lucy was out with a friend from school and her friend's Mum, whom I know well, she had spotted the little figure with the wording "Hotei" beside it. So she bought it for me – and was highly pleased with herself for finding it. Lucy loves giving presents, and she wanted to tell me the tale of her quest. I watch her porcelain skin and rosebud lips as she smiles at me, and a brief pang of exquisite pleasure stabs me in the pit of my stomach.

I glance at Maria, who is drinking her coffee and staring in an unfocussed way at her daughter that indicates, as I know well, that she is actually thinking about some thorny problem for which she has to use her ingenuity to resolve today. I love their mother very much, even though she has forgotten my birthday. Maria had given me a rueful smile when she saw the two little packages in birthday paper propped up against my cereal plate on the breakfast table. I am surprised that neither of our two little angels had the foresight to remind her. They are used to her pre-occupation with work and her lack of recognition of what we know to be important family occasions. Perhaps their decision not to remind her gives them a chance to feel superior. "Mummy really ought to remember," they will say solemnly shaking their heads in judgement.

She may remember to bring me back some flowers or a book when she comes home – always assuming she has time to take a break and get to a shop during her long and arduous office day. I busy myself opening the gift from my son and this activity hides my disappointment. Robbie loves to watch the reaction on my face as I unwrap the paper and extract the gift, so I play up a bit, taking my time and placing an expression of surprise and delight on my face. The delight is genuine. He has given me a wooden paper knife with an owl painted on the handle. I am touched by his desire to please me. I tell him that I think it the most beautiful owl in the world, and that the knife will come in so useful to open all the letters I get (few enough, in fact – most are for my wife). This token of love is infinitely precious and I give my son a cuddle in thanks for his gift, feeling with acute pleasure the sturdy frame beneath his fragile confidence. In utter contentment I watch my wife who, looking beautiful and distracted, has just located her briefcase behind the children's satchels.

Lucy, who thinks I have spent enough time examining Robbie's present, brings me back to hers. "But Daddee, you do love Hotei, don't you?" she pleads, placing her small hand on my arm. I nod vigorously whilst squeezing Robbie with my other arm. Maria looks across the kitchen at her family tableau. She has half-heard Lucy's remark whilst she was putting on her suit jacket. She is about to leave for the office and has just enough time to be mystified. "Who is Hotei?" she asks with her eyebrows elegantly raised.

"You," I say to my goddess of selfless toil. "And the children" – but I don't utter the last three words – I am a considerate man.

I blow her a kiss, and before Robbie or Lucy have a chance to explain to their mother about the little god, the door closes behind her. She is not a paragon but she is the breadwinner, and I do love her. At these times, I mentally pat myself on the back and consider myself a model of parenthood and understanding, whilst also being aware that I am sometimes a little smug. Sighing at Maria's lack of perception I gather up discarded wrapping paper and dirty plates from the table before driving my children to school.

EVANESCENCE

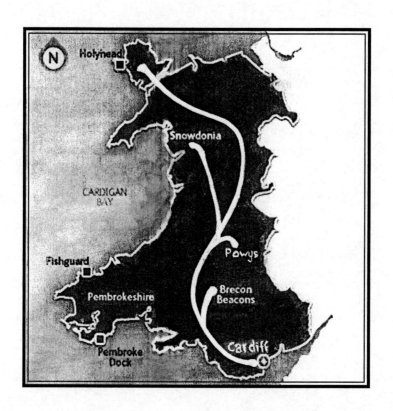

Evanescence

It was a dark night somewhere in the Atlantic Ocean. The sailing vessel was heading westwards, and had been close hauled on the wind for over ten days. The sails were set, one of the crew was at the wheel and the others on deck ignored the light rain and the occasional spray. The night watch debating society comprising four members of the crew was in full swing in spite of the damp and the darkness. Topics covered that night had ranged from the universal heights of "Can there ever be a justification for war?" to the personal depths of "What I dislike most in the world."

The former had evolved into a discussion of political ideologies, with Bryony sitting under the spray hood beating her socialist feminist pacifist drum whilst Shane, lounging on the windward cockpit seat with his long legs stretched across and braced against the other seat, branded himself as a warmongering racist reactionary in order to have a good argument and wind up the others. Bryony and Shane enacted their usual game of taking totally opposing views, but whereas Bryony tended to argue from conviction, Shane did so out of perversity. Xavier, who was standing whilst he helmed, listened in his usual taciturn way and Ian from the leeward cockpit seat argued for tolerance of other people's extreme beliefs. As usual the debate descended into mud slinging with Bryony accusing Shane of "being somewhere to the far right of Colonel Blimp or Genghis Khan."

Shane responded by saying that it was clear to everyone Trotsky would be her hero. This was guaranteed to irritate Ian who demanded, in the angry puzzled way he adopted when he felt that his lack of education was under attack, to know, "Who the hell is Trotsky?" As usual no one replied to his sneering rhetorical question and at that point the bows hit a particularly awkward wave drenching the cockpit and crew in curiously warm water. The ensuing wail of dismay doused the political debate.

The boat had been on passage for nearly three weeks, and everyone aboard was used to the conditions that had prevailed for some days. When the sails had been adjusted and the course checked, there was not much to do except chat. It was too wet for a Sony Walkman and books could be read only during off-watch hours below when sleep eluded, though this was seldom because of the tiring regime. So talking, recounting stories and imparting opinions were the normal routine for night watches. During the day watches there was generally work to be done – bosun's work repairing or servicing gear, sail mending, cooking and cleaning below, and – the most unpopular of all – washing up greasy plates in cold sea-water. On deck, of course, there were frequent sail changes and the constant sail trimming, but at night enthusiasm for these diminished and the crew combated tiredness by lengthy discussions about life with a capital 'L'.

Xavier, a quiet French Canadian who was the watch leader, asked Ian to ease off a bit on the main sheet as the boat was heeling over a bit too much in the strengthening wind, and he then put Shane on the helm before he went below to make a note in the ship's log on the chart table. The crew members took half hour turns helming at the large wheel situated in the stern of the boat, which had an aft cockpit. When Xavier came up on deck, there was a lull in the conversation whilst sails were checked and re-trimmed. The sailing boat – called 'Artemis' – was 60ft in length, and there were nine on board including the skipper. The crew were organised into two watches of four which alternated every six hours and the skipper did the navigation and helped with sail changes and problems. That night the skipper was on "golden kip." This was an uninterrupted night of sleep, which was taken by each member of the crew in rotation once every nine days. It happened to be skipper's turn so he was below. This meant that the habitual night watch chatter was less constrained than it would have been in his presence.

In the last hour of their watch, Ian dozed on the bridge deck sheltered by the spray hood, but the other three kept themselves awake and alert by chatting. The Hippos, the friendly nickname for 'A' watch, who were always accused of wallowing in self-pity in preference to seawater, had the first half of the night on deck which started at 2000 after supper and lasted six hours when they were all wearily aching to climb into their berths in the cabins below and get some sleep. They had had a sail change early on as the wind increased, and to their disgust two of them had got thoroughly wet on the foredeck, but otherwise their watch was uneventful.

It was Bryony who had instigated the "What I dislike most" topic which soon turned into a competition as to who could best lampoon the boat (for which they had great affection) the watch leaders (both of whom they admired) and the voyage (which they were enjoying hugely).

Shane, whose tall frame was slightly illuminated by the low light of the compass on the binnacle in front of the wheel, carelessly pushed back the hood on his oilskins from his blonde hair and said: "What I hate most is a boat where you bash your head on a low bulkhead every time you walk through the cabin." Shane's height and his clumsy co-ordination in the constantly moving vessel meant that he was forever hitting his head and incurring bruises. "When I make my million I'll have a luxury motor yacht – not subject to the vagaries of the wind – and with plenty of head room."

Bryony, her lank hair plastered to her pale face, her fastidiousness well known to her crewmates, announced that in her opinion, "Cleaning teeth in seawater is one of life's nastiest experiences."

Ian, who was renowned for having the smelliest feet aboard, then said: " Washing in sea-water is definitely a worse option than not washing at all."

This produced a response of, "Filthiness is next to Godlessness," from Bryony and a nod of agreement from Xavier who shaved every day and deplored the habit of the younger men on board of retaining their stubble in the hope that a beard would grow.

The depths of triviality having been plumbed, it was discovered that only twenty minutes remained before watch changeover, and Bryony was deputed to go below and wake up the other watch, but reminded not to disturb the skipper who was, "On golden".

As Bryony pushed past Ian at the top of the companionway steps, he woke up and said. "How much longer until the end of the watch? I can't wait to get those bloody Rhinos up here getting wet instead of me." 'B' watch were insultingly known as the Rhinos who unaccountably lacked aggression and hard grit.

Shane, who was getting the full brunt of the frequent spray from the waves pointed out that Ian was the only one in the dry. This produced only a grunt, and a comment from Xavier that if Shane helmed with more concentration he could avoid hitting so many waves and deluging his fellow crew members so often.

At watch change, the oncoming Rhinos traded the usual insults with the Hippos as they went off. "What, only 43 miles in 6 hours – pathetic!" This was greeting with a comment along the lines of "Reluctantly we must hand over to the amateurs."

The Rhinos took the second night watch – the one which involved dragging themselves out of their hot bunks in the fetid forward cabins at just before 0200 to come on deck in the chilly darkness and which ended at 0800 by which time the watch were ravenous for breakfast at the end of their stint. The first part of the watch was usually quiet whilst the crew adjusted their eyes to the dark and woke up fully.

Midway through the watch the blackness of the overcast skies were beginning to lighten to that dull metal greyness which preceded dawn. The sails had been adjusted for a slight shift in wind direction about an hour before, and a reef had been put in the mainsail to reduce canvas for the rising strength of the wind. So there was nothing much to do except talk desultorily amongst themselves. They were almost in the tropics, so it was warm, but a light drizzle and the odd wave over the deck meant they had to wear their oilskins to keep dry.

Ralph was on the helm. Small in stature he stood with his legs planted apart to keep his balance, his slender hands holding the big wheel, his elfin features visible in the light from the compass. Tina, the dormouse of the crew who loved her sleep above all, was curled up and dozing in her favourite position – on a damp sail bag on the cockpit floor out of the wind. Evan, the watch leader, was sitting up on the windward side his arm round a winch to keep his balance and keeping an eye on the sails. Nigel was lying full length on the leeward seat, with his head propped up on a coiled rope – something which the skipper had said was dangerous. Lying down was not allowed because the tendency to drop off was strong – and all crew on each watch had to stay awake and keep vigilant whilst on deck. But when the skipper was below – or having some kip, one of two members of the crew flouted the strict rules in order to relax the muscles for a few minutes which were usually taut with the effort of balancing on a lunging boat heeled over at an angle of thirty degrees, which was chopping through the waves and being slewed over by the swell or a strong gust of wind.

Evan had initiated the topic of conversation, which was about having a change of direction in life. He thought that a sailing voyage gave one a different perspective on things and prompted an alteration in attitude and values which was refreshing.

Ralph, in the intervals from his careful concentration on helming, had thrown in the odd comments about his situation. Until recently, he had worked in an office in the centre of Coventry and said that, though he had been brought up in an urban environment, he would much prefer to live in the country or in a small town with a job which did not wholly engross every minute of every day but which allowed him some leisure and quality of life.

The conversation had then drifted from Nigel's reminiscences about working in pubs to his speculations about how long it would take to get to their destination port and how many girls he might be a able to score with when he did get there. Nigel was very keen on sailing and was taking time off to do this voyage before he looked for another job in a pub that was nearer the sea. Under his open yellow oily jacket he was wearing his grubby white tee shirt with the words "Real sailors drink real beer" across his broad chest. In order to tease Tina, he announced from his prone position that his order of preferences were firstly sailing, secondly boozing and lastly womanising.

In order to cut short such drivel Tina sat up and asked Evan if he thought the wind was going to strengthen. Before the latter had a chance to reply, Nigel chipped in with his favourite expression: "It's a definite maybe". Evan then said that he thought that the wind would probably decrease around dawn.

Having finished his half hour spell on the helm, Ralph handed over to Evan who, buttoning up his jacket against the wind, grasped the wheel in his bony hands. Ralph reminded him of the compass course, and then sat down on the vacated seat and stared into the middle distance trying to see if the horizon was yet visible. He was hungry – and breakfast was over two hours away.

Evan, whose tall thin frame belied his strength, tended to helm sitting on the raised edge of the cockpit on the windward side so he could see the sails. At night when it was dark he occasionally asked one of the others to shine a torch on the sails so he could do this. Having looked around and assimilated a small change in the wind direction, he asked Nigel to adjust the foresails – a high cut yankee and the staysail. This done, he settled down and, whilst helming and keeping up the boat's speed, he also managed to take part in the general chat, which at this moment centred round what they were all going to do the first night in port. Nigel wanted to go to a nightclub and see if he could pick up a girl, Ralph said he would go for a long solitary moonlit walk and Tina opted for a night's sleep in a soft bed after a long hot bath. Evan thought he might have a meal in a restaurant in good company with a good bottle of wine.

At the mention of food, Tina, reluctant to relinquish her much coveted position out of the wind, and knowing that Ralph was always hungry, asked him if he would nip below and bring up a packet of biscuits. A few minutes later they were all munching away and Tina was regaling the others with a description of the type of biscuits she liked best – none of which – to her disgust – had been included on the provisioning list for the boat. Food talk – always a vibrant topic of conversation – lasted about half an hour and was succeeded by the ever popular subject of sex, and in particular an old edition of Mayfair which was lying dog-eared on the saloon table below. Did Nigel fancy the brunette on the front cover as much as Evan did? In much the same way as he had declared that he liked custard more than cream, Ralph announced that he preferred the blonde in the centre pages who was sitting naked on a wooden chair to the dark haired cover-girl who was bending down wearing red high heel shoes and nothing else.

Tina kept silent during these pathetic and banal discussions – she had already decided to lob the offending magazine overboard at the next opportunity. The howl of rage this would induce would be worth enduring the boys' subsequent teasing. Bryony, the only other girl on the crew, would be on her side – she was just as sick of these chauvinistic comments – and had recently announced with an aristocratic yawn that the conversation on board was so boring – and that all anyone could discuss was the five "ings" – eating, drinking, sleeping, shitting and screwing. Even Nigel, who took pride in being more foul-mouthed than anyone else on board, had blinked in surprise when he heard this utterance in her irritatingly classy voice, but he had to admit she had hit the nail on the "effing" head.

In order to raise the tone of the conversation from the topic of girly magazines Evan said, in his oddly quiet but commanding way, that he had been thinking about immortality. This remark was greeted with amazed silence which was inevitably broken by Nigel who chortled: "It must be all those stars which we haven't seen tonight that brings this on this aberration in our revered watch leader."

"Well, it isn't given to many people to be a Rembrandt or a Mozart. Or Einstein or Shakespeare," said Tina sitting up and joining in what she thought would be a more interesting discussion. "How else can one achieve immortality except by creating or discovering something which lives on after one's death?"

Evan smiled. "I suppose what I really meant to ask you all was essentially this….." He paused to duck the spray from a wave, which deluged the cockpit and evoked a screech of dismay from Tina who took a direct hit. When the protests had died down he continued, "You're all young – what do you want to achieve in life? Here we are on a boat passing from what used to be called the old world to the new. Life is like a sailing passage – transitional. In the grand scheme of things we live for only a brief moment in the enormity of eternity. We're just a speck on the horizon or a drop in the ocean. But we each have our fleeting time on earth and what we do want to make of it?"

Nigel, always the first to respond, blurted out, "This sort of conversation makes me feel distinctly uncomfortable. I never think of myself as insignificant but perhaps I'm biased!" He laughed and patted his pectoral muscles with his big fists. "But to answer you, I suppose my goal in life is to have fun, to go sailing, to have a pie and a pint in my local pub and to be surrounded by those who enjoy a laugh like I do. In fact I'd quite like to help other people to enjoy themselves."

Evan looked affectionately at Nigel's good natured sunburnt face in the pale pre-dawn light, before leaning over the wheel to look down at Tina who was sitting on the cockpit sole with her back to the compass binnacle facing away from him, "What about you, Tina?"

"I want to be respected," she said slowly. "I want to have a reputation for being good at what I do and for being honest." They all knew that Tina had been at art school and was interested in painting. She had a sketchbook aboard and often made sketches of her fellow crew members. The opportunity to undertake this sea voyage had presented itself and she had taken it. Though inexperienced and unsure if she really liked ocean sailing, she was determined to be a competent and valued crew member. She was uncompromising, tough, critical of herself and often disappointed in her efforts. "I think what I would really like to do is to create art – enduring art," she concluded.

Nigel at this point got to his feet and clambered onto the deck by the stern rail, to urinate over the side.

Annoyed at what she saw as a crude reaction to her serious declaration, Tina said snappily, "The men on this boat pee an inordinate amount."

"And women on this boat nag an inordinate amount," said Nigel placidly as he zipped up his flies. "Come on, Ralph, let's hear what a man wants to do."

Ralph whose reticent shyness and diminutive stature meant that he never put himself forward, was now relaxed enough with his teasing but kindly ship-mates to be able to respond. "I'm not ambitious," he admitted. "I don't want to set the world alight. I admire Tina for her desire to achieve recognition through her artistic talent, but I would like to be ordinary. To blend in and not arouse hostility." He paused to think and then continued reflectively, "I think I'm more at home in the natural world than in a man-made environment and I don't want to go on working in an office. I like the sea and this adventure but feel more at home on land. I want to live and work in the country. Yes – perhaps I'll grow things," he concluded with a wistful look, waving his hand gracefully.

Evan, who had listened carefully with his usual focussed frown to what had been said, encapsulated their comments in the same way as he had always summarised the points taught at the end of a lesson when he had been working as a teacher. " So Nigel wants to enjoy himself and help other people to do the same. Tina wants to be respected as a creative artist, and Ralph would like to live in the country and work with nature. That seems to be the essence of what you're all saying."

"It's your turn now, Evan", called Tina. "You can't ask us questions and then cop out. Time to bare your soul."

"That sounds a bit chilly," said Nigel promptly and stopped to wait for the laugh, which duly came.

Evan smiled and replied that he had no intention of baring his soul to anyone but that he thought he would like to create something that would live on after his death. "I hope that isn't arrogant."

Tina interrupted him. "Of course it isn't. Lots of people want to leave something behind them. I certainly do. But for the majority of non-creative people, the easiest way is by having children who will outlive their parents and march forward into the future."

"Well, tragically I haven't found a wife yet," said Evan with mock sadness in his voice. "But I definitely would like children – lots of them."

Looking at his watch, he announced that the skipper had said that they should tack about an hour before the end of the watch and get everything set up for the oncoming Hippos who would have to prepare and eat breakfast before they came on deck and took over. The Rhinos made ready in their usual efficient manner and Evan called "Ready About", and swiftly spun the wheel round, whilst the others freed the sheets and winched in the sails on the other side.

When this manoeuvre had been completed and the sails re-trimmed, Evan put Tina on the helm and went below for a minute to note the tack and the new course in the logbook. When his head re-appeared in the companionway hatch, it was to ask if anyone by any chance would like a cup of tea. This was greeted with "Yeah!" in unison, and a timorous request from Ralph for another biscuit. As he went below to put on the kettle, Evan smiled to himself. He was fond of the youngsters – they were a good team – including those on the other watch. He was some fifteen years older than them and he enjoyed their exuberance and affectionate jokes in the same way as he had always liked enthusiasm in his pupils at the school where he had worked before he took up yacht deliveries and sail training cruises. He was adept at controlling eager crew members who thought they knew it all, and gently encouraged and taught those who lacked confidence and experience.

The current crew were a likeable bunch who were interesting characters though all very different, and he felt a real bond with them all because of the bad knock down they had suffered a week earlier, when with all hands on deck they had behaved with courage and efficiency. Evan had been washed over the side of the boat though still attached by his lifeline, and three of the lads had pulled him back aboard. He was grateful for their quick reactions and strength. Seriousness and responsibility lay below their light-hearted jesting behaviour. The camaraderie was as genuine as the mutual respect and affection.

When Evan was back on deck having distributed hot mugs of tea, and Nigel was taking the last half hour trick on the helm before the end of their watch, the discussion about aims and ambitions continued. For the first ten days of the voyage, until he swapped with Xavier, Evan had been watch leader on the other watch, with Bryony, Shane and Ian. He told his listeners that he had asked them the same question about what they wanted to achieve in life.

"I expect those toffee-nosed Hippos were rather more highbrow than us," said Nigel with a grin. He was on good terms with everyone aboard.

"Tell us what they said, then," said Tina, who was curious.

Evan recalled the scene in his mind. Bryony, usually so cool and confident, had revealed a disappointment in her young life. She had said, "I had hoped that one day I might become a doctor, but I found it so awfully hard doing exams and I didn't make the grade into medical school. I'm not much good at anything else except cooking, so I'll probably end up as a caterer." Inevitably the boys had jeered when they discovered that their feminist crew member had resigned herself to being a galley slave. Bryony shouted at them, "I emphatically do not want to prepare food on this boat! No one appreciates my culinary skills and subtlety – none of you have any taste or discernment – all anyone ever wants to eat is bloody custard and crumble."

To his listeners on the other watch, Evan said: "Bryony wants to be a doctor."

Tina then asked what Ian aimed to do in life. Ian was passionate about travelling and had already wearied his fellow sailors with descriptions of an overland trip to India. Evan remembered his enthusiastic statement: "I want to travel – to every Continent and live and work in different places. I want to explore and discover and cross boundaries." He had been on the helm and was steering rather erratically having lost concentration in his vision of a peripatetic life in exotic places. "I'm nearly 24 and I still feel poised on the threshold of life. I want to get on with real ....." At this point the bow of the boat took a lunge in the wrong direction, the sails backed and he had broken off and muttered an apology whilst he got them back on course.

Shane had made his habitual caustic comment saying, " Off course, off balance – our Ian's not poised at all."

Bryony had laughed saying, "Not so. He's achieving his ambition right now – travelling between two Continents."

Sullen and aware of their constant teasing, Ian had doggedly concluded, "I don't care for rain and cold climates. I want to live in the sun."

"Ian would like to travel and live in the tropics." Evan related to the other watch, " And – no surprise here – Shane wants to be a success."

Shane made no secret of the fact that he wanted to make a million. He was the youngest on board and his insecurity about being thought immature manifested itself in his assumption of an easy over-confident charm. All his young life he had become used to his handsome face and blue eyes being admired. So he quite enjoyed the others on the crew who teased him good naturedly about his "ugly mug", about his lofty ambitions and his desire to be a high flyer in the city, where had had spent some months working as a office boy in a firm of stockbrokers. On board he was often accused of being lazy, but in fact he tried to avoid tasks in which he knew he would not excel. He craved praise and hated criticism. He wanted to be popular and on rare occasions when he was not taken seriously, his brittle sense of humour deserted him and he became moody and rebellious.

Nigel said kindly "I like Shane – he's unashamedly materialistic."

Ralph was scornful of the pursuit of worldly wealth. "I simply cannot understand why anyone wants to be in the City of London in a high powered pressured job which demands working all hours God made. It would send me crazy."

Tina commented laconically that so far Shane had shown no signs of overwork.

Evan laughed and said: "Shane's alright. He just wants

to grow up fast." What he left unsaid was that Shane wanted above all to avoid failure.

The following day, the wind decreased and they had their first day of sunshine for a week. Around the middle of the day, the off watch came on deck to enjoy the sun. Shane and Ian who were on watch had removed most of their clothes and Nigel was quick to do the same when he emerged from below. Ralph who was more self-conscious never stripped off, and Evan and Xavier rarely did. The two girls retained their clothes and their dignity, though the skipper who was on the helm was a champion of nudity and demonstrated his commitment. In his presence there were some muted jokes about six packs and showing off, with flexing of muscles and questions to the girls such as "Don't you fancy my body?"

This produced the inevitable howl of denial by Tina and a brisk retort by Bryony that, "Familiarity breeds contempt." The skipper roared with laughter.

At this point Evan, who had been the last to wake up, showed his face in the companionway hatch, and smiled as he realised that the crew were again engaged in their usual joking banter. A query from Shane as to why Evan didn't join in by stripping off, elicited a quick insult from Nigel, "Because he's an ugly Welsh git who's too thin by half," and a rueful laugh from the target of this remark who was well aware of how apt it was.

The skipper, with his usual heavy-handed humour, asked if one of the two female members of the crew might be prepared to alleviate the boredom by doing the dance of the seven army blankets. The girls dutifully laughed and shook their heads.

Ian asked them why they wouldn't oblige, and Nigel inevitably chimed in with, "Because their tits are too small."

This produced a withering rejoinder by Bryony, "The only thing that guys with small brains ever think about is girls with large breasts."

Then it was general insult time. Tina was a repressed female, Nigel a boorish oaf, Shane a chauvinist pig and Bryony an arrogant snob. This then led on to an enjoyable heated argument about stereotypes, and whether people grew into predictable roles. Ian was definitely going to be a wild rover, Evan was certain to be a crusty bachelor and no doubt Shane would become a male model!

Xavier, pointing at the battered check shirt he wore, laughingly said in his delightful French accent that he might become a lumberjack. This was greeted with howls of derision and delight, and though mystified as to the cause, he was to be teased about his remark for the duration of the passage. Ralph, looking up at the mast and squinting at the white sails bright in the sunlight, said he would rather grow trees that hack them down.

"Ralph," said Tina smiling at the young man, "Always tries to change the subject to something more uplifting. The other night he started telling us all about phosphorescence in the sea. In the end we couldn't decide whether the phenomenon was evanescent or effervescent, and we had a good debate about onomatopoeia in words."

"What the hell is that?" growled Ian predictably.

Ignoring his querulous interruption, Bryony yawned and said "Anyone trying the elevate the conversation on this boat is fighting a losing battle. Even if we start talking about celestial navigation, we always get back to sex in the end! It makes me want to go back to my bunk, sleep and oblivion. Whose turn it is to be on Golden Kip tonight?"

"That sleepaholic Tina," said Evan. "It might be a peaceful night watch for a change."

"Wonderful," retorted Tina with a grin. " I can't wait for a twelve hour break from all your interminable rubbish." This precipitated howls of derisory laughter. Then the skipper asked one of his crew to go below and get him a beer. The vessel sailed on.

* * * * *

It was grey windy day in Cardiff some thirty years later. Autumn had come early and the trees were turning colour. Tina was watching others arrive and assemble, each looking either awkward or serious. She caught sight of a tall pale-haired woman hurrying from the car park with an elegant rolled black umbrella in one hand and an expensive looking leather bag slung over her shoulder. She paused to look at the face beneath the neat black hat and instantly recognised Bryony, whom she had not seen for over twenty years.

"Bryony," she called out as the figure drew near. "It's me, Tina," she said using a nickname she had dropped long ago when she had reverted to her real name of Tatiana.

The woman stopped and peered at the small dark haired figure some twenty yards off. She fished into her bag and brought out some glasses and having put them on, she focussed on the woman who had addressed her, and with a yelp of surprise she walked up to her and said, "Good grief, it's you, Tina. I'd no idea that you knew Evan."

"If you remember," said Tina dryly, "We all sailed across the Atlantic together once many years ago."

"Oh yes, I know that. What I meant was that I didn't realize that you still knew Evan."

"We're not the only ones who kept in touch, it seems," said Tina, indicating a balding man who was waiting on the grass near the gravel path with his hands in his pockets. "Isn't that Ian? Over there by the railings. He's rather bald now, but it's him alright."

"The chap he's talking to seems a bit familiar," said Bryony peering through her glasses. "I think it's Nigel."

"It is," said Tina. "You can't mistake that paunch. He's put on a lot more weight, but that was always going to happen."

At this point, a black suited figure emerged from the chapel and, calling out in a loud but reverential tone that the guests for Mr Pritchard's funeral could now go in, he ushered the waiting group towards the door. Ian caught sight of Bryony and Tina as they went in, and gave them a discreet wave, which Tina returned. Nigel, who had been astonished but delighted to meet up with Ian ten minutes earlier, gave an inappropriately broad grin when he caught sight of the two women, and was unable to resist an over-loud stage whisper, "Hey girls, see you afterwards."

Tina winced and nodded at him as they filed into seats on the opposite sides of the small aisle. The recorded organ music doused conversation and the guests fastened their eyes on the coffin before them, and quietly watched as Angharad, the wife of the deceased, entered the chapel and sat down at the front.

Twenty-five minutes later they were all outside again. The congregation had filed out and were standing around, some with the usual bewildered opaque expressions of those who have been moved but are trying to control their feelings, and others who had given way to their sorrow and loss and were either crying quietly into their handkerchiefs, or were trying to rearrange their faces and retrieve their dignity.

There was a chill north-easterly blowing and Tina, who still avoided standing in draughts or strong winds, positioned herself near the side wall of the chapel, out of the cold. The other three joined her, and they all stared, without speaking, at the flowers and wreaths that were laid out on a small lawn beside the chapel just below them, the bright colours leeching into the soft dark earth as a slight drizzle or tears blurred their vision. Nigel had been crying and blowing his nose noisily and Bryony eyes were red behind her glasses. Tina and Ian were dry eyed and looked sombre.

"Well, that was a good little service," Nigel blurted out, keen to break the silence and trying the get his emotions under control.

Tina said "I thought it soulless. I can't stand crematoriums, and these dreary conveyer belt services. They're all the same."

"Shane's service wasn't." Bryony spoke with an unsteady gulping sound. "It was very 'off the wall', if I remember rightly. And the wake afterwards was wild."

"That was a long time ago," Ian spoke for the first time.

"Twenty five years," said Tina in a clipped voice. "Shane's been dead for a quarter of a century."

Nigel nodding furiously and blinking hard, remembered the other tragedy – of a young life cut short

"Why the hell do we only ever meet up at funerals?" Ian said putting into words his anger against whatever force it was that had caused the death of his closest friend.

Ignoring his rhetorical question, as she had always done, Bryony took off her glasses and wiped the moisture off them. "I always howl at funerals. I feel so sad and empty."

"Me, too," said Nigel with a watery smile. "I feel as if I've lost my best mate."

"And you can't believe you're never going to see him again," sympathised Bryony, putting her gloved hand on his arm.

"Never going to have a laugh or a drink with him again. He's not going to be there to pat you on the back or listen to your troubles," continued Nigel. "Evan was a great guy."

They all nodded, and watched as a car drove up and Angharad and an elderly couple, who were probably her parents, got into it. Some of the other guests began to wander off and disperse quietly and with dignity. There were no children at the service to lighten the tone, as there had been at Shane's funeral, when his younger half-brothers and sisters had been so melodramatically distraught.

Suddenly, Tina called out. "Look – over there. It's Ralph." She hadn't noticed him during the service, his lack of height and self-effacing manner as ever having pushed him into obscurity, but she caught sight of him standing alone under a tree, when those who had been in front of him walked off down the path.

Nigel spun round, still agile for such a big man, and yelled: "Ralph, we're all over here." The slight figure came slowly towards them – he was aware they were there – he had seen them all in the chapel and knew they would eventually notice him.

Tina rushed up to him and kissed him on the cheek – she had not done this to any of the others – but Ralph looked vulnerable as always and seemed to need a very overt sign of recognition. He blushed and shook the others' hands, smiling at them in turn.

"It's good to see you all," he said, but what he didn't say was that he was very surprised that they were there. He was unaware that Evan had kept in touch with the other members of the crew – the older man had certainly never mentioned them in all the years he had known him. The crew of Artemis had split up after the sailing voyage and gone their separate ways. A couple of reunions and Shane's funeral had brought them briefly together during the first few years, but then he had lost contact with them. All except Evan who had kept in touch, and become his firm friend and wise mentor.

To the others, Ralph appeared to be the same quiet person – but a little more self-possessed and still looking young, having aged less than the others. Tina was thinner and her uncompromising character was deeply etched into her lined face. Bryony was a handsome middle-aged woman in her fifties and, with a smile more warmly generous than it had once been, she appeared less brusque and more compassionate. Ian, though sun tanned, looked tired but with the same questing look he had always had. He had tried to conceal his baldness by cutting what remained of his hair very short. Nigel's laugh lines round his eyes had proliferated and his belly was now fat instead of muscle, but he exuded the old familiar geniality and goodwill, which had always meant he was well liked.

A light rain began to fall and the smoke from the Thornvale Crematorium blew away over the group of yew trees the other side of the garden of remembrance with its carpet of depressingly damp floral tributes.

"I think the rain might get worse," said Tina looking up at the clouds.

"That's a definite maybe," Nigel chipped in quickly and two of the others smiled remembering his by-line on the boat.

"Getting soaked together seems unavoidable," murmured Ralph, recalling their sailing voyage, but no one heard the joke.

"Are we going to the gathering at Evan's house?" asked Bryony. "I mean Ahgharad's house – as it is now."

"I don't really know her very well – which is odd considering how often I've seen Evan in recent years. We always seem to meet – we always met – in pubs," said Nigel.

"I don't know her at all, but I don't think I want to. She has no taste in funerals," said Tina.

"It wasn't too bad," said Bryony. "I liked the Good Samaritan reading, though it's a bit odd at a funeral."

Ralph said with quiet intensity, "It was awful. The dignity and enormity of death to be reduced to a cramped twenty minutes, wedged in between other hurried funerals, with piped organ music and that awful whirring sound when the coffin slides forward and the curtain parts. No thanks. When I go, I want to be buried under a tree with no fuss and plastic frills."

"I need a drink", said Nigel, who felt uncomfortable with their critical comments.

In the end, they decided to go to the local pub, which Nigel had earlier spotted just down the road from the wrought iron gates of the crematorium and its grounds. The rain was falling more steadily, so they walked away together and a few minutes later arrived at The Three Elms.

"Not a very accurate name," remarked Ralph, looking at the five trees near the pub. "Not one of them is an elm!"

Nigel inevitably bought the first round of drinks, and Tina and Ralph found a table beside the window and sat down. Bryony went to the cloakroom to wash her face and Ian hung up his raincoat.

"Have you come far, Nigel?" asked Tina, when the big man had sat down.

"Not too far because I live in Wales. I run a small charter business – sailing boats – small cruisers. It's up in Holyhead."

"How amazing. I moved here too. I've got a cottage in the Brecon Beacons." Tina did not say that she shared the cottage, which was owned by her partner Paul,

Then Ralph said in his diffident way, "I live in Wales as well."

"You don't! Where?"

"I'm up in Powys – I used to work for the Welsh Forestry Commission, and I stayed on in the area after I set up my own business." Ralph was a tree specialist – and had recently written a book on conifers. But he did not mention this.

Bryony came back to the table and Nigel handed her the glass of wine she had asked for. "Where have you travelled from, then?" he asked her.

71

"Oh, only a few miles. I live in Cardiff – on the other side of the city. I married a doctor – he's Welsh – was born in Swansea. I'm a doctor too, now," Bryony added.

"Isn't that what you always wanted to do?" said Ian. "Or perhaps you wanted to be a chef. I can't quite remember."

"None of us is Welsh and yet we're all living here – how strange!" said Tina.

"I'm not," said Ian. "I'm a man of no fixed abode," he added with a note of pride in his voice.

"Still the rolling stone, eh?" said Nigel giving him a slap on the back, to which Ian managed not to react with aversion.

"Yep," he drawled, taking a large swallow of his beer. "I've lived in Indonesia, Venezuela, Nigeria, Australia and Norway. I'm in the oil business. I live where the work is." The others reacted with politely raised eyebrows of congratulatory surprise.

"Norway sounds the odd man out, Ian." said Bryony. "I thought you favoured hot climates."

Ian laughed as he looked round at his audience. "I was desperate for a job when I took that contract." He had been very surprised to see the other crew members of Artemis from all those years ago. Evan had never given him an indication that he was keeping in contact with the others on the boat – he had never referred to them in his letters. But here were four of them – thirty years older but essentially the same.

But not Evan. Ian felt a spasm of loss. It was Evan's death that had caused them to meet up once again after so long. My goodness, he thought, we all look exactly the same. We're a bit fatter or thinner or greyer, but physically, people don't change that much. "My round," he said aloud. "Same again?"

Ralph put his half-pint down on the table and turned to Tina. "So what do you do on your Welsh mountain?" he asked with a smile.

"I'm a sculptor. After the voyage, I tried to make a living as an artist, but my paintings didn't sell so I took up teaching, which is what I was doing when we last met – at Shane's funeral. I remember Evan talking to me at that time and later he suggested that I go back to art school and change to sculpture. I took his advice and it was the best thing I ever did."

"So what do you make?" asked Nigel. "I expect it's very modern and full of bits of metal and string." He waved his empty glass in the air tracing the line of an imaginary work of art. "Something which I wouldn't understand."

"You certainly would recognise what I do – it's figurative and human. I manage to make ends meet by making sculptures of people." Tina was in fact a moderately successful sculptor, who was in demand with her distinctive portrait heads, for which she got commissions, and which were usually cast in bronze. "Perhaps I was inspired all those years ago on Artemis by all you guys stripping off. Although I sneered at the time I do admit now that you were all in prime physical shape, except for the bruises and the beards. Perhaps it was all that crappy photography in those porno magazines you all looked at, which made me to take up life classes to see if I could do better."

Nigel and Ian laughed and then stopped, remembering why they were all there.

Suddenly everyone felt a bit guilty – they had forgotten to talk about the person to whose funeral they had come. Then gradually they explained how and why they had kept in touch with Evan and what he had meant to them.

Nigel said that Evan had done a lot for him – he had persuaded him to stop working in pubs and to do an instructor's course in sailing. He'd gone on from there. "Evan told me that if I did what I liked best, then I would do it successfully. So I started teaching kids to sail and later moved on to running a small fleet of charter boats. Evan found me a backer and it's because of him that I managed to get going. He always kept in touch and encouraged me – he was easy to talk to and we were good mates. I'll miss him like hell."

"I'll miss his letters," said Ian. "Evan has been a wonderful correspondent. Wherever I've worked in the world he always wrote to me. I have a stack of his letters – witty comments on people, informative about affairs at home, amusing anecdotes – they were not always lengthy but they meant so much to me. He kept me in touch with my roots when I felt lonely and far away. On my trips back to the UK we always met up and he was interested – as no one else ever was – in where I'd

73

been and what I'd done. He used to say that he didn't need to travel because he could sit in an armchair and read my letters to him." Ian coughed to conceal a slight wobble in his voice.

"Vicarious enjoyment," murmured Bryony thoughtfully. "Very much Evan's way."

Tina bought them another round of drinks, overruling Nigel's protest. "No, Nigel. I insist – it's my turn."

"Evan had a big impact on my life," said Bryony. "He introduced me to my future husband." She had been working as an auxiliary nurse at a hospital in Swansea. Evan and Angharad had invited her over to supper where she had met an attractive and ambitious young doctor. At the time Gareth was a junior registrar in the Heath Hospital where he was now a consultant. "After we married, both he and Evan urged me to go back to college and study to become a doctor too." She remembered how Evan had offered to look after baby Adam whilst she was studying for her finals and Gareth was working in Casualty. "We've got three almost adult children – the youngest wants to become a doctor too. It's an exhausting life – juggling career and children – but very fulfilling."

"I've got kids too," said Nigel. "They're not too good at schoolwork – neither was I – but they're great little sailors. Do any of you still sail?" he asked, looking round.

The women shook their heads and Ian said, "I did a bit of sailing out East but not any more. Water skiing is more my line."

"That voyage across the Atlantic was a one-off for me. It made me realise how much I love the land," Ralph said in his modest way. "After we got back, I decided not to return to work in Coventry, and moved down to Somerset, where my sister lived. I worked on an estate as a junior gardener, and learnt a lot from the head guy there. I became interested in trees – Evan leant me some books on the subject – and then, with his support, I went off to do a course on forestry. Afterwards, I went to work for an arboretum. I now specialise in conifers, and in fact I've written a book on the subject."

"I'll bet you've produced the ultimate treatise on trees," joked Tina looking curiously at his small hands that were able to rear trees and write books.

Ralph laughed and modestly denied this. "Evan loves trees too," he said. "He asked me to put in some specimen trees in his garden, even though the area was a bit small and rather suburban. But when I was over there last spring, they were doing well. At least they'll live on." He paused and there was a small silence. "I'm going to plant an elm tree for Evan. They were decimated by disease some years back, and in common with people like Evan, there aren't enough of them around. It will be my memorial to him. It could live for a couple of hundred years."

Nigel spoke in a portentous voice, "'Oh mighty Oak – if you could speak what would you say to me?' said the lover of trees. 'I'm not an oak, I'm an elm,' replied the tree." The big man shook with boisterous laughter at his own joke.

"That's a really bad one," groaned Ian.

Ralph glanced at Nigel affectionately – he hadn't changed at all! On the boat he had played the role of the jolly joker – defusing awkwardness and creating laughter – he was an amiable man without an ounce of malice in him. He just wanted to have fun. But he too, in his sentimental but sincere way, had loved Evan – the big man had cried unselfconsciously during that mawkish service.

Tina felt it was now her turn to tell the tale of how Evan had made a difference to her life. She, who had so despised nude women in dirty magazines and naked men in the crew, had become a figurative sculptor. "Evan had a friend who ran a small foundry in Herefordshire and enabled me to cast my clay models into bronze. It's a wonderful material – almost indestructible – and I'm amazed to think that my work will probably last forever, like Greek sculptures."

"Unless it receives a direct hit from a nuclear bomb," murmured Ralph.

Tina swept on. "I was working in London at the time. Evan had a contact who owned a small gallery in Hampstead and that was where I had my first exhibition. He came to the opening – all the way from Cardiff – and bought one of my small bronzes though he probably couldn't afford it. Later on, after I moved to Wales, I sculpted his gaunt bony hands. His helping hands. I've still got them – cast in bronze. They're timeless and they'll live on – unlike him," she sniffed. For a moment they were all silent in appreciation of their dead friend.

"Such a lovely man. Ugly on the outside. Beautiful within." Bryony whispered, as she finished her glass of wine and put it down clumsily on the table. "That could be his epitaph."

Ralph gazed out of the pub window across the road towards the gardens of the crematorium. The smoke from its chimney, just visible over the top of a gracefully drooping deodar cedar, was blowing away in the wind. He turned back to the table where Bryony had just bought them some more drinks. He shook his head – he had to drive back.

Tina was still talking. Alcohol, which made Ralph and Ian more withdrawn, made her effusive and Nigel more expansive. "I see it all now," she announced. "Evan was a communicator. He kept in touch with us – he helped us all – encouraged and inspired us – writing letters and giving advice. In the world's eye he didn't really achieve much but in fact it's what he gave to others – and to us – which is his legacy."

Evan, as they all knew, had been a teacher, and after retiring at sixty he had run a charity to help the homeless. He had never earned very much – and always lived in the same place in the city. He had married another teacher called Angharad who still worked in the local primary school. They were childless, although they had given many foster children a temporary home.

"You're right," Nigel brought his fist down on the table to emphasize his point and making the empty glasses chink as he said, "Evan was our watch leader many years ago on the boat and he's been keeping watch over us ever since. He brought us all to Wales – except you, Ian – where he could keep an eye on us."

Bryony said slowly, "He helped us achieve our potential. He spurred us on and picked us up when we fell. I now understand why the reading in the service was the parable of the Good Samaritan. That's what Evan was. I thought it was because of his teaching kids and his work with homeless people. But he touched all of us. We are his successes. He never failed us."

"He didn't succeed with Shane though," Ian suddenly said.

There was a moment of silence whilst they remembered the other absent crew member – the one who had died so young. Five years after they had returned home from their transatlantic voyage, Evan had organised a reunion party. It had been a pleasant evening initially, but of course Shane had drunk too much and spoilt things.

"Remember that party Evan threw?" said Nigel. "Shane got paralytic and smashed up a glass coffee table. Didn't he pick some sort of silly quarrel with you, Ian?"

"He punched me," said Ian. "Can't remember why – but then Shane didn't need much reason to lose his temper. He'd been out of work for two years and probably drinking steadily on Daddy's money. He was insecure and totally uncontrollable."

"We all knew that Evan had been trying to help Shane to kick his alcoholism and save him from ruining his life. He was very distressed by the quarrel and the ensuing fight. Evan was such a peacemaker," said Tina, slurring the last word.

"Shane was such a drunk," Ralph said disapprovingly.

"Such a beautiful young man", said Bryony sadly.

"But without a beautiful mind," said Tina.

Shane had been killed in a car accident a week later, leaving behind a distraught family and lots of debts. No one knew whether it was suicide or drink – probably both. All the crew of Artemis, including Skipper, had attended Shane's funeral. It was the last time they had been together.

"Poor old Shane," said Nigel heartily, trying to conceal a belch. "Lazy – but great company."

"Always last on watch," said Ian, recalling how this had rankled him.

"Dreadfully chauvinistic," said Tina.

"Never washed his hair," said Bryony.

"Poor Shane," they murmured together.

To change the subject Nigel asked, "Whatever happened to Xavier?"

"He went back to Canada," said Ralph.

"Perhaps he became a lumberjack," Ian spoke this with a French accent.

This was greeted with laughter. They remembered the teasing and the jokes and the friendly banter. They recalled that it was Evan who had instituted the night watch debating society.

"All those many nights at sea when we talked and put the world to rights. We were so young and so sure of where we wanted to go." Bryony said sentimentally, forgetting entirely how unsure they had all been about what they had wanted to do.

"Talking of going, I must get on my way," said Ralph, standing up "I've a longish drive. And I haven't drunk as much as you lot."

"Don't go, Ralph," chorused the others, but he smiled and shook his head. He looked down at them sitting round the table. How easily, he thought, they had fallen back into their stereotyped roles on the boat: the jovial joker Nigel, the gentle womanly Bryony, the tough guy Ian, the touchy feminist Tina and the quiet shy one – him. He gave them a wave and slipped out of the pub, forgetting to leave them his telephone number.

"Goodbyee," called Bryony who knew she was inebriated – something which rarely happened these days with her responsible roles as a doctor, wife and mother. She was quite enjoying the lapse.

Tina, who for a few minutes had been quietly trying to sober up a bit, turned to Nigel and asked, "Do you all remember that night on the boat when Evan started talking about immortality? I was on watch with you and Ralph."

"I do," said Nigel, "It was all about what we wanted to do with our lives."

"It was all to do with creating something which would last – and isn't that what Evan has helped us to do?" Tina had reached the emphatic, arm-waving stage of intoxication. "Ralph's got his trees, I've got my sculpture and you've got your boats. Bryony's a doctor and Ian's a traveller – which is what they wanted to do."

Ian stared at the dregs in his pint glass, and tried to focus on what Tina had said. He vaguely remembered the conversation taking place on his watch with Bryony and Shane. "What I do recall is that Shane wanted to make a million."

"Poor old Shane." Nigel had reached the repetition stage of drunkenness. He frowned in an effort to remember. "What was it Evan wanted?"

Tina raised her head with a pleased look on her face having pulled into the present a statement from the shadows of the past, "He hoped to create something which would live on after his death. He wanted children – lots of them."

"Poor old Evan," brooded Nigel. "Died of cancer. He never did have any kids".

"Don't you see?" exclaimed Bryony, flushed with sense of enlightenment. "Evan was like a father to us. In essence we are his children."

"That's so true," slurred Tina.

Ian suddenly looked at his watch. "I gotta go. I've probably missed my train." He stood up carefully, holding the edge of the table. "Good to see you all again."

"Keep in touch, Ian. Now that Evan's gone, the link should be maintained – we're almost brothers and sisters," implored Tina. But Ian left the pub without giving his address because he didn't have one.

"Good old Ian," said Nigel.

Bryony smiled at him affectionately. He was older and fatter, but still the same cheery beery Nigel. Salt of the earth.

They were all a bit drunk – and Tina had closed her eyes. She was leaning slightly on Bryony who noticed streaks of grey in her dark hair. "I'm a bit sleepy," she murmured.

On the boat Tina had been obsessed about sleeping. She was always dropping off in corners and dozing on watch. She was known as the dormouse. On the other hand, Bryony had found sleep difficult. The berths were narrow, hard, and fetid. She had tried every bunk in the boat in the hope that one might provide her with a good night's rest. The boys had teasingly accused her of sleeping around.

Nigel, another pint miraculously having appeared in front of him, nudged Tina, who opened her eyes glassily and looked at him. "Remember Golden Kip?" he said. "We took it in turns to have a night on 'Golden'?"

Tina sighed. "How wonderful it was to go off watch and know you had a whole night of uninterrupted peaceful hours to lie down, relax those aching muscles and drift off to blissful sleep."

"I always envied you that ability," said Bryony with a yawn.

"Here's to Evan," said Nigel, brandishing his tankard and downing his drink.

Tina nodded and muttered, "To Evan." A few seconds later she added with a choked laugh, "And I hope that's where he's gone."

"He's on everlasting 'Golden'," Bryony said with tears in her eyes.

"It's a definite maybe," said Nigel.

MIRROR IMAGE

Mirror Image

"Presentiment is the long shadow on the lawn
The notice to the startled grass
That darkness is about to pass."

Emily Dickinson

Louise opened the door of the room and walked in purposefully. Then she stopped and seemed to hesitate when she caught sight of a familiar photograph on the chest of drawers beside the window. She glanced out of the window, then at her watch and with a little nod, continued across the room, round the bed and sat down at a dressing table in front of an elegant gilt mirror.

It was about five o'clock in the afternoon and the autumn sunlight filtered in through the window, dappling a pattern of glazing bars on the pale green carpet. She had about an hour before she ought to leave, and her thoughts briefly flickered over the prospect of the next few months, but without alighting for long on any image, as if wishing to wait until she had time and space in which to luxuriate in this pleasing vision of the future. Or was it because, if she dwelt too long on it, she might realize that the plan had some flaws that could spell disaster?

"That's just what Mary would say," thought Louise. "But she's not here now, and shouldn't get back before I leave, so I won't have to listen to her trying to dissuade me from going." She opened a drawer and took out a small bag containing make-up. She cleaned her face carefully using cotton wool and lotion, and then contemplated her face before deciding which image she wished to project for this momentous enterprise.

"I'll just whack on some war-paint," her mother used to say, and throw it on she did with swift carelessness. Her sister never bothered with cosmetics, denouncing make-up as a calculating disguise or a mask of artificiality.

"She makes me feel," thought Louise, "that I am doing something reprehensible and false, when all I'm really doing is putting on something to cover up blotchy skin and make my eyes look bigger and my cheeks a little less pale. It helps the confidence too – and that's what I need at the moment. Will it enhance my natural features, as it says on the jar?" She gazed at her reflection questioningly. "What are my natural features?" She asked herself. "They seem to change, just as my image of myself seems to alter. Do others see me always in the same way, or do they see me as I see myself in all my myriad poses? I feel that one day I shimmer into vision as an elegant creature of dragonfly grace, and on another I slip into view as a shy opaque woman with a hint of mystery."

She made a decision – she would put her hair up – it would give her poise and stature. She began to brush her hair and looked thoughtfully round the familiar room. Would the little house be solitary after she had gone? Would it be available if she came back? Did she still care about all the pretty works of art that she had collected once with so much care and elegant taste. Did they matter? No. What was really important was her peace of mind.

Louise turned on the lamp beside the mirror, found a box of pins and set to work on her hair. She had recently dyed it a rich blond colour, and looked anxiously in the mirror to see if any of the darker roots were growing through. She satisfied herself that this was not the case and went back to pinning up her hair, sticking in the long thin crinkly hair-pins with little confident jabs into the French pleat that she could not see at the back of her head. She had worn her hair long for some time now, and often wore it up when she wished to appear more business-like and efficient than she really was. But she planned to let it down when she arrived in the warmer climate. She might even have it cut short and go for a radical new look to match her outrageous new life.

It was undeniably outrageous to go away and leave so many responsibilities. But they weighed her down and limited her choices and freedom to do as she pleased. She thought of her father, frail and sad, who had been so lonely in the years since her mother had died. Mary had visited him often during this difficult time, and sometimes Louise herself nobly sacrificed one of her precious days in the city to descend on the rural village where he lived and bestow her whimsical caring persona on her ailing parent. His love for her had always been special and he lavished it on her pretty face and sparkling personality whilst poor practical Mary had never been favoured with more than his affection. But after a few hours of flitting about the cottage, chatting about her life in town and provoking smiles and gentle laughs, she became bored of the querulous demands and the local gossip. With an apologetic smile and a show of regret, she explained that she had to get back to cook Arnold his evening meal when he came home from work. The duties of a good wife were invoked to excuse the lapses in a dutiful daughter.

But things were different now since her brother had come back. William had been working in Africa, and had had a frightful accident in his jeep. He did not talk about it much, but clearly he had been trapped for some hours before he was found and extricated. He had spent months in hospital both in Africa and in England. He was now a paraplegic and lived in a wheelchair. He had come home because for the moment there was nowhere else to go, and he was still there after two years, gradually re-habilitating himself and becoming resigned to a different kind of life from the one he had envisaged. With his son under the same roof, her father was less solitary and they seemed to enjoy one another's company. But her brother was now showing signs of restlessness and, having come to terms with his permanent disability, was beginning to think about the rest of his life – he was still a young man. Louise was afraid that, when he moved out, her father would make the demands on her and Mary that had largely been absent during the last couple of years of William's residence.

She realised that she was being selfish, but she hoped that, if she left now, then she would not be branded as the deserter of the family and perhaps William would come to see his real purpose in life as a companion for his father, in the absence of another contender for the role. Yes, she certainly must go now before her brother started flexing his bruised and clipped wings. He should be able to learn the part of the filial carer without too many regrets. His father's gratitude would be some recompense and reward. She wouldn't mind if he punished her desertion by cutting her out of his Will. She wouldn't need anything because someone else would be looking after her for the rest of her life. William would inherit the cottage and its fields and he could perhaps buy some animals to graze it. Certainly, he must stay. It was, after all, his turn – he had had a number of years of freedom in his beloved game park.

Her brother had been the adventurous one but that had changed and now she would be taking up the mantle of the traveller of the family. She would be the one who would spread her wings and fly off to far-flung lands. She exhaled slowly to keep her excitement in check. When Arnold heard about her elopement, he would be very surprised. "I didn't think Louise had it in her," he would say. "She's flighty and unstable but not courageous."

"But I am," thought Louise. "He doesn't know me. Even after five years of marriage, he didn't know me. He didn't understand the imaginative and impulsive side of my nature. He repressed my natural 'joie de vivre' with his mundane comments and his need for a regulated existence. Now I come to think of it, Mary would have suited him better with her practical and conventional approach to life. But clearly he was more attracted to me. I offered him passion and glamour. Mary would have given him stability and security. But the lure of my unpredictability and my beauty tipped the balance. Arnold chose me and not my sister." Looking back on it, Louise decided that he had made a mistake and so had she. Mary would have been the better wife and the marriage might have lasted.

But Louise had been the victor and had carried him off. She had married him in a hurry – keen to get away from the sadness of their home after their mother had finally died of the cancer that had caused so much suffering. Arnold was good-looking and had a strong personality that promised protection from worries and threats. He was kind in an austere sort of way, but she discovered quite soon after the wedding that he was rigid and uncompromising. He wanted order and she dabbled in chaos. He liked safety; she yearned after risk. "I'm surprised our marriage lasted as long as it did," she said aloud. "He was so impossible." She replaced the hairbrush in the drawer and closed it firmly.

Hassan was very different. With his olive skin and black hair he was physically desirable in a way that Arnold, though handsome in a tall pallid way, had never been. He was shorter but slimmer than the Englishman and he dressed more flamboyantly. Arnold had been serious and sardonic. Hassan had a good sense of fun and made her laugh. And he was the more ardent and inventive lover.

She had met him at a drinks party given by Mary, and Louise had immediately targeted the exotic foreigner who had arrived on his own. That evening, she had chosen to be a cool, sophisticated woman with lots of eye make-up and mystery. She occasionally adopted this role when invited out as it gave her poise and minimized the ignominy if she remained without a man to take her out to dinner at the end of the party. Hassan was clearly fascinated by her. It wasn't until he drove her home that evening and mentioned that he had known Mary for a few weeks, that she realised she had perhaps stolen her sister's boyfriend. It was an innocent mistake, she told herself.

Hassan explained that he was over in England for a few weeks on business and pleasure. But he rarely did any work, and stayed at a small but expensive hotel, so he clearly had private means. He quickly decided to ignore Mary and concentrate on her more exotic sister. Louise, who rarely felt any guilt, embarked on a hedonistic affair with energy and enthusiasm. Her marriage had broken up a year before, so she only had herself to please. Hassan filled her empty days – and nights – with pleasure.

She remembered the day when she realised that her rapacious, devil-may-care attitude began to transform into a more tender and dependant one. She started to need Hassan and made the mistake of becoming emotionally involved. Of course, he said he loved her – but they all did. She had had two lovers since the end of her marriage but she had carefully remained uninvolved. She had enjoyed the opportunity to act different roles and to portray herself to one as the long-suffering rejected wife who wanted comforting, and to the other as a waif who had been starved of affection and needing only love and kindness to enable her to blossom. They had both professed love for her, but she had had her fun and sent them on their way.

Hassan was very different. He was so romantic and yet very passionate. He sent her expensive flowers and gave her unusual presents. He vowed that she was the most extraordinary woman he had ever met, and that he would love her forever. She knew he flattered her but she adored the attention.

She glanced at her watch, and then at the gold bracelet on her wrist – it glinted in the lamp light. She flexed her fingers and smiled. She unscrewed the top of a jar and began to apply some foundation on her face. She wanted to look radiant and attractive for Hassan.

It was on her birthday – she told him inaccurately that it was her twenty-fifth – that she had fallen in love with him. He arrived outside her little terraced house which she had just finished decorating and indulging her own predilection for pretty ornamental things. He had showered praises on her taste and discernment and announced that, although he was charmed by her lovely home, he wanted to take her out for the day. He invited her to a picnic on the river and drove her out of town to a small restaurant on the river bank. The 'picnic' consisted of a sophisticated meal, served up beneath a sun umbrella by waiters on the restaurant lawn. It was all delightful. After the meal, he fetched a wicker basket from his car and gave it to her with a huge bouquet of red roses.

When she asked him what was inside it, he told her to open it. She did this carefully, and was surprised to see at least a dozen white doves inside. When she asked him what she should do with them, he replied, "Set them free". And so she did, and as they fluttered up into the air she looked at Hassan and he gave a white smile. She became suffused with a choking feeling and stared dizzyingly at her lover who took her by the arm to steady her. He had given her white doves to set free – but she was no longer at liberty.

Of course, Mary disapproved of her sister's affair. Whether she was jealous or whether she felt that Hassan was not going to honour his commitment, Louise did not know. Hassan had told her that he would have to go home to his own country, and that he had some work to do in the Middle East. He needed to explain to his parents who were devout Muslims that he had met the woman he wanted to have as his wife. He asked her earnestly whether she might be able to convert to Islam and live with him in his land away from her own people. With only a show of hesitation, she promised she would do this for him. She told him she would have no regrets, though privately she felt a bit selfish and guilty that she would be denying her family the opportunity of seeing her. She wouldn't miss them, of course.

There was a sudden slight draught, pulling her back into the present, and Louise realised that she had left the door unlocked. Had someone come in downstairs? She listened carefully, but after a while, seemed reassured and decided that she need not put any rouge on her cheeks. She would look pale and interesting for her journey.

Two months ago, Hassan had departed and left her with his love, his promises and his address. He would contact her and tell her when to come to join him. She believed him totally. Since then he had written two short but passionate letters which were reassuring and wonderful but which gave no specific reference to the date when she would be joining him. She quelled a lurking unease in the pit of her stomach, and wrote back loving words to him and requesting more details about when their life together would begin. She missed him – and his adulation. More recently a gold bracelet had arrived from him, but she had not heard anything for a month now, although she had written twice. He had said that it might be awkward if she telephoned him, so had given her no number. In the absence of any more definite plan, she had decided to go to him at his home and arrive as it were – a 'fait accompli'.

During the two weeks when she was making preparations for her flight she managed to ignore her misgivings and convince herself that his lack of complicity in her plans was unnecessary and that he would be surprised but delighted at her audacity and loving commitment and would enfold her into his arms and his life.

At this point she turned round and glanced at her small travel bag which stood in the corner. She could see her airline ticket – one way only – tucked into the side pocket. Her passport was still in the top drawer and she took it out now and put it on the glass top of her dressing table in order not to forget it. Her large suitcase was downstairs, packed and ready to leave. She tried to envisage herself as she would appear at the airport – a lone beautiful woman, leaving her country and her past, to strike out into the unknown and to take up a new life with the lover who would soon be her husband. Her look of resolute eagerness for adventure would be tinged with faint regret and a hint of past sadness. She leant forward and began to apply some eye shadow. Those who felt compelled to look at her would wonder at her air of mystery and calm detachment. Yes, that would be the right note to strike. Another persona.

A sound on the stairs interrupted her pleasing thoughts, and a few seconds later Mary's face swam into view in the mirror into which Louise was looking. Without turning round, Louise gave a sigh of exasperation and said rather sharply:

"What are you doing here at this time? Have you finished work early?"

Mary did not reply to these questions, but stood behind her sister and quietly asked, "Where are you going with that suitcase?"

"None of your business," responded Louise sharply. "If I choose to take a little holiday, that is no concern of yours. I'm a free agent and can do as I please. In fact, I don't know why you don't take the odd break – it would do you good – it would give you something new to talk about." She had paused whilst she was saying this, but she then continued with her eye make-up.

Mary wandered round the room, and glanced at the small bag with its prominent ticket. She said, "I have work to do," emphasizing the word 'I'.

"Well, I don't," retorted Louise. "I hate working and don't believe in the work ethic. I'm free of all that mundane repetitive stuff. In fact," she announced triumphantly, "I'm getting away for good." She found she could not resist telling Mary and inviting the inevitable censure. "I'm going away with Hassan. We're going to start a new life together – in his part of the world. I'm leaving in under half an hour." She glanced at Mary to see how she was taking this revelation, and felt almost pleased with the look of disapproval she saw there.

"I suspected you might do this," said Mary's reflection in the mirror.

"You aren't going to dissuade me this time," said Louise in a firm tone, whilst examining her eyes. "I'm really going. I need a big change in my life and this is it. You can all do without me. Daddy and William manage fine together and you're always around. I don't need all this anymore," she said airily, waving her eyebrow pencil at the room. "I can do without all these possessions. I want love and I want a simple life. I don't want complications and sophistications," she insisted, as she opened her eyes wide and applied mascara to her lashes.

"You're being irresponsible," said Mary.

"You're trying to make me feel guilty – well, I shan't. You always pour scorn over my plans. Well, you won't change my mind this time. You probably think Hassan won't stay with me, but I know he will. You don't know him as well as I do. You once said he was a philanderer. Oh yes, I know he's charming. But I say that even philanderers can change when they fall in love." In the face of Mary's silent denunciation she continued, "You are so pessimistic. You want me to return to Arnold – you've always said that he gave stability to my life. Well, I don't want stability. I don't want common sense and realism. I want imagination and dreams and love." Louise dusted some powder onto her face and some of the fine powder drifted up into the air, then settling on the face of the mirror.

91

" I think you should go back to Marsh House," said Mary soothingly. "You're starting to get panicky and defensive. I told Daddy that I thought you should not have discharged yourself. It was too soon. Are you taking the tablets?"

"To hell with the tablets. They depress me. Can't you see I've got to go away? It's my only chance." A note of disquiet had crept into Louise's voice. "If I stay behind, you'll only pull me down with the force of your dreary practicality. I must have my dream, and I will have it – however fleetingly it lasts." She picked up a lipstick and carefully applied the red gloss to her narrow lips.

"I've been talking to Arnold," Mary continued in the same pacifying tone as before. "And he agrees with me. We both think you need the calming influence of your medical advisors. It's no good running away. Hassan is bad news – we both know that. You don't really trust him. You're full of doubts and fears. You know he's not going to marry you – he's probably got a wife already." It seemed to her sister that Mary knew, as she often did at this point in their many disputes, that she was beginning to get the upper hand.

"Stop, stop," shouted Louise putting her hands over her ears. "I'm going to get away from you, Mary. You haunt me with your home truths and bleak advice."

"But I keep you sane," said Mary.

"You depress me. I've got to go. I must try to make it work." Louise stared at her reflection in the glass. Her face was perfect, even though there were cracks behind its facade. "I'm going to leave you behind," she said fiercely, tapping with her long fingernail at Mary's face beside hers in the mirror. "You and I have been too close. We've got to go our different ways."

"Don't break this mirror," warned Mary. "Remember the one you shattered at home seven years ago."

"You were the cause of that, not me," muttered Louise.

"Not true," said Mary. "You broke it in one of your uncontrollable rages. You always smash things."

Louise did remember that other mirror which sat on the table in Alice's room in their family home. It was a day in

July just after term had ended and she and her twin were in the bedroom discussing college life. They were both at the same university, though Alice was studying English and Louise was doing History of Art. They even shared a student flat – they would not be parted.

Louise was drying her hair in front of the mirror and Alice was lounging on her bed. Mother had called them down to lunch but they had ignored this. In exasperation, Mary had come upstairs and into the room to tell them to come down at once. As the twins stared at her in silence with their peculiarly irritating way of excluding outsiders, she lost her temper with their selfishness and their total lack of remorse.

"You waste time up here when you could be helping downstairs," Mary had said accusingly. "You're always together – always reading books, looking at pictures or watching films. You two spend your lives seeing shadows of the world," she sneered.

Louise had turned her back and leant forward to the mirror to address Mary's reflection, each deliberate word accompanied by a sharp tap of the glass with the end of the hair dryer. "You ... spend ... your ... life ... being ... bossy." On the final word, the mirror splintered and the shards of glass fell forward onto the surface of her twin's dressing table.

Alice said solemnly, "The mirror cracked from side to side," and Louise joined in mournfully with, "The curse has come upon me! cried the Lady of Shalott." They began to titter simultaneously, whilst Mary left the room to tell her mother. "Seven years bad luck," the twins crowed in unison, and their demonic laugher pursued her downstairs.

And bad luck had followed. The next February, their mother finally succumbed to lung cancer, after years of heavy smoking. They were all distraught and Louise, in her effort to get away from the lingering misery of their bereaved family, married the wrong man. She abandoned her degree course for the novelty of matrimony. That was over five years ago. It was during the honeymoon with Arnold that Alice disappeared. She had gone walking in Peru on vacation during her final year at college, and never made contact again. Louise felt wretchedly guilty and tormented herself with the notion that Alice had run away because she felt forsaken by her twin. After nearly a year the family decided to abandon the search for her. Louise endured the appalling separation with an almost physical pain that no amount of Arnold's loving sympathy could dispel. The next disaster was her father's business, which finally went into liquidation having suffered from the neglect of its proprietor during the months of his desperate and abortive quest for his lost daughter.

The bad luck had still more time to run. Three years ago her brother had damaged his life forever by the accident which left him paralysed and this tragedy crippled the family even more. Louise was distraught by William's affliction and she missed Alice as much as ever. It was all too much to bear, and the next year Louise had a serious mental breakdown and had spent various periods in a psychiatric hospital. She became increasingly alienated from her husband who, she felt, had been insensitive and uninvolved in her suffering. One year ago she left him. He had generously accepted that she needed space and time, and rented for her the small house in which she now lived. He continued to hope that their estrangement would be temporary.

Mary was of the opinion that Louise should not live on her own, and had decided to keep an eye on her and visit her frequently. Louise was disturbed by the fact that she felt dependant on conversations with Mary but also felt an irrational dislike of her sister's surveillance.

The seven years since the broken mirror had now passed, thought Louise, and it was time for a new beginning. Their lives had been shattered and it was time for her to escape from it all. Mary would survive her absence and would hold things together – that was the part she had to play. Louise's final act in the drama was to run away as she believed her twin had done and create a new life apart from the others. Louise examined her face in the pool of light and applied some powder. She quickly gathered up all the cosmetics and dropped them into a bag, snapping the clasp shut. She rose to her feet.

Mary emerged from the shadows at the back of the

darkening room. She had been thinking and had decided now not to dissuade Louise from going. She had suddenly realised that perhaps this was the way to get rid of her problematic sibling. But a sudden change of heart would alert Louise who knew her well and knew how rarely Mary was persuaded to agree. To suddenly give encouragement now would invoke suspicion. Mary knew she should continue to pretend and said in a calm bossy tone, "This is a very selfish, silly plan. You know from experience that it won't work. It's just another one of your performances. I can see that you're watching yourself now and wondering if you can carry it off. But I know your resolve is weakening. You don't really believe you can do this." She was goading her sister. This was the way to banish Louise forever.

"Oh yes I do." said Louise, predictably taking the bait. She walked over to the window and looked out at the darkening sky. She pulled the curtains shut and then looked down at the photograph on the chest of drawers. The young woman was a mirror image of herself – her twin Alice – who had been lost or dead for five long lonely years. She picked up the photograph, kissed it, and handed it to Mary. "Here you are. Something to remind you of us both."

For a moment, Mary lost control, and cried: "Don't Louise. Don't go. Please."

A brave false smile appeared on her sister's irresolute face. She grasped the travel bag and, slinging it over her shoulder, ran across to the dressing table and snatched at her passport. Her hand was shaking so much she dropped it, and it fell open under the light. In the seconds before she picked it up, they both read the name: Mary Louise Hyde.

Louise grabbed the passport and ran swiftly out of the room. Mary carefully put the photograph down. She no longer wanted to be Alice's replacement – she wanted to be a person in her own right. She drew the curtains and sat down in front of her dressing table. She breathed out slowly and a sigh escaped from her lips as if from a departing ghost.

She looked at her image in the mirror, and quietly began to remove all the make-up. She wouldn't need it now. She noticed the jar of tablets which had been pushed behind the mirror. She must remember to take them. If she forgot, Louise might return to disrupt her life. If she could keep things on an even keel, in time the medication would not be necessary. Arnold would be pleased at the progress she was making. In a few months she might consider returning to live with him. But she needed more time to consolidate her position and to be sure that Louise was gone permanently. There were still difficulties ahead that needed to be overcome.

Mary thought of Hassan. He would not have been right for her any more than Arnold had suited Louise. No, Hassan had made his exit and would not be there for Louise. Her dream would die. But Arnold was still there, waiting to see if Mary would come back to him. He was a patient man. She thought of him with a sentiment that bordered on affection and decided to give him a ring in the morning. Perhaps she would go down to the country and see her father on Friday and give William the opportunity to take the weekend off. He needed time to get to know his new girlfriend.

With her face now devoid of any mask or artificiality, Mary switched off the lamp and left the room. She descended to the hall to lock her front door. She saw that the passport – the key to Louise's new life – was lying on the hall carpet, dropped in her hasty flight to be gone. Mary hoped fervently – but without absolute conviction – that Louise would not come back for it. The absence of her alter ego was novel and refreshing. Perhaps this time it would last.

FLY BABY

Fly Baby

A country at war attracts adventurers and opportunists but it can also lure the curious and the foolhardy. Even the majority of those who are appalled by the horror of pain and suffering admit to a guilty fascination about war zones, though they would probably not wish to visit one. Youthful ignorance and the blind belief in immunity from danger result in bravado and rash behaviour that age and experience would avoid.

In 1970 Cathy, young, adventurous and unwise, decided to go to Laos. She was living in Thailand at the time, working as a teacher in a Bangkok language school. She had spent her University career in Belfast, before the city had descended into major conflict. Student life in Northern Ireland might even have been described by some of her fellow students as dull. Cathy had studied Classics and Ancient History. For three years she had relived the ancient battles and embedded herself in the history and culture of the Greek and Roman Empires.

When she had obtained her degree, Cathy decided she needed change and excitement – and the twentieth century. Eighteen of her twenty-two years had been spent in education. Family holidays had been mainly in the United Kingdom, with occasional forays to Spain and France, and university vacations had included a trip to Greece, and ski holiday in Austria. She felt a need to go further afield, and began to search for jobs abroad. There was some work available in Prague, behind the iron curtain, which would be unusual, but it was still Europe. So Cathy opted for the other job offered to her – a more exciting attractive proposition of teaching English as a foreign language in Thailand, some 8000 miles away.

She had the usual European illusions about the Far East and schoolgirl dreams of the strange exotic orient. A degree course had not prepared her for confrontation with a world as ancient as the one she had studied, and with values and outlook so alien from the one she had lived in.

Her arrival in Bangkok was a revelation and a disappointment. Unfettered development had allowed the skyline to become lopsided with high-rise modern blocks alongside low-level traditional buildings. A short-sighted policy of infilling the 'klongs' (canals) meant that in the wet season the water often remained knee deep on the filthy roads. The fumes from the traffic jams caused by the numerous battered buses, cars and 'samlors' (three wheeled motorised rickshaws) rose up into the air and mingled with the myriad human smells that emanate from any hot, humid and dirty city.

She was not disappointed, however, in the house that she was to share with another teacher at the school – a Scottish girl called Jeanie. It was a Thai style house on one storey made of wood, with a large overhanging roof, set in a little garden green with exotic shrubs and bright with flowers. The screens instead of windows gave a sense of space and openness. Her initial delight was only slightly dampened when she discovered that without air-conditioning the heat was intense, and that large ants marched through the outhouse kitchen, whilst mosquitoes, lizards and cockroaches managed to penetrate the screens and roam happily round all the other rooms. The garden, attractive in the dry season, became a boggy morass full of noisy frogs in the wet season, with muddy water through which she had to wade to reach the steps up to the door. She understood then why the house was raised slightly above the ground.

The humid weight of the huge fetid city pressed down on her by day as she tried in the sticky heat to concentrate on teaching her pupils that the third person singular of verbs had a 's' on the end. Direct method teaching meant that one did not explain grammar, and she had to resort to a bag full of props such as a rubber snake which she used to flourish with a loud hiss when her more obtuse students persisted in saying "She write" or "He drive". This usually managed to bring smiles to their habitually serious faces, but she often had the uncomfortable feeling that to them she seemed something of a clown – an overweight white clown.

Cathy, with her liberal views and professed lack of racism, was initially embarrassed that she found it difficult to distinguish between her students, but after a while her perception of the oriental features widened and she became more attuned to them, and so learned with relief to recognise and know the differing characteristics of those around her. It also came as something of a shock to discover that she herself was the outsider here – and that the muttered 'farang' (foreigner) that she heard people say to her as they passed was almost an insult.

The noise of the city during the days enveloped her: the constant roar of traffic and hooting of horns, the different cries and sounds identifying the various street vendors, the whining nasal singing of Thai pop songs. At night she used to lie awake listening eagerly to the strange and alien sounds which surrounded their seemingly fragile house – the constant sibilance of the grasshoppers, the sudden onset of the frogs' chorus during the rainy season, as if some conducting frog had waved its baton, and its equally abrupt cessation. She heard too the "chock-chock" of the lizards as they darted up and down the wooden walls, and the sounds of the scurrying animals in the roof space and behind the house. She was horrified when Jeanie told her that these were rats in the open drains behind the house, and only slightly reassured when she was told that they "never came inside".

Although the two young women were both very modestly paid in their teaching jobs, they still had a servant – indeed, they discovered that even lowly paid families had some sort of servant. Lek was small and nimble – and worked tirelessly. Three of her five children came to live with her in the one room allocated to the servant, and later on Cathy and Jeanie discovered that there were four other children living with her husband and his other wife in a one-room slum in the dockland area of the city. Cathy and Jeanie decided to buy the school uniforms and books for the resident children to enable them to go to school. No fees were payable, it seemed, but a uniform was obligatory. Cathy was able to write home and inform family and friends that she and Jeanie had "adopted" three Thai children and were educating them. It sounded so philanthropic. She hoped but also doubted that those back in England would be interested. In any case, she really did enjoy the company of the children whose nicknames were Dang, Noi and Tut.

Jeanie always wore a smart miniskirt or dress when teaching, but liked to wear a 'pahsin' – the Thai long straight skirt – when at home, and Cathy took up the habit with alacrity, and much enjoyed buying lengths of pahsin material in the local market. She was charmed by the many eastern customs she learned, and very embarrassed when she transgressed social rules. She realized the importance of being correct and polite. Shoes were always removed before entering any house and, if the sole of one's foot was allowed to face any person, this was an insult. One did not shake hands – or indeed touch any part of another person's body and in particular the head because it was most sacred. Greetings were courteous and elaborate and strictly observed. Cathy was particularly fascinated by the tradition of putting down food for the monks who walked by at dawn with their begging bowls, and Jeanie felt that it was important to have a spirit house in the garden for good fortune.

Cathy was initially enthusiastic and always assiduous with her work. This was her first teaching post, and therefore much preparation was required. She needed to become familiar with the special problems of grammar, intonation and pronunciation that were common to this part of the world. Her students were mainly adults working in various businesses round the city, although she did have one class of children. Some of the larger companies had decided to provide English language lessons as a part of staff training, and so the teachers working for the language school found themselves travelling all over downtown Bangkok to conduct classes at their students' workplaces. This involved an energy-sapping journey in the heat, weighed down by tape-recorders and other teaching aids. Taxis were cheap but involved much bargaining to get the drivers down to the correct fares, as advised by the school, nor was it any good trying to persuade a Thai taxi-driver to take one down to Chinatown, since only Chinese drivers would venture there. Huge traffic jams were everyday occurrences and patience was stretched to the limits amidst honking vehicles and belching fumes. To Cathy this was a rude awakening from the tranquil beauty of the orient of her dreams.

The weary repetitiveness of language teaching, once she had amassed a large collection of lesson plans, meant that her interest in the school life, which had absorbed her totally when she first arrived, began to wane. She was obliged to wake before dawn, so that she could travel far across the city to her early morning class which was held during the hour before work commenced for the day; her students consisted of selected employees of a large company. Late afternoon and evening classes at the school were held after office hours for those students of English who paid for themselves. The pattern of Cathy's days therefore meant that her mornings and most of her evenings were spent working. During the middle of the day it was too hot and she was too tired to do anything other than stay in her shady house, lie on the bed, and chat to Jeanie, whose work schedule was similar. She took frequent showers – this involved scooping up water from a large 'klong' jar and chucking it over herself. The water, having been in the large jar for several hours was far cooler than that from the tap since the tank was in the roof under the baking sun.

Sometimes she would venture out after the heat of the day had waned somewhat, and walk down to the nearest market to buy food. The romance of buying strange foods and exotic tropical fruit was slightly tarnished when she saw the rats scurrying below the wooden duck-boards on which everyone walked to keep their feet out of the dirt and mud. She occasionally took buses downtown to the major temples and wandered around them with a determined effort to see everything. Elegant as these temples were, they displayed a wearisome sameness – all bright orange and green in colour, with gilded and golden Buddhas everywhere. Her interest in Thai culture waned with the advent of the hot season and, as she was becoming more confident with her Thai language, she decided to make efforts to get to know people.

Cathy occasionally visited the houses of some of her students but these were usually far out in the suburbs and involved long and exhausting bus rides through un-picturesque streets lined

103

with concrete or wooden houses to spend a few hours talking in stilted English (theirs) or stilted Thai (hers). She wanted to know more about the Thais, to see their homes and how they lived, and to have discussions about their culture and art, but was disappointed to find many of them interested only in western pop music, fashionable clothes and the latest films. It was easy to become acquainted with them – they were easy-going and pleasant – but it proved difficult to become friends. The differences in the way of life, culture and values flowed like an impassable river between them.

Though she did manage to make friends with some Thais, she found similar difficulty in getting to know other people from overseas who were living and working there. The foreign community was small and close-knit, and its members invariably socialized with each other. From time to time she came into contact with travellers passing through the country whose freedom she rather envied from the lofty heights of her superior status as a Bangkok resident. But she did still feel isolated and anomalous.

Jeanie was becoming less available as a confidant, because she had become involved in a love affair with one of her students. Cathy would never have admitted that she was lonely, since she had long ago decided that "lonely" was a negative word. But she used the word "solitary" to describe her state, this being in her view a positive word, since it was possible to choose "solitariness", whilst "loneliness" was inflicted. Surrounded by teeming life, she felt herself to be apart and different. She began to feel constricted by the huge city, and hemmed in by the sheer numbers of the urban population.

Cathy felt that her life as a single foreign female in Bangkok was restricted and that her days and her job were becoming repetitive. Clubs and bars could be indulged in easily enough, but too many late nights undermined her ability to cope with the very early start to her working day. Her weekends, however, were for the most part free, but after a few months, she felt she had exhausted all the possibilities within the city, having visited with great dedication all the major temples, the various markets, and important buildings. She had even tried flying a kite – the national sport – in seedy dusty Lumpini Park, but it was always kidnapped by other more deft kite flyers, and she grew tired of buying a new one each time and being jeered at when its line was cut.

Her passion for novelty was thwarted, so she decided to escape to the rural areas as often as she could. Her curiosity and eagerness to explore the country took her at weekends and on the many religious and public holidays to parts of Thailand that she could visit in the time span of two or three days. With an independent spirit and considerable organizational ability, she planned these trips with care, and soon began to look beyond the borders of the country. Burma was difficult and expensive since one had to fly in and out. Vietnam was at war and she had seen enough G.I.'s on "Rest and Recreation" in Bangkok not to wish to visit their battleground. She had already taken some local leave and visited the Angkor Wat temple complex in Cambodia at Siam Reap, but that country too was on the brink of war and devastation. Malaysia, less attractive because it had once been an English colony, lay a long way to the south.

To the north lay Laos, a country of considerable attraction – remote jungles and old temples – where the tentacles of guerrilla conflict were not yet too restricting. She discovered that there was an overnight train that would take her from Bangkok up to Non Khai, the border town on the River Mekong. From there she could take the ferry across the river to the Laotian border post, an easy seven mile bus ride from the country's administrative capital Vientiane. This would be her goal.

Whilst planning her first sortie into Laos, she met up with a couple who had spent some weeks there and were delighted by the bizarre and the beautiful that they had encountered. Living in Bangkok, the so-called sin city of the East, Cathy had become used to the excesses and public pleasures of the flesh on offer to men. But these two Australians, who had been in Laos, told tales of the rather less obvious but more wicked activities to be had in its capital. Vientiane was reputedly full of opium dens, gold smugglers, spies and strange people. She

105

must stay at the Constellation – a French Hotel, where there were mosquito nets, tight-lipped barmen, and mysterious meetings. Cathy, a moderately sensible human being, thought all this would be good for a laugh, and felt sure that she could not come to too much harm. Travelling alone as ever, she might even be able to pose as one of the twilight crowd. There were endless possibilities for a little adventure.

The train journey – first class could not be afforded nor would it have been desirable – meant journeying with crowds of other passengers in cramped conditions. She took the overnight train which departed an hour after her last evening class ended on Friday. After a weary week and a long day's work, she ached for sleep but with the train stopping and starting throughout the pitch dark night, and her neighbours on the hard seat jostling her, and her excitement at the prospect of seeing Laos for the first time, it was impossible to sleep much. Nor was she able to maintain her aloof cool poised world-weary traveller look when squashed between a betel nut chewing peasant woman and a small briefcase carrying young man dressed in a shiny suit who was trying to practice his few words of mangled English on her. The Thais, and indeed most Asians, are unaware of the Western concept of and need for personal privacy. Wherever Cathy went she found herself assailed by the constant attentions and close proximity of those around her.

Her first visit to Laos was fruitful and amusing. On arrival at dawn in Non Khai, she took a tricycle rickshaw from the rail head down to the wooden pier on the banks of the Mekong. No boat was waiting to leave, but it very soon became apparent that the way to get across the river and into Laos was to buy a seat in one of a number of long wooden canoes with long-shafted outboard engines on the back, controlled by young men in tatty shorts, who navigated their craft at terrifying speeds across the murky brown waters to Tahdua, the Laotian border post on the other side. In company with seven or eight impassive locals she was transported into another land.

From there she was given a lift in the back of a rusty truck to Vientiane, the main city of Laos. Cathy had found out that Vientiane was the administrative capital – the nerve centre of politics, business, education and communications in the country. She also knew that the other main city, Luang Prabang was the seat of the royal family and the religious capital, making it the cultural, spiritual and traditional centre of Laos.

She had explored Vientiane, looking at the buildings and temples. It amused her to note that there was still a strong French influence there. She was delighted by the fact that, unlike westernised Bangkok, many of the inhabitants walked barefoot and wore traditional clothing – the 'sampot' for men – baggy knee length trousers worn with or without a shirt, and the 'sin' for women – a long skirt or sarong worn with a blouse. She saw the market where on the ground, among the fruit and vegetables on offer, small piles of marijuana of different quality were displayed on scraps of material. She drank local tea in seedy cafes, and tried out spicy Laotian dishes in small pavement restaurants.

Her interest in religion and places of worship led her to explore the various temples where she encountered rows of Buddhas, their faces calm and complacent, the position of their hands indicating whether they were meditating, subduing 'mara' (evil), or forbidding relatives to fight. She had encountered another temple devotee – an American called Bill who said he was working for USAID. They struck up a friendship based on their mutual interest in local culture.

On her second visit to Laos, he arranged a trip downriver with a medical unit from the Dooley Foundation to some Meo tribes who had been relocated there from areas disrupted by the war. They trekked through the forest to village clearings where the tribes-people sat round and listened impassively to advice they would subsequently ignore. This was all a far cry from the sophistications and decadences of Bangkok, and was soothingly and sympathetically at variance with the noisy humdrum of teaching at the language school.

Each visit to Laos involved some time and expense since it was necessary on each occasion to obtain a visa and tax certificate to prevent her leaving Thailand without paying

107

her annual tax. In her effort to avoid a couple of hot hours spent in a fetid Bangkok office an hour's taxi ride away, Cathy discovered that entering Laos could be done easily, unobtrusively and unofficially. On her next visit she left the overnight train at dawn one stop before the border town, and followed a track down to the banks of the wide brown Mekong River. Here there were numerous boys in long wooden boats, who for a few Baht or Kip (Thai and Lao currency) would paddle her across the river into Laos illegally. This was much more enthralling, with its element of danger, but would be inadvisable after the monsoon rains came.

Cathy became obsessed with Laos. Her American friend, Bill, told her about the political situation. Laos, he said, was a fragile buffer squeezed between Communist and non-Communist countries, sustained in a precarious but officially recognised neutrality largely by United States aid. The Royal Government pinned its hopes for survival on the preservation of its neutralist stance (in connection with the war in South Vietnam) whilst trying to implement a national unity that the country had never enjoyed. He explained that it was an underdeveloped land passing through a process of modernisation and change, the difficulties of which were complicated by the state of crisis in the country caused by the fact that the Pathet Lao controlled much of the territory.

The Pathet Lao were a shadowy guerrilla force about which Cathy realised she knew very little, considering them to be the Laotian equivalent of the Vietcong. Bill informed her that the Pathet Lao (or the Laotian People's Liberation Army), who had waged insurrectionary warfare against the Royal Government since the early 1950's, were inspired and backed by the Communist government of North Vietnam, and that they held more than half the country in a sort of military stalemate, with sporadic outbursts of fighting. The territory controlled by them was inaccessible to the Royal Government and indeed to neutral observers. He pointed out that they even held some of the land which separated the two main cities.

Cathy of course was intrigued and challenged by this news. Another visit must be made, so that she could reach the beleaguered religious and cultural capital of the country, Luang Prabang. Here there was a spectacular mother temple, the royal palace, elegant traditional houses and much to see. In July, in spite of the fact that this was the start of the three month rainy season in Laos, Cathy again headed north for a long weekend. Arrangements for onward travel to the royal city could be made only in Vientiane but she soon found that this was not easy. She heard that the city was cut off from vehicular access by "communist infested jungle" surrounding it. The Pathet Lao controlled the only road, and access to the ancient city was by air only. Undaunted, Cathy soon found out that there were three airlines that flew ageing aeroplanes up into the hills to Luang Prabang. Royal Air Lao, the only official state-run airline, had both its aircraft out of commission, Air America operations were not running passenger aircraft at the time, but Lao Air Charter (non-Lao owned) was reputed to run a flight each day.

In the event, and against the advice of Bill, whom Cathy found less than adventurous, the intrepid young woman hitched a ride on board a light aircraft from Continental Airways (they were in the country under contract to the U.S., and rumour had it that they were a CIA-run outfit), having bumped into an obliging American pilot in a bar in downtown Vientiane. The fact that he was somewhat drunk, limped and had a scar on his face only added to the disreputable glamour of it all. She heard that the CIA's main base was at Site 20 up near Luang Prabang. She was offered a lift there and back, and although she had slight misgivings about his motives or his aircraft's reliability, it was just too exciting an opportunity to miss.

The flight proved to be disappointingly uneventful and the enigmatic pilot deposited her at the desired destination – to her dismay without making even a half-hearted attempt "on her virtue!" But Luang Prabang was everything she had hoped for – beautiful, remote, dangerous and quiet except for the regular noise of military aircraft taking off on sorties to bomb the surrounding countryside where the Pathet Lao lurked. These planes had been given to the Laotians by the Americans, who claimed to have no servicemen on the ground. This was a fallacy. When Cathy booked herself into the Phousi Arkane hotel (the only one she could find), there were a number of Asian Americans slouching around in flying gear, who told her they came from Hawaii. No doubt, thought Cathy, the U.S. military had specially selected these pilots, believing that Hawaiians would look oriental and blend into the background more easily than Occidental Americans. They were wrong. These pilots, who were there unofficially, were too awkward and flamboyant ever to merge unobtrusively with the graceful Lao people. Their combat dress and loud American voices jarred and obtruded.

Cathy was enchanted to discover that she was in the city during one of the major religious festivals: Khao Vatsa, which marks the beginning of a period of retreat for the 'bonzes' (monks). This echoes the time when Buddha and his followers retired to Jetavana in the rainy season. There were extensive formal processions, solemn in spite of the rain and muddy streets. Everyone was flocking to the main temple with its glorious curved triple roof outlined against the low clouds on the surrounding hills. Here there were prayers and offerings, and Cathy was able to see the Lao royal family who were present and to listen to the melodious and muted instrumental music accompanying the ceremonies.

The next day at midday she went down to the Prison Bar located appropriately by the city prison, which was where her pilot friend had arranged to meet her. She was somewhat apprehensive about the area in which it was located, and the bead curtains and generally sleazy look of the bar did not for once delight her. After a nervous hour in the place, she realized that her pilot was not going to turn up, and indeed nobody seemed to know him at all. His name did not appear to be familiar to the barman, whose pock-marked face was devoid of expression. She wondered if he was being obstructive, secretive or merely surly.

Cathy was worried. She needed to get back to Vientiane so that she could cross the Mekong, catch the overnight train down to Bangkok and the next morning take her class, who were becoming used to their first lesson of the week being given by an overtired zombie. She decided to go to the small airport and see what might be arranged. There she was told by an American that the aerial bombardment from the airport was to be stepped up and that probably no commercial traffic would be allowed. Somehow the prospect of being stranded in Luang Prabang did not enthral the intrepid traveller. She asked around the dusty airport building and was informed eventually that there was indeed one flight out down to Vientiane that afternoon, but that it was fully booked. She pleaded with the stony-faced individual, but to no effect. Accustomed by now to local ways and knowing that very little could be accomplished with officials without the payment of a bribe – known as 'tea-money' – she offered a small sum in addition to the modest fare, and soon found herself in possession of a ticket on a flight in an old Dakota due to leave in fifteen minutes. She was pleased but flustered by the imminent departure.

She then spent the next two hours waiting for the plane to arrive, and when it did to discover that there was some delay before it could leave. Finally late in the afternoon, she clambered aboard the DC-3 only to discover that it was far from full. Only a dozen passengers were on board including two men in military uniform, and only one other woman with a child. The last four rows of seats in the antiquated aircraft had been taken out to accommodate crates of Coca Cola bottles, sacks of green vegetables, some assorted and ill-wrapped packages, a few brightly coloured plastic buckets, and an old bicycle. No one spoke English or Thai, so Cathy, enveloped in a fog of incomprehension, chose a window seat with a plastic cover that was not too badly split, and the plane subsequently ambled off into the cloudy sky.

The distance between the two cities was some 140 miles and the flight south to Vientiane's "international" Wattay airport would take less than an hour. It was with some surprise therefore that after some 20 minutes, Cathy noticed the aircraft descending, and listened with apprehension to the steward announce something in Lao which she did not understand. His smooth face was devoid of any expression, which worried Cathy who knew that that the local reaction to a problem was

111

either total hysteria or absolute blank acceptance. In rising panic she looked out of the window, and saw that they had descended through the clouds and were circling over an area of thick dense forest. What was happening? Were they going to make a landing and if so, where? What if the guerrillas lurking below shot at the aircraft? Suddenly she caught sight of a narrow grassy strip hemmed in on each side by the thick dark forest, and she realized with sick fear that they were going to attempt to land.

In the event the landing, though bumpy, was accomplished without any problem, and Cathy, white-faced, tried to ask one of the other passengers what was happening. She received no reply. The steward motioned them to get out of the plane, and shaking with fear Cathy obeyed, convinced they were all to be taken prisoner and marched off into the jungle. In fact, once the engines stopped the plane would become very hot, and the steward merely wanted his passengers to sit under the wing on the ground out of the sun. The two soldiers disappeared, and the other passengers crouched down in the shade. Cathy saw that some of the baggage at the back of the plane was being unloaded. Surely these boxes contained guns or ammunition or perhaps food supplies for a guerrilla unit based nearby. Her imagination ran riot and any minute she expected armed Pathet Lao to emerge from the surrounding watchful trees and to run towards the unprotected plane sitting quietly and defenceless in the sun. How vulnerable they were but how calm they all seemed to be. Was this oriental stoicism or just unconcerned ignorance? Surely they must be aware of the imminent peril?

Half an hour passed, and nothing happened. By this time, Cathy was bitterly regretting the whole adventure. How stupid of her to swan off into unknown territory without thinking of what might go wrong! How arrogant to always imagine herself immune from disaster. Perhaps her good luck was finally running out. She would simply disappear. "Oh God, get me out of this mess," she murmured, "And I promise I won't be so stupid again." She felt very lonely, very vulnerable and found to her chagrin that some salty tears were sliding down

112

her face. Her inability to prevent herself from crying when faced with adversity was always a horrible embarrassment to her. Two of the other passengers sheltering under the wing stared at her expressionlessly, so she looked the other way and tried to compose herself, though her heart was thudding with terror and apprehension. She did not want them to know of her acute anxiety, and tried to think rationally about the possible outcomes.

Though the young woman was very frightened, she could see some grim humour in the situation. She remembered that she had told nobody where she was going for the weekend, and that she had entered the country illegally by not going through the border post. To try and cheer herself up she began to speculate on the possible Bangkok newspaper coverage of the strange disappearance of an English girl seen leaving her Thai house on a Friday evening – and never returning. Of course she would never be heard of again. The search would take place in the wrong country!

At this point there was the sound of a motor, and a green jeep emerged onto the airstrip and drove slowly up to the plane and the watchful but silent group under its wing. There were three people in it, a driver and two young men with rifles – or did one of them have a machine gun? Cathy's heart sank with terror as the two gunmen got out and sauntered towards the front of the aircraft. The tension mounted, but the driver of the vehicle and the plane's steward casually began to load some of the bottle crates into the back of the jeep. There was an interchange of Laotian gabble from below the cockpit, and then, as in some bizarre dream of an earlier life, Cathy thought she heard the words: "Stop blathering – I don't understand a word," spoken in a thick Northern Irish accent. She had no trouble recognising it, having spent four years in Belfast. But had she really heard it?

Again the voice cut like a scythe through the heat and quiet, and said, "Okay, so this is all you can pay me. I'm bloody well going now." After a couple of minutes the two soldiers climbed back into their jeep, which bumped across the airstrip and disappeared into the dense wall of trees.

The steward starting waving his hands to indicate that the passengers could re-board. Cathy surreptitiously dried her eyes. Hardly able to believe that they might yet make their escape, she was yet unable to contain her curiosity and darted forward to the source of that startlingly incongruous voice. There stood the pilot, short and stocky, his back to her, in a grubby shirt and creased trousers. But with thinning reddish blond hair! He turned round and presented to her a bleary, weary, lined face devoid of any charm, and remarked, "You're the American passenger, then?"

"No," stammered Cathy, "I'm English, in fact."

"That's much more unusual here," said the pilot, breathing out whisky fumes. "Do you want to join me in the cockpit for the last hop to Vientiane?"

"So there's no problem, then?" gasped Cathy.

"Not so long as this battered old crate can take off on this short strip without clouting a tree or two," said the pilot cheerfully, pushing her onto the plane and climbing in after her.

They walked through to the cockpit, and Cathy, stunned by the sudden disappearance of an armed threat, found her previous terror quickly substituted by the fear of flying with this disreputable looking Northern Irish drunkard in charge. Even the excitement of being in the cockpit of a plane for the first time could not diminish her apprehension as they took off, but once in the sky she felt more relieved, and they began to talk.

He was evasive when she asked him why they had made their unscheduled stopover, but in the end it appeared that he was doing a little business deal over some Coca Cola and canned food. Disappointed at the mundane reason for their mysterious detour and embarrassed because he had laughed at her unfounded fears, she changed the subject and told him about herself. He then reciprocated by telling her that he had once worked for "bloody Aer Fungus" but that they didn't want to train him to fly jets so he had worked variously for airlines in Bolivia and Peru, then in the Gulf, and now he had "reached the end of the road" being reduced to working for a pathetic little company with clapped out aircraft in "this poor little country with its petty war." His disillusionment must have led him to drink, thought Cathy, who remained anxious until he miraculously brought the plane down onto the tarmac at Vientiane airport in the gathering dusk. Thanking her rescuer fervently, she hurried off to get a taxi to take her the few miles to where she could hire a small boat to take her across the Mekong River from Laos to Thailand. On the other side, in the velvet darkness she ran up the bank to the railhead where she was just in time to catch the slow night train back to Bangkok.

In the still dawn, the "Express" lumbered into Hualampong station, and Cathy was glad to be back. For the first time since the months of her defection to Laos and her love affair with danger, Bangkok seemed a welcome and familiar haven. Soon afterwards, Cathy decided that she had seen as much of Laos as she wished to see, and when her restlessness prompted her once more to look outside Thailand she turned her attentions to Malaysia far to the south, and planned a week's holiday relaxing by a beach in Penang. This would give her time to plan the production of a play that she was to direct for an amateur dramatic group in Bangkok. Thinking that verse drama might be unusual, she had chosen Christopher Fry's "The Lady's not for Burning". The title seemed appropriate – and in the play the heroine wanted to live too.

To Jeanie she embellished the story of her trip to Luang Prabang and omitted much, and in her letters home she recounted the tale with panache and exaggeration. Privately she recalled with chagrin her overactive imagination and the unnecessary fright she had inflicted upon herself, though she managed to forget her lapse of insouciance and her embarrassing tears. It was also irritating that the hero who had delivered her from the clutches of fear had been such an unromantic individual. It seemed less than fair that he should have been so ordinary, so unattractive and not at all "dashing". In her diary she altered the role of the pilot to one that suited the story better, and the mundane commercial transaction became gun running, the two soldiers became a band of armed guerrillas. It could and should have been like that. After some time and repetition, the fiction became the real story and the distasteful duller facts slid into oblivion. Tampering with the facts made it a better tale.

Many years later she was able to dig into the recesses of her memory and admit the truth. Cathy at last learnt to laugh at her youthful yearning for mystery and fear, and to admit that the real story might be just as amusing as the invented one. But in both versions, Laos always remained in her psyche as a land of shadowy dreams and averted dangers. She did not want to go back – reality would never live up to her memories. And anyway, the war was over.

SCARS

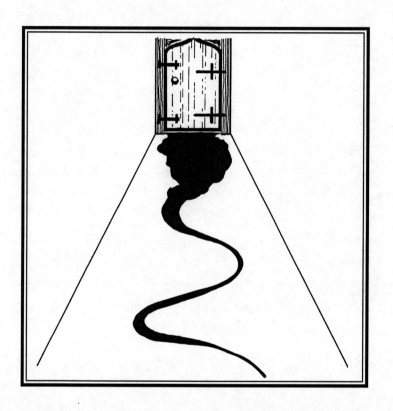

Scars

I've never been very good about coping with blood. It always makes me feel faint. I don't know why I have this silliness when I'm really a very practical person. I can chop wood, change plugs, put up shelves, fix gadgets, clean out garden sheds and service the engine of the lawn mover – plus all the usual jobs in the house. But the sight of blood reduces me to a bumbling idiot. This revulsion never really bothered me until I had children but then I felt that I should try to get control of it, and at least be able to function if a family crisis happened.

I felt quite sick when Stephen, my husband, described to me what he had experienced watching, as it were, from the sharp end when I gave birth to our son. I remember the bloody sheets and cringe even now from the shock they gave me. He wasn't present for the earlier birth of our daughters, who were, thankfully, born whilst I was under anaesthetic – so I don't remember much except the pain beforehand. But my problem with the sight of blood came about much earlier in my life.

I came from a male-orientated family – both my mother and I were tomboys as children – and we both had brothers to contend with plus many male cousins. My childhood was full of toy trains, cars, bikes, football, air guns and model aeroplanes. I had few girly toys – and had little time for those I did possess. I far preferred the construction kits and racing cars that my brothers had. I ignored my doll's house and my dressing up clothes, and with my brothers we performed operations and amputations on my Barbie dolls.

My mother happily never really qualified as a sensible grown-up. She was superb at organising mad-cap expeditions: late-night barbecue parties on beaches with tides coming in, constructing rafts with rope and oil drums to paddle across to an island in a local lake, picnicking on a mountain railway whilst listening for the train, constructing tree houses far too high up, and generally encouraging us to run as wild as she had done during her childhood in Kenya. She inspired me to climb trees since it was an effective way of hiding from the boys when things became too rough even for me.

Inevitably scrapes, cuts and bruises were a part of life – and at first I didn't really mind witnessing them. The occasion that must have traumatised me took place whilst we were on holiday in the Isle of Wight. It was evening and getting dark; we had all been out sailing in small boats. My oldest brother, who had capsized his dinghy and was cold from the sea, decided to have a bath to warm himself up. The rented cottage had the bathroom on the ground floor and its door had two panes of heavy frosted glass. My brother slipped on the bath mat, and whilst falling tried to save himself by lunging out with his arm which punched a hole in the heavy glass door of the room.

Blood. It spouted out like a fountain. My mother, who had once been in the army, did the tourniquet thing, and aware of my squeamishness she told me to go into the kitchen and telephone for an ambulance. This I did, but I could not bring myself to return to the room where the blood was – and later on my mother left me in the house (after telling me to shut up, calm down and not be hysterical) whilst she went to the hospital with my brother.

He had severed an artery and the blood had sprayed about. I found a mop and a bucket of water, and I bravely tried to clean up the mess off the floor, walls and ceiling. I felt gutless and inadequate that I had to push myself to do this. I then abandoned the mop in its gory bucket, and decided to try to knock out the rest of the plate glass which had been shattered and which was clearly a danger. This job was preferable even though I found the odd shred of bloodied skin. With a hammer I tried hitting the broken glass panel out but it kept splintering and sending shards around me. I then put on an old dressing gown, a pair of sunglasses, and started thumping the glass out at arms length with the end of a broom. At this point, my younger brother, who had been de-rigging his dinghy, walked in. I stopped, broom handle poised to thrust. He looked at me – my odd attire, the sunglasses, the broom handle, the broken glass door, the bucket of bloody water and the reddened mop, and he started laughing. I joined in weakly.

My elder brother survived alright but ended up with a twisted scar and a difficulty with using corkscrews to open bottles – which proved rather inconvenient for him when he ran his pub later in life. But the "blood bath" episode scarred me too, and was, I think, the cause of my phobia.

I have never been able to look at accidents when I encounter them in case there may be a lot of blood. I feel guilty that I cannot assist as I should be able to do. I detest violence in films and photographs. I am unable to bandage myself if I am cut but always ask someone else to do it for me whilst I look away. A passage in a book describing someone who was hideously injured in the First World War lingered in my mind and haunted me for weeks. Although I was very good at drawing diagrams of the human circulation system in biology classes at school, I was hopeless when we had to dissect reptiles or parts of animals. Blood makes me feel dizzy and sick.

* * * * *

One summer day not so long ago, my daughter Jenny ran into the house to find me. She was in tears because she had cut her knee and had not yet reached the stoic age when such hurts could be either ignored or borne with heroic dignity. I steeled myself to look at her knee, which turned out to be a shallow cut oozing gritty blood. I grabbed some kitchen paper and held it over the wound, whilst calming her – and myself – by saying in a soothing voice that it wasn't that bad. I sat her on the old kitchen sofa and chatted insouciantly while I found the necessary items to deal with the cut. The ragged white edges repelled me but I swallowed my repulsion and dabbed away with some wet cotton wool to remove any mud or dirt. The soft palpable pinkness visible through the tear soon stopped leaching blood and I then found some lint and a roll of plaster and with relief stuck it across the hurtful blemish on my daughter's knee. I felt oddly angry that her young skin should be so despoiled. I then sat down beside her and stroked her leg whilst telling her that it was not serious enough for the doctor, that it would be alright, that the pain would soon go away, and what a brave girl she was.

Jenny asked me if she would have a scar – something which I would never have been concerned about when I had been a child – but then Jenny is much more conscious about her appearance than I was. No, no, I reassured her – it was nothing like the cut I had sustained at her age when my brother and I had been chasing sheep on a hill. It ought to have had stitches, I tell my daughter, but no-one could be bothered, so I ended up with a purple uneven jagged scar across my knee, which I again showed to her. I have many scars on my knees – mainly from falling out of trees – but I do not recollect the actual incidents when I got them. Perhaps I have just eradicated them from my mind.

Some of my stories Jenny has heard before – and she asks me about the Y-shaped scar on my heel which commemorates the occasion when I was only six and a seesaw crushed it. I gently tell her again about that summer's day long ago when I first climbed on to our new seesaw with my brother at the other end. I wrapped my legs round the plank and when it came crashing down, it landed on my own foot! This is definitely one of my earliest memories. I show her the scar on my heel and she touches it with her finger and listens to me.

Whilst sitting there companionably with my ten year old daughter, I think of other children who, by accident, have been cheated out of the decade of loving life that has been my child's good fortune. Today, whilst listening to the radio, I heard someone translate the words of a small boy in Ethiopia who was saying calmly that he expected to die because his family had no crops because of drought, and no money and no food, and that he hoped he would die soon. I felt so keenly the huge gulf between that child's experience and mine or my daughter's. I also recall another child whose life was cut short – and I cringe inwardly – for this is my story and, though Jenny does not know it, it is her sister's story.

Jenny and Ellie were twins and their birth was painful and protracted. I eventually had an anaesthetic whilst forceps were

122

used, but after their traumatic birth both girls were healthy though small. I was ecstatic about my tiny daughters – and very protective. I was a typical flustered first-time mother. I found it hard to leave the house, I did not want anyone else to hold the twins, and I even felt apprehensive when Stephen picked one up. There was no real reason to feel worried like this because initially I had support and reassurance from the district nurse. When she left I became very tired and after a couple of weeks a friend persuaded us to hire a maternity nurse to help me through the exhaustion barrier. She was a no-nonsense Australian who took over and taught me a lot. I began to relax. She left when the girls were six weeks old and by then I was confident enough to bath them and even trim their tiny soft nails.

When the twins were nearly three months old, I started to want to leave the house with them. I had confined myself to our home during three cold winter months with only the occasional walk round the garden and the surrounding lanes. We were living in a terraced cottage on the outskirts of a small village. One Tuesday when my husband was at work I decided to go shopping and take the twins. Such expeditions were rare, as I was still nervous about these tiny beautiful babies who were my responsibility. My husband had left the car parked outside the house and had got a lift to work with a friend because he knew I wanted to go into town to shop. It was only the third time I had used the car since coming out of hospital. Stephen or the nurse or various friends had done the shopping, but now I wanted to buy some clothes for my babies and some toiletries for myself and to get used to buying the food again.

I had two small reclining baby car seats which were buckled into the rear seats, and in which Jenny and Ellie lay strapped in whilst we drove. I had a collapsible double baby buggy in the boot of the car and into which I would put the twins when we had parked and wanted to go into the shop.

I was nervous, I remember, for no particular reason because there was no longer any ice on the roads and it was not raining. I drove slowly along the quiet lanes towards the main road. I

123

started to enjoy the sense of freedom combined with a proud feeling of responsibility, though I did keep glancing over my shoulders to see if Jenny and Ellie were alright – they were too low to be visible in the mirror. I must have been doing this when a large van hurtled round the corner ahead. When I flicked my eyes back to the road, it filled my vision and seemed so threatening that I panicked and aimed for the verge on my side, turning too sharply and too much. The van shot past, missing me easily and disappeared down the road without seeing my car plunge into the ditch with a juddering impact and become entangled with the overhanging thorn hedge beside it.

I was stunned for a few moments until a horrifying wail from one of the girls began. I turned round and saw a large branch of the thorn tree had broken the window and thrust itself into the back of the car. Jenny, who was in the car seat which was uppermost had her face covered in blood and was howling. I felt dizzy and faint and my heart was thudding but I managed to pull myself round the steering wheel, thrust open the driver's door and climb out of the car. I was nearly sick with shock. Shaking with fear and dread at the state of the babies, I tried to open the offside door. It would have been impossible to get at the other door which was down in the ditch. After scrabbling ineffectively for a minute and sobbing with frustration, the door suddenly clicked and opened. Little Jenny's face was badly lacerated but Ellie seemed to be alright – she was lying in her seat making only a few whimpering noises while Jenny, who was clearly the more injured of the two was shrieking with a frightening intensity. Her face dripped blood from the many scratches, and with a tight feeling of terror in my chest I broke away a couple of small branches from her, and unbuckling the strap, carefully extricated her from the seat. This all took more time than it should have done because I was so upset and fumbled ineffectively. Then I had Jenny in my arms, and glancing across at Ellie, I told her shakily that I would be right back to get her. I staggered up the bank and put Jenny down on the grass verge – but it was a cold day – so I pulled off my jacket and wrapped it round her. I examined her to see if anything serious was wrong – I had no way of knowing if there were any bones broken. But there seemed to be a lot of blood and this unnerved me so I dabbed at it with a sleeve of the jacket.

I looked down the empty lane hoping desperately that someone would come along and help me. Perhaps ten minutes had passed since I had blundered into the ditch with my precious cargo. Surely another car would appear soon. Jenny was still crying loudly but I had to get Ellie out too, so I climbed down into the car in order to undo Ellie's safety harness. She was strangely quiet and I felt a stab of pure terror as I picked her up. Her eyes were still open – there seemed to be nothing wrong with her – but her head was more floppy than usual. She was so small and still, she was so defenceless and still … beautiful but … not breathing.

I do not know how I got out of the car, but I was found some minutes later standing beside the road, wailing to the winds, with my bleeding living untwinned daughter at my feet and my pale dead daughter in my arms.

Jenny has never known about her sister. We were so traumatised about Ellie that we could hardly talk about her, and very soon, she became a taboo subject – the pain was too great. I don't think – but I can never be sure – that Stephen blamed me – he has never given me any indication that he does. But he did not – and still does not – want to talk about it – at all.

Perhaps we have been wrong here. Possibly we should mention her again from time to time – otherwise she might never have been alive. Her death was so appalling that I have failed to come to terms with it. This is my dark secret. I suppose that one day I shall have to tell Jenny – but not yet, not yet. But I cannot help wondering if Ellie would have looked different, or if she would have had the same colour eyes. I feel so guilty that I cannot remember what colour they were. What would her character have been like? Her personality never had time to develop and by my carelessness I denied her a life.

We moved away from the area – we could not bear the sympathy that our friends and neighbours lavished on us.

Their kind looks and careful comments were a daily ordeal. But Jenny herself was the greatest reminder of her sister – they had been so alike as babies. I often wonder if they would have grown up to be different or similar. Would Ellie have been as confident as her sister or would she have been shyer? Jenny is interested in outdoor things and loves sport. Would Ellie have shared these pursuits or would she have been more artistic or musical? Jenny likes singing but has already given up with the recorder. Would they have been the two sides of one coin or two halves of one apple? I'm never going to know.

I find myself looking down at Jenny and noticing that the colour has returned to her cheeks. By this time she has calmed down, come to terms with the shock of her wound, and is beginning to be restless – she does not want to stay any longer beside me on the sofa. This child could be Ellie. I kiss the top of her head and urge her to take care, and she limps dramatically out of the room. She has been comforted and I have been saddened. My loving serenity propels her forward to her next action, escapade, adventure. She is for the moment secure in my love and care. I shall not fail her as I once failed her sister.

Am I scarred by this tragedy? Yes. I am. My weak spot is my inability to forget and forgive myself. How can I heal this wound which still bleeds after ten years? Do I really try or it is easier to suppress it all? I argue with myself. At length, and as always, I take the cowards way and push it to the darker corners of my mind. I don't want to agonise over it for too long – Ellie is my Achilles Heel. But I must try to hide my vulnerable secret because I have to go on living – with all the accumulated baggage of life, the bad times, the good memories, and the emotional scars.

It is time to go and collect little Adam who has been spending the afternoon with a friend who lives in the next street. I shall not leave Jenny alone in the house for the ten minutes that it will take me to walk there and back. I know I am over-protective but I remember that other ten minutes. For a decade I have remembered them with pain. Jenny does not suffer too much from my over-solicitude – she is used to it and will come without a murmur. Adam and Jenny love me – I am their rock and for them I can do no wrong. Children have a predisposition to love their parents and I would never do anything to undermine my children's innocent affection and trust. I am a good mother.

Trying to forget is not easy. The image of that dreadful day is etched in my mind and will not be obliterated. I wonder if Jenny's twin had survived whether she would have forgiven me for what might have ensued – at worst a serious disability or at best a disfiguring scar. I think she would have, but I cannot be sure. I need to turn and walk away from that long corridor in my mind that leads to the door that I keep locked. Inside is blood – the red death of my daughter – and in my nightmares it seeps out, dark and sticky on the cold senseless floor. I must lock the door, seal it and ignore it. I hope I'll always have the strength to do so. I will stay calm; I will be strong.

Yet again I suppress the memory of tiny Ellie and turn to the living. They have no scars yet – and they need me.

NOISE

Noise

I will tell you the story of Fergus and Marion. It is a moral tale with a beginning, a climactic middle and an end. Before the year in which these events took place and afterwards, their lives flowed serenely without drama, so for them nothing very much changed after all. For me, it is different – my life will never be the same. Fergus and Marion do not realize that anything momentous took place and that they missed a chance to become real people. But I do not condemn them – there have been missed opportunities in my life too. It is not always easy or possible to grasp the nettle of change. It was painful for me – but ultimately enriching.

It was during the unsettled seventies when the world was a difficult place. It has never been easy – life on earth – but it was at this time that dissatisfaction fell like a disease on the Royal Borough of Kensington and Chelsea. The comfortable values and habits of a decade were disrupted by the incursion of Worry: worry about the Bomb, worry about the Rainforests, worry about Northern Ireland, and worry about the London Traffic Problem.

Fergus and Marion lived in Barnabas Mansions – and they probably still do. It was one of those medium-sized red brick blocks of flats along the Earls Court Road, with uniform metal window frames and a large draughty entrance hall in need of some refurbishment. Their flat, Number 46, had previously belonged to Marion's mother, who had been a friend of mine. She had left it after her death to her son and daughter. He decided that nothing would induce him to reside in such a dump, and after his return to London from working in Spain, he decamped to taste the less formal delights of life south of the Thames. His sister paid him a modest contribution of rent, and had shared the one bedroom with a girlfriend until her marriage to Fergus.

Fergus, a contented childhood spent in East Sheen, gained with adulthood a dissatisfaction with his whereabouts, and was as eager as his brother-in-law to cross the River, but in the opposite direction. Upwardly mobile, the prospect of a residence north of the Thames was a not inconsiderable factor among the many reasons for getting married to Marion.

Companionship and status were the reasons that Fergus and Marion made an early marriage. It is inconvenient, awkward and solitary to be single, as I know – having had a lifetime's experience of this state. They knew that as a married couple they would be a more acceptable social entity, and felt that more doors would be open to them. Children, however, would come later. Sensible and careful, they realized that some years should elapse before embarking on a family, in order to give them time to plan, save money and savour their independence.

After five years they were still living in Flat 46, comfortable, complacent, and self-satisfied. But the world was intruding and life in Barnabas Mansions was becoming a less cosy place. The superpowers were threatening war, their own government seemed precarious, and the service charge in the mansion block was going up yet again. After five years of self-centred introspection, Fergus and Marion were ready to become aware of the world situation and to open their ears and eyes. What they saw on television, which they watched with their backs to the world outside the door of their flat, was really happening, not some strange shadow play. They watched News programmes now instead of American thriller series. It was more relevant, they said.

Fergus worked in the account's department of a firm in Chiswick, while Marion worked in a department store in the West End. She herself would never have described her job in this way – she told her acquaintance that she worked for Liberty's, as indeed she did. Such status as she did have was within the confines of the Linen Department, where she was now Senior Sales Assistant. They left for work at the same time, and returned home within half an hour of each other; except on Tuesdays when Fergus played squash at the local club, and on Wednesdays when Marion struggled with Spanish at an evening class. Other evening occupations included cooking supper, flat cleaning, watching television, planning their next holiday or weekend, or Discussing the World Situation. Sometimes they went out, had a meal with friends, visited Fergus's parents, saw a film or went to a pub. Life did not seem to be uneventful – indeed it appeared to be positively active and full. They often said to each other, "We never seem to have a minute for ourselves." The truth was that everything they did centred round their needs. They viewed every international crisis or natural disaster from the perspective of how it might affect them. Selfishness was the core of their being. It's sad to say that they were no different from many others who lack the vision to look beyond themselves.

It was during the seventh year of their married life that it became apparent to Fergus and Marion that it was now Time to Question Values and become Concerned about Issues. Or perhaps it was just a touch of boredom that set them on the road which led to their obsession. They needed to get hot under the collar about something, and it had to be a Joint Protest, because, "United we stand and divided we are less effective," Marion used to say. So this is what happened.

The problem was on their own doorstep. Earls Court Road had always been busy, with traffic routed one-way down it, past the tube station towards the Brompton and Fulham Roads. The Borough Council had done its best to ensure that parking was kept off this route to try to keep traffic moving, but the buses had to stop and start, and a new bus stop was positioned just below the second floor windows of Flat 46, Barnabas Mansions. The squeal of braking and the whine of accelerating double-decker buses was a constant irritant, and it was mingled with the general roar of heavy vehicles and lighter traffic, and the discordant horns of impatient drivers as they writhed with frustration in their stationary vehicles.

On the other side of the narrow street which led down the side of the Mansion Block, and opposite the corner where Fergus and Marion's flat was situated, there was an old local pub. This had recently been taken over by a large brewery, who

133

had "tastefully renovated" and "themed" it, using much shiny brass, many items of carefully designed trendy junk, and "old fashioned" new shiny brown leather buttoned pub furniture. A powerful hi-fi sound system was installed playing taped music of the popular but bland variety acceptable to the majority of the clientele. The pub became a "Tavern" with a new young ambitious profit-motivated landlord. Chairs and tables on the wide pavement outside gave it that attractive "Continental" flavour but without the weather to complement it. Even so the pub became a popular early evening haunt. And it became noisy – bearable early in the week, but offensively loud later in the week, and horribly intrusive over the weekends.

The area around Barnabas Mansions began, in the view of some of the residents, to "go down". Noisy bed-sit dwellers moved in to the block next door, and the old building opposite was converted into a student hostel. In the mansion block itself there were various changes of tenancy which brought in a younger, more active group of people. Indeed it seemed to some of the longer-term residents as if some of their number were becoming infected with this feeling of change and behaving with less decorum. There was more music wafting through the corridors: classical and operatic in evidence as well as rock and reggae. It was evident that some of the tenants were actually playing musical instruments inside their closed doors. (I was a culprit here. I had to practice – it was my profession.) Fortunately, because the building had been constructed well before wafer-thin walls became the norm, these sounds were muffled. But it was a worrying period of attrition. The older residents sighed and grumbled.

Even worse, it appeared that more of the tenants were having families. Before, sounds of children had been comfortingly rare, and the few couples who erred by having children were schooled by the silent disapproving majority into keeping them quiet and under control. But now, there was a disturbing increase not only in the numbers of younger persons, but a corresponding decrease in the ability – and even inclination – by the parents to depress the decibel level of their offspring. Children made noises from the other side of their closed doors, and occasionally in the erstwhile sacrosanct corridors! Where would it end?

Another factor was the invasion of electric gadgetry which was seen being delivered to certain flats. Elderly residents' wirelesses sedately settled on the Home Service or the Third Programme were now less frequent than the newcomer's stereo radios tuned to Radio Luxembourg or the Light Programme. Records and gramophone players were giving way to cassettes and turntables with amplifiers and loud speakers. Colour televisions were more in evidence, and some people were actually buying toys and games, which emitted noises that seemed to penetrate everywhere. The once quiet and orderly corridors echoed with a myriad jumble of sounds. To some – and I count myself amongst them – this was a welcome indication of the resurgence of noisy normality after an era of repression, but to others it was alien invasion of the privacy and tranquillity that had been theirs for so long. To a solitary man such as I am it was pleasant and companionable.

Fergus had read an article in a magazine about the damaging effects of very loud and high-pitched sounds. He became concerned and sent off for a report on noise and stress, researched and published by a reputable academic institution. He offered to lend me this report, so I might be aware of the dangers of excessive and persistent noise in our lives. I was warned of high decibel levels and weighed down with many indigestible statistics. I returned it largely unread.

It seemed to Fergus and Marion as if all sound within Barnabas Mansions was becoming penetrating – shrill bells, shrieking children, thumping music, and as if everything outside was becoming louder and more aggressive – police sirens, screeching brakes, car horns, tube train thunder, traffic rumble all combined to produce an unbearable cacophony. In reality the noise was not so very bad; it had not increased appreciably, but what had decreased was Marion and Fergus's tolerance of it. It didn't really bother me much.

I am a musician and music is my life. I am an experienced and able professional flautist. My career has been rewarding though I have had some failures. For many years I have tried, in addition, to compose music but success and recognition elude me. Perhaps I am not passionate enough, as my attempts often seem too subdued, too inhibited. I suspect that my creativity has been cramped by an obsession with structure, and that my compositions are too controlled and lack vivacity. So now I am content to play and interpret music composed by others more talented than I.

My philosophy is that music has no limits – it is so much more than mere notes, scales and melodies, small pieces or mighty works – it encompasses all harmonies and discordances that are the rhythm and music of life. For someone who lives on his own, the sounds that surround me make me feel a part of the world I inhabit and that is very comforting.

The couple's intolerance of noise became apparent to me when, having shown little interest in my work previously, they started referring to my profession. I had been practising in my flat for years without anyone mentioning it or seeming to be aware of it. But Marion, knowing that I played the flute in an orchestra, began to imagine she could hear me. Her increased sensitivity in her hearing did not seem to be matched by a similar increase in her logical faculties.

Now that I have made my debut into this drama, I should tell you how I came to know the players. I had been living in Barnabas Mansions for a number of years before they appeared on the scene. I had known Marion's mother for many years, and also her husband, Vincent, who had been a moderately talented conductor. Three years after the death of her husband, when her two children had just left home, Helena was seeking a comfortable flat in which to live. I alerted her to the sale of a two-bedroom flat almost opposite mine on the first floor. She bought it and moved in, becoming my neighbour – and bringing colour and companionship back into my life.

I appreciated her for her unconventional remarks and witty indiscretions whilst she found in me an admiring listener who didn't criticise or complicate her life by trying to become more intimate. I was immensely fond of Helena, but knew better than to wreck our renewed friendship by becoming amorous, though God knows I had the inclination. After a few years she became ill and died, and subsequently I became acquainted with her daughter, who moved into the flat.

I choose never to be disappointed with life and I realize that women of charm and originality like Helena are rarely encountered. Marion had neither the personality nor the looks of her mother, but I am a man who is prepared to take what life brings along. And she was nice enough, not un-amusing in her naiveté, and pleasant to have coffee with. I'm sure that she used to tell her girlfriend who initially shared the flat that she had "inherited this dear old chap" from her mum. Occasionally I met her brother who was more interesting because of a certain unpredictability that he had probably inherited from the delightful Helena. He had the knack of needling his sister with calculated but seemingly spontaneous remarks or purporting to have outrageous views always diametrically opposed to those of his sister. She was so easy to tease. One always knew exactly what Marion was going to say or do.

Then she met Fergus at a drinks party somewhere, and no doubt thought that his bland mirror-image of her own views constituted a ideal basis for marriage. Naturally, he was of the same opinion!

I saw less of Marion after her marriage, though occasionally they would invite me in when they were short of a man at dinner parties. She probably said to her friends, "He's a bit older but awfully sweet!" I admit that I went because I was sometimes bored with my own company; always eating on my own was tedious, particularly as I cannot cook very well. Marion was an excellent provider of meals, and even if the conversation could not match the quality of the food I went along for the inner amusement of listening to their guests whose blinkered views of the world were hideously fascinating. Political standpoints were often somewhere to the right of Enoch Powell, and many of them were for bringing back hanging, and staying out of Europe, not to mention wiping out Russia with a nuclear bomb before they did it to us! It was all excruciatingly and entertainingly predictable at Fergus and Marion's!

137

So it began to interest me when they became obsessed. I now realize that something like it had always been a possibility. They thought they needed to care deeply about something – to become Involved and Committed. The slight increase in sound levels provided them with a theme. What did surprise me was the intensity with which they pursued their crusade against NOISE. It was an un-winnable war. Protest letters to the town council, leaflets delivered to the other flats and surrounding dwellings, lineage advertisements in the local paper, an attempt to form a local anti-noise campaign committee – all these proved ineffective in the face of overwhelming apathy in those from whom they hoped to recruit support. The local vicar was simply not interested in disbanding his keen bell-ringing group. London Transport could offer little hope that the brakes on their buses would be better lubricated. Marion came across the landing to my flat more than once to complain that people were despicably lazy and not prepared to fight for peace in our time.

Inevitably Fergus became as disillusioned as Marion. They always did everything together. The lack of dissention in their personal lives must have been so enervating. They needed some spice and discord to give flavour to the insipidity of their existence. Not that they thought their days were dull – I am convinced they saw their roles as full of activity and purpose. But their enthusiasm for a silent world and a quiet life was dampened by the massive forces arrayed against them: the might of Car Manufacturers, Motor Bike Dealers, the Breweries, London Transport, and the human desire and compulsive need to communicate, make music and produce the myriad sounds of daily life.

On one occasion on a Sunday afternoon, before they became critical of the "noise" of my flute playing, I invited them over for tea. Another friend called Clive was there too – he lived in a flat on the ground floor and was a person for whom I had much sympathy – though I never let him know. He had become deaf in his forties and was therefore cast into the wilderness of exile from the world of sound and music that gave my life all meaning. He was a calm and thoughtful man with a passionate interest in gardens. Though he lived in a London flat, every fine weekend was spent visiting gardens round the southern counties, and in the winter he read books on his subject.

Fergus and Marion were introduced and upon realizing that Clive was deaf and therefore lip-reading, they addressed careful and simple remarks to his face, whilst ignoring his mind and sensibilities. Of course the conversation turned to their aversion to noise. To my amazement, this unwise and tactless couple chortled on about how wonderful it must be to have such perfect peace and silence all the time. Clive thought, at first, that they were joking in some kind of bizarre bad taste, but when he realised they were serious, he dismissed them as mad. It was an awkward afternoon.

In enlisting support in their anti-noise campaign, they had some limited success with a couple of their friends. In the corridor outside our flats, I met Marion one evening with a pallid young woman whom she introduced as Sally. They had just returned from the Spanish class which they both attended. Marion had invited her back to show her a sample letter which she had persuaded Sally to write to her Member of Parliament. It seemed that Sally too was disturbed by The Traffic Noise Problem, and was being driven to distraction by The Squealing Buses. I thought she looked a bit of an easy convert, with her neurotic harassed manner and obsequious desire to please her friend.

Then I met Rod, who played squash with Fergus every week. One Tuesday evening he called round to collect Fergus who had taken his car into a garage to have a service done or perhaps to try to reduce the engine noise! I was in their flat, borrowing some milk and chatting to Marion, when Rod rang the new buzzer that had replaced the bell. He was a big fellow with one of those hearty booming voices so I didn't give him much chance of continuing as a friend if he didn't tone down the decibels. He seemed pleasantly normal, and I was rather surprised to hear him tell Fergus that he'd managed to get hold of the mailing list of Squash Club members from the Secretary. I discovered that Fergus planned to write to them all about the aviation noise from the jets taking off at Heathrow and flying over the club premises which lay below the flight path. Fergus was going to point out that there was a serious environmental problem, and urge them to write to their Members of Parliament.

None of this really bore fruit, and inevitably Fergus and Marion reduced their target area to their own locality and when this too proved unsuccessful, they concentrated their protests on their own dwelling. They even gave up trying to make me practice my flute elsewhere. As ever, they were oblivious to the insulting nature of this suggestion – and I, as ever, decided not to take offence. It amused me to follow the progress of their quest, smile at their follies and witness the eventual debacle.

You may be wondering why I took such an interest in this foolish couple. I shall now reveal both a secret and a mystery in my life. Some twenty-five years ago, when Helena's husband was on a tour in Australia, she and I had an affair. It was an intense and wonderful experience for me, though I later realised that for her I was just a friend who became something more for a fleeting period when she was lonely and in need of love. When Vincent returned after a few months, I was cast off. Feeling angry and rejected I terminated my friendship with the pair, but never revealed her unfaithfulness. My love affair with Helena became a golden but painful memory. I never married because I could never find anyone who mattered to me as much as she had.

Some months later I heard that Vincent and Helena had had a child, a daughter to be named Marion. I became convinced that the child was mine, and particularly after I was invited to the Christening. Clearly I was not to be asked to be Godfather as that would have been too obvious. Though curious to see my child, I declined to attend. Only once, some years later, did I ask Helena if Marion was mine, and raising her elegant eyebrows, she refused to reply. She was always so intriguing and so infuriating. If she decided to keep a secret, nothing would persuade her to divulge it. I suspected but I never knew for sure. Needless to say, after Helena's death the truth died with her, and I never felt that I could mention to Marion the shocking fact that I was probably her father.

To return to the tale of the War against Noise, they now waged the campaign in their own home. Marion, who had always been a disappointingly bland and easy-going person, became irritable and fussy. She explained to me that her nerves were on edge, and that she found certain intrusions quite unbearable – the ring of the door bell, the shrill alarm of their bedside clock, the buzzing timer on their cooker, the pips on the radio. Fergus, who had always been able to cope well with minor problems round the flat, took an irrational dislike to the tiled floor in the kitchen because their footsteps clacked across it. The vocal enthusiasm of the plumbing came in for a lot of criticism – radiators that bubbled with joy when the heating came on, a lavatory with a flush that was arrogantly over-exuberant and taps that gushed too jauntily. But the one thing that drove them quite demented was the blaring voices on television. They needed to watch it, they said, in order to keep up with the important events taking place in the world, but it caused them pain and anguish to do so because the volume had to be loud enough to hear above the nightmare of the noise outside their flat:- aeroplanes, traffic, brakes, horns, cars, songs, people, life.

I had always wanted to see Marion or indeed Fergus really get angry – to the point where they behaved with some kind of normal spontaneous reaction. The time was drawing closer. Muffled shouts of irritation were heard behind their closed flat door, and once a savage "Go Away" was heard to echo round the landing when someone had had the temerity to ring their doorbell on a quiet Saturday afternoon when Marion was having a rest. They seemed to be falling apart because they were unable to control the volume of life.

And so we come to the fateful night. Various other flat owners on the same floor had become aware of the increasing strain under which their neighbours in No 46 were living. Indeed, we had all been subjected to various visits by either Marion or Fergus, initially with eager requests to join their crusade and subsequently rude demands to reduce the noise levels behind our flat doors. We were all aware there was a time bomb ticking away waiting to blow up. We just hoped the fallout wouldn't disrupt us all too much. Flat dwellers are a selfish lot.

I heard about the explosion from a young acquaintance of mine who was a student at the Royal Academy of Music. She lived in a bed-sit opposite Barnabas Mansions, and one October evening she was looking out of her open window at the movement and lights below in the Earls Court Road when her attention was caught by a window being thrown open in the block opposite. Two people appeared to be shouting and gesticulating, silhouetted against the orange glow of the lighted room behind them. It seemed they were trying to lift up a heavy object – and with a sickening feeling, the young woman thought she was about to witness some horrific crime. She stared transfixed unable even to call out. What was that large object they had hauled up onto the window ledge? At the last minute before it plunged to the street, she shrieked out across the busy road, "Look out!" Only one person heard – and he miraculously looked up and dived for the kerb. A huge chunk of heavy black plastic and glass crashed down onto the spot where he had stood two seconds before, and imploded. Stunned pedestrians thought a bomb had gone off and they dived for cover. A few shrieks were heard, but for half a minute there was no movement. Then the man who had so narrowly escaped picked himself up from the gutter and swore loudly as he surveyed the wreckage of a large and forever silenced television set. The traffic on the road inexorably crawled by unconcerned about life on the pavement.

There were, of course, repercussions. The man who had narrowly missed being killed by the television made a complaint to the police, who paid a visit to Flat 46, from where the missile had been ejected. By the time they arrived the howling fury and pent-up frustration of the couple residing there had somewhat diminished as full awareness of what they had done broke through and enabled them to realise that they had narrowly missed causing the death of another human being. They were evasive about the reason for their actions, but suitably contrite and in the due course of time they were convicted for their crime – and paid the fine. The near-victim

142

lost interest in the protracted proceedings and went to Spain for the winter.

The next step was inevitable too. Having failed to enlist others to aid their crusade to diminish the sounds of city life, they realized there was little they could do, and so they simply decided to turn their backs on it all. They would insulate themselves from the world and its noise. They had plenty of experience in ignoring reality and shutting out unpleasant truths, so this new move proved successful in some respects.

First they started with their flat – their island of sanity and tranquillity in a world gone mad with the effect of brutal and excessive noise. They convinced themselves that the sounds had increased to the level where they were unbearable to live with, though the rest of us hardly noticed any difference. They were almost magnificent in their self-delusion. Fergus, who had always been a regular at DIY shops and stores, created not a little noise by putting in double glazing, insulation in the form of ceiling tiles, and they went to the expense of lifting their carpets to have top quality foam underlay laid down under it. Marion purchased much yardage of heavy material, with which she made curtains, lined and interlined. She even hung a thick velvet curtain in front of the flat door. Fortunately, this was in November, and summer and the need for ventilation seemed a long way off. Fergus explained to me, one Saturday afternoon when he had come across to ask whether I still played the flute or listened to music, that they had managed to eliminate almost all sounds from outside the flat except for the occasional recalcitrant bus.

"We're rather proud of ourselves," he said. "We can now enjoy a meal in peace." I was duly invited round to share a meal and inspect their insulated world. They had indeed done a thorough job, and the sounds of normal life were subdued and muted. I was interested to note that they had targeted food as well, and selected a meal the eating of which would maintain a dignified silence. Nothing was allowed which might offend by giving rise to the odd slurp (so no soup), the rasp of a knife across porcelain (so no steak). The rustle of a crisp salad was unacceptable, celery with the cheese proved too crunchy, and crackers were definitely out. I began to wonder what they did about breakfast, as this meal seemed to be fraught with potential auricular problems. No doubt cereals had been banned, but what about crisp bacon, not to mention toast? Had these been expunged also? I shuddered.

Whilst drinking coffee (very carefully) I noticed that the attractive chiming bracket clock which Marion had inherited from Helena had stopped. It was too handsome a piece to remove and hide away, so they had immobilised it instead. Silent timepieces were easy to arrange. There was no evidence of a radio (and we all knew what had become of the television!), and some of Marion's more noisy kitchen gadgetry had been removed. I wondered what they had done about the telephone – surely they would not have cut themselves off to the extent of disconnecting it! Fergus was keen to explain that there was available on the market now a telephone which could have the bell turned down or indeed off, and that, expensive though they were, he had one on order. It was important to leave lines of communication open, he declared pompously. I wondered if he really knew what that meant.

Conversation that evening was in the usual vein and echoed the meal – flabby politics, soggy religion, dreary films, dull reminiscences. Of course, Noise as the arch villain was predictably condemned. But I was tired, and though momentarily cheered up by the, albeit diminished, sound of a car hooting right below their window, I needed to return to reality in the form of my own flat with my record player, the Third Programme, or the sounds of a London evening through an open window bringing in fresh air and normality. So I thanked them both and escaped.

Having tackled the noise of daily life in their home and the food in their mouths, they turned their endeavours to their work and their leisure. I believe Marion transferred to the lingerie department, where salespersons conducted their work in hushed deferential whispers. Fergus had always worked in the comparatively quiet world of accounts but he probably made efforts to silent any irritating calculators or persistent coughs. Quite how they made their respective journeys to their workplaces I do not know – perhaps they wore ear-plugs.

144

And for hobbies, they took up chess, tapestry making and photography. Marion discontinued her Spanish lessons – the language was too Latin and anyway Spain was too raucous. Fergus continued with his squash but refused to play with players who shouted or cried out. Before all the noise nonsense, they used to go occasionally to concerts and plays, but now they never attended these and rarely went to films and musicals, which they had always enjoyed before. They shunned loud parties and other social events and entertainment, preferring, they claimed, a quiet evening at home. They found it hard to find restaurants where meals were eaten without noisy diners and, even worse, accompanying music. So they ate out less often.

One January evening I knocked quietly at their door to ask if I could borrow some curry powder, and whilst Marion was looking for it, I was invited in and noticed a pile of holiday brochures lying on the new velvety soft carpet. They had always been keen on their annual holiday and had enjoyed winter evenings spent poring over possible destinations – usually a nice hotel in Jersey or a self-catering apartment in Teneriffe with some friends. But now my opinion was asked about painting holidays in Switzerland or Finland. Which country did I think would be most tranquil? Marion had been reading about trips to Lapland and Iceland – she thought snow might be very peaceful. They had often gone to Spain or Portugal before, but holidays in the sun did not now appeal. Chillier climates promised less clamour, it seemed. Would bicycling in Belgium along canal paths be too energetic? What about a cruise along the coast of Norway? I muttered something about the steppes of Russia and retreated, silently leaving them to their quiet deliberations. They knew nothing about the loneliness of single people.

I have to admit that I did almost admire the dreadful duo for their idiotic obsession with creating their own silent world. They had stopped trying to convert the rest of us and had placed themselves apart. I gave up trying to imagine what their evenings would have been like. With no television and radio, they must have had to talk to each other – it was hard to imagine what they might say, having by now long since run out of the self-congratulatory descriptions of how they had achieved their haven of tranquillity amidst an alien world.

But they could not keep it up. Their silent world bored them. They had banished and denied one of their five senses. They had compounded this crime by being deaf to advice. They did not listen. They did not want to hear why other people disagreed – they did not want to admit that they might be wrong. Never distinguishing between the few really unbearable noises and the many myriad marvellous sounds of people and their lives, they turned their backs on reality. The demon of discord from which they fled pursued them in their heads. Their tempers frayed. Their lives shrivelled.

I encountered Marion one Sunday morning in the entrance hall shouting at one of the newer ground floor occupants, who was struggling with a crying toddler whilst trying to extricate a bawling baby from a pushchair. The young mother was quite astonished by the vehemence of the other woman. She retreated with her children into her flat, and Marion stamped out of the building without even noticing me. But then lots of people don't notice me. Perhaps I'm too self-effacing – I seem to be positive and visible only when I'm playing my flute. But my neighbours don't see this. In any case, I've always felt more interest in other people than in myself.

Marion and Fergus had often talked about having a family when the time was right and, though not enthusiastic, they had never before shown antipathy to children. However, now their vendetta was extended to include the noise of families, and no doubt they put off yet again their decision to have a child. It would have required them to overcome their selfishness.

In that year of their obsession, they dismissed from their lives the sounds of laughter and sorrow, songs – harmonious or discordant, music and musical instruments, natural sounds and mechanised sounds, birdsong and human singing, high notes and high hopes, low jokes and low giggles, loud shouts and soft whispers – the marvellous musicality of life. I didn't laugh at them any more. Indeed, I felt very sorry for them. How they must have suffered!

But they didn't admit it. No, not them. Spring with all its vitality returned to England but not to the suffocating enclosed world of Flat 46, Barnabas Mansions. Marion's brother returned from a two-year job in Brazil and came to see them. On my way to buy a newspaper, I passed him in the corridor – he did not recognise me. I suppose I was looking older. I can remember on my return hearing the roar of laughter that managed to escape through the heavy door curtain and through the door itself – like an trumpet emitting common sense.

Having no sense of humour themselves, Marion and Fergus did not like being laughed at. She did not mention her brother's visit to me the next time I saw her. They wanted to be taken seriously and his ridicule had upset their equilibrium. The seed of doubt had been sown. It grew as rapidly as the young shoots on the trees in the nearby square. The wind of change was blowing in harmony with the rubbish that blew along Earls Court Road.

I was away on tour for a few weeks. Shortly after my return, one morning in May as I remember – I heard music coming from their flat. Astonished and also pleased, I knocked on the door. The sound was throttled. Fergus opened the door and, looking a bit guilty, he said he was having a few days off work. The radio was sitting innocently on the table behind him, silent as an admonished child.

A few days later, whilst returning from the shops to the Mansions, I looked up in surprise to see the windows of their flat open, and curtains drawn to let in the fresh air. Number 46 must have become unbearably stuffy. A change was in the air. The cloak of silence that hovered round our end of the corridor began to lift. I played my flute with as much alacrity as ever, but I felt that my music now had an audience – which if not enthusiastic was at least accepting. Marion smiled more and I even heard Fergus whistle occasionally as he used to do.

They had booked up a painting holiday in Holland and off they went in June. I didn't hear much about it after they came back, which was unusual because Marion had always taken pleasure in regaling me with the details of their various holidays. I can only assume it was silent and dreadfully dull – neither of them having any creative instincts or any real interest in art. They were probably telling their friends at work how marvellous and peaceful it had been! Fergus decided to frame up two of Marion's drawings, and they asked me round to look at them and advise as to where they should hang them. Having cooed tactfully over the windmills, I suggested the dining room wall (where they would be observed less often), and Fergus started to hammer in the picture hooks. The plaster was hard so it took a bit of time, and their neighbour from the adjoining flat, no doubt pleased to have the opportunity to get some revenge, thumped on the wall to express her irritation. Fergus was devastated. Marion was despatched to apologise. "How could we have been so insensitive?" she said to me.

"Because you always are," I wanted to say, but didn't.

After that the fall from grace, the abandonment of their principles, the flight from silence gathered momentum. They re-connected the doorbell and they re-tuned to the Home Service. A new television was surreptitiously delivered which no doubt allowed them to abandon their recent awkward habit of talking to each other in the evenings. The horror of being thrown on their scarce inner resources receded.

They broke out of their prison of silence but remained unaware of the perimeter fence of their limited aspirations. They pulled back into their lives all the sumptuous sounds they had banished. They did not seem to feel any embarrassment or shame – they felt no need to move away and live somewhere where people wouldn't laugh at them. In fact, I don't think they even realised that people found them comical. Or perhaps it was only I who felt ashamed for them – laughed at them. I am ashamed of myself too – I sought the company of those I despised because I am a pitiful and lonely man.

Or was it because I felt the tug of a father's affection?

One Saturday lunchtime, I was surprised and pleased when Fergus rang my bell and suggested we go to the pub for a drink and said that Marion was out shopping. I thought perhaps that

148

he was trying to eradicate any ill-feeling I might have as a result of their previous intolerance of my music. Over a pint of beer, we swapped confidences and I mentioned my regret that I had never managed to compose anything really fine. He mentioned his disappointment that he had not made it into the club squash team. We commiserated with each other.

Then he said something that made me sit up and listen. Marion had had a deep disappointment too. A few years back, she had discovered amongst various papers a notebook of her mother's, and she had been distressed to find that her mother's husband, Vincent, whom she had always thought was her father, was not in fact her real father. She had learnt who her natural father was.

Here Fergus paused to take a swig of his beer. I held my breath. Had Marion then always known about me? Then Fergus delivered the coup de grâce by uttering the name of a well-known politician, long since retired and now dead. He probably should not have mentioned it, I heard him say through the red haze of my mortification, because Marion had chosen to dismiss the whole unsavoury disclosure.

But I knew it was true. Life had dealt me the unkindest kick of all – the revelation that fatherhood had also eluded me. I felt betrayed. Muttering something about feeling a little unwell – my drink was too bitter to finish – I slunk back to my flat, licking my wounded pride.

For a couple of days I stoked my anger and nursed my grudge against the world. Then, needing some retaliatory act to assuage my vexation, I decided to tell Marion that her mother and I had once had a torrid affair. The chance came the next evening, when Fergus was at the squash club and Marion, bored with her own company, invited me over for a cup of coffee after supper. My ill humour was at eruption point and without preamble I told her that once I had been her mother's lover. To my amazement, she laughed and refused to believe me. Then I lost my temper and for the first time ever I told her exactly what I thought of her. She went white with anger at my insulting and acid remarks and threw me out.

149

I was incensed with the stupidity of the woman, and stumbled back to my own flat, boiling with frustration. There was a pounding in my head, an insistent beat of fury. For a long time a savage music ravaged my soul, and then a period of sweet peace ensued, after the chaos and pain. I picked up my flute and began to play.

Eventually I became more clear-headed and could write my music down. After some time and effort, I produced a completed work. The first part was strident, passionate and angry, the second part reflected the emptiness of despair and disillusion, and finally came acceptance and the balm of healing. It was good. It was probably the first time I had ever composed anything worthwhile.

My cosy existence had been jolted out of its groove. Perhaps, in order to create, to achieve, it was necessary to get involved with other people, to feel pain and ecstasy, and not stand back and be the wry commentator. Though I never expected to, perhaps I had learnt something from Fergus and Marion – the need to throw out the stumbling block in one's life. My problem was that I had lacked the courage to move on, that I clung to comforting old habits, that I put up with Marion because I loved her mother. My aspirations to parenthood were misguided. I never did relate to her but I became infected by her insensitivity. One should avoid the company of tedious people – it rubs off!

So I gave up my long-standing job with the orchestra. I had been there too long. I sold my flat and moved to another part of town – to an area less desirable but more vibrant, where I rented a house. It was hard to have a change of career at my age, but I was lucky and managed to secure a post at a large school where I took up teaching music to those pupils who showed an interest. Some of them had ability and enthusiasm that needed encouraging. I found to my surprise that I had a talent for teaching, and to my amazement I actually enjoyed it. Of course I had problems and troublesome students, and I became tired and tetchy. But on the whole I relished the whole experience of moving out of my comfortable niche.

The unpredictability of the working day in my new profession gave my life zest and it gave my music bite – a necessary edge. I am pleased with my progress as an aspiring composer. One of these days I might get my work performed. Who knows what will happen? I might even achieve acclaim, but that matters less than it once did.

I had always been conservative in appearance and modest in my ambitions, but now I decided that, in order to make an impact when giving lessons, I needed to become eccentric and little flamboyant. I assumed quirky little mannerisms and took to wearing orange or red shirts and mismatched brightly coloured socks. The pupils loved it. I became known as the Pied Piper, and I soon had a following of devotees. Most of the children laughed at me but some of them liked me. I made friends with a couple of the teachers, one of whom moved into my house. It was companionable, and I learnt to share things and care about someone else other than myself.

I rarely thought about the past and the dusty old life I had led for so long in Barnabas Mansions. It amused me to imagine Marion, having decided to forgive my rude outburst, knocking on my old flat door, and getting no reply. I had gone. They would feel curiosity but no guilt. And I was free of them and of my pathetic illusion that I had meant something to them. They had not deserved my friendship and I had withdrawn it.

The moral of this tale should be that Fergus and Marion learnt humour and humility. Of this there were incapable. What happened to them? I knew little and cared even less. They will never again achieve the ludicrous grandeur of their obsession with noise. No doubt they retreated into the vast selfishness of their sterile sluggish lives and nothing changed. Change is vital and it is a crime against life to remain unmoved. That is a lesson I have learnt.

DRAGON'S MOUTH

Dragon's Mouth

I'm not easily frightened.

It's easy to say this and the statement has a satisfying ring of bravado about it. But I have to admit to having a latent fear of the dark ever since I was a child. I have tried to submerge this panicky instinct and indeed my family did their best to suppress it. My sister and I were told not to be silly or spineless. My parents robustly decided not to foster fears by pandering to such childish worries, and so whimsical night lights or low wattage lamps in bedrooms were not encouraged, and indeed soon became banned. We had to cope with the unalterable fact that night was dark, and that was usually when we slept.

Had we shared a bedroom, coping with "Lights out" and the instant descent into blackness might have been easier. We would have had each other to bolster up confidence and we could have whispered together. When we tentatively suggested that we might share a room, we were informed how fortunate we were to have our own bedrooms, and that was the way it was. My sister managed to grow up quicker than me, and she didn't seem to mind the dark – or so she said. And I was left – the only wimp in the family, who pulled up the bed clothes over my head when Mummy left the bedroom having kissed me goodnight, because the warm small darkness under the covers was somehow more acceptable than the huge echoing black void that was the rest of my bedroom. I remember whimpering silently to myself on windy winter nights when the sounds of the vast blackness outside the house intruded into my bedroom.

When I was quite small, I was obsessed with the horrible conviction that I had a crocodile under my bed. This frightening fantasy was very real, even though logic and the cold light of day should have dispelled it, and it may have arisen from the fact that we had rather high beds with trendy iron bedsteads and big empty spaces below. It may also have been fostered by the wonderfully terrifying tale of "The Enormous Crocodile" by Roald Dahl. I was petrified to get up in the night and go for a pee, lest the "croc" caught me and bit my leg off. Later on, I bought myself a small torch so that I could switch it on and check out the ominous void below the bed before I ventured to put foot to floor.

Later on I managed to conquer the crocodile nightmare but then became obsessed with lurking spiders, wood lice and cockroaches. When we were about ten years old, my mother suggested that I use a duvet. Although my sister had been acquiescent, I resisted this change and was allowed to stay with sheets and blankets, which I far preferred because they could be tucked in all round me, so that no creepy crawlies could get in unseen and lurk around my toes.

I suppose I must have grown out of worrying about the darkness in my bedroom at some point, because I don't really mind it any more. But that could be because I now have a lover to lie beside me in bed and kick out any terrors of the night that occasionally still inhabit my head. Before I met him, I used to live in a small village in a cottage on my own. This was brave stuff, and I felt a real grown-up person coping so well with the solitude. That, as it happened, was never the problem – I rather like my own company. It was arriving home after work in the winter months when it was dark that I found difficult. There were no street lights in the road, and I had to park my car in the lane and walk through the gap in the hedge, and up the garden path to my back door. When the headlamps were dowsed and if there were no stars or moon, then it was a very black walk with hidden dangers lurking behind every shadow, bush or tree. I knew that I could have used a torch but that would have meant admitting to a very silly anxiety. If I walked slowly with measured steps I could control the unease, and then unlock the door and go in, switching on all the lights very quickly. But if I allowed my terror to get hold of me, then I ran from car to door, and my agitated pounding steps echoing on the stone slabs brought on panic. In distress I would fumble with the keys and finally fall in through my door and bang it shut behind me in a blue funk, my heart thudding with alarm.

156

I don't think I was worried about anything in particular – murderers or monsters. It was just that fear of the unknown and the threat posed by lack of vision. Again, I have managed to conquer my horrors and subdue my overactive imagination. In fact, I pride myself now on how cool and calm I am. Experience has shown me how groundlessly stupid it is to be so apprehensive. I can, I reassure my adult and confident self, rise above such cowardly and immature worries.

Except that I find I now live with a man who is obsessed with sailing. And I don't mean messing about in dinghies, day sailing on reservoirs or in harbours. I mean sailing across large expanses of water, involving many days and nights at sea. I have discovered that I love sailing – well, most of the time. It's often wet, cold and bumpy, but it is also challenging, adventurous and fun. On the whole I've learnt to manage quite well in a small boat on a big ocean – I often surprise myself about how adaptable and resilient I am – and I've learnt a few things about boats, weather and compatibility. I have also learnt how to cope with tiredness and loss of energy – eat lots whenever a hint of hunger is felt. I am quite young, I sometimes think, to have managed to do all this and explore a wonderful and loving relationship for the first time in my life. Though "MJ" and I spend much of our time on the sea, as yet we have had remarkably few bad experiences together.

My biggest problem is night sailing when we are just the two of us. It means that I am on my own for a night watch, whilst my lover is asleep. Sailing at night can sometimes evoke waking nightmares, caused either by internal fatigue or external stimulation. And the vast dome of blackness above, even when star studded, can be very unnerving. I've tried to talk to other sailing people about this spooky feeling in the dark at sea but few are prepared to admit in the clear light of day to frightening hallucinations in the dead of night. Men often laugh indulgently at my feminine fears, so I now tend to keep quiet about them. It is clearly something I have to come to terms with on my own.

Recently we both decided to change jobs, and have put our budding careers on hold whilst we go blue water cruising for a year. We flew to the West Indies, and bought an old 38ft sailing boat in Martinique. She was battered, comfortable and affordable. Most importantly she sails well. We headed south with the prevailing wind on our quarter, giving us a comfortable ride down the Windward Islands.

After a couple of weeks at anchor in various lovely harbours in Grenada, we have decided to sail on down to Trinidad and Venezuela. I am getting pretty confident and competent by now, and able to handle the boat on my own. So we are setting off on a southerly passage of some ninety miles from St George's, Grenada to Trinidad, where we plan to spend some time before moving on westwards.

We are on our own, since our crew – a couple of friends from home – have left ship in Grenada to fly back to Europe. It has been a hectic day but we have decided on a night passage, in order to arrive in the morning, and not in the dark. Approaches to islands in the Caribbean are best made during daylight hours, as navigational lights are not always functioning, and the coasts are often rocky with coral reefs.

There is little wind as we set off across Grand Anse bay at dusk, but it picks up as we approached Saline Point, the south western tip of the island, by which time it is dark. As we round the point, a huge black phantom shadow with two bright staring eyes flies towards us at frightening speed from the west, and thunders low overhead to land on the runway at the international airport which extends to the very shore. For one terrifying moment we think the aeroplane will hit the top of our mast. This is an illusion which we often have when passing under bridges, when the mast seems so tall, and the obstruction so low. So this is an unnerving start to a spooky night.

After a meal, during which the few lights on the southern shore of Grenada fade, I take a few hours kip, and leave MJ on watch. When I come up for my stint at midnight, the wind is fresh on the port beam, and we are making good progress. MJ retires below, and here I am, a bit sleepy, with little to do, a slight feeling of uneasiness – for no good reason – and an over-active imagination. It takes a little while for my eyes to adjust to the dark after the cabin lights below which have now been dowsed. The black glinting waves undulate all around the boat. I feel we are an insignificant dot in the vast immensity of the sea under the arching void of night.

When we are on night watches, if there are two or more of us, we tend to talk. There's not much else to do once the sails are trimmed and any necessary adjustment to course has been made. Under the cloak of night there is a tendency to divulge secrets and make unwise disclosures that one might not do in the cool light of day. It's something to do with the intensity and immensity of the ocean on all sides under the black dome studded with myriad stars. When I'm on my own, I still chat – to myself. It seems quite normal. And reassuringly companionable. Occasionally I speak out loud but usually it is an internal monologue. Tonight is no exception.

"It's pretty dark out here – hardly any stars – and slick black water swishing along our hull. The boat's going fine – though the wind may build and I may need to reef. How long have I had of my watch? What, only ten minutes! Perhaps I can have a piece of fruit or a biscuit in half an hour – just to keep me going. It's warm enough though – there's nothing worse than cold night watches – but this is the wonderful Caribbean. .... Perhaps I'll just take a peek at the chart below. Maybe make a note in the log. Careful down the companionway steps – hold on. MJ looks peacefully asleep, lank damp hair on pillow. Lucky man.

"Good grief – what's that noise? Get on deck immediately. Anything broken? .... Nothing I can see. Oh well, probably a sea bird. Or do dolphins make that sort of noise? Could it be a whale – are they this far south? Well, at least it didn't wake MJ. And I caught my shin coming up the steps too fast. Painful. Concentrate on sailing. Check the course and ensure the Autohelm is behaving. Trim sails.............

"I can't see anything, but the boat seems to be charging like a blind bull into the unknown. Do the local fishermen show lights? I'll bet they don't. Would they see ours – that little modest tricolour way up sixty feet? No. Anyhow, surely we must be too far offshore for any little craft. .... What

159

about big boats or ships? There seems to be pall of blackness enveloping the boat. Calm down – there's no reason to be anxious. Oh do stop being so jumpy. There's nothing out there. But we're going very fast and what if there were a large piece of driftwood or a half-sunk container floating in our path – or even worse, a huge whale? .... Stop this silliness, right now! Three deep breaths. Think about something else. Such as sunshine and flowers. Totally irrelevant to this situation. What situation? There is no problem. Calm down. Try a piece of chocolate. The water looks so black. ....

"Oh dear – the topping lift seems to be loose and flying about – I'd better go forward and hoist it up a bit. Why am I doing this, slinking cautiously along the deck, risking my life just for a loose topping lift? I'm mad! .... Better – I've taken up the slack in it and I'm back in the cockpit. Wind getting up – so I'll have to put a reef in – perhaps not quite yet. The wind might drop. .... But it doesn't, so I really ought to bang one in. .... Coward. Lazybones. No I'm not: I'll do it now. Remember Rob James who always said 'If you've thought about it twice, you should have done it.'

"Well, it's in and all's well. The boat seems to be going just as fast as before – with nearly 25 knots of wind. I slipped slightly on a rope on the coach roof – very careless of me. I should wear my harness, but its so restricting! Without it, if I had tripped up I might have slithered over the side. It doesn't bear thinking about – MJ waking up three hours from now, and not knowing whether I was five minutes or four hours astern. Not to mention about what I would be feeling – knowing I was going to drown, and wondering whether the sharks would get to me first! What a nightmare. Why do I do this? I'm risking my life every time I go sailing. This is self-indulgent stupidity. I've a family thousands of miles away that need me – I must be crazy!.........

"You certainly are crazy to let your thoughts run on like this. Driving a car on crowded roads is probably more dangerous than a solo night watch. Yes, I know. But here I'm alone. I'm also in charge. MJ trusts me, and he's vulnerable while asleep down below. .... I think I can hear him breathing from where I'm sitting on the bridge deck – rather comforting. I can always call him. But there's no reason – everything's alright. .... Get a harness ready and put it by the spray hood. Just in case. No real need to put it on yet – the wind's not getting up. No, I'm not scared.

"I still feel a bit strange. There are no stars now. The night is very black and we seem to be hurtling round in a huge circle – that is the sensation I have, although I know from the compass that we are on course in the right direction. The wind has gone a bit further forward, so the impression of speed is increased – but I do so dislike this dashing into darkness. I wonder what there is up ahead. .... Perhaps we are closer to Trinidad than we think. We are making for the Boca del Dragón – the Dragon's Mouth – which is the gap between the north-west tip of Trinidad and the north-east arm of Venezuela. Strung with islands and many rocks, tides and hazards, it is the entrance to the Gulf of Paria and our port of destination, Chaguaramas on Trinidad's western coast.

"We seem to be racing towards a huge black cavern. I have an odd sensation that we are going downhill. Fear. Keep it under control. I must be very tired. I'm getting things out of all proportion. Perhaps another little snack will cheer me up. ....my blood sugar level low and all that!

"Is this watch never going to end? I've still got over an hour. I think I can see a curious kind of light over there – not a single light like a vessel, more of a luminous haze. There are no such things as UFO's, and its too low for an aircraft. Is it a big ship and how far away is it? .... You silly cow, its the moon rising – behind a low cloud. You really are suffering from hallucinations. I know. But this is a horrible night. .... It could be a lot worse. But it's me that's the problem – maybe I ate something that has stimulated my imagination. It's like a dream that I can't control. I keep thinking about how far we are from anywhere, if we needed any help, or if the boat were to sink. .... Stop all this and go below and write up the log – something concrete to do prevent over-stimulated brain from inventing dangers.

161

"Only twenty minutes before I can wake up MJ. I've un-reefed, as the wind abated a bit. I shut my mind to the nasty possibility of falling overboard and just got on with it. I don't normally have these nerves. But to-night I have this mental picture of our tiny boat being sucked down the gorge of a gigantic and evil sea monster. I wonder if there is a strong current pushing us faster and faster. Of course not, you idiot! I'm tired. It's nearly 0400. Not long now to my berth, and hopefully oblivion. Time to wake MJ. He's so sensible. I won't tell him about all my fears and fantasies – he would think me dotty. It's just been so dark."

I'm lying down, having clambered into MJ's sleeping bag, which is warm and smells comfortingly of him. We had a cup of tea together and he has told me that we are on course and will not be anywhere near any navigational hazards until morning. My fears have subsided and my pulse has returned to normal. I am sleepy and feel a sense of contentment that comes after a night watch, when muscles relax, and the need to be alert recedes. I am no longer in charge. I trust MJ totally and I can now let go. Over the chart table is a soothing red light that goes out as I close my eyelids. But I know it's there. A tiny beacon in the darkness. .... The boat surges forward towards dawn.

* * * * *

It's daylight and I can see the sunlight flickering on the wood bulkhead beside my berth. I can hear the sluice of waves past the hull beside my head. A feeling of well-being pervades my heated body cocooned in its sleeping bag. I glance across the cabin – MJ is at the chart table writing, and listening to music on his headphones. He smiles at me as I extract myself from the berth and stretch. Light has already filled my head and banished the darkness of my fear.

I murmur "good morning" as I clamber up onto the bridge deck and look around. It's a lovely day – the sea is glistening – the sky is a mottled blue – and there on the horizon in front of us are the islands of the Dragon's Mouth – the visual reality dispelling the ghost of my nightmare. The north coast of Trinidad is low to windward on the port bow. We'll be there in a few hours. I really do like sailing. All is well. Below MJ is making bacon sandwiches. Smells good. I'm ravenous.

The wind is cool on my skin. The white sails are taut. Night has given way to day. But I know that old dread will emerge again at dusk. The mind monster and its gaping jaws – my fear of the dark and the unknown – won't go away for more than a few glorious hours. Until then I'm in control, brave and free.

REQUITAL

Requital

I dislike being cheated. My husband does too, but he retaliates. Unlike me. I just find it all too difficult to object and make a fuss. My neighbour, Serena, says I am too timid. I get very embarrassed in restaurants when Clive demands a better table than the one he has been allocated which is next to the entrance to the toilets or in a draught from a door. He tends to get his way – which I do applaud. He is a large intimidating man whose strength I admire, but I feel sorry for those who get the edge of his temper. Sometimes this is me.

Last year, a travelling salesman came to the door to sell some new type of cleaning fluid. I made the mistake of opening the door to him, and within a minute or two he was sitting in my kitchen drinking a cup of tea. He was so convincing that I ended up buying four bottles of the stuff because he gave me such a good discount. I always find it hard to say no. After he'd gone I tried some on the stain on one of the cushions of our sofa, on which Clive had spilt some black coffee. It not only failed to remove the stain but it took all the colour out of the material, and I had to hide the cushion so as Clive wouldn't see my blunder. I knew if Clive discovered I'd bought something from a door-to-door salesman that I'd never hear the end of it so I hid the rest of the bottles away in a cupboard. Such a waste of money. Sometimes, I think Clive is right – that I am as stupid as he says I am.

But I'm getting more cautious, or rather suspicious. The other day, while I was scrubbing the wooden chopping block – which Clive always tells me is a harbour for germs – the telephone rang. I took off my rubber gloves and answered it, and someone at the other end began by asking me if I was the owner of my house. Well, of course I told him that perhaps he ought to speak to my husband, who was at work. Though later I realised that I was in fact part owner of our house and could have said so. He then started going on about things such as security for the future, optimising assets and maximising potential – in the end it appeared that he was offering financial advice. Well I told him straight that my husband took care of all those sort of things. He said he would phone back and speak to my husband, but he never did. I don't expect Clive would have listened to him anyway – he doesn't like taking advice from anyone. He is convinced that these self-styled professional people are swindlers who are trying to take him for a ride. He has no time for bank managers, solicitors, insurance brokers or estate agents. "I can get by very well without all these charlatans," he says firmly.

Sometimes I think Clive is a bit hard on people who are only trying to earn a living. He's often very suspicious in shops too – though he doesn't go shopping very much, except to the local hardware store to buy tools or nails and to the off-licence to get some more beer. When he's in The Handyman Shop, he asks all sorts of awkward and tricky questions about the object he's buying. I won't go with him any more – I find it too embarrassing.

Clive says he can't bear to shop with me because I dawdle and dither. This is a little unfair. Of course, when I buy presents for people I have always tried to find unusual and pretty things so I tend to take a lot of time. Clive teases me about my lists and my preoccupation with finding just the right present for a particular person. He doesn't realise that it's important to me – that I care. I like shopping and I like to get it right. Last month I spent two hours trying to buy his father a nice birthday present and Clive told me not to be too pernickety and to get a move on. I thought that was slightly unkind of him.

Recently I've started buying by mail order – it's much less stressful. When I am looking for clothes, and want to try things on, I always feel somewhat intimidated by shop assistants. It seems so rude to say that you know they are wrong when they tell you that something looks good on you when you know that it doesn't suit you at all. I like to shop by catalogue because then I don't have to see people face to face – and it's easier to send things back if they aren't right or don't fit.

168

But with food shopping I really do need to check out the quality of the fresh items and the price of my groceries before I buy them. My friend and neighbour, Serena, seems to come back from the supermarket with lots of items which she doesn't really want – she laughs about this and says she can't concentrate on it all because it's just "too boring." I disagree, though I don't tell her to her face. I rather like my twice-weekly shopping trips. First of all, I plan ahead and decide which shops I'll go to. Then I make a list and keep to it, and don't get distracted by offers for things that I don't really want. I'm sure lots of people buy things they don't need at all because they get lured by the so-called "savings". Finally, I check everything I've bought carefully to prevent making any mistakes. I'm normally very vigilant about "sell-by" dates and damaged packaging, so that I don't have to go back and complain later. Not that I ever complain much – I find it hard to tell someone that they've sold me something faulty. Even though I know they are in the wrong, I always feel bad about it myself.

Some weeks ago I went for a cup of coffee round at Serena's house. We were sitting in the front sitting room – she clearly didn't want me anywhere near her kitchen, which was probably in its usual state of chaos. But anyhow she often uses her front room – much more than we do ours. This time she and I drank our coffee out of her best cups and saucers. I felt a bit bad because when she comes over to my house, we usually drink our coffee out of mugs, although they are bone china – the ones I bought two years ago with the gardening motifs – with pretty delicate handles. But mugs never the less. Memo: next time she visits me I must get my second best cups and saucers out of the top cupboard. Anyway, on this particular day, Serena admitted that these were the only cups and saucers she had – very pretty with gilt borders – probably quite expensive – and I was rather touched that she should waste them, as it were, on her old friend and neighbour who wouldn't have minded a mug.

I said to her, "Serena, you don't need to get out the best china for me – I'm ever so happy with a mug in the kitchen."

To which she cheerfully replied: "Good Lord, Barbara, I can't let you into the kitchen – or the dining room at the moment – we had a dinner party last night and I haven't got round to clearing it all up yet." That amazed me! She seemed to feel no embarrassment that she and Greg had left everything and gone to bed without so much as carrying the dirty crockery and cutlery into the kitchen. I expect she'd picked up the glasses from the sitting room and plumped up the cushions only ten minutes before I arrived. And perhaps she had used the best china because everything else was dirty!

This led me to reflect that, firstly, in our house the washing up would have been done by me that evening after the guests had left, however tired I was. Clive would have gone to bed – he never does things like washing up. Secondly, we rarely have dinner parties any more because I don't like not being able to calculate when my guests might choose to depart (and I don't like leaving things to chance). Thirdly, and this reflection slightly upset me, that although Serena often has me round for coffee, she and Greg never invite us for dinner. Even though Greg and Clive often chat over the fence on Saturday mornings when they are washing their cars, I'm not convinced that Greg likes Clive. And finally, dinner parties happen on Friday or Saturday nights when people don't have to get up early and go to work the next day. And this was a Thursday!

So there we were, Serena and I, drinking coffee in her sitting room, whilst she had all that washing up and cleaning work to do. I couldn't have sat there as calmly as she did – I would have been itching to get on with it all. It was good coffee too – real coffee – and I felt a pang of guilt that I always give her "instant" when she comes round to me. Perhaps some had been left in the pot after the dinner, and she had re-heated it – yes, that must have been what she'd done.

I glanced down to the tray with the elegant china coffee pot, and a little silver milk jug. Serena followed my gaze and said rather sadly, "The matching cream jug for this set got broken some years back, and the pattern's not available anymore, so I use this little silver jug which was a wedding present."

"It's a very pretty jug," I responded with enthusiasm, so as to dispel any awkwardness over the careless loss of the china jug and the use of a precious wedding gift when any old jug would have done. "I do like silver. And it's been cleaned very well. What product do you use?"

Serena stifled a yawn – which I thought a bit impolite until I recalled that she had probably been to bed very late and had to get up early to get Greg's breakfast before he went to work – and said, "I don't remember – something which comes in a small blue bottle."

To make her feel better, I then told her about some small items of silver which I simply couldn't get clean at all, however much I tried. She hadn't really got any advice and changed the subject to the latest episode of "Dallas" which we had both seen. Serena said she only watched what she calls "mope operas" to cheer herself up, and we often chatted about them and speculated about what might be going to happen. We both enjoyed disliking J.R. who was such an awful cheat and liar. I don't like cheats and frauds.

Clive won't watch "Dallas" – he says it is melodramatic rubbish. For me it's compulsive viewing and I put up with his sarcastic comments in the same way I endure his endless criticisms of the way I roast potatoes. It seems that I'm never going to reach the pinnacle of perfection, which his mother clearly did week after week during his childhood. It's just as well that she died before Clive and I met, or else I might have been tempted to murder her! Only joking, of course.

Serena was round at my house the other day, and we were having some coffee and biscuits in my kitchen. Before she arrived I had washed the floor but I was a bit ashamed because I had been cleaning the silver at one end of the table which was covered with cloths and newspaper. I like the kitchen to be clean and tidy with things in their proper place. Whilst wiping the work surface near the kettle with a blue Spontex cloth because I had spotted a small spillage of coffee on it, I apologised for the mess on the table. However, Serena didn't seem to mind. I've noticed that she does leave her kitchen in rather a state, but then I suppose I should make allowances

171

for the fact that she has a part-time job and I don't – so I've probably got more time to devote to household tasks. Clive always tells me that I fuss over the house too much, but if I didn't we'd live in a pigsty, because he has never pushed a vacuum cleaner over a carpet in his life. "Women's work" is what he says.

So there we were, sitting in my kitchen – I really prefer it to our sitting room, because it has a nice view over the rear garden which was looking very pretty. I had the day before planted out some pansies in the borders. (Clive doesn't really have time to do any gardening). I regret to say that Serena and Greg's back garden leaves much to be desired. Greg makes an effort with the front patch, but their dog is left to roam around at the back, and the grass is rather worn, and the borders untidy and overgrown. This might also account for the fact that often Serena likes to use her sitting room with its view out over the street. In our front room, we tend to leave our best three-piece suite with their dust covers on, so as to keep them from getting soiled and faded. Clive and I like to use the snug settee in our conservatory off the kitchen. He often sits there to do his football pools. That's where we have our television too. I always think that it's a bit tasteless to have your TV in your best room. Though to be fair, Serena and Greg manage to do this by having it tucked away in a smart cupboard with panelled doors.

Anyway, we were chatting about this and that, and because the silver was on the table, I reminded her of our previous conversation and said that I was having trouble cleaning the small silver cruet set. She looked puzzled – and I indicated the small salt, pepper and mustard pots, which were on the newspapers waiting to be cleaned. They were very tarnished and I was trying again to see if I could shine them up, because I couldn't possibly use them as they were. She didn't seem to understand the word 'cruet' – and I remembered that my husband once said: "Silly dainty word – cruet." I have an uneasy feeling that perhaps it isn't correct to call the salt, pepper and mustard a cruet.

172

Serena leaned over and picked up the mustard pot, with its little glass container. She examined the surface and the blackened stains, and casually asked me if it was silver or plate. I hastily reassured her that it was indeed silver – I had bought it some years before and the silversmiths had definitely sold it to me as silver. I pointed out the little marks on the base. "These are the silver marks," I said, explaining to Serena about silver marks.

She listened with apparent interest, but then it turned out that she knew much more than me about silver. Looking at the base with a thoughtful look, "I think you've been had," she said. "The base ring is undoubtedly silver – but it's probably the only thing which is. The bases have been hallmarked and attached to the three items of silver plate subsequently. It's an old trick to give the impression that the whole item is silver. Which it isn't, or it would be possible to clean it."

"And look," she said showing it to me, "The base ring's not tarnished like the rest. There's the proof for you."

I was surprised, as you can imagine. I was also upset – to discover firstly that the cruet set was not wholly silver, then that I had clearly been cheated and thirdly that my friend knew enough about the subject to expose the fraud. Serena always surprises me with her know-how. She knows about things like psychology, government policy and stained glass windows – which amazes me. She explained about GNP to me to other day though I'm still a bit hazy about what it is. She knows where to look these things up. I admire that, and though it does make me feel a bit of an ignoramus, I don't resent her putting me right. I'm amazed that she has the time to find out about it all – I never seem to have a minute even to read the newspapers – how she ever gets all the washing, cleaning and shopping done as well as going to work beats me. Well, she skimps a bit on the cleaning and no wonder!

After she'd gone, I looked at the three pieces of silver again, and it did look suspiciously as if she was right. I felt very annoyed because I had been deceived. I had inherited a few hundred pounds from an aunt of mine about ten years earlier and I spent a part of this on the silver cruet set, something I'd

173

always wanted which I thought would lend a bit of style to our dining table. Not that we use the dining room much these days – Clive calls the room his study and resents having to tidy up his desk in there when we need to eat round the dining room table. That's why we don't entertain much any more. I find this rather a shame as I never get much opportunity to use our best china dinner service with the pink and gilt border pattern that I saved for so long to buy.

The silversmiths where I had bought the cruet were in the centre of a town some twenty miles away – they were called Falstaff and Sons Ltd. I recalled that they had given me a receipt at the time with a brief description of the items and the sum I had paid for them – £155. If they were only silver plate, then they were worth only about £30. It was about nine years ago and I had thought at the time that they might be a good investment, which would go up in value as the price of silver rose. I mentioned this to Clive to try to justify my extravagance, but he just said that if I wanted to waste the money I had inherited, then who was he to stop me? I searched my dressing table for the receipt because I keep them in there or the kitchen drawer because I don't have a desk – Clive doesn't see that I have a need for one – and he's probably right. I couldn't find it, but then it was some years back. I'm normally very careful about retaining receipts, especially for valuable items which might need to be insured, and it was probably tucked away in a large envelope of old papers which I kept in a box in the attic.

I was incensed about being cheated even though it had happened a long while before. I decided not to tell Clive because I knew what he would do. He's such a short-tempered chap that he would go round to Falstaff's, shout at the manager and probably end up punching the man on the nose. That would put us in the wrong rather than them. Clive is a bit too belligerent at times with people he thinks have "done him down." He threatens to give them "what for", though I'm not sure what he means by this. I'm never aggressive because I'm rather petite. And I don't shout at people – I leave that sort of thing to my husband. I get a bit annoyed when Clive comes home with muddy shoes and walks all over my clean newly washed Amtico floor tiles, but I rarely lose my rag. I did once, when he promised to be home in time to meet my parents from the station and forgot. I can drive, but Clive needs the car more than me and I don't mind walking to the shops though the bags do get a bit heavy at times. So I had to get a taxi and was late at the station. They were upset at having to wait for ten minutes – which I thought was unreasonable. So on that one occasion I lost my temper with Clive when he got back from work, and I was mortified when he turned to my parents and said that they could now see what he had to put up with.

Anyway, to return to the problem of the cheating silversmith, I decided to be more subtle. I wanted to get the shop to admit that they had defrauded me, and to take back the items and repay me in full. I would then tell Clive who, for once, would applaud what I had done. He doesn't like being swindled any more than I do. My plan of action would involve finding the original receipt, wrapping up the tarnished silver and taking a bus into town, and going into Falstaffs and asking to see someone in authority.

While I was envisaging the sequence of events, I hit upon a brilliant idea. In order to get them to look at the silver items and tell me honestly what they were, I would pretend to want to sell them. They always have a notice in their shop window saying that they seek to acquire silver items. After nearly a decade they would not remember having sold them to me, and then I would ask them what they would give me for them. I took pleasure in imagining what would happen.

I would enter the shop hesitantly and ask to speak to the proprietor. He would then appear discreetly from the back room and I would then modestly explain to him that I'd had these silver salt, pepper and mustard pots for about ten years and was thinking of selling them, and was wondering what they might be worth. The gentleman would then look at them through that little eyepiece which is a magnifying glass and, with a slight sneer, he would mention some paltry sum. I would then look horrified and say that as they were silver surely they would be worth much more than that. Indeed I had paid much more for them originally.

He would then put a pained expression on his face, and say something like: "Indeed, madam. You are mistaken. These items are not silver but only plated." I would then protest and point out the silver marks on the bases. He would then examine them more closely, and with a knowing smirk he would tell me that I was undoubtedly the victim of a fraud, as only the bases were silver and the rest was plate. He would then say something along the lines of: "This is one of the tricks of the shady end of the trade. You should go back to the unscrupulous silversmiths who sold you these as hallmarked silver, and demand your money back."

I would then flourish the receipt, which I had miraculously kept over the years, and calmly but firmly name them as the perpetrators of this fraud, exposing them in front of the other customers who would look shocked and horrified and instantly leave the shop.

The silversmith would have to grovel and make profuse apologies and he would then offer unconditionally to take back the items and give me back the full sum I had paid for them. He might even beg that I should not take the matter to the law or the local ombudsman. How satisfying it would be. Memo: should I ask for interest on the sum of £155 over ten years?

I must admit that I felt a bit nervous about doing this, but when I finally managed to unearth the old receipt from the box in the attic, I felt as if I was embarking on a crusade. I was the injured party and they were in the wrong, and I ought to assert my rights. Though I am a small woman I was determined to stand up for myself.

I didn't tell Serena what I was doing or that it was her who had opened this can of worms in the first place. I would tell her all about it afterwards. She would be amazed!

The following week, I packed up the fake silver items in some tissue paper and put them in a bag, and I put on my second best overcoat – the one with the velvet collar – and set off. I started to feel a bit jittery on the bus, but by the time I was walking into Falstaffs, I was resolved to see it through.

There was a woman behind the counter. She was smartly dressed in a black pinstriped trouser suit. I stood there quietly waiting whilst she re-arranged some silver serviette rings in the glazed cupboard on the wall behind the counter. She must have known I was there, but it was only when I coughed slightly that she turned round, pretended that she had just noticed my presence and then, fixing her eyes on my velvet collar, asked with a bland smile whether she could help me. I said that I wanted some advice about some silver I might wish to sell. She rearranged her face from the ingratiatingly courteous expression intended for potential buyers into one emitting slight contempt combined with feigned sympathy for those persons who were unfortunate enough to have to dispose of their silver.

"Would you care to show the items to me?" she asked smoothly.

Well, I could not think of any way to refuse, so I took the pieces out of my bag and put them down on the counter. "They're rather tarnished," I started saying apologetically.

She didn't even pick them up, but looked down on them and said: "It's not really quite the sort of thing we would be interested in."

This was not working out according to plan. So I asked politely if there was a qualified silversmith who could look at them and give me an idea of what they might be worth. With a look of exasperation she said that she supposed that she might be able to get young Mr Falstaff to come through and give a value. Slowly she walked through to the back office, locking the shop door first to ensure that I didn't steal anything and run out of the shop. How insulting!

I picked up my silver cruet and wrapped them up in the cloth in which I had bought them, and waited quietly until the bossy woman returned and said that Mr Falstaff would come down in about five minutes. Without offering me a seat, she turned back to continue with her re-arrangement of the display case. I sat down carefully on a chair with a blue upholstered

177

seat and after seventeen minutes, I heard some heavy footsteps coming down a staircase and then a rather overweight young man of about thirty came through from the back of the shop. He was wearing a smart three-piece suit with the buttons done up which made him look even fatter. He emanated a smell of some rather odious after-shave lotion.

He gave me a lofty appraising look and said in an oily voice, "Well, what can I do for you, madam?"

Before I had time to respond, the smart shop assistant said, "Madam would like you to look at a few small items she wishes to dispose of."

"Indeed, and what might they be?"

"Madam has a set of silver plated table condiments," Mrs Bossy interposed before I had time to speak.

Mr Falstaff turned to me with a tight but tolerant smile and said, "I'm afraid we wouldn't be interested in.....", and here he gave a little pause before uttering with a note of distaste in his voice, "Plate and EPNS."

At last I found my voice, and said rather too loudly, "They're silver. That's what I was told when I bought them. That they were real silver."

The portly young man held out his soft clean hand, and I put the crumpled cloth containing the silver into it. He placed it on the counter and unwrapped it revealing my poor little discoloured items, which he carefully placed in a line in front of me. Then he picked up each of them in turn and examined them carefully.

"Oh dear me, no." he said with a feigned sympathetic smile. "Not silver. At all. Really not worth anything. So sorry." He turned away.

"Wait a minute." I said with my heart thudding with indignation. "I bought them from you some years ago and you sold me them as silver."

The man turned round slowly, and with a frosty smile, uttered interrogatively, "Indeed?"

"Indeed," I repeated his words, and was sorry that the only audience that I had for his inevitable embarrassment was the bossy woman who worked for him and would probably side with him to condone criminal deception. I continued with a

178

note of triumph in my voice, "And what's more, I have the receipt to prove it."

"May I see it?" he asked in a quiet but brittle tone. I noticed he had dropped the "madam".

I opened my bag, took out the old receipt and flourished it in front of him.

"It must be a forgery," said Mrs Bossy, in her interfering way.

Mr Falstaff twitched with irritation at her interruption. He took the receipt from my fingers and looked at it carefully.

"No, Mrs Goodbody," he said, "The receipt is signed by my father and it is in order."

Now it is coming, I thought. Now I am going to get the admission of guilt, the grovelling apology and the recompense. I felt vindicated. I cheered my victory in my mind. I looked at his face expecting to see some confusion and some humility. But instead, I was surprised to see a stern expression appear on his features. There was no indication that he felt any guilt.

Mr Falstaff cleared his throat and continued. "But it is clear to me that the silver I see in front of me now is not the same as the silver for which this is the receipt."

What a brazen remark! I was incensed. "But I tell you that it is," I protested.

"There's nothing on the receipt to indicate that it is the same three items. There are many silver and silver-plated salt, pepper and mustard pots which might fit this description. So I think, Madam," he said with an exaggeratedly polite sneer on the word 'Madam', "That you must be mistaken."

I was astounded. He was calling me a liar. Here was proof of his firm's treachery, and he was implying that I had substituted the silver items with others of less value.

Then I realised that the wording on the receipt would not uphold my accusation of deception. He knew that and smiled slyly. "A firm of our repute and integrity would take a very serious view about an unfounded accusation like this. We would take full legal recourse against the person concerned."

179

"How dare you," I began. But stopped. He had the receipt in his fingers and was holding it as if it was proof of my guilt. I stared at him in horror.

"I think you had better take your items," he said looking down his fleshy nose at the sullied objects on the counter between us, "And leave my shop. If you are very lucky I shall say no more about this attempt on your part to blackmail this firm. In fact, you are fortunate that I have decided to treat you leniently and say no more about it."

Then, very decisively and quickly, before I could prevent him, he tore up the receipt into small pieces and threw them in the waste paper bin behind the counter. He stared at me aggressively and then leant menacingly across the counter at me, and raised his chin. He pointed silently towards the door. His after-shave lotion gave off a whiff of sulphur. The shop assistant came round the counter, quickly wrapped up my cruet in its cloth and handed it to me. I was so surprised and discomposed that I took it and retreated to the door, which I found I could not open.

I had a moment of panic that they might be going to arrest me after all. At this point the woman came smoothly across, unlocked the door with her passkey, and opened it for me with mock courtesy. They both looked at me without speaking.

"Can't you see what a crook you work for?" I hissed at her as I scuttled out and stood shaking on the pavement outside the shop.

I heard the door close smartly behind me and, to my huge chagrin, I also heard some muffled laughter. My revenge had turned to dust and ashes. I had let myself be bullied and bundled out of his shop. I was furious.

I don't know how I got home. When safe in my own house, I shoved the beastly cruet set into the back of the kitchen drawer – I never wanted to see it again. I felt cheated and humiliated and soiled by the experience. I had to have a bath to wash all his lies and my shame out of myself. I had been frightened and I must admit I had a bit of a cry too. I was so shocked and shaken by what had happened that I had to resort to eating half a packet of biscuits. Biscuits have always been comfort food for me, but I try to eat very few, as I am proud of my dress size ten. I sat on the sofa, ate the wretched biscuits and drank two cups of tea. I was so distraught I didn't care about dropping crumbs amongst the cushions.

I was still there and still upset when Clive got home. He was surprised and a bit put out that supper wasn't ready.

"Anything the matter, Babs?" he asked whilst looking round for his newspaper.

I really dislike the way he calls me Babs. "My name is Barbara," I often correct him, but his lapse was not high on my agenda that evening. I needed to tell him what had happened and I knew that he would be incensed by my treatment. My husband would believe me and defend me, and act if I asked for his help.

For the second time that day I was in for a huge disappointment. He didn't seem to realise that I'd had a horrible experience at the hands of a bully and a cheat, and he muttered something about the fact that now the incriminating receipt had been destroyed that there was no proof and in any case he could not be bothered with all the hassle.

I am a small woman but I have a big heart. I have feelings. I flicked the biscuit crumbs off my lap onto the pale green carpet as I stood up, and then told Clive that I was extremely upset. I was aware that we might get nowhere by trying to argue with Falstaffs. But I had been cheated, insulted and my honour had been called into question, and I thought that he should do something symbolic to protest about my ill treatment. A look of wary uneasiness appeared on his face, which changed to amazement when I calmly told him, "I am asking you to go into the silversmiths tomorrow and punch Mr Falstaff on the nose."

"I bloody well won't," he said. "What a daft idea."

"It may be. But I want you to do it for me."

It was a test to see if he loved me enough – and if he had the guts to do it.

He failed on both counts.

I ought to have realised that Clive would decline to retaliate. He's all bluster and bluff and no action. I thought

181

I had married a strong belligerent aggressive man, and I find out he's a gutless wimp after all. Do I feel cheated? Yes, I do. After all I've done for him over the years, he refuses to do this one thing for me. I think I might divorce him. I feel quite resentful.

I may not get my revenge on the jewellers, but I plan to get my own back on my husband. I want my home to myself without him cluttering it up. The grounds for divorce are a problem. It's rather a shame that he's not been cheating on me – with Serena for example – then I could get rid of him for adultery. Perhaps mental cruelty would be cause enough. Now I think about it, he's driven me mad for years. All those muddy footprints. Clive is so lazy and – I'm going to say it – selfish. My husband is very selfish. I'm surprised I've put up with it all for so long. Living on my own will be cleaner, quieter, better. The worm turns and wants retribution. Or is it requital? I must look it up in the dictionary. When I have a minute to spare.

I shall clearly have to work on how to get rid of my husband. Permanently. At the same time I might also dump Serena – I sometimes feel that she isn't really my friend at all. I'll just tidy up the house and then I'll make a nice cup of tea and give it some thought.

SAUCE

Sauce

It was surprise to everyone when Oliver married Susan. Cultivated in mind and graceful in appearance the young woman was utterly different from his previous girlfriends whose personalities were often an echo of his own – wild and unpredictable. His friends felt that Susan simply did not fit into the pattern of his usual interests and preferences – dangerous sports, drunken parties and beautiful but outrageous women.

For Oliver, it might have been her soft voice that made her seem vulnerable and desirable, or perhaps her quiet and dignified manner was a much-needed antidote to the waning attractions and increasing excesses of a bachelor life in London. Uncomplicated and undemanding, she soothed his restlessness and boosted his ego. He felt weary of the female selfishness and jealousy that, he claimed, had marred his earlier disastrous love-affairs. Oliver liked Susan – she was refreshingly different. She was good for him. He subsequently fell prey to her obvious adoration of him. Though adept at turning his back on problems, he was not good at disentangling himself from a trouble-free and comfortable relationship. So he moved into her flat in Camden, which in any case was convenient for his commute to work. When, after a rare disagreement, she threatened to throw him out, he panicked and promptly proposed. Desperate in case he should lose this gem of a woman, he married her, happily and without hesitation.

In appearance, small and fine-boned, Susan was not conventionally beautiful and her pale skin and huge eyes rescued her features from mere prettiness. However, to everyone who came to know her it was apparent that beneath this calm exterior there was determined and resourceful character. Whether or not she was aware of his likely deficiencies in the role, she wanted Oliver as her husband. A quiet young woman leading a pleasant life in London, she had met Oliver at a charity dinner, which he had inadvertently promised to attend, and then found he could not extricate himself from the obligation. By happy accident he had a very quiet but attractive dinner table companion who was charmingly attentive to his every word. Even so, he would probably not have bothered to further the acquaintance if she had not taken the bull by the horns and telephoned him to invite him to a supper party. One thing led to another.

Susan soon realised the improbability of their paths crossing without design, and contrived to remain within his orbit. She not only found his personality immensely attractive and his milieu more amusing than her own, but also really loved him. Having got him to the altar, this seemingly frail and submissive wife was to need all her underlying strength and forbearance to see her through the maelstrom of marriage that followed.

It was during the early years when their children were young, and when life was tiring, unpredictable but enjoyable, that the couple went through the 'house party' phase. It was inevitable that Oliver, with his flamboyant personality, handsome appearance, and undoubted charm would be an asset at a weekend in the country. Susan with her pearls and her pretty manners was an appropriate adjunct. A solitary child, brought up quietly by elderly parents in a country village, she had developed in the company of her husband a taste for things more gregarious and opulent. She enjoyed these weekends, perhaps even more than her over-indulged husband, as a taste of life to come. Sadly her dreams of a conventional life, settled in a large family house, were never to be fulfilled, and so she adjusted to a peripatetic lifestyle with adaptable children but an uncontrollable husband. In his flawed careless way Oliver did love his wife, though his affection was never as deep nor as unselfish as the love she lavished unrewardingly on him.

On this occasion, when their children had again been left with their patient and resilient grandmother in London, they went to Buckinghamshire to the home of Mr. and Mrs. Pope, whose daughter some years earlier had been one of Oliver's girlfriends, though she was now married and living abroad. Her mother had always liked Oliver, and been flattered by his

186

charm and amused by his pretensions. Though well aware of his faults of indolence and selfishness, Leonora Pope valued his unique ability to entertain and shock her friends and had decided to continue the acquaintance. She liked his calm and unusual wife, even though the latter had supplanted her own daughter, and found Susan attractively modest, kind and polite – an excellent counterbalance for the more extrovert guests. A woman of style and intelligence, Leonora was uncompetitive, and not only delighted in the extravagant personalities that she attracted to her house, but also appreciated the quieter, thoughtful and well-mannered individuals who passed through her door. A kind-hearted and generous woman who loved to entertain, she invited to her house a motley selection of people of differing age, education and occupation – anyone in fact that she found interesting, regardless of worth or wealth. Well aware of her own idiosyncrasies, she was tolerant of eccentricities in others. She had many friends and seemed happy to accept all comers into her home. Her husband, a pleasant and reticent man, cheerfully accepted and funded his wife's main preoccupation and indulgence – hospitality.

The couple lived in a large and handsome house with all the accoutrements that their taste selected and their wealth enabled. Elegantly furnished yet pleasingly informal, the house was open for friends and family, guests and dogs to wander through the many rooms at their will. The grounds too were uncluttered and spacious, with a walled garden, fine trees, rose beds, croquet lawn, and an unobtrusive swimming pool. Weekend visitors and dinner guests were made to feel comfortable and relaxed, whether they were the performers or the observers. A preponderance of the former made for a more extrovert social event, and if there proved to be too many of the passive variety, Leonora was able to throw in her own considerable contribution of wit and flamboyance to counteract any possible lapse in pace and entertainment. She was renowned and respected for her organisational abilities and social graces.

Oliver and Susan had very much enjoyed an earlier visit six months before, but this weekend would be different, with the highlight being a large party on the Saturday evening, with many guests coming from the local area. Oliver, for whom social engagements were an antidote to boredom, and who sparkled when in company as he never did at home, often amused his friends in town with stories of wild and wonderful parties which his imagination embellished and enhanced, for he never believed in spoiling a good anecdote for the sake of truth. His error was in announcing the details of parties and events in advance, as some of his less socially acceptable friends were apt to "jump on the band wagon" if they thought they could get away with it. In this case, with the tolerant and generous Leonora as hostess, they had every chance.

The dress code on this occasion was Black Tie, but the two uninvited guests arrived in Costume, in the belief fostered by their chum Ollie that this was a Fancy Dress Party. The double blunder – the gatecrash and the odd garb – was accepted with great good humour by the Popes. No one minded the presence of the Monk and the Friar – it added a lugubriously amusing touch to the evening, especially as they had arrived on a motor bike. Oliver, though obviously the cause of this intrusion, was unrepentant in his usual fine form, glass in hand and stories in full flow. Enjoying the admiration accorded to her husband, and echoing his performance in a minor key, Susan, too, was found to be witty and attractive, and compliments on their double act were a source of considerable pleasure for her.

Their hostess wandered through the assembled guests gracefully attired in a long green dress, dispensing drinks, flattery and charm. Some guests had been requested to give a hand, and they took it in turns to run the bar or assist the young women who were laying out the platters of food for the buffet supper in the large dining room. After dinner a couple of local amateur jazz musicians set up in the drawing room and entertained any who chose to listen. It was late summer so guests wandered round the garden and a few braved the coolness of the English night air and took a dip in the swimming pool. Everything seemed to be pleasantly spontaneous and apart from a few bursts of raucous laughter or drunken argumentativeness, the continuous babble of party chat and discussion remained at a controlled decibel level where everyone seemed to promote the pervading atmosphere of amiability and good manners.

Just when there seemed to be a slowing of momentum, a breakfast barbecue was served on the terrace. This was refreshingly informal, with a carefully thought out "transport cafe" appeal featuring sizzling bacon and sausages with hunks of bread washed down with cups of strong tea. Large catering size jars of tomato ketchup and English mustard were plonked on the trestle table with rolls of kitchen paper for napkins. No-one really needed anything more to eat but the smell was irresistible and by now the boredom factor had set in, and the guests could stoke up their enthusiasm for continuing the revelry by indulging in further food and conversation around the "camp fire".

Later on there was some desultory dancing to music in the drawing room, a few earnest discussions emanating from the depths of the library sofas, and the continuous chatter and laughter from the hard-core party regulars who were practised in the ability to pace themselves throughout the evening and keep going on and on.

Some of the older guests left the party at the usual "not too early and not too late" acceptable time, thus guaranteeing themselves further invitations. Within an hour the majority of those remaining departed after bidding goodnight to their hostess – their host having gone to bed as soon as he could decently do so without incurring the displeasure of his wife. A few insensitive types hung on for a little longer ignoring or unaware of Leonora's raised eyebrows, and seriously prejudicing their chances of remaining on her guest list. Eventually they got the message and took themselves off. Only the house guests remained.

Of those who had been invited to stay overnight, two couples had retired at an appropriate hour, but some, including Oliver, had thought it kind to keep their hostess company until the stragglers had all gone. Of these, a few thoughtful ones – including Susan but not her husband – decided to give a hand clearing up and perhaps winning a few grateful smiles from the rather daunting lady of the house. But Leonora, though exceedingly tired but giving no sign of it, chose to make no distinction between those who were clearing and clattering plates and those who were still drinking and clinking glasses. The guests who were helping became discouraged by the lack of appreciation for their efforts, mumbled their excuses and drifted upstairs to bed. Finally, the drinkers realized that that party was at an end, and decided that prolonging it further might prove unwise.

As for the two uninvited guests – Mick the monk and Tony the friar – they had attempted to leave during the general exodus, and had set off on their bike, but under the influence of whatever intoxicant or substance they had indulged in, they succeeded in steering their machine into a dark ditch a quarter of a mile down the lane. Stumbling back to the well-lit house, they were pronounced unfit to return to town, and meandered around without showing any inclination to pass out or any wish to sleep. Shrugging her well-bred shoulders, Leonora accepted the inevitable, unearthed some rugs and allocated a couple of sofas to them when they should feel the need to lie down. Their presence denied her of her usual role – that of being last to bed. She requested their silence, forbade them to drink any more, and leaving them the freedom of the ground floor, she climbed the stairs purposefully but wearily to bed.

Susan woke up the next morning and washed and dressed thoughtfully without drawing the curtains which might have disturbed her prone husband. A curious sound from the garden made her lift a corner of the curtain and look out of the window. A bizarre sight met her eyes – the drunken monk and friar of the previous night's gate-crashing escapade were throwing a frisbee to one another on the croquet lawn, their long skirts handicapping their mobility among the hoops. Lurching around in a strange manner, they made whooping bird-like cries, their strange behaviour induced either by drugs, drink or the light-headedness that come from staying up all night, or indeed all three. Concerned because the presence of these two young men was Oliver's fault, she woke up her husband, risking his habitual morning irritability. Bewildered and bleary, he staggered over to the window to look at the spectacle but, inured to the idiocies of his friends, he flopped back to sleep whilst his wife decided to descend and follow developments.

A strange and more disconcerting sight met her eyes when she entered the kitchen. Leonora Pope, resplendently clothed in pink dressing gown and red-faced indignation, had clearly lost her habitual composure and good humour. Outraged and overtired, she was trying to identify who was responsible for the state of her kitchen. Someone had pushed her best feather duster through the enlarged neck of a catering size jar of tomato ketchup and painted the walls and part of the ceiling of the kitchen. The perpetrator was clearly absent. The sauce was spattered everywhere and red gobs had dripped onto the table and floor. A tall thin man in a crumpled blue shirt, one of the house guests, was attempting to reduce his hangover with a cup of coffee whilst vaguely trying to placate his hostess. A woman called Theresa, who worked as a cleaner, was clattering dishes and cutlery in the sink, her hair tied up in a floral scarf. Susan timorously offered to help clean up the mess, but Leonora was more interested in discovering who had committed this monumental folly. Susan had already deduced that the two young men who were prancing around the lawn were probably responsible, but chose to remain quiet.

A small window looked out from the kitchen through the branches of a magnolia tree across the rose garden and lawn. It was only a matter of time before Leonora glanced through it and caught sight of the obvious culprits. She made an inarticulate exclamation of fury attracting the others in the kitchen who joined her, and they all watched the ghostly pair, who were stumbling around the croquet hoops waving their arms like sleep-walkers.

"Ooh, Mrs Pope," said Theresa in a suitably shocked tone, "I wonder if it's them who've made all this mess."

"It most certainly was those two very silly and very drunk young men!" her employer replied with a grim expression.

"Perhaps an appropriate punishment might be the modern equivalent of tarring and feathering," suggested the tall thin man. With a small smile he indicated the large jar of sauce with the cane-handle feather duster still reposing in the remainder of the sticky contents.

"Good idea, Colin," said Leonora seizing on the idea and needing some action to alleviate her irritation. Immediate retribution was to be dispensed by the four of them.

A back door led out of the kitchen, and from it a path led up some steps and round the end of a wall to the side of the lawn. Susan, feeling that she and Oliver were in some measure marginally responsible for the crime committed by their friends was eager to win forgiveness by playing an active part in their punishment. So she volunteered to go on ahead to call the delinquent pair over to her, whilst Leonora, the laconic Colin, and an overexcited Theresa lurked behind the wall out of sight. The lady of the house was carrying the large jar of tomato sauce with the handle of her best feather duster jauntily emerging from it.

Susan beckoned to the clerics who broke off from their play, and an odd little dumb show followed. No word was spoken but she beckoned and they looked at her and then each other. She continued to beckon and they gradually came closer. When they were beside her she took hold of the monk's left arm and the friar's right arm and turned them round to face the judge and jury, who walked out from their recess in a bizarre and colourful procession: voluminous pink leading the trio, blue beanpole in the centre, and floral turban at the rear.

The young men stood impassive and silent as they waited for interrogation, sentence and punishment. In a curious gesture of defence or perhaps defiance, they pulled up their hoods. Her dressing gown flapping in the morning breeze, Leonora advanced on the pair, holding the incriminating evidence in outstretched arms. Stopping immediately in front of them, not without some theatricality, she demanded, "Who did this?"

Without hesitation and without apology, Mick in monk's garb said, "I did."

Spacing out with emphasis words that she was not in the habit of using, Leonora Pope loudly declaimed, "You   dirty rotten   stinking   little   bastard!" Then she put the large jar down on the grass and drawing out the dripping feather duster from the neck, as if it were a sword from a scabbard, she proceeded to smear the red sauce all over the recalcitrant young man. Guilty but not ashamed, he took his penance with growing horror until her final lunge besmeared his face and his hair, the monks hood having fallen back. With a ghastly shriek, his over-stimulated brain snapped to the conviction that this was blood, and he broke away and ran flapping across the lawn like some demented banshee. Leaping over the rose bushes and a low wall, he threw himself with desperate abandon into the swimming pool. The avenging party could only hear the splash and had to imagine the water becoming polluted and stained with the monk's dripping gore.

Theresa scuttled up to the pool, breathless with delighted horror and eager to be the first one to see the corpse. The other three remained on the lawn, but Tony, his friar's costume torn and grubby, slowly wandered away down the path toward the kitchen garden, uninvolved and incurious. Mick, of course, swam slowly round the pool, dispersing the red liquid and somewhat clearing his befuddled brain with the chill clarity of cold water, and clambered out on his own, much to the disappointment of Theresa.

During the daubing, Susan had relinquished the arm of the culprit and his friend, and stood back to be out of the limelight and also to avoid being splashed by tomato ketchup. The scene reminded her of watching a sketch in a revue in London some years earlier in which two of the actors, pretending to be English lords in a Shakespearian battle were fighting with swords, and one had shouted "O Saucy Worcester"! She emitted a small nervous giggle.

Upstairs Oliver, still unconscious, was unaware of the events being enacted in the kitchen below his room until Mick's loud howl disturbed him. Feeling blurred and nauseous, he reached the window and throwing open the curtain, he was just in time to see his friend, still in monk's costume, running wildly across the lawn until out of his line of vision, pursued a minute later by a small frizzy haired woman in a floral apron until she too disappeared around the corner of the house. On the grass

193

stood three motionless watching figures, one of whom was his wife. His tired brain simply could not understand what was going on and he decided he would find out from Susan later. Whatever had happened could not possibly have anything to do with him, so he shut out the daylight once more and, never feeling any necessity to rise early in other people's houses, he returned to bed.

Punishment having been meted out to the guilty person, those who had partaken in the little drama felt able to return to the kitchen, clean the worst of the mess off the walls, and eat breakfast. They were later joined by Mick himself who had dried out, changed into some clothes borrowed from Oliver, and seemed none the worse for his ordeal. No doubt the effects of what he had taken – which had triggered his aberrant behaviour – were now lessening. He was hungry and cheekily ate the last rashers of bacon. Leonora even spoke to him, perhaps in an effort to try and allay what she might later admit, only to herself of course, to be a rather hysterical over-reaction to a minor misdemeanour. She gave no indication of the acute annoyance she felt that two of her guests had witnessed the loss of her renowned poise and observed her lapse from the serene detachment and easy-going tolerance she portrayed to the world. It was galling.

Later, Mick and Tony retrieved their bike and took their hangovers and their habits back to London. Their chastisement, of course, had no lasting effect on them. It merely fuelled their wayward desire to shock and enlarged their repertoire of maniacal pranks which they could boast about to their drinking pals.

The stigma of their misdeed, however, remained on the couple who had carelessly allowed them to abuse a friend's hospitality. Susan and Oliver – "the goose and the gander" – were never to be invited back. They had committed the ultimate social indiscretion – they had caused their hostess to lose her temper.

BLIND LOVE

Blind Love

The door opened. A tall grey-haired stranger wearing dark glasses stood on the threshold looking over her head. Helen had rung the doorbell, waited for a minute and, hearing no approaching footsteps, had turned away and was descending the steps when the door opened. Helen turned again, stepped back in surprise, and almost tripped on the low steps.

"Who's there?" asked the man in a soft but clear voice.

"I'm a friend of Jane's – Mrs Clifford," she explained. "I was hoping to catch her in."

"She's had to go out for half an hour," the man responded, "But you can come in and wait for her if you wish."

Helen hesitated. He was now looking down at her but still not directly at her face. She then said carefully, "Do you mind my asking who you are?"

"I'm the piano tuner. I come every six months, and have done so for some years. I am trustworthy," he said with a small smile. "Do come in."

She stepped inside and he stood back courteously to give her room to pass, and then he quietly closed the door. It was a grey winter afternoon and the trees in the square were tall but there were no lights on in the hall and front rooms to dispel the dimness. In the half-light, Helen realised that what she found curious was the fact of his dark glasses. She turned to look at him, and the realisation came to her – he was blind.

As if echoing her thoughts he said, "I'm blind. But I do know my way around this flat. Would you like a cup of tea?" He walked slowly but confidently into the kitchen, and across it to the worktop where the kettle stood. He fumbled a little trying to locate it, and then grasped it, turned and walked to the sink – she could almost hear him mentally count the four steps to it. He found the tap, filled the kettle, and then returned it to the base and switched it on. "Mrs Clifford is quite happy

197

that I make myself tea when I have finished with the piano," he said. "When she is not here, of course. Would you like tea?" he repeated.

Helen, who had been watching him with interest and curiosity, suddenly realised she needed to reply and blurted out a slightly embarrassed "Oh yes," feeling she had been caught out with a prurient interest in his disability. "Yes, thank you," she said more confidently. She then looked at him as a person. He was a beautiful man – tall and straight backed, but with a fluidity and grace that surprised her because she had a notion that all blind people stumbled and walked with uncertainty. His face had a slightly blurred feel to it, as if his lack of sight had somehow given him less distinct features, but his skin was clear though pale, and his grey hair perhaps made him look older than he was. She guessed that he was probably in his early forties. The dark glasses were disconcerting because she had no indication of what he was thinking. She had examined him furtively, as she often did with people, so as not to embarrass them, but then she remembered that he could not see her and was not aware of her perusal.

She took off her coat, relaxed a bit and said, "Would you like me to make the tea?" A mistake, she instantly realised, feeling disappointed with herself.

He did not reply, but pulled out a chair for her, so she sat down murmuring a contrite, "Thank-you." There was an awkward silence while he felt around in one of the cupboards and found two mugs.

"I'm Helen," she announced rather too loudly, "I'm a teacher," and waited for his response.

"I'm Matt," he announced. "I'm from Ireland." Not 'I'm Irish', she noted. And no accent either. Curious.

Again, as if reading her thoughts, he says " Your accent – are you from the North East?"

Helen was surprised. " I didn't know it was still that strong – I've been down south for some years now. Yes, I'm from a small village between Newcastle and Durham."

"Ah, Durham," he said in a mellow voice of recollection, "Those wonderful stained glass windows in your Cathedral."

She found this observation odd, in view of his lack of sight, but let it pass. Maybe he saw them before he lost his sight.

She was slightly unnerved when, as if hearing her thoughts, he volunteered the information. "I've been blind almost all my life but I still have vague recollections of colour and form which my imagination conjures up and illuminates." As if to forestall her question, he then said, "I lost my sight in an accident in my childhood. I was about five." He said this simply and in a matter-of-fact way, as if he did not want to enlarge on the subject. It was in the past – a fact, nothing more. He did not want sympathy.

The boiling kettle intruded, and slowly and with great care Matt made two mugs of tea and placed one near her on the table. Then he, too, sat down, pushing the milk jug across the surface in her direction.

" Do you play the piano?" asked Helen, looking at his hand holding the mug. She noticed his fingers were slightly dirty. He would be unaware of this, she realised.

"But, of course", said Matt, "And also the mouth organ." He put his other hand in his hip pocket and pulled out the small instrument. "It's nothing compared to the piano but I can carry it about with me. You can't do that with a piano! And I don't own one anyway." Again, said without any hint of seeking sympathy. Just factual.

"Where do you live?" asked Helen.

"In this town – in a flat near Hospital Road," he replied. "It's quite small, and it has no view, but it suits me." Again, she was surprised that he mentioned the fact that there was no view – it would, she thought, be irrelevant to him.

"That's not very far from me," she responded. "I'm round the corner in the High Street – in a small house which I rent. I share it with another woman."

Having found some common ground, they then discussed the area in which they lived. They had both been there for about two years. They liked the same bread shop and both avoided the cut-price supermarket, preferring to support the smaller local shops. He lived on his own, and she shared with a nurse called Amy. Whilst they were talking she noticed that he became less formal and more animated. He seemed interested in her reactions to his comments on the Patel's corner shop, and she understood that the place was too noisy for him – it was always crowded.

They drank their tea, and then, as if they had exhausted the topic which related to both of them, they fell silent. She rose and picked up both their mugs and put them in the sink. He stood up too. She noticed that his shirt cuffs were frayed, and realised with a pang that he probably did not realise when his clothes needed mending or replacing. She looked at her own arms and wondered what it would be like not to be able to see oneself. Would she forget after some time what her face looked like?

"Would you like to hear me play the piano?" he said. "I usually practice for a while before I go. It's quite a good piano and it has an pleasant tone." Emphasising the word "quite", he could not have damned it more effectively. She followed him to the sitting room, and he ran his hand along the boudoir grand as he passed it. He sat on the stool and played some classical piece that Helen did not recognise. But then, she admitted to herself with a feeling almost like remorse that her knowledge of classical music was quite limited. She stood leaning against the doorjamb, watching him.

He played well and she enjoyed listening to him and, she admitted to herself, looking at him. He seemed at home with the piano but he did not sway as some pianists do. He was still except for his hands. He appeared odd and austere – looking straight ahead with his dark glasses, but his hands gliding and running over the keys with a fluid grace that charmed her eyes as the sounds pleased her ears.

A thought suddenly came into her head. She did not wait for him to finish, but said, "There's a piano in our house. No one plays it, but its in good condition."

He had stopped playing when she started to speak, and she felt a little embarrassed for interrupting his music. But he didn't seem to mind. As if continuing her thought, he said: "Perhaps I can come round and play on it sometime?"

200

"Yes. That's a good idea," she said a little breathlessly, and feeling a tiny stab of delight. "That would be nice," she said in a more measured tone, aware that the bland word 'nice' did not describe how she was feeling.

"Would you like my address?" she asked. "I'll write it down for you."

"Tell it to me," he said. "I have a good memory." She had done it again.

"I'm afraid you must think I am very stupid – and unfeeling," she said ruefully.

"Not at all," he said cheerfully. "You'll get used to it – to my blindness. It takes the sighted a bit of time to stop feeling guilty and start to accept."

She felt a warm glow. He had said, "You'll get used to it." So she would have time and he would give her time. She told him her address and he nodded with a concentrated look – as he committed it to his memory. He asked her if she would put her telephone number in his mobile, and he told her how to get a voice tag set up. When, in order to record the tag, he spoke her name 'Helen' in his quiet but firm voice, she felt as if her heart gave two quick beats instead of one.

Putting the mobile in his pocket, he pulled out his wallet and extracted a small sticky label from it, which he handed to her – it was his address and telephone number.

"It's been good talking to you," he said in his direct way. "I think we might become friends."

He put his hand out towards her. She took it and for a second or two they held hands.

His fingers were cool and firm. She thought hers might be trembling and almost sighed. She looked up at him – his calmness had an edge of confidence. It was as if a dream had flown moth-like in through the dusty window.

"I will learn – to understand," she said.

"That's unlikely – but it's good that you have an open mind. And anyway my lack of sight won't really matter when we get to know each other better," he smiled.

"This is all a bit rapid," Helen muttered in her confusion.

"And is that a problem?" Matt asked quietly.

"No, I suppose not," she said hesitantly, and then more firmly she continued:

"I'm home after six in the evenings – and I'm usually around at weekends."

"I'll call round," he said.

"We don't have a bell – only a knocker on the door," she told him. He nodded.

She did not ask him how he would find his way – she was learning.

At this point, Matt turned his head and his expression altered. She then heard the front door open and realised that his acute hearing had picked up the sound of someone coming up the steps to the house. Jane walked into the hall calling out, "Its only me, Matt – I'm back." Matt walked into the hall and Helen followed.

"Hello, Helen," Jane said catching sight of her, "No doubt Matt let you in. How good of you to come round."

Jane was pleased to see her friend and said that she should stay for some soup or cheese, asking her how long her lunch hour was. She paid Matt twenty pounds for the tuning he had done, and he quietly departed, without looking at Helen – or indeed at anything.

"Now, come along into the kitchen," Jane said, "And tell me what's new in your life."

But Helen did not, of course, comply. The newness was too special to be chatted about. Helen kept silent about her embryonic friendship as if, by mentioning it, the spell would break.

* * * * *

Ten days later, at about 7 o'clock in the evening, Matt knocked on her door. It had been a long ten days. She had felt as if she was in her teens again – yearning for a boy, to whom she felt attracted, to contact her. It was a pleasing realisation that she could still feel like this twenty years later. The man – with his blindness – fascinated her. She had nearly called him twice, but she wanted to be sure of his interest in her, so that she would not make a fool of herself.

Her heart lifted when she saw him on her doorstep. "Hello," she said.

They sat, drank coffee, talked. He played the piano and she listened, and they talked more. There was laughter and teasing and soon she realised that he did not mind if she was caught out treating him as a disabled person. He gently put these lapses aside and concentrated on getting to know her. She, however, was acutely aware of his blindness – it was almost part of his attraction. He was so different.

The next time he came round, she was out – and when Amy said that a man who was blind had called at the house, she felt a surge of disappointment – as if she had been cheated. So she telephoned him. He answered and they talked for a while. She was surprised that this felt completely normal – and realised why – all people are blind to each other on the telephone.

They decided to meet a couple of days later. Amy would be off duty and at home that evening, and as Helen did not wish to share him, she suggested that they meet elsewhere. He promptly invited her round to his flat. She said that she would make a meal – and he gently said he would organise food. She acquiesced.

It was getting dark as she walked to his house on the evening arranged. With some nervousness – or was it nervous excitement – she rang the bell and heard his footsteps descending some stairs. He opened the door and she noticed immediately that he was not wearing his dark glasses. With some relief, she saw that his eyes were quite normal looking though rather expressionless. She had feared he might be disfigured from the accident, which had caused his sight loss, but this was not the case.

"Hello Helen. My flat's on the first floor," he explained. Closing the front door behind her, he turned and she followed him upstairs. "The ground floor is occupied by a woman who works in a solicitor's office. She's got a small child. The top floor flat is empty at the moment." He stopped just inside the open door to his home, and let her pass him while he closed the door quietly behind them. She found herself in a pleasant sitting room with a kitchen area at one end. There were two doors leading off it – presumably to a bedroom and bathroom. There was some modern but muted music playing quietly on a sound system. The curtains were drawn as it was almost dark. Then it occurred to her that they might always be drawn – it would make no difference to him. He wouldn't even need the two table lamps which he had probably turned on for her. He was always in the dark so why bother with lights? A rather mundane thought came to her that he must save a lot on the electricity bill.

He was standing in the room, and held out an arm for her coat – it was a chilly April evening. She took it off and he hung it on a hook beside the door. They both sat down – she on a chair and he on the sofa. Feeling a bit awkward, she started chattering about her day and telling him about some unruly children in her class. He asked a few questions to put her at her ease, although he seemed to her quite relaxed.

After a few minutes, he rose and went over towards the kitchen – again no hesitation marred his graceful movements – and he opened a bottle of wine and slowly poured two glasses. He had decided what they would drink – and she found this calm assumption of decision-making very attractive – she was being looked after by him and he was taking control – it was, after all, his home and his environment. He passed her a glass and putting his down on a table, he changed the music. She recognised Gershwin, and said how much she liked it. He smiled and finding his glass he raised it to her and said simply, "Welcome." They drank, and she started to relax.

In subsequent weeks, when she got to know him better, she realised that this calm confidence extended beyond his home and pervaded everything he did.

That first evening, he had arranged an Indian meal. Mr Patel at the corner shop had a cousin with a small business selling take-away meals – they were well known in the locality – and one could choose a meal over the telephone. Matt told her that he had already been out to collect what he had ordered, and it was keeping warm in his eye-level oven. He smiled at the phrase describing his oven and this made her realise how many expressions use the word eye: – eye-level, eye-catching, eyesore, eye-opener, eye-witness. She remarked on this, and he laughingly agreed, saying that sighted people invented language, but it didn't bother him or other "eyeless" people.

She looked around the room that at first seemed normal, if a little bare, but then she realised that it lacked any pictures and there was no television, although there was a large radio and hi-fi system. There was a shelf with some books – which surprised her and of course, there were tapes and talking books. In the kitchen area there were a few gadgets, which she saw were modified to enable use by a blind person. The kitchen was small and tidy but not very clean. It was clearly difficult to know if things were dusty or greasy if you could not see.

Uncannily he then said, " I have a friend who comes in once a fortnight to give the place a good clean – obviously I cannot know what it looks like. But I do keep it tidy and organised. If I leave things in the wrong place, I tend to forget where I put them, and then spend hours searching every surface. It took a few months when I first got this flat before I stopped knocking things over, but now I know where everything is." Instead of looking around as a seeing person would, he stared straight ahead as he said this, and then his serious expression was illuminated by a smile.

It was a lovely evening. It was redolent of love – but not desire. At least not on his part, she thought with slight disappointment. As far as she was concerned, she was aching for him to make some physical contact. After they had eaten, they sat on the sofa, and he asked her if he could touch her – but, as he explained, only so that he could find out what she was like – her shape and texture, her skin and hair. Without waiting for her assent – he had probably realised that this was what she wanted – he began an exploration of her face and hair in an extraordinarily gentle yet detailed manner. His fingers traced her face – he felt her nose, her lips and her cheekbones – he ran his forefingers over her eyebrows and eyelids and then stroked her hair and ears.

"Very sexy," she murmured.

"I called it exploratory," he said with a smile. "I can get to know your mind by talking to you. But unless I touch you I have little idea of what you are like physically."

"And what am I like?" she asked curiously.

"Well," he said with a mock frown, "Your head is a good shape and you have prominent cheekbones. Your skin is firm but soft, and your mouth is large. Probably good for kissing – we might try that later. And you smell nice," he added suddenly leaning down and burying his nose in her neck. "Mmmm, I thought so – but you've almost sunk your own smell with some expensive perfume." His breath and words were close to her skin.

She giggled. "You're tickling me." He then kissed her gently, but not passionately.

He then rose to his feet and went across to change the music. He chose some modern jazz piano music and then sat down again beside her but without touching her. He listened to the music with an intensity, which she could not share or understand. She almost felt jealous of the sounds that so completely drew his attention away from her. But wisely, she kept quiet. When it had finished, he asked her if she liked it, and she nodded, "Yes, but I find it difficult to understand." She said this quickly as if embarrassed by ignorance.

"You don't need to understand it. Just listen, and you will either enjoy it or not," he told her.

At around midnight, Matt said they should probably "call it a day" – an expression he rather liked, he said, because he had no real notion of day or night, and he found it amusing to suggest that a sighted person could call night day – which is what he often did. Helen noticed he did not wear a watch and wondered how he could tell the time, but she did not ask. Such practical questions could wait until another day – or night.

She lived too close to him for a taxi to be worthwhile, and in spite of her protests he walked her home. They said goodnight on her doorstep.

"Will you find your way back alright?" she asked with a hint of anxiety.

He said accusingly, "You mean, in the dark?" Laughing quietly, he held her face and kissed her forehead, then walked away. He raised an arm as he turned the corner, but did not look round, of course.

* * * * *

A few days later, Matt telephoned Helen to ask if he could come round at the weekend to see her and play the piano. She had been planning to go home to her parents who now lived in Newcastle, but promptly decided to put them off for a week.

She recalled how full her weekends had been last year, when David was still with her. She remembered afternoons spent fishing, evenings in pubs and in front of the television – all so predictable. David, with his loud laughter and friendly disposition had been affectionate but occasionally a little dull. She had become exasperated by his easy-going temperament and self-indulgent indolence. They had rented the flat together, and bought the piano because he wanted to learn to play. He hadn't done so – his enthusiasms were usually short-lived – and after he had gone, it remained – a reminder of another relationship that hadn't worked out. She felt quite raw after the break-up. He had been very fond of her, and was devastated when she put an end to it. When he had finally moved out, she had put a notice in Patel's for someone to share the flat and Amy had answered.

Amy was an agency nurse and her working hours changed on a regular basis but this weekend she was on nights and usually started work at around 6 pm. By now, Helen was quite keen for Amy's approval of her unusual boyfriend. She wanted to talk about Matt with someone else, and to find out whether other people reacted in the same way as she did to him. She did not want to involve Jane Clifford who would probably disapprove. "But my dear, he's my piano tuner." So she asked him over for lunch on Saturday, when Amy would be there, and suggested that perhaps they might go for a walk afterwards.

He arrived around noon, wearing a dark polo neck sweater over jeans and, with his dark glasses giving him an air of mystery, he seemed quite exotic though sombre. As if he wanted to dispel this image, and almost as though he realised that she wanted him to impress Amy, he was amusing and captivating during the meal. She had bought some crusty bread, and made a Greek salad with French dressing. They shared a bottle of red wine, and she noticed that he was careful to wipe his face with a cotton handkerchief after eating or drinking. He was clearly a fastidious man but his blindness limited his ability to keep his appearance as trim as he would have liked. His nails were clean but he was unaware of the mud on his shoes.

Amy was clearly charmed but also well aware of the unspoken warning emanating from Helen that clearly said: "I'm glad you like him. But hands off – he's mine."

Not that Amy was any competition – she was younger than Helen, but shorter and of a stocky build, and with a rather brisk manner, an irritating giggle, and a mind focussed on trivia. She read women's magazines rather than books, and was inordinately interested in the lives of film stars and sports personalities. This prurient interest was unlikely to strike any chord in Matt, though he listened politely to her as she talked about a favourite celebrity and some photographs of him that she had seen in Hello magazine.

Amy said she was going to get some more sleep before going on duty, and the two of them went for a walk. She held his arm, and it felt as if he was leading the way. He did, however, ask her to explain what she saw, and she started saying which street they were in and what the buildings were like, until he asked her if there were other people about.

"Yes, quite a few," she responded. "Would you like me to describe them to you?"

"Yes, please," he answered. "I always like to hear about other people – what they look like, or rather what you think they look like."

It pleased her that he was interested in her assessment of those they passed, and after a few minutes she warmed to her task, and started joking about one or two odd characters they encountered. She even started to embellish her descriptions a bit, to make them more interesting. But after one of her most extravagant remarks, she saw him frown, and fearing his disapproval, she toned down her comments. He did not want a performance from her – he just wanted to get a flavour of what surrounded them and of the people they encountered. He could, she realised, make his own assessment from what she said. It was important to be truthful and she felt guilty of departing from this in her effort to entertain and make him think well of her.

"There is a man over there with two small children – he looks tired and unhappy but they don't seem to be aware of this. They are running about and he is trying to stop them going into the road. I think he is sad – perhaps his wife has died or left him, and he can't cope," she added.

"You don't know that," he said. "That's just your imagination running away with you."

"I can only see them through my eyes," she said. "I can't help the way I think about them nor my speculations about their life. I always wonder why people behave in the way they do. What's wrong with a bit of imagination, anyway?" she asked.

"Because it's not true and it's misleading. I might think from your remarks that you knew him and were aware of his circumstances."

"Does that matter? Anyway," she shrugged, "It makes it more interesting – for me."

She suddenly remembered another man who had criticised her for an having an unbridled imagination – and that this was his euphemism for telling lies.

They returned from their walk, and she made some tea for them. Amy came out of her room dressed in her nurse's uniform and they drank tea and listened to him while he played the piano to them. Shortly afterwards, Amy left for the short walk to the hospital. He continued to play and she sat drowsily on the sofa. She felt as if he had moved into another realm apart from her, but was content that he should do so, because she knew he would return to hers in due course.

They went out for a meal to a nearby Italian restaurant, and she told him about her family and her childhood. He asked various questions and she was flattered by his interest. Later, when she was on her own, Helen realised that he had been much less forthcoming about his own background and resolved to show more interest the next time they met. She must stop being so self-centred, she said to herself. Then she decided that he'd been rather guarded about his past and this added to his appeal.

She had hoped he might suggest that he stay the night, and was rather disappointed when he didn't. Did he not find her attractive? She wondered. Did he disapprove of her for some reason? She examined her feelings. She was strongly drawn to him – she liked his company, found him unusual, knew him to be kind and thoughtful. And yes, she desired him – she wanted him to make love to her – she wanted to see him and hold him and have him inside her. Matt was not a shy man but he was keeping her at arm's length. Perhaps he just needed more time. He was more reticent than she and perhaps he enjoyed the initial "getting to know each other" phase before the storm of a sexual relationship. She told herself that she would wait till he wanted to take it further. She would wait for a green light.

* * * * *

A week later on a rainy Sunday, he telephoned her and suggested that she come round in the afternoon. There was a note of anticipation and roughness in his voice, which she immediately picked up. He sounded as if he wanted her – sexually. She had a bath and took some care about her appearance and then laughed at herself when she recalled that he would not see her. The habit of making an effort with her appearance was ingrained in her, and she wanted him to think her attractive. She knew she desired him and wanted to see him naked.

Matt did find Helen attractive, but he wanted to get to know her better before starting an affair. His relationships with women tended to end disastrously because they could not cope with his disability, and mistakenly assumed a superior role.

210

He was not prepared to subdue his strong personality when women found him attractive but pitied him and tried to look after him. He was looking for someone who would ignore his blindness and focus on him as a person and not the embodiment of a sad blind handsome man, bravely coping with a terrible problem, who needed the ministrations of a selfless angel. He managed very well with his life, but he could not manage to find someone who would treat him as an equal.

He woke up on that Sunday morning in early spring, and decided that it was time he seduced Helen – not that she was averse to this happening. He knew very well that she wanted to go to bed with him, but he wanted her on his own terms and on his own territory. He telephoned her and made the assignation. He then changed the sheets on his bed, and had a shower, washing his hair. He wanted her to think him desirable and he wanted her to discover that, despite his recent apparent coolness, he was sexy. He was fond of Helen and he hoped he might learn to love her. Perhaps she would be the one he was looking for.

In order to create the right atmosphere and because he thought his flat might be dusty and dull, he decided to draw the curtains in the sitting room and to light some candles and joss sticks in the bedroom. The latter not a very easy exercise but he could feel for the wick, listen for the match igniting, and smell the candle flame. Let her be under no illusion from the moment she walked in the door as to why he had wanted her to come round. He wondered whether she had any odd scruples about making love in the daytime – it mattered not a jot to him, but some women were less inhibited at night. He hoped that Helen would not be a woman who minded being able to see him when he could not see her. This would be a test. It was easy to accept his lack of sight if they were both in the dark – and he wanted her to accept his blindness even when making love.

They were both nervous – Helen when she rang his bell and Matt when he opened the door to her. He took her hand without a word, and led her upstairs. They both knew what would happen, and they both wanted it to be special. He

211

closed the flat door and led her across to his bedroom. He was pleased, when she saw the room and the candles, that he could feel her trembling.

"I think I love you," she said.

"I want to love you," he said, "And I want you to love me."

The glow of the candles and the pungent smell of the incense were exotic and arousing. They undressed. His body was pale, lean and his manner gentle but persistent. He saw her not with his eyes but with his hands. She had never known such sweet lovemaking – and she suppressed the worrying thought that he must have had plenty of experience to pleasure her with such finesse. It was a magical afternoon. After hours of lovemaking and love murmuring they were languorous but hungry, and laughed when they discovered they had both been too nervous to eat anything earlier in the day. They sat naked on the bed and ate what he had in his fridge – cold chicken and pears. They talked, they kissed, they caressed. It was magical.

Helen stayed the night and was late for work the next morning. Matt cancelled his first appointment for piano tuning. He needed some sleep. She managed to get through the school day in a state of blissful exhaustion.

They slept together often after that, but the mysterious excitement of their first time was never re-created, although they grew to know each other's preferences and habits better.

A few weeks later, when the novelty of the sexual element in their relationship had diminished somewhat, and when they were prepared to enjoy themselves in other ways, he asked her to a concert. He had clearly chosen it because the composer was well known and the programme something which he felt she could easily respond to.

He had discovered that she knew little of classical music and he was trying to educate her. She did not resent this – she knew that her taste was deficient or undeveloped in the appreciation of music.

Helen liked the concert but found she enjoyed watching the musicians as much as listening to the sounds they produced. She watched Matt too and could see that he became involved in the music and appreciated the performance in a way that she was unable to. He sat still with an inward look on his face and a slight tilt to his finely shaped head.

She had always preferred the theatre and, as she explained to her lover, there had been a time in her life when she had considered studying drama and trying to become an actress. But she had known that she would not make the grade and therefore had decided to become an avid playgoer.

Matt surprised her by suggesting that they might go the theatre in a nearby town to see a play. She was eventually persuaded that he would find it interesting, and she bought tickets for a play she thought might amuse them both. She drove him there in her small car. When the performance started, Helen found herself whispering to him about what the set was like and where the characters were and what they were doing. He listened to this for about fifteen minutes, and then gently told her to desist – she had told him enough and he could understand from the dialogue what was happening. She felt rebuffed and inadequate. She then closed her own eyes to see if she could understand what was happening on stage from the words. She soon found that she had to open them – and that she needed the visual as well as the aural picture. Matt listened with an intentness that she found both attractive and galling. At these times he withdrew his attention from her and she tried to accept that this was necessary.

During the interval it was clear that he knew very well what was happening on stage – and commented that two of the actors portrayed their characters more convincingly than the others. She had a moment of supreme irritation that he seemed to know more about the play and the performance than she did, though she admitted to herself that this might be because of the distraction caused by her feelings about him and her experiment with voluntary blindness. The evening was not a success – she felt he had invaded her territory and had not sought her help. He sensed that she resented his not needing her assistance.

* * * * *

213

In May there was a warm spell, and one Saturday they took a picnic into the countryside and ate it beside a small brook. Helen knew of the place because she had once been there with David who had spent all afternoon trying to fish, although she did not mention this. She lay in the grass looking up at a tree, and Matt played his mouth organ. Then he sat on the bank and let the water trickle over his feet. He told her that he had once been to the seashore and been confused by the waves breaking on the sand. He had never bathed in the sea – it was not an element in which he felt safe, but he did like swimming in the confines of a pool. She then asked him what he did for holidays, and he told her that he went on coach tours round Europe.

She sat up, astonished. "But why do that? You can't see anything."

"But I meet the other tourists on the coach tour," he explained. "And I borrow their eyes and their viewpoints. There are always at least twenty or thirty other people, and because we are travelling together, I meet most of them. Every day I ask someone different to be my eyes, and to sit next to me beside the window or to accompany me when we are walking round. I ask them to tell me what they see and what they think of what they see. No-one minds doing this for only a day – it would be very arduous to undertake such a task for an entire holiday, but usually my fellow travellers are happy to oblige for a day or a few hours. They like to be needed. Everyone likes to be needed," he added.

"What a wonderful idea," she said. "But how do you relate to what they are describing?"

"It doesn't matter," he said. "I learn, not only about the places through which we are passing or visiting, but also I hear about what they are interested in. One person will be enthusiastic about buildings and architecture, whilst another will be interested in gardens and nature. Many will like landscapes and vistas, whilst someone else will describe the people or animals they see. I receive a wide variety of different perceptions and feelings and opinions. My companions vary enormously – some are intelligent and sensitive, whilst others are more trivial or limited. I listen to people who are outspoken, shy, amusing, dull, enthusiastic, bored. I am fascinated about what people leave out or what they notice or what they choose to talk about. I ask questions and they reply in different ways. I have 'seen' the Eiffel Tower through the eyes of someone who is interested in painting. I have 'seen' the Colosseum through a man who saw it as a symbol of Christianity. I have 'seen' the Swiss Alps through the eyes of three women who were interested respectively in films, food and wild flowers."

She was filled with admiration for this man and his ability to make the best of his hard path in life. But there was this anomaly – he did not mind asking for help and receiving it, but he often rejected it when it was offered. When he did this with her, she often felt rebuffed and slight resentment from the implication that she was unable to decide correctly what he might need. But he did seem to need her. He did ask her for information about their route when they were out walking but, if she gave too much detail or became too lyrical, he cut her short. Then she felt aggrieved and insecure, in much the same way as she did as when her head of department reprimanded her for a noisy classroom, after she taken considerable pains to get her students to participate in a class improvisation.

She was, actually, proud of Matt and enjoyed being seen with him. Her reasons were probably twofold: – she liked to accompany this enigmatic self-assured man in his dark glasses and she also fancifully envisaged herself as a loyal woman supporting a man tragically afflicted. One thing did bother her – Matt did not seem really to care for his appearance. He washed himself and wore clean garments and was careful when eating, but he took no interest in his clothes, which she thought were hopelessly out of fashion. He wore polo neck sweaters and cord trousers. She tried to persuade him to let her buy him some clothes, but he was adamant that he did not want this.

"You only want me to buy fashionable clothes because then your image with me will be improved. It won't change anything. I should, I hope, still be attractive to you in my old and comfortable clothes. So what's the point?" he asked.

215

"You don't bother about your appearance because you can't see," she was stung into replying. "I have to look at you in that dreary sweater and baggy trousers."

"Well, you don't have to," he replied. "You could go and find someone else who is better looking."

"But you are good-looking," she insisted, " You just don't care about these things. You live in the mind. And I can't blame you for that, I suppose."

"Because its all I have," he said her unspoken words. "Don't be too over-solicitous and don't mother me. I can buy my own clothes. I can always ask the advice of the shop staff. I don't find it a problem."

"What I find a problem," she retorted in a rising tone, "Is that you exclude me. I want to help and you won't let me."

"You should realise," he said quietly, "That I have come to terms with my blindness and its limitations. But you have not come to terms with your misconceptions about the blind. It seems you cannot accept me as a normal person – which is all I want."

His soft voice condemned her outburst. He was in control and she had lost her cool.

"I'm the one who is disabled," she thought miserably. "I'm the one who is blind – I can't see him and treat him the same way as I do other people. I can't ignore his sightless eyes. I'm incapable of treating him normally."

She decided to try to understand what it was like to be blind by spending a few hours at home wearing a thick bandage over her eyes. The first half hour was exciting but then she began to feel progressively disorientated and kept bumping into objects. She was not content to sit on her sofa but felt she should try to behave normally, and found she was unable to do the simplest things. After a demoralising hour, she tore off the bandage and then felt ashamed. The gulf between them seemed so huge – she had sight and he did not.

She didn't realise that his blindness and his courageous acceptance of it was the main reason why she loved him but also the reason why she could not see him as her equal. She felt sorry for him, whilst knowing that he did not need or want this sympathy. He had a positive attitude and coped very well. He managed to find his way around when walking even though he rarely used a stick, and he organised travel to some of his appointments by taxi. She knew of blind people who made no effort to work or earn a living, so she admired the fact that he did. The local taxi firm knew him well and their drivers guided him up steps and to front doors. He had managed to build up a small number of private clients who wanted their pianos tuned and he worked one day a week in the large music emporium in the centre of town – tuning their stock pianos and the occasional harpsichord.

The school where she worked was not far from the town centre and she decided that during one of her lunch breaks, she would call in to see what he was like in his work environment. She stood outside looking in through the window and saw him sitting at a piano near the rear of the showroom. She admired the deft, measured and intent way in which he went about tuning the instrument. It began to rain. She ventured inside to be closer to him – knowing that he could not know she was there watching him. The sales assistant glanced at her but made no move to approach her so she was free to wander about and covertly watch her lover. His dignity and detachment accentuated the blindness that she found mysterious and appealing. She felt sad that he would never see, and guiltily disappointed that he would never see her. She wondered if all sighted people felt guilty when they saw those who had no sight. As she stood there reflecting, some ten yards from Matt, he slowly raised his head and turned it in her direction. He slowly breathed in through his nose and, rising to his feet, quietly said, "Is that you, Helen?"

She felt a stab of guilt, as if he had caught her red-handed, and replied, breathlessly, "Yes, yes it is." It was her perfume – she always used the same one.

"I smelled your scent," he said predictably, with a smile. He stood there, waiting, while she approached him and gave him a kiss on the cheek. He put his arm around her and unhurriedly kissed her on the lips. The sales assistant was watching with interest. Helen felt awkward, but Matt was kind and did not ask her why she was there, but stroked her hair and said into her ear that he lusted after her but he had three pianos to tune before he could go to bed with her. She giggled and said that she had four lessons to teach and should be on her way. The rain had stopped and the sun came out as she walked back to the school, smiling to herself. He had made her feel happy. It was summer and she was in love.

* * * * *

A week later, Matt suggested that they meet up with a couple of friends of his for a meal, and she was pleased at the idea. She was keen to do so because she wanted to see how his friends related to him. She did not make the mistake of asking if they were sighted, knowing that this would be an irrelevance for him. Susie and Paul met them in a small restaurant, and she could see that they were not blind and not inhibited in any way by the fact that Matt was. They clearly knew him well, and he even took his dark glasses off, which he rarely did in public. He had told her that he did not mind whether he wore them or not, but they did indicate to people that he was blind and this helped others to avoid walking into him.

Paul was a musician and Susie worked in a bookshop. She had clearly helped Matt with obtaining Braille and talking books. Matt chatted very naturally with them, and Helen was drawn into the conversation from time to time. They showed interest in her teaching and the problems of discipline in schools. But after a while, Paul and Matt started talking about music and Susie and Helen fell silent. The difference between them was that whilst Susie appeared comfortable in her listener role, Helen wanted to participate and to contribute. She felt at a disadvantage because of her meagre knowledge of classical music and her inability to relate to what they were discussing. Matt was clearly enjoying the conversation and she felt petty and selfish.

At one point she tried to change the subject, but Matt frowned at her over-loud interjection, and she fell silent and felt awkward. After the meal, they walked home and she pretended to feel what he genuinely felt – that it had been an enjoyable evening. What she did feel was resentment.

Later on, in bed, Matt made love to her with his usual dexterity and muted passion. All was well, she thought – he did love her with all her faults. And she loved him – in the dark together where they were both equal.

On another occasion, she asked Matt if he wanted to join her and some teaching colleagues for a drink in a local pub. He agreed to the plan but slightly annoyed her by failing to conceal a small flicker of reluctance. It was a Friday evening, after work, and Matt arrived late because the taxi booked to collect him from a piano-tuning job had been delayed. She was sitting at a table in the corner with four others and, when she saw him hesitate in the doorway, she swiftly went to him, took his arm possessively and guided him to where they were all seated. She introduced him to them in turn and could see him making a mental note of their names. He sat down and chatted a little with the woman on his left and answered questions about where he lived and what he did. But it was apparent to her that he found the pub too noisy for his sensitive and acute hearing. Instead of sympathising with this problem, she was irritated by it, and felt he was rejecting her friends and her milieu. In retaliation, she started behaving in a very extrovert way, and laughing a lot and slightly flirting with one of the men. Matt raised his eyebrows over his sightless eyes and knew very well what was happening. He fell silent and did not join in. He could not hear well – there was too much background noise. He felt that Helen should have known that a boisterous pub would have been difficult for him and he felt some disappointment that she seemed unaware of this.

But she was aware – and could not help herself. She wanted him to show himself off as gracefully dignified and accepting of his fate, but he was shrinking into his corner and behaving as if he could not cope. She was disappointed that he was not making an impression on her friends. And he was disappointed that this mattered to her. She teased him about his old jacket with its frayed sleeves and was mortified when

219

he gave her a weary and watery smile. He tried to talk to the man on his right and she interrupted them with a question about a new film, and then chatted to the man whilst Matt listened, watching her with a guarded look, as if he could not understand why she was behaving in that way.

Bad behaviour has curious momentum of its own, and even some of her colleagues looked a little uncomfortable as she talked about his love of music and accused him of not being curious about the visual world. He smiled and shrugged but did not think it necessary to respond. When he rose and said he found the pub a bit noisy, she looked at him pityingly as if he lacked courage to stay but then, in a rush of guilt at her behaviour, she quickly said goodbye to the others and left with him.

On the way home he said nothing, and his silence burned in her gut. They left the busy street and turned into a quieter road, taking their usual route. Matt stopped walking and turned to face her.

"I don't mind you teasing or belittling me," he said slowly, "If it makes you feel better. But what I want to know is this. In what way have I hurt you so that you tried to hurt me back? I don't understand."

"You didn't like my friends and you made no effort," she accused him.

"You know that's not true – I'm just not able to participate if there's a lot of background babble. I made an effort and you should give me credit for that."

"Why are you so bloody noble?" she shouted. "You make me feel ashamed and guilty. And I don't like being reminded of my bad behaviour and selfishness. And worst of all, you don't seem to mind it."

"Oh, I do mind," he said quietly. "I mind very much that your vision seems to be more limited than mine. I want a loving relationship and I want you to forget my disability – ignore my blindness if you can. I don't want to play emotional games and I find these loud histrionic outbursts disturbing. I'm not prepared to put up with them."

"So you can't live with my noisy emotional outbursts," she said bitterly, "Which is a typical male trait, and I can't live with your long-suffering acceptance. We're just very different. You are a saint and I seem to be cast in the role of a sinner. I can't live up to you. I'm sighted and you're not. And though you're probably right when you say I'm the one with limited vision, I don't like feeling inferior."

"You are creating a rift with this polarised view of our relationship," he said sadly. "It's destructive. Why are you doing this?"

"You don't need me," she wailed almost in tears. " You don't need my eyes. You manage very well on your own. We're not going anywhere together anymore."

"No, I don't need your eyes," he said, raising his voice in anger at last. "That's not what I want from you. I want a loving relationship between two equals. Is that too much to ask? I'm visually impaired, not emotionally disabled."

She stood shaking with misery because she knew she could not resolve the dichotomy. It was his potential vulnerability, which had engendered her love for him, but it was his physical imperfection that denied him equal status and required him to need her. His self-confidence, the quality that at first had so attracted her, now infuriated her. She saw him solitarily and stubbornly not admitting he needed help. He denied her, and she was the loser. She turned and walked off down the road. He could find his own way home! That he would, she had no doubt.

* * * * *

Over the next weeks, as summer gave way to autumn their loving relationship deteriorated. He was puzzled and disappointed by her wanton destruction of what had been of value though fragile. They still slept together but less often and there was a kind of rough desperation in their couplings. They could not find peace in their lovemaking any more than in their conversations. The natural companionship of their earlier period together had evaporated, and it soon became clear that neither of them was going to alter sufficiently to enable the affair to flourish.

221

"We don't seem to agree about anything anymore," he said dejectedly when they had had an argument over education, and Helen had become upset because he would not accept that she probably knew more about this subject than he did. "You may disagree with me but I am entitled to my opinion." Then with an attempt at humour, he went on, "We just don't see eye to eye." He smiled sadly when she did not respond, but merely shrugged her shoulders.

One day in late September, they were walking beneath some trees. They were talking of mental pictures and visualisation. She still remained curious as to how he "saw" things in his mind. She asked him what he imagined a tree was like. How did he understand the concept of colour? He tried to explain that he was unconcerned about things that he could not understand and could never experience, but she thought his answer evasive.

"Do you want to know what I look like," Helen said, hoping for an affirmative answer, needing his curiosity.

"Not really," he said. "I like you – that is enough."

"But you don't love me any more," she said quietly. "And you're still so special and important to me."

"If I'm special to you, it's because I am me, not because I am blind. You should love me for myself, not for my disability," Matt said in exasperation. "I don't want to be an exotic experiment or an object of pity."

Later, on another occasion, she said to him: "I've often wondered if you know that you are a good-looking man."

"I see you are still obsessed with appearances rather than reality," he said dryly. "But for the record, yes, I have been told by more than one woman that I am a handsome beast. Perhaps it's my dark glasses that they find sexy and mysterious."

"It did occur to me," she said, "That you could be a serial womaniser. You know you are attractive, and you could trade on women's sympathies and capitalise on their guilt and their desire to help. Your lack of sight is no drawback in bed in the dark. You could have been a real philanderer," she continued, looking at him with interest.

"How do you know that I'm not?" he said with a smile.

"Because I know that what really interests you is the head not the heart," she replied honestly. "Though you are good in bed, I always feel that your performance is calculated rather than passionate."

"What a cruel thing to say," he said, but he did not deny it. He had thought that his lack of desire had been well concealed by his expertise and was surprised at her perceptiveness. It cooled things even more between them. She was relieved that there had never been any suggestion of living together – they had both decided that they wanted to preserve and inhabit their own space.

It was in November, when their meetings had dwindled to once a week and their occasional sexual encounters had become perfunctory, and they were sitting in his flat drinking coffee, that she felt a slight difference in him. It seemed as if he was suppressing a latent excitement, a guilty secret. Her intuition told her he had met someone else. It was almost a relief. She could now let him go and feel no culpability because he would not be alone for long. She was not surprised when he gently broke the news to her that he had met a woman whom he liked a lot, and he wanted to be free to get to know her better. Her name was Celine.

"We both know," he said, "That our time together is at an end. It hasn't worked – and I wish it had been otherwise. I hope you won't be lonely," he asked, echoing her worry about him.

"Don't worry, Matt," she said, and patted his arm. "I'm not heartbroken, though I would have been six months ago. Shall I tell you why?"

He nodded and lent back in the sofa. He was a good listener and she wanted to tell him.

Helen got to her feet and paced about his room. "I've found it impossible to live up to your vision of the ideal woman – one who can forget about appearances and not worry about the visual world. I can't deny my five senses, any more than you can be interested in the one sense that you lack. The fact is that I've still got my eyes and I like to use them. I like watching people and their expressions; I like looking at the countryside and nature; I want to be dazzled by beautiful things and I want to be horrified by ugly things. I like to read books and look at photographs. Damn it, I want to watch TV and go to films. I'm just ordinary but you're extraordinary. And so hard to live with!" Here she took a deep breath and continued in a calmer tone. "I shall miss your calmness and your intelligence and your kindness, but I shan't miss feeling inferior. I have to believe that I'm worthwhile and I want to be able to like myself. My self-esteem has taken a battering whilst I've been with you. It's demoralising living with a saint – especially a blind one. I'm fallible and I like it that way. You've transcended your disability and I admire you for that, but I'm not prepared to forgo my fascination with things visual because they don't matter to you. I wish you luck with Celine – but don't be too hard on her. Don't be as critical as you were with me. I honestly think the only woman who could fit the bill of your exacting demands would probably be blind herself."

"She is," he said.

* * * * *

She did not see him for a few weeks and then one day she caught sight of him in the street. She waited for the pang of regret and was pleasantly surprised when no such feeling arose. In fact, his sleek, tall, dark-eyed form almost repelled her. She hoped he had found what he was looking for and she now felt relief that she had not filled the vacancy.

Helen did not see Matt again after that. Perhaps he had moved in with his new woman; perhaps it had not worked out or he had gone away. She missed the lovemaking but not the lover. She did not lament his loss for very long.

That chilly winter, David, comfortably fallible, amusingly mundane, blind to her imperfections and still loving her unconditionally, came back into her life. He was reassuringly familiar and refreshingly unpretentious so she sighed and put him on again like an old coat, worn and warm.

POSTE RESTANTE

Poste Restante

Léonie adores writing letters.

Even though she is now fifty, and the era of the fax is already waning and the age of e-mail has arrived, she still loves writing letters in longhand. Her adult children tease her that she is living in a different century and that she is stuck in a time warp, but she takes no notice and still replies to their e-mails with an old-fashioned letter. She detests the computer, dislikes the telephone and loathes what she sees as the "fad" of texting on mobiles. She enjoys the process of composition and the satisfaction of saying exactly what she wishes to impart in well-chosen words written in an attractive flowing hand.

As a child in the nineteen sixties, when the letter was the usual method of communication, she discovered the excitement and pleasure of sending and receiving letters. English was her favourite subject at school, and she enjoyed writing essays. Creation was her passion and she had a fertile imagination. She had an urge to communicate but an even stronger desire to describe her life and feelings. She loved choosing words and painting pictures with them. From compositions she went on to develop her skill at writing a good letter. Here she felt free to write what she wanted, relating incidents without the limitation of having to be accurate or truthful. She could bend the truth and add exotic detail or omit what sounded dull. She could be chatty, dramatic, funny, frivolous, serious – as she pleased – and with no teacher to criticise her style or demand a particular topic – which is what happened in English lessons. It was rare that any of her letters were actually posted. She invented exotic imaginary recipients, all of whom were enthralled to hear about her life. The enjoyment was in writing the letters and keeping them in a blue ring binder she called her Missive.

The tools of the trade had also thrilled her. She liked the crisp white pads of paper that her father gave to her, but preferred the thicker cream sheets with matching envelopes that she "found" in her mother's desk. Her Godmother had given her an elegant fountain pen, with a zigzag pattern on the barrel and a gold coloured nib, which she never took to school but which she always used for letters. She liked the even flow of her handwriting across the page and embellished her capital letters with extra flourishes. She enjoyed seeing a whole page covered in her stylish sloping writing in the colour of ink that was her current favourite. She would spend a month with green ink and then on a whim change to purple. She felt this gave her letters a visual distinctiveness.

She had a penchant for owning all the other ancillary items – spare nibs, paper clips, erasers and different coloured pencils. As a small girl she had a desire to accumulate brand new or unused items – chiselled square rubbers, long pointed pencils and smooth wooden rulers. She remembered, with only a flicker of guilt, that at the age of ten she had regularly stolen such things from a stationers shop when her mother and the shop assistant were not looking. She "borrowed" paper clips and stamps from her father's desk. She used to hoard her acquisitions at the back of her desk drawer, and take them out furtively from time to time and gloat over her collection. She had now stopped obtaining her writing materials by this unorthodox method. Her father had become aware both of her passion for writing letters and her "jackdaw" habits, and so he supplied her with all she needed – except an appreciation of her efforts. For of course, living at home, she did not write to them and so they were ignorant of her talent, though indulgent in what they perceived as a childhood craze.

Above all, Léonie enjoyed the thrill of saying what she wanted with no one interrupting her. Conversation at home during her childhood was demoralising and dissatisfying. Her three older brothers were all larger than her in stature and more forceful in character. She was shouted down at table and knocked down at games. She was never allowed to finish a sentence. Though her frustration was evident to her mother, who was occupied trying to control her noisy sons, and to her father, who sat quietly and disapprovingly at one end of the table, they did not intervene. She had to fight her own battles. So she gave up, remained silent and took her revenge at leisure, destroying them by word in her letters. The fact that they were unaware of the savagery to which she regularly subjected them on the page was mildly annoying, but this irritation was countered by the benefit of no retaliation. A bruised ego was better than a bruised arm.

But unread prose, however brilliant, was ultimately unsatisfactory. She now wanted to post her letters to a real person and to get a response. She began to correspond with her Godmother, and she found comfort in unloading her worries and her feelings on paper, knowing there would be a sympathetic reader.

Her Godmother enjoyed receiving weekly salvos from Léonie. She felt sorry for the girl having such an unappreciative father and such uncivil brothers. She encouraged her Goddaughter to write letters and communicate with friends outside the family who would appreciate her epistolary skills. She found her Goddaughter's style entertainingly florid and the content interestingly percipient. Her biggest asset, from Léonie's point of view, was that she wrote back. Over a period of three years, she regularly corresponded with the young girl, but then she re-married and the exclusive link was broken, and their exchange of letters petered out.

Léonie's main problem was lack of correspondents. Very few of her friends seemed to want to write to her. Her Godmother had been very kind and had always responded – and she was immensely grateful for this. However, what she craved from the replies was not so much news from the writer but a reaction to what she had written to them. All children are monstrously self-centred and Léonie was no exception.

When she had started writing letters she had invented imaginary friends to whom she could say anything and everything. But she then developed a wish to post letters in the big red letterbox at the corner of the street, and needed a reliable person as a recipient. She managed to persuade the occasional friend to accept her letters and even to reply. One year she had met a girl on the beach during one of their summer holidays and had happily carried on a correspondence with her for a while, but the interest on the part of the other child dwindled – or perhaps she was discouraged by the Léonie's eloquence and effusiveness with which she could not compete.

By now, one-sided correspondence had ceased to amuse Léonie. Receiving letters assumed a greater importance – she really did want to hear back from those on whom she lavished her beautiful and witty letters.

At about this time, her father decided to take a job abroad. Her two elder brothers were then at college and the youngest brother, Thomas, and Léonie were to attend boarding school for a few years. For some reason, Tom was sent to a school a long way from his sister's. One of the consolations of this arrangement, as Léonie saw it, was that she would need to write to her brother to keep in touch. She knew that the older two boys would never bother to write to her, but she had hoped that Thomas would do so. Sadly he never responded at all to her letters and after a while she gave up. She was not going to waste her efforts on an impolite and indifferent sibling.

She had better hopes of her parents. She would now have the opportunity of lavishing her eloquence on them. Surely they would write regularly to her! At her boarding school, it was obligatory to write home each Sunday afternoon, if the child was not out on an "exeat". The other girls in her house moaned about this rule, and wrote with reluctance and brevity. But Léonie found no problem with this obligation – the only problem was that there was rarely any response.

Her father never wrote at all – no doubt he was too busy with the important affairs of life, his work and the outside world to put pen to paper and communicate with his only daughter. Léonie did not excuse him, but she thought he probably came from an era when Englishmen did not think that writing letters to their children was their responsibility. The lords of creation had weightier matters to deal with, and left any letter writing to their minions – wives and secretaries.

Her mother was French, full of good intentions but delightfully disorganised. Annick was a gregarious woman who was had great enthusiasm for life and a genuine affection for people. She was very capable of arranging brilliant dinner parties or charitable events, but on the domestic front she started projects that she rarely finished and her house was always in a state that bordered on chaos. She seemed to have time for everyone, always offering help and sympathy for those with troubles. She squandered hours of her day drinking coffee with neurotic girlfriends. Inevitably, she was admired and valued by her friends, and adored uncritically by her children.

Annick's time was divided between listening to other people's problems, working on her latest project (making tapestries or digging a pond or learning the oboe), sitting on her charitable committees, and occasionally talking to her husband. She loved her children, but out of sight they really did slip out of mind. Perhaps it was the relief of having only one man and not four in her disordered house that made her occasionally forget that she had a daughter.

Her desk was always covered in letters and bills which had arrived and been opened but which had not become urgent enough to persuade Annick that a response was needed. She was unmethodical and impulsive, and was unable to prioritise – frequently spending hours helping a stranger, whilst finding no time at all to write to her youngest child. Corresponding with her children had never become habitual. For the majority of their childhood, they had been living at home and when she found herself living aboard, her main contact with her children was responding to her sons' pleas for more pocket money or an increase in their allowance. She was amused by her daughter's flowery and entertaining letters, but never seemed able to find the time or to make the required effort to write back on a regular basis.

When at home together, Annick and Léonie had related well. The mother taught her young daughter how to cook, and instilled in her a taste for French literature. Though Léonie pretended to dislike her French name, she was secretly pleased when her friends said they thought it foreign-sounding and exotic. As she grew older and mastered her other language, Léonie decided it was unusual and useful to be half-French. She became interested in her mother's family background and loved to hear Annick's stories about the family home in the Auvergne.

Childhood stories are also an important part of the lives of Léonie's children. She tells them in both written and spoken words not only about her own childhood in England but also about that distant time when their grandmother was a young girl living in rural France. Léonie's sons and daughters have heard some of these stories many times, but there is a family convention not to remind the person recounting the story of this. Everyone is aware of the pretence that the story is being told for the first time, and no one is indelicate enough to mention the repetition. Anyway, the old stories are comfortingly familiar. Even Alain, Leonie's husband, who is more assertive than his wife sometimes likes, is quietly supportive of the reiterative tradition, which he values. He is a thoroughly modern man who uses all the latest communication processes, but he is tolerant of his wife's addiction to the old-fashioned methods. Indeed he encourages her – it gives him an edge.

Looking back again at her childhood, Léonie realises that her time at boarding school was not the happiest part of her young life. With an enforced absence from her family, Léonie found that letters meant much more to her and what she really wanted was a short letter regularly to assure her that they loved her and were thinking of her. Her other friends received weekly letters from one of their parents, but Léonie was lucky if she received more than two a term. She became quite upset when post after post arrived with nothing for her. She began to sprinkle her weekly letters with bitter comments such as: "Thank you for your letter – I'm sorry it got lost in the post," or "Question: Guess why I am unique at school? Answer: I am the only one who does not receive letters from home." These remarks did occasionally shame her mother into writing a letter, which mainly comprised complicated excuses as to why she had not found the time to write earlier, with very little other news.

These days Léonie is still obsessive about communicating with her own children and she writes to them often. She and Alain have lived in France since their marriage, and the children were educated there, though they have now moved away or live abroad. She recalls how she always wrote to her children when they were at "en pension" at the Lycée, which was in a town some forty kilometres from their village. She remembers how neglected she had felt at her English school with no letters from home, vowing that if ever she had children of her own, she would always keep her promises and write them letters.

As a teenager, Léonie never did manage to educate her mother and eventually became mature enough to accept the fact that most people disliked or resented writing letters. The year her parents returned to England and bought a house in Surrey, Léonie went to University in Scotland to study English and French. She developed an appreciation of the diaries and letters of some of the writers she studied, and the letter was elevated to an art form. During her years at university she wrote home every couple of weeks, whilst knowing that her artistic and sensitive letters would get no written response. However, she was prudent enough to keep a copy of the ones of which she was particularly proud because she had no faith that her parents would keep her words safe for posterity.

A new student far from home, she found the lack of communication from her parents at first annoying but then convenient. There was no telephone in the flat and personal mobiles were a thing of the future, so Léonie got on with her life without parental interference. If she went to an all night party with the hard drinking set, or if she went climbing mountains with inappropriate companions and insufficient kit, her mother and father would never know. In her letters, now somewhat briefer, she omitted to mention reckless activities so as not to worry them. The girl failed to realise that her parents' apparent lack of interest and concern about her actually showed that they were very aware that their daughter was a responsible individual who could take care of herself. Léonie had never made the demands of them that her brothers habitually did.

233

Clearly she was self-sufficient and so, although they did care, they did not worry about her.

She used to come home for the winter and spring holidays, and get a holiday job. Her father gave her a bit of financial help occasionally, but he usually forgot and she did not ask. Student grants were available and Léonie rather liked the challenge of seeing if she could manage. In the long summer break, she would take off round the Continent with friends from university, having earned the money to do so. She "discovered" postcards and, although she felt they were poor substitutes for a proper letter, they obviated the necessity of carrying round pen, ink, paper and envelopes. She spurned facile tourist views and bought art cards, but even these she rather despised although she felt that her parents deserved no more.

In her final year at college, Léonie informed her parents that she was renting student accommodation in the town. In fact, she was living in a flat with her boyfriend – an attractive but conceited youth who was studying philosophy – but she didn't bother to mention this in her letters home. It was not that she felt her parents would disapprove – whether they did or didn't would not have bothered her – but she occasionally punished them by shutting them out of the important things in her life, in the way she felt they had excluded her from theirs. When the painful relationship with her lover broke up, she turned to her friends for comfort. She had never involved her mother in her private affairs, and did not do so now. She did not know that her mother, whose sons had now flown the nest, might have been glad for an appeal for emotional support from her independent daughter. However, Annick was not given the opportunity. She had left it too late.

Léonie passed her final exams and achieved a commendable degree. Her father was too busy to come to her graduation, and although her mother had intended to come north for it, some big charitable event precluded her from doing so. Léonie neglected to give them the photograph of herself wearing gown and mortarboard – and they failed to ask her if they could have one.

Her university years had been hard work and now she wanted a bit of travel before settling down to a career. She had not taken a gap year, so she applied for a job abroad, teaching English as a foreign language. Her parents had moved house again, and her father was commuting to London from their new home in Croydon. Léonie had no intention of residing in a suburb. She had an offer of a job in Europe and another in the South East Asia. She chose the latter. The Far East beckoned with promise. And it was further away.

Léonie would not miss her brothers. The eldest was now working in America, and her second brother was living in Sheffield with his partner who had two children. The young men made minimal contact with home and now, far apart in miles and in years, their sister felt that she hardly knew them. She had seen little of Thomas during her student years in Scotland. He was now living in London but never made the effort to share with his parents anything of his life other than mounds of dirty shirts on the occasions when he returned home for the weekend to eat proper meals and catch up on sleep. When at home their youngest son was not forthcoming about work or friends, and he returned on Sunday evenings to his separate life. Léonie, who had been washing her own clothes for years, had little in common with her nearest sibling.

Her contract for the teaching post was for two years, and she would not be returning home during that time as it was too far away and too expensive. She also planned to take several months travelling round the Far East and overland back to Britain afterwards. Surprisingly, just before her departure, her parents asked her if she would continue with her habit of writing home. Their last little bird was about to fly the nest, and the news and details of their daughter's life in the letters, which she had sent them for so many years, had now become habitual and necessary.

Léonie, surprised by their admission and touched by their loving interest, decided to make a bargain. If they wrote to her, she would write to them. They agreed – there was some justice in the demand. The daughter departed and for a few months they did keep their word, but soon their letters became

235

infrequent and Léonie rarely received replies to her eloquent descriptions of life in her corner of Asia. There was no access to telephones where she lived, and the telecommunication system in the city was inefficient and inaccessible. In any case, Léonie was averse to telephones. She knew that she would detest a hurried conversation with someone she loved which was distorted by a poor quality connection or interrupted by an incomprehensible operator, and fractured by the pips which heralded disconnection. A brief fleeting talk with one of her parents would elicit little information whilst being emotionally upsetting. Letters were more effective, discursive and a much more satisfactory method of communication. On their part, it would not have occurred to her parents to telephone their daughter even if they had been able to. In those days international telephone calls were just too expensive.

Now, when Léonie tells her children that for over two years she never spoke to her parents, they can hardly believe it. They live in the world of mobile phones with instant and constant communication. Technology has moved on so far that her listeners cannot comprehend that there was a time when telephoning was rare. Today it is normal to keep in touch with each other frequently. Back in the seventies, things were different. Léonie had tried once to book a call at Christmas from the local post office, but despite many frustrating hours waiting for her connection, she had not got through. Perhaps her decision not to try again was also because she felt her parents did not deserve the required effort or cost on her part. She never knew whether they ever felt the need to talk to her – this seemed unlikely in view of their reluctance to put pen to paper.

When Léonie started travelling, after her teaching contract had ended, she decided to use the worldwide system of Poste Restante – a service provided by the post offices of main towns in most countries to accept and store incoming mail intended for travellers who, passing through that town, could call in to the Poste Restante desk or office to collect their letters or packages.

She was a solitary young woman who had a few friends in England, none of whom corresponded with her. She did,

236

however, prefer to travel with a companion and usually managed to find someone on the same road as her with whom she could share a few days or weeks. She decided that it would be a kindness to let her parents have some method of contacting her in case there was an emergency or in the very unlikely event of their actually writing a letter to her to tell her their news. So she planned her route calculating the approximate dates when she might be in certain countries and cities, and wrote a letter to her parents giving this information and saying that she would check for mail at Poste Restante in these various places. Even if they never wrote, at least they would know which country she was in. She took with her a small pad of airmail paper and some thin envelopes – she was travelling light and on a low budget.

She kept a diary, writing in it whenever the mood took her or time allowed, sitting beside the road waiting for a bus in Malaysia, at a grubby table in a cheap travellers' hotel in Singapore, or lying on a beach in Goa. She used to copy excerpts from her diary into her letters and post them off into the silence. She made a big effort to get to Poste Restante in the General Post Offices which she had nominated but it was very rare that anything was waiting for her, and she used the opportunity to buy stamps and post her letters and cards. Her persistence in continuing with outgoing mail in the face of nothing incoming made her feel more than a little self-righteous.

These days, she is rewarded by replies from three of her four children – only one has rebelled against the tyranny of answering letters, an obligation that Léonie tried to instill in them as a habit for life. They know that their mother has been scarred by her own parents' disinclination to correspond with their child – she has told them about it many times. They love her and therefore make the effort.

This is a letter which Léonie has just written to one of her daughters. Marie is just twenty-four and the same age as her mother was at the time of the incident which is described in the letter.

237

"Darling Marie,

"So you are twenty four. How does it feel? Did you receive the flowers? I have something a little less ephemeral to give you when we next meet - it's too fragile to send!

"I hope you celebrated in some way - an intimate dinner or a riotous party - something to remember. One's life is made up of just such memories - and these eventually will be transformed into stories, amended, polished and probably embroidered.

"The other day, I was clearing out an old box of letters, brochures and cards and I came across a bundle of items which dated back to my time in South East Asia in the 1970's. I found something there which reminded me of a day over thirty years ago when I was on my travels in Indonesia, after I finished my teaching job in Malaysia.

"You know that in my twenties I had spent two years working in the Far East - which I found both fascinating and exhausting. I used to teach adults and therefore my classes took place mainly in the early mornings and in the evenings. Instead of resting in between as most of the other teachers did, I used to go out to the markets to buy fruit and vegetables, or wander the streets, or visit married female friends who lived in air conditioned flats and were fortunate in that they did not have to work. At weekends, I avoided the British Club and other haunts of the "ex-pat" community, and travelled up-country. It was beautiful and remote and was refreshingly different from life in the city with the smells, the noise and the prolific humanity.

"I always preferred the countryside to the cities, but when I started travelling after my job came to an end, I found that it was always necessary to go first to the major city or capital of the country that I was visiting because that was where one could meet other travellers, obtain information about what to see and how to travel, change money on the black market, but more importantly to experience the culture and customs and to meet the people living at the heart and nerve centre of that particular country.

"The experience which I am about to relate, took place in Jakarta, the capital of Indonesia, which was then one of the most unpleasant cities I had ever visited. Java was a beautiful, fertile and highly populated island. Jakarta was a big city with lots of slums, similar in noise, dirt, humidity and traffic to Bangkok in Thailand, which I had visited a couple of months earlier. I far preferred travelling round Java and Sumatra to spending time in the capital city, but on two occasions I did spend some time there. General Sukarno had gone, and another horrid military dictator – General Suharto – was in power. The Chinese had been ruthlessly suppressed, and one had to look down side streets off the beaten track to find the noodle shops in which I preferred to eat.

"After a nasty experience in Bangkok (I'll tell you about that another time), I was rather wary of Jakarta. In those days it was an ugly sprawling city full of brutal concrete buildings and hideous monuments built by Sukarno at vast cost. Housing had been demolished to construct wide grand squares and new avenues, but these were uncompleted as was a huge useless empty stadium and an expensive prestige hotel for the new emerging regime which was just as inflexible and corrupt as the earlier one. In those days, there were hardly any high-rise structures – buildings were large and low and invariably unfinished. The essential services were antiquated and inefficient – power cuts were frequent. It was all gigantic in concept and chaotic in construction.

"And so many people. Everywhere. Thousands of people thronging every street, square, and open space. I felt oppressed by the multitude, jostled by crowds – there seemed to be respect for personal space. I later felt the same in Calcutta where there was never any chance of being on one's own. There were no-go areas: the port and Chinatown were poverty stricken lawless areas and it was dangerous to venture there. And the city dwellers were different. Though I had found the Bataks tribes in Sumatra easy-going and friendly, the Indonesians I came across in the capital in Java were suspicious of or indifferent to foreigners and I felt alienated.

"I had been forewarned, so I had taken the unusual precaution of arranging somewhere to stay before I arrived – a flat belonging to businessman who had been one of my pupils. He had been employed in Kuala Lumpur but had been moved to the firm's office in Jakarta. The flat was in a block in a suburb of the city – an area which was a rather more salubrious than I could usually afford. I was travelling with an Australian girl called Susie whom I had met in Singapore, and we slept on the floor in the spare bedroom. There was no bed but the room had air-conditioning – blissful! I was suffering from a painful eye infection and stayed in the flat for a couple of days – it was April, the hot season – and it was blistering outside. Susie used to bring me mangos and sticky rice to eat. She decided to visit Bandung for a day, and with my eye a bit better, I decided to venture out and see if I could manage the task of visiting the General Post Office and Poste Restante. This was to be my goal that day – a traverse across the city and back again – probably fruitless.

"I had discovered that apart from walking, the only cheap way of crossing the city was on one of the overcrowded buses which careered madly down the crowded streets and which usually took you somewhere you didn't want to be. The other method, only slightly more expensive, was to take a bicycle rickshaw. They were called Bejaks – three-wheeler affairs, painted in different colours, with a seat behind

the driver who pedalled furiously weaving in
and out of the other road traffic, the street
sellers and the market stalls. I had found out
that Bejaks painted in blue were only permitted
to take fares in the "blue" area, and that if one
crossed zones, one had to change Bejaks, and
there were yellow Bejaks for the "yellow" area,
and green and red also. It was complicated
and tiring because each time one changed
Bejaks, one had to communicate in Indonesian
and bargain to establish a reasonable fare to
one's destination or to the next zone. On this
occasion, recovering from my eye infection,
I thought I would avoid the exhaustion of
walking, the crush and uncertainty of riding on
the buses, and would take my chance with the
bicycle rickshaws. I had to change Bejaks three
times, and after nearly one and a half hours,
I was deposited in a huge dusty market area,
across which I could see a wide grey building,
which I understood was the GPO.

"My various travelling companions used to
tease me about my persistence in locating and
visiting the main post offices which were often
a long way from where we were staying. Whilst
my fellow backpackers were chilling out in the
shade or dozing in the cheap bedrooms of the
shabby low-budget hotels we used, I would spend
hours, walking across hot dusty teeming cities
to check with the Poste Restante office to see if
any letters had miraculously found their way
there. I would use the occasion to buy stamps
or post a letter home, but I invariably returned

242

to my small hotel empty-handed. I developed
a strategy of non-expectation and tranquil
acceptance to cope with what I once might have
termed disappointments. Somehow the effort
still seemed worth making – almost as a test of
my inner strength and patience.

"Patience was necessary because visiting
government post offices in different Asian
towns and countries in hot humid conditions
was a time and energy consuming business.
The offices were usually situated in poor
overcrowded districts in huge dilapidated
buildings with peeling wooden shutters
hanging off gaping unglazed windows.
Opening hours were erratic, and those
working there were often wearing uniforms
and impassive expressions whilst working
at a measured pace designed to intimidate
and irritate customers by its overbearing
inefficiency. Sometimes the various services
were housed in different buildings or huts,
but they were always, always full of people,
crowding the entrances, waiting in queues,
lounging on the steps, wandering along
corridors, talking in groups or just sitting
staring vacantly in the fetid air. The sounds
of muted conversations within, the cries of
food vendors outside, dry coughing and noisy
spitting, mingled with the tapping of boots on
stone floors and the banging of rubber stamps
onto official documents. The interiors were
often thick with dust and flies, being moved
by ancient fans slowly turning the heavy air,

which bore the same sweaty spicy smell that I
always associated with Asian cities.

"I pushed my way through the myriad
market stalls and the throng of buyers and
sellers, and found myself in front of a typical
government building such as I have just
described. I climbed up the cracked and stained
steps to enter the large entrance door. My
heart sank – the main concourse was full of
people – and there was very little indication of
where I should go. I waited in one queue for
about twenty minutes, only to discover that I
was in the wrong area – and I was directed to
another hall. Here I waited again, managed to
buys some stamps, and upon enquiring about
Poste Restante was waved through a door.
Here I found myself in a large low room, in
some kind of annexe to the main building, in
which about thirty or forty people were sitting
at desks, typing on old metal typewriters or
writing laboriously in ledgers or shuffling
official forms. I stood at the counter, quietly
waiting with about seven other people, until
one of the workers condescended to approach
us and deal with our various requests. Time
passed and eventually my turn came. My
request was met with blank incomprehension
on the face of the man behind the counter, and
after a consultation with another uniformed
colleague, he told me that the Poste Restante
was housed in a room somewhere off a corridor
in the main building. I returned there, feeling
very demoralised and irritated, and wondering

why the hell I bothered to do these stupid things. But having come such a long way and wasted the best part of a day, I was determined to persevere. I was directed by another official through a doorway and down a long corridor. This seemed to connect the main building with another older and even shabbier building to the rear.

"By this time, I was getting tired and quite convinced that I was wasting my time. I asked yet another impassive face at yet another counter and was silently waved through yet another door, which led outside the building. In front of me was a small shack in what seemed like a yard where discarded cardboard boxes and rubbish had been thrown. There was a small wooden door with peeling green paint on which I cautiously knocked. No reply. A louder knock, and still no reply, so in a fit of frustration I pushed the door sharply. It swung back and crashed against some obstacle behind it.

"I stepped inside and was confronted with a small room piled high with ancient rusty filing cabinets, a large battered desk and a pair of small grimy apertures for windows. An elderly Indonesian man sat behind the desk, wearing the ubiquitous crumpled grey green uniform, and looking up at me expectantly. He did not seem perturbed by my assault on his office door, but waited patiently for me to speak.

"In desperation and with no confidence at all that I would get a positive response, I asked yet again: 'Poste Restante?' He nodded slowly, and gave me a small smile of encouragement - the first sympathetic sign I had received that day. I could hardly believe it, so I repeated the words, and again he nodded. I leant down and slowly wrote my name on a slip of paper which I then handed to him. Silently - I began to wonder if he was mute - he leant down and opened a dented filing cabinet. From inside, he drew out two small wooden boxes or trays, which he placed on the desk. I saw, with a sense of total futility, that the boxes were crammed with old dirty dog-eared envelopes. Here was a repository of forlorn letters that had never been and would never get collected. Some of them looked as if they had been there for years. How often, I wondered, did anyone find their way here and actually collect one of these battered relics?

"The man bent his balding head over one of the boxes and riffled through the contents as he had clearly done many times before. He seemed to have no confidence in matching an item in his care to the person enquiring for one. Neither did I. He thumbed his way slowly through the grubby envelopes, whilst I turned to stare out of the door at a gaunt dog which was rooting through the rubbish. An exclamation made me swing round, and I saw a slow smile spread over the face of the Poste Restante clerk as he extracted a pale blue air mail letter from a place in the box and held it aloft with a look of pride. Now I was the one who was mute - with astonishment!

"With a flourish he handed me the letter, and I glanced down to see my name in my mother's handwriting. The words blurred and my tears started to fall. A look of alarm and concern replaced my companion's triumphant expression. I could not explain – I lacked both words and the language to do so. I gulped my thanks and tried to smile in encouragement and gratitude. He nodded nervously, and I turned to go, clutching the precious letter. I was so stunned that I nearly tripped over the threshold. He came round his desk and steadied my arm. Impulsively I gave him a hug. The shutter immediately came down and his expression became blank and politely unconcerned. A mistake. I knew that one should never make physical contact with strangers in Asia – it always produced a frozen rejection.

"After I left the tiny office I went and sat on the grimy steps at the front of the main hall of the GPO and opened the small miracle from my mother. The content was unremarkable but what was wonderful was that here in this alien world I had received a most unlikely revelation – the assurance that my mother had thought of me and loved me enough to send her words half way across the world to reach me. She could not have known what this small token meant to me – alone and a long way from home.

"Well darling, I must tell you that I felt a nostalgic pang when I set eyes on that very letter again a few days ago. It brought it all back to me. I have very few letters from my

247

mother but that is one which I shall always treasure."

Léonie signs off the letter to her daughter who lives in England with her husband. She glances through the four pages of her careful script in blue ink – she no longer uses red or purple inks – it's too "jeune." She carefully folds the letter, places it in a thick cream envelope and sticks a stamp on it. But her mind is on that day long ago in the Poste Restante office in Jakarta. She picks up the faded old envelope which contains the letter from the past – an ordinary chatty letter sent from Croyden in England detailing domestic events and local gossip – which found its way to her in Asia across thousands of miles. A seemingly ordinary letter but for her a rarity, an affirmation, a consolation, a moment etched in time. She remembers her tears in that dingy shack and the distress of the elderly clerk who thought she had received bad news, and how she was unable to communicate with him.

She thoughtfully looks at both letters – addressed to daughters of the same age but living in different times. She kisses them both and puts one in the drawer and the other in her bag. She will walk to the village post box – there is only one collection a day and the letter may take three days to arrive at its destination. This does not matter – she is happy to entrust a morsel of her life to the vagaries of the rural French postal system. Her words will travel across the space between herself and Marie, and for a few moments will re-connect them in their mutual love. She can no longer do this with her own mother. She has been dead for years.

A letter informing Léonie that her mother was ill with a brain tumour arrived at Poste Restante in Ankara, but for once Léonie did not manage to visit the capital city. She was more interested in getting to Istanbul and, travelling with friends, she took a steamer there from Trebizond on the Black Sea. She would soon be back in Europe, and congratulated herself that she had travelled the whole way there overland. She was

248

now eager, after a long time on the road, to be back in England. She would spend a couple of weeks in Turkey before going on to Greece, from where she planned to fly home on a student flight.

Annick died three weeks before her daughter arrived home from her travels. Léonie received the terrible news when she telephoned home from Athens to tell her parents that she would be arriving home in a couple of days. The elation of her imminent return and her reunion with her family evaporated the moment she heard the devastating news. Missing the urgent letter in Ankara meant that she had lost the opportunity to see her mother once more and to say goodbye. Her guilt took a long time to diminish but her sadness and regret lasted longer.

The Jakarta letter turned out to be more precious that ever – it contained the last words she was ever to receive from her mother. Léonie remembers this and writes every letter to her children as if it were the last.

SOUL TRADER

Soul Trader

Last year my annual bonus was £341,230. It will be less this year – there was that downturn in the Adora hedge fund. But my salary will have increased. It always does. I have a good job – it's exciting and demanding and I do it well. I'm highly remunerated and I'm proud of my success. My investment account is steadily rising in value, my own personal portfolio is worth in excess of half a million, and my savings and current accounts always have a worryingly large balance. It's been hard achieving all this, and don't I know it!

My problem is that I don't have any time to spend the money. I work far too hard. I'm "cash rich and time poor," as they say. My penthouse flat in a converted warehouse overlooking the Thames is already perfect and needs no more spent on it. I really splurged out on it three years ago – and the upholstery, carpets and curtains still look brand new. I hardly ever use the gleaming stainless steel and black granite kitchen – I'm far too tired to cook when I get back from work – and often it's nearly 10 pm which is too late to eat anyway. Regarding other expenditure, I buy myself three extortionately expensive suits each year for work, together with appropriate shoes and belts, and a couple of well cut pairs of jeans and whatever else I need for chilling out after work. I really have no time to trawl round shops and I prefer having a limited but select wardrobe of clothes. Less choice takes less time, and though I always look smart I'm not convinced that anyone takes any notice of my appearance. This is rather sad, considering the care I take with it. This is not to say that if I turned up at the office crumpled and casual that there wouldn't be a few raised eyebrows. There would be. It's just that they expect me always to look smart, cool and immaculate. So when I turn up at work there is no comment – just acceptance that I keep myself as sharp and smooth in the fashion side of things as I am on the dealing side. It's all a part of the image.

I thought I might collect art and invest some of my well-gotten gains in paintings, but this involves going to galleries, and trying to conceal my absolute ignorance about it all, whilst hoping that I'm not being ripped off. Anyhow, I'm now the proud owner of an Ivon Hitchens, a John Piper, and a Patrick Heron. I quite like them, though I'm not sure about the Hitchens, which has a rather muddy feel about the colours. I was rather talked into buying it by the suave self-assured man at the gallery in Bond Street, who said it would be a good investment. Well, that always persuades me. The Heron abstract is rather loud – the colours are vibrant and lurid and it's rather "in your face". It impresses. I'm sure I paid far too much for the Piper, which is spooky and surrealistic. It is definitely my favourite. The pictures, framed up, are big, but then my walls require something dramatic. They're insured, of course, along with everything else I have. I don't know why I do this, because I don't really care for my possessions. I suppose I ought to like books and sculpture. Bookcases are considered a bit naff these days, and I don't really have many books – I've certainly no time to read them if I did own a lot. The trouble with sculpture is that people might criticise my taste – and though I have no problem at all defending my business decisions, (probably because they usually turn out successfully) I get a little perturbed trying to justify or explain my cultural or artistic acquisitions. I wouldn't want to be accused of borrowing other people's taste. That would be a bit "low-brow."

The other big item of expenditure, as I read recently in a Sunday newspaper article, is the annual holiday. Not for me! I rarely ever have one. Occasionally the office insist that I take some time off, so I fly off to Paris or Rome, buy some clothes, visit my favourite uncle in Versailles, or my friend Susie who works for the embassy in Rome, yawn my way round some art galleries, binge on croissants or pasta, and return to London, wondering how one ever meets people. I'm not unattractive but I suspect that in social spheres I might be thought shy. I can hold my own with the guys at work, but I'm not too good at making contact with members of the opposite sex, and initiating relationships. In fact, I suspect others might think me anti-social. I'm not – it's just that I don't choose to get involved. Relationships take time, and time is a commodity I'm short on. Just now I'm into my career, and personal things have to take a back seat. They'll be time for those later on when I've made a million. Well, perhaps my third million. Then I'll be able to relax and look around and set the emotional side of my life in motion.

That's not to say that I have no social life at all. I do, of course, get invited to parties and dinners, and I like to put on some smart gear and make an effort. At drinks parties or in pubs, I occasionally put in an appearance and, though I find it hard to participate in too much inane frivolous chatter, I do try to fit in and be amused by it all. The trouble is that it doesn't stop there. Even after a pleasant evening of social interchange, I get embarrassed if someone makes a direct proposition, and I tend to steer clear of starting an affair. These things play havoc with your ability to keep a clear head at work, and an unemotional cool head is the secret of success. Not to mention the importance of sleep. A few late nights and it shows around the corners of my eyes and the edges of my concentration. I cannot afford to let a tangled human relationship play hell with my performance at work. In my position, I would be in the firing line. Some of the others manage to get away with concealing the messiness and disruption caused by a destructive affair, but it takes its toll, and the end of year bonus will reflect that lack of dedication to the job. Of course some of them are married, and one can easily discern the stress caused by juggling the demands of a wife and children with the priorities one has at work. No, I have to play it cool and calm. I need their respect and their admiration. I don't want criticism and I can't take gratuitous advice. I can't rock the boat; I can't afford to relax and be different. I need to fit in with the company team and feel that I am one of the select few with talent and drive. My ego needs boosting, and I need that thrill of success and accolade that comes from working at my 100% best.

But, and there is a "but", I do feel that sometimes I'm undermining the human and caring side of my character. The

255

part of me that should love and laugh and relax. I conceal this from my work mates, but I have an uneasy feeling I'm not a rounded person, and that there are aspects of my nature and my personality that I'm suppressing. I really do intend to "let it all hang out" at some time in the future. But not now. Not yet. I can't.

My worry is that perhaps I am damaging my ability to interact with people, to love and become involved with someone to whom I'm attracted. So from time to time, I indulge in a weekend off. Or rather, it might be more accurate to say that I subject myself to human intercourse outside my work. It's rare I do this, and that does concern me. I'm still quite young – in my thirties– and I feel the need to reassure myself that I can – when I want to – find someone to marry and have kids with. That need asserts itself more often recently, which is why I accepted an invitation to go to Somerset for a long weekend over the spring bank holiday.

"Somerset, I ask you," I moaned to a colleague at work. "All that way to spend the inevitable rainy weekend in a borrowed Barbour jacket and muddy green boots talking about the savagery and anti-social behaviour of hunt protesters or hunt followers, depending on which point of view you have. But then again it just might be fun," and I thought to myself that I might meet some interesting people with whom I could become friends. I ought to make an effort. Because people regard me as aloof, I tend not to get too many invitations, so I need to respond in the affirmative. Or else, I'll turn into a loner.

But I knew it would almost certainly be a disappointment.

I once spent a disastrous Easter staying with an old school friend married to a Norfolk farmer. Minutes before my arrival, they had just had a huge row about a proposed new radiator in the hall, she wanting a larger model, and he not really wanting anything at all. The atmosphere was as chilly as the farmhouse, but not quite as cold as the temperature in the local mediaeval stone church at Good Friday's midnight mass. The air was thick with infectious streaming colds wafting cloudily upwards towards the mock candle bulbs. On Easter Saturday I declined to join the shooting party who set off unseasonably early. My parents once paid for me and my brother, Ralph, to have lessons in shooting when we were teenagers. I was rather better than him at knocking down the clay pigeons, and he understandably got rather upset about it. But that was years before, and I'd probably lost the knack. In any case, I felt that my presence wasn't really required so I stayed, had coffee with Sarah and read the newspapers whilst Roger went off with the lads.

Later, we joined a noisy crew of locals in the village pub, and then returned to the chaotic overcrowded farmhouse for an overcooked lunch, amidst over-excited dogs and irritable teenagers. I almost sprained my ankle on Easter Sunday, trying to be jolly and help the younger children with their egg hunt amongst the bushes and slippery lawn. Though in considerable pain on the drive from Norfolk to London in my Porsche, I was immensely relieved when I arrived back on Easter Monday evening to my well-heated, clean, sparsely furnished and, most of all, blissfully empty flat. I turned on some music on the new Bang and Olufson, and had a long hot bath to ease the ankle and wash away the country dross. I think it was Wordsworth who talked about the "bliss of solitude".

Anyhow, I propose to try yet again. It has to be a weekend, because I can't socialise during the week. I need my sleep – I must keep the hard edge at work. I cannot let them think me vulnerable or soft. It's tiring, that image I need to promote, and it requires total effort. So as the office will be closed anyway on Monday – no trading – I might as well take off and try to indulge in something more carefree and liberating than I usually do. I expect to regret the venture but I'll go anyway.

My friends in Somerset who have invited me, Karl and Susie, say there will be a party and I should bring some "glad rags", so I shall take my Armani jacket and some elegant beige trousers. Probably unsuitable – too chic – I rarely get it right. But it gives me confidence when I wear expensive clothes and look my best.

257

Before I tell you about the West Country weekend, I think I should come clean and mention why I was having this campaign of social endeavour. I ran into a friend called Nicky a few months back – we met up at a restaurant at the birthday dinner of a mutual acquaintance. Nicky had recently married a university lecturer and they seemed happy and contented. My single state was mentioned and joked about, and then I was given some advice. A management consultant friend had advised Nicky, who was always involved with or recovering from stormy relationships, to go about the business of finding a suitable person to share love with and perhaps life, using method instead of madness. One should decide what type of person one was and what kinds of men or women would attract, amuse, interest. Using headhunting tactics, and following up all social contacts and useful leads, one could eliminate unsuitable or undesirable persons, carefully concealing the use of interviewing techniques in getting to know possible candidates, and then select a short list and go for gold in getting to know them in order to choose the right one. Of course, at the very end of this exercise there had to be the spark of chemistry, a mutual attraction, and if that were lacking, then you cut loose and moved on to the next name on the shortlist. This exercise had been successful for Nicky, and it might work for me, so I thought I'd give it a try.

Well, I know this seems a bit mechanical, and too cool and calculating by half, but it made sense. I have long found that it's very difficult to meet the right type of person who is intelligent but not a geek, educated but not stuffy, attractive but not conceited, sensitive but not soppy, fun but not frivolous. I would not, on principle, use the Internet, because it's far too revealing about oneself, if you tell the truth, and it's self-defeating if you don't. And anyway, I'm really more into "face to face" contact. It's the eyes that tell you so much, and I do like good-looking people.

Feeling a bit foolish, but not really worried because no-one will ever know, I've made my list of preferred characteristics, physical and otherwise, and I have targeted all my friends and contacts who could introduce me to the right sort of person who might fit the bill. I've crossed off my list all those well-meaning people who have spent years trying to team me up with a horror job for a partner. The couple in Somerset are ex-city people who have gone down to the country and intentionally "dropped out" of their rat-race lives in London. They intrigue me, and they might have some interesting friends, so I've engineered an invitation, and I propose to give it a whirl. I have nothing to lose and, as Martin at work always says, "It might amuse."

* * * * *

Three years have passed since I typed the above in my private computer diary. Three extraordinary years of unexpected and inexplicable events. Definitely X-rated!

That weekend in Somerset changed my life. Initially I thought that what happened was a disaster, but now, looking back, I realise that it was providence, enchantment and my redemption as a human being. There are defining moments in one's life, and this was one of them.

We met at the party on that Saturday night, and the rapport was instant and mutual. I had no idea that I could be attracted to someone like Simon. He was so charming, so gentle. It was a whole new ball game. I went into free-fall.

I took a week off work – I was owed many days holiday – and stayed on. I just had to get to grips with this new feeling, this startling change in me, this irresponsibility. Karl and Susie's reactions to the affair were very different. Karl watched it unfold with sardonic amusement whereas Susie was angry with me. She was very protective of Simon, who was her favourite brother and who lived in the same village. However, he had been there for some years before their defection from the City, and no doubt felt he could look after and look out for himself.

It was almost summer. With butterflies, birds and bees. Simon and I frolicked in the hay, and shocked everyone. It was a totally new experience. It was also a problem. He was the vicar of the local church. His congregation were shocked by his unexpected behaviour, his desertion of his single status and his perverse alliance with a city slicker, a good-looking affluent successful bond trader. He had, they muttered mutinously and inaccurately, "abandoned all his vows of poverty, chastity and purity." It was a scandal. Shocked whispers snaked their way round the congregation when he smiled at me in church.

But that's all we did – we smiled, held hands, embraced, talked, but there was no sex. He was an Anglican clergyman. It would have been "sinful". But we were in love and nothing could stop our feelings. All those jaded female members of his congregation who had hoped he would choose a local wife, ground their teeth with jealousy, their condemnation mixed with fascination. It was difficult for Simon – he had never expected to be so attracted to an outsider, to someone so unacceptable, so inappropriate, so "wicked".

I know now that what I did was wrong. I lost my temper and my sense of proportion. Perhaps it was because I felt we were unfairly ostracised, and our love sullied by all the innuendo and gossip. For whatever reason, in a moment of madness, I accidentally and intentionally set fire to the parish hall – a building hideously utilitarian – a place of festering resentment and un-Christian attitudes. And Simon, coming in to the hall as I was trying to decide whether to fan the flames or stamp them out, could not prevent the fire from spreading. Forced to retreat from the heat and smoke in the building, and watching from under a nearby tree whilst waiting for the fire brigade to arrive, we were sadly unable to stop the village hero – a postman by the name of Bert – from dashing inside to see if he could single-handedly put out the blaze. The fireman got him out alive, but he was quite badly burned and was rushed to hospital. Thankfully, he survived.

The conflagration was dramatic, destructive and damaging. In the fallout, the police treated me like a criminal, and far worse – Simon kept his distance. I decided to resign from my job, and paid for my offence with fractured friendships, loss of earnings and savings, and – more bitter – disruption of my peace of mind. But in the end I didn't lose Simon. He stuck by me.

It was a difficult few months but we got through it together.

I think the office were, in fact, quite pleased at my departure and my ignominy. I had been too successful, too skilful, and I was never one of them. They were delighted to discover I had feet of clay and passionate secrets; my reputation was tarnished and they could push me off my pedestal. It had always been hard for them to accept me, a woman, in their closed and high-powered domain, and now that I was married to a country vicar, pregnant with twins, and being prosecuted for arson, their laughter must have echoed all the way to the Isle of Dogs. But I didn't care, I had found my all – my friend, my femininity, my lover, my life.

The arson prosecution was finally dropped through lack of corroborative evidence (my husband could not testify). I forfeited my career – of course. I would have given it up anyway. I don't miss all that money, but what was left has made motherhood marginally more comfortable. I don't have to go to work, and with twin boys every minute of the day is crammed full. I don't have all the time in the world, but I never did. If anything, being a parent makes even more demands than my hectic city job. It's certainly more energy consuming, time eroding, and a whole load trickier. The children are more devious than my old boss, more nosily distracting than the trading floor, more emotionally draining than the office party. They are, simply, more real. Living with another – a lover – is more enthralling (as being "in thrall") than the freedom of being single, and a family is infinitely more fulfilling than the forthcoming bonus.

Through knowing Simon, respecting him, and learning about his faith, my life has gained a spiritual dimension. It's called believing in God. It is supremely important to me, but I think it unwise to dissect my new and fragile faith – it's a mystery. It seems to defy logic and rational explanation. Human love, though imperfect, is simply more understandable than heavenly love and divine grace.

I love the boys and their father – these three men in my life. I used to think, when surrounded by all those power-hungry

261

hard-working male colleagues, that one day I would have female friends, and perhaps a daughter or a sister-in-law. But no such luck! I am happily condemned to these three alpha omega males who use me, love me, drain me, fill me. There is so much constant communication between us all that it makes me heady – and often gives me headache. And now I have a loving relationship with God to work on and enjoy. That is the priority. He should come first, but Simon, Tom or Jude often elbow him out of the top spot. Simon tells me this is wrong and I know he is right, but I am a "frail" woman and cannot help it, wilfully putting my men, with their muddy feet, on pedestals. Where God should be.

Motherhood dragged out of my core a selflessness that I never knew was there. The desire to protect, cherish and nurture soon dismantled that hard-nosed, self-sufficient carapace. I became blissfully vulnerable. There is pain too now, in my life, caused by fear. Fear for my little boys in this world that I know, from my earlier life that seems a hundred years ago, is a big bad place. Simon tells me that my fear means that I still haven't yet learnt to trust God. Surrendering my will and relying on someone else – almighty but invisible – is hard for me. But I have been trying. They say you don't change, but I have changed. Or perhaps I have merely discovered things inside my head that I never knew about: reserves of patience, repositories of innate motherly wisdom, stores of energy, and fathomless wells of love. As you can see, I am adopting the clichés of love language.

I am a new person; I have started anew. How fortunate that I've had the chance. A chance encounter in Somerset. A path that led me away from a selfish, brittle, hollow existence that was also, I confess, exciting, challenging and intense. However, excitement, challenge and intensity are still in my new life – but they are different, deeper and enduring. With my role as the wife of a hard-working vicar, the demands of my two tyrannical toddlers, my voluntary work at the local nursing home, and my involvement in dozens of local causes, societies and committees – tittle-tattle and little battles – I feel I have at last learnt about multi-tasking and many layering. I must not forget to give myself and my God some private time when I can be at peace or rest, and so re-charge my batteries and let my soul sing for the sheer joy of being alive in this evolving, eternal, painful and pressured world.

My family have put poetry and words back into my life. I fall over with tiredness. I brim over with love. I often lose my rag when I become overtired and things get out of proportion. My peace of mind is often precarious and my newfound good-nature can unravel. My nails are chipped, my shirt is un-ironed, but my real standards have not slipped. I still admire hard-working people, still aim to please, and still try to be good – if not the best – at what I do. Though now I have more honesty and less pride. I can admit to myself, if not to others, that I am no more the perfect parent or spouse now than I was once the high-flying successful bond trader. I try to live each day as it comes – and I try to remember that I too have a need for space and spirituality. My life is better than it was, so much better. Perfection is not possible – we should learn to be satisfied with what we have. I don't regret – well perhaps just for a moment – the loss of my Bang and Olufson. My life and values were horribly materialistic and self-centred. We all make mistakes.

I have to admit that I did set fire to the hall curtains. Curiously I didn't feel at all sorry for my lapse, at the time, though recently I have had to ask for forgiveness. Although the insurance company understandably refused to pay out, we managed to re-build the parish hall. I had to sell my gilded London flat to raise the money, but after paying the mortgage off, my final bonus from work was also needed to cover the total cost of the new hall. It is a far better building and much more user-friendly, so in time I hope the village will forgive me. I decided to sell my overpriced paintings to help out the family of the man who had to spend so many long months in the burns unit in that hospital near Bristol. Thank God he is now much better, and may soon be able to return to work. I feel so guilty about that.

The consequences of my action were more far-reaching than I could ever have imagined. It was a few months after the birth of Tom and Jude and with the encouragement of my husband that I drove on my own to Frenchay to visit the poor man whose life I had so wilfully disrupted. It was on the way back that I had the car accident that maimed me. I've always though the word "paraplegic" rather ugly sounding, but the reality is even more stark. Life in a wheelchair is not exactly what I expected, but I am continually amazed at how much I can do living as I do on two wheels. You also need a sense of humour. And acceptance without self-pity. And God most of all.

Simon is, of course, a saint. I am the sinner he is saddled with, and yet, amazingly, he still thinks he is blessed with me. I know that I have a soul and that God loves me unconditionally. My activity has been curtailed in one way but my mind can still somersault. Though unable to walk, I have better balance. I am calmer. I have more love for others than I ever had before. I certainly receive more than I deserve. I took risks. My path is different from what I imagined it would be and I travel it with less agility but more dignity. I am less independent but I've been set free. Jesus says to us, "I have come that they may have life, and have it to the full." I traded one life for another – and in truth this is the better one.

POKER FACES

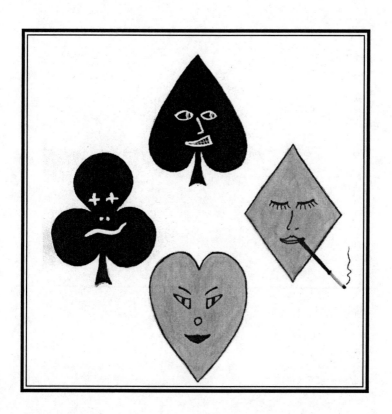

Poker Faces

'Last chance saloon'

Smoke billowed across the dining room. Some of the guests coughed. The children's eyes smarted. Molly's sharp voice cut through the murk. "That's it. You've had your last chance. You've done this too many times. I'm confiscating the toaster."

The watery rays of the spring sun passed into the Victorian bay windows filtering through the dissipating fronds of burnt bread smoke. Breakfast time at The Fells Hotel was a ritual. Not too much talk, except for the giggles and sniggers from the children's table, but a lot of crunching and munching. Crisp bacon, noisy toast, lips slurping tea, knives scraping on squeaky plates. The odd newspaper shaken out after a page turned. Occasional murmurs. "More toast, dear?" "A little more butter if we may." "Porridge for me, I think."

Each table in the large dining room had a plug let into the floor beneath it. For dinner small electric lights with globe glass shades were placed on each table, but for breakfast, these were replaced by individual toasters – the old fashioned type without timers. Vigilance was required because, if left too long, the toast burnt. It was a novel idea – and ensured that each table had fresh warm toast when it was needed.

The disadvantage was that children enthusiastically loaded their toaster with slices of bread and then forgot to remove them, resulting in smoke, smell and even flames on occasion. Molly had a shorter fuse than the other hotel staff who tended to be less severe when disciplining the children for their many raucous misdemeanours. The reason for this leniency was that the six children were the nephews and nieces of the owner who was surprisingly tolerant of the invasion of two families and their noisy city children in his quiet hotel haven. Uncle Vivian invited them and their parents to stay for ten days or so each year, early in the season, when his holiday hotel was not yet full. The children looked forward eagerly to the annual visit north to the uninhibited freedom of the Lake District and the open-hearted welcome at The Fells, whilst the generosity of their uncle was much appreciated by the parents who could not have afforded to go away to a hotel on holiday. For the two families, it was time of liberation from the restrictions and restraints of home and a temporary escape from urban life and pressures.

'It's my lucky day'

Towards the end of breakfast, Molly appeared again at the debris-strewn children's table just before their noisy exodus, and deposited a large white envelope in front of Chris. "The way you behave, you don't deserve this," she said sternly, but then negated her pretended reprimand by smiling and murmuring, "Don't spend it all at once!" as she turned away.

Six pairs of eyes focussed on the envelope, which Molly had placed leaning up against the milk jug. Chris, who was the wild one of the gang and never did anything without a display of drama, learnt forward and picked it up slowly with a gratified smirk on his face. It was his fifteenth Birthday, and he had already received gifts and gratifying attention from his brother and sister and his cousins before breakfast in the attic bedroom that he shared with his cousin, Geoff, who was one year older.

"Go on. Open it," pleaded Freddie, his younger brother, impatiently tapping his spoon on the table.

Tantalisingly and very slowly, Chris picked up a knife, used a napkin to wipe off the jam and butter smeared on it, and inserted the blade into the top of the envelope. There was a sharp intake of breath from his sister, Ella, as he ripped it across to reveal the contents: a large card depicting a fishing rod, bag and dead salmon – Uncle Vivian's choice of card – and inside the salutation, "Happy Birthday and Good Fishing." This was a bit odd, as the only fishing they ever did was for minnows in the stream using an old champagne bottle with the inverted end bashed in and stuffed with bread, to lure in the prey. But much more interesting was the crisp new ten pound note attached with a paperclip to the inside of the card. A collective sigh greeted the sight of yet another example of Uncle Vivian's generosity. Chris's eyes glittered in triumph. They had all suspected for many years that they had a rich uncle, and there was much speculation about whether he had a safe concealed somewhere on the premises, stashed with cash, though they had never managed to locate it.

'Follow suit'

As a young man, their uncle Vivian had learnt his trade working in a seaside hotel in Bournemouth. His first hotel he managed was in the Welsh borders, and it was here that he developed his skills and evolved his philosophy of success. After twenty years, having amassed the necessary savings to enable him to borrow further finance, and having acquired a trim and astute wife named Jean, he bought his own hotel and moved further northwards to pursue his career as a solid respectable country hotelier in the Lake District.

The Fells was a solid Victorian structure built in grey and pinkish-red granite. From a child's perspective, it seemed enormous with a huge entrance hall with open fire, a broad staircase with solid wooden bannisters marvellous for sliding down, a lounge with large but comfy battered chintz sofas, a traditional dining room conservatively furnished with sensible tables and sturdy chairs with faded velvet seats, and long dimly lit corridors with numbered panelled doors. The hotel stood imposingly on the side of a mountain at the top of a long winding drive, looking across the valley to a famously beautiful lake with distant mountains beyond. The view was spectacular and the hotel stood in some acres of pleasant grounds, with terraces, a stream, and a putting green. It was magical! The fells reared up behind the hotel, with rocky steep pastures and shaggy sheep, dark fir plantations and chill mountain streams.

Uncle Vivian, as he frequently reminded his relatives on their annual visit, had no wish to run a hotel for travelling salesmen. His was a robust traditional family hotel to which his guests often returned year after year, metamorphosing over time from honeymoon couple to young married and then family with children. Repeat business was his forté. He used to say that he could not think of a nicer occupation than the hotel business. "My guests want comfort, pleasure and peace, and I enjoy providing them with what they seek. Everyone is happy – what could be better?"

He was an expansive genial man, generous but not unwisely so, an astute businessman and a good hotelier. He and his wife, who was an excellent caterer and cook, worked hard and they did well. His secret for success was: clean bedrooms nicely furnished (but not too luxurious), with good nourishing food (though not too exotic) and at a realistic affordable price.

'Full house'

Vivian came from a large family whom he adored. He was one of seven siblings – five brothers and two sisters. He had married Jean, a laconic industrious woman, but they had not had children. He never appeared to regret this, but instead bestowed his love and largess on his relatives. One of his brothers had died as a child, one had left to live in India as a young man, and another now lived in Canada. His elder sister had been a famous beauty and had married a wealthy businessman, from who she rapidly became estranged, taking her one son with her to live in a claustrophobic flat in New York. His much younger brother, Godfrey, lived in Swansea with a beautiful wife and three children. The younger sister, Maureen, was his favourite sibling and she had married an antique dealer and lived in Bristol, and they too had three children. These last two families were the ones who were invited to The Fells each spring, and whom, as Molly often used to bemoan, their uncle "thoroughly spoilt".

'Three of a kind'

Molly shooed the six children out of the dining room, and told them to go outside and get some fresh air. They rather

270

enjoyed her mock disapproval and mild discipline, because they knew, with the confidence of fortunate children whose families gave them time and love, that really she adored them. They ran out into the garden, squawking and strutting about like chickens emerging from their henhouse. Sooner or later Chris or his cousin Geoff, the two oldest, would be voted the leader for the day and call the shots.

Molly had joined the husband and wife hotel team as a young woman and had never left. It seemed as if she could do everything – she took orders and served at tables, organised the laundry and cleaning, answered the telephone and typed letters, worked in reception and ran the games room bar after dinner. The younger children never quite questioned why Molly was in such a position of authority, though their parents were well aware that this attractive but formidable woman was the power behind the throne. She was Uncle Vivian's secretary, right-arm, confidante and mistress. Jean, an intelligent but undemonstrative woman, knew all about Molly and her husband, and viewed the liaison with amused tolerance and perhaps some relief, as it freed more time for her bridge sessions, her flowers and her painting. Indeed she liked the younger woman. Nevertheless she did not allow Molly to trespass in her kitchen – that was her domain, as was the garden.

Molly was an attractive plump woman, slightly sloppy in appearance but "oozing sensuality", as Geoff put it, whilst slightly unsure of what he meant by this. She was an indolent person who forced herself to work hard. She adored Vivian with an unswerving devotion over many years – she was argumentative, kind, sharp-tongued and selfish but above all, passionately in love with her boss. Over the years she became absorbed into the family sometimes as a daughter and sometimes as another wife. It was an uncomplicated ménage à trois – the three of them occupied separate numbered hotel bedrooms in different parts of the upper floors – and they worked, ate and lived together in harmony and mutual affection, with only the occasional tiff when jealously briefly intruded on their habitual good-natured tolerance. In recent years, the older children had

271

become aware of the slightly unconventional arrangement and in private sniggered about it, and spent hours spying on Molly and their uncle, trying to catch them out.

'I'll see you'

After breakfast, the "Fells Gang" met to decide what they were going to do. Their parents had gone off together for the day, leaving the siblings and cousins to their own devices – under Molly's vague supervision. She was content to let them play unfettered in the grounds, her only stricture was that they should not stray too far from the hotel.

The two sets of parents felt they deserved a respite from entertaining their young. The day before, Godfrey, leaving his wife reading her book in their room, had driven his three children on one of the ritual family excursions up a narrow mountain road to Ashness, from where thoughtless Geoff had leant out over the sheer cliff above Ladore Falls, torturing his father who suffered from vertigo. Dan had collected a number of oddly-shaped stones which he piled in the boot. Then, siblings squabbling in a battered car, they had continued up to Watendlath at the end of the road, and ruined its peaceful tranquilly with raucous shouts and coltish wild behaviour. Carrie, sitting on a gate, observed as her boisterous brothers ran riot, and then they left, the echoes of their insensitive exhibitionism fading with the noise of the car engine as they departed from that quiet place.

Maureen, on her own because her husband had a headache, had taken her brood up to the top of the grim and grey Honister Pass, another annual escapade. Here they always stopped to run along the rusty rail tracks and explore the old slate quarry workings. Freddie had unearthed a rotten sheep's skull, and Chris had fallen, cutting himself on a rock. He and Ella slithered down the unstable slopes with fear and exultation, whilst their mother leant against the car smoking a cigarette and watching, trying to conceal her anxiety and pride.

'Straight Flush'

On the morning of Chris's birthday, the activity they chose involved using the bike he had received from his parents. They had given it to him at the start of the holiday – it had travelled up on the roof of their car – so that he and Geoff (who had brought his bike too) could go biking together. Though obviously second or even third hand, the bike was robust though it had no gears. Geoff's bike seemed to have no brakes. In a shed near the dustbins round the back of the hotel kitchen, Freddie had found an battered cart on four small wheels, and this gave them the idea of having races down the drive.

The little ones, Dan and his cousin Ella were banned from participating, because, at nine and ten, they were "too young". Though disappointed, the pair chose to spend the morning down at the stream building dams, diverting water and creating a miniature island. The day before they had amused themselves hiding in the bamboo clumps and making houses in the long grass in the adjacent field. Dan was passionate about construction and water-courses, and would spend hours down in this heavenly haven, long after Ella had become bored and wandered off to play in the hollow oak.

At the top of the drive or racetrack, Carrie was deputed to be the official starter, but soon she got bored with this role, and wandered off to sit on the terrace, and read her "Lays of Ancient Rome" in the spring sunshine, escaping into her beloved world of gods and goddesses whilst avoiding the boisterous boys, bruised legs, and the inevitable arguments.

Chris and Geoff, hurtling down the long steep drive at breakneck speeds spraying gravel and grit as they braked, crashed into the undergrowth when they lost it on a corner, or shot out of the drive entrance into the main road. Then they toiled up to the top and did it all over again, passing Freddie descending in his wobbly cart, as they pushed their bikes back up to the top. Chris thought it brilliant fun to frighten guests as they walked under the trees or drove their cars slowly up the long drive to the hotel. Emerging at speed from round a bend, red-faced from the wind in his face, he shot straight past them, shrieking with aggression and fuelled with adrenalin.

Around noon the children converged on the hotel, thirsty and hungry, and went straight to the place where these needs could be met – where everyone congregated, and where everything happened.

This was the owner's sitting room. It had two doors: one which was panelled opened into the main hall and reception area, and the other, baize-covered, led into a corridor leading to the dining room. This room was the nerve centre of the whole operation. At one end was the hotel office with an old desk piled high with papers where occasionally Molly would sit, looking disapprovingly over her spectacles at anyone in the room who was disturbing her. There was a sagging leather sofa, a large armchair (sacrosanct as no-one sat in it except uncle Vivian) and a round dining table with a number of mismatching upright chairs, at which occasional informal meals were taken but which was also used for evening card games. A pair of French windows, with brown velvet curtains, opened out onto a terrace and looked across to the small putting green.

This room was marked "Private" on both doors, but it was not secluded at all. Quite the opposite. Though the paying hotel guests never intruded, the family used it all the time. Jean chatted to her bridge-laying friends whilst sitting on the sofa. Uncle Vivian watched the racing on his small television. Molly bustled in with drinks and snacks. It was where family read newspapers, smoked, chatted and drank coffee. The children instinctively knew that this was a place where noisy games were not allowed. It was where decisions were taken about plans for the day, and it was where they could always locate someone with information about meal times, lost gum boots, who had borrowed the comics, and where one could find a plaster. This room was the hub of the hotel and it drew the family like a magnet. The children slouched on the sofa – if someone else hadn't got there first, or lay on the floor reading a book. They chatted to anyone who was in the room who cared to listen, played patience at the table, and "stole" the peanuts and crisps unaware that these had been put out for them.

Just before lunch, there was the exciting announcement that the two uncles were going to include Geoff and Chris in a game of poker that evening. This was a family ritual from which the children had been excluded until now. They had been given lessons in the game and had been allowed to stay up and watch, but now the older boys were to be allowed to join in the adult game. The year before Vivian had taught them the rules of poker, which they eagerly assimilated together with the jargon. Uncle Vivian played only draw poker, saying he had no time for "fancy stud poker". This year he had told them about the betting, explaining that the game of poker had two parts: the original staking – deciding whether to play or not, and the betting after the cards were drawn.

The first part, he told them, was mathematical, and the second psychological.

"Your bets are determined by how you read the way in which the other players are behaving, and by your judgement as to how the others are reading you." He grinned, putting his hand on Chris's shoulder. "This is where you need a poker face, old son."

"What's that?" asked Geoff, wanting to get his uncle's attention.

"A face devoid of expression, so that the other players won't be able to guess what you have or what you might do." Vivian tapped the boy's chest, " You might find that hard, Geoff, but it's vital."

Freddie, aged twelve and the accepted boffin of the gang, who wanted to be a psychoanalyst, was a little disappointed to be excluded. So he announced that he had evolved a theory that each member of the family belonged in one of the four suits: spades, hearts, diamonds and clubs. He would be formulating his hypothesis and making his classifications during the day and after the poker session that night. This gave him a cast iron reason for staying up to watch the entire game.

'Ace high'

As the weather was fine, the six children were given a packed lunch, which they ate together sitting on the stone wall which bordered the terrace. Dan was trying to persuade Ella to swap her chocolate bar for his apple, and Freddie was busy airing his views and pursuing his theory about personalities and suits. "Chris is very competitive and loves to win. He wants power and bullies us into agreeing to his mad schemes." At this point Freddie pulled up his jeans and showed Carrie the bruises and grazes he had sustained during the morning's crazy racing down the drive. "Chris," he concluded, "Is definitely a Club – probably the Jack of Clubs."

"What am I?" shouted Dan

"What about me?" squeaked Ella.

Recalling that Dan had trailed up the path at the end of that morning, covered in mud, pleading with his siblings to come and see the canal he had dug from the pond, Freddie promptly declared his younger cousin to be Spade, whilst his little sister who adored helping people and feeding animals was certainly a Heart.

"Uncle Vivian is, of course, the Ace of Hearts," Freddie proclaimed, and they all nodded in agreement.

'Have a flutter'

In the afternoon, all of the children decided to walk up the fells on Skiddaw, behind the hotel. This was Carrie's domain and she was queen for the afternoon. When she wasn't immersed in her many books of myths and legends that she so adored, the fourteen year old, who later danced her way round Europe, used to race up the steep pastures and along the mountain stream in bare feet leaping like a joyful mountain goat from stone to tussock to hummock, her face radiant with health and excitement. None of the others could catch her as she ran through the birch wood weaving her way round the slender pale trunks, laughing, calling, "Catch me if you can." And they tried. But they couldn't. Further up there were waterfalls where she enthroned herself on a rock high above the others, her straw hair tangled and wet with spray, her smile flowing down towards her minions, her long legs gleaming through the bushes and her giggles babbling over the stones.

276

Carrie, distantly benign, laughingly elusive, languidly beautiful was idolized by her youngest cousin, little Ella. Aloof from the ragged band of devotees who followed her golden lead up the mountain, like an exotic bird Carrie floated on silver streams and chose not to dive into deep waters. Who needed dark dangers when there was an airy element up there to inhabit? Geoff, with his anguished introspection and frustrated ambition to appear calm and worldly-wise, envied his sister her joie de vivre, that luminous unconcern, her careless confidence. Carrie was unmistakably a Diamond, thought Freddie.

'Bluffing'

On their return from the fells, at around teatime, the tired children descended on their uncle's sitting room. There they were confronted with a large iced cake with fifteen candles on it. There was a rowdy rendering of "Happy Birthday", after which Chris dramatically blew out all his candles and almost set light to the paper cake frill. He then stabbed the large cake knife into the middle of the cake and hacked off a couple of huge and uneven slices, before Molly grabbed it from him and took over.

The hungry children gobbled their cake and slopped their orange squash, leaving crumbs on the sofa and mud on the carpet. Though Vivian was remarkably tolerant of the havoc they played in his domain, Aunt Jean was less easy-going, but usually ignored them rather than let them annoy her unduly – she knew their visit was short and soon the normal calm tenor of life would be resumed. No-nonsense Molly called them "untidy grubby kids" as they tumbled out of the room. Freddie whispered to Carrie that Molly was plainly a Club.

Uncle Vivian's sitting room was also used as a short cut. It was quicker to nip through it to the dining room if late for dinner. It knocked off thirty seconds getting to the front hall from the back service stairs. It was a very neat route to the terrace if one wanted to avoid encountering guests or if one wanted to bag the putting green ahead of them. It was an arterial road junction, and they darted through it all day long.

About an hour later, Dan ran though en route for the terrace. Uncle Vivian was sitting quietly in his big battered chair with his eyes half closed, seemingly dozing, but as his nephew hurtled past, his arm shot out and clutched an arm, holding it fast in an iron grip. How Dan squirmed, how he wriggled, how he loved it! The benign uncle looked into the boy's eyes, and uttered one word, "Stop." This was a game, and Dan knew he had to freeze and remain immobile for exactly two minutes at the end of which he would be released, when he could leap and lunge away, shrieking with laughter and delight. In fact the children often ran past their uncle's chair just to see if he would catch them, but he didn't always rise to the bait, which made the game so much more delightfully unpredictable. Vivian had great affection for his brother's and his sister's children. He was sometime stern, often fun, and they loved him.

'A pair of aces'

The children ate supper with their parents at a large table in the dining room.

Geoff and Chris were excited about their admission to the poker game that night, and were warned again by their parents that poker chips were not used, and the family tradition meant that real money was bet at table. Not large sums, but one had to be careful. Uncle Vivian had a huge jar filled with coins, and those playing could exchange notes and large coins for smaller coins to bet with. Another rule was that no one lent or borrowed money. If you lost all that you had brought to the table to play with, then you left the game.

After the meal, Maureen and her husband went down to the hotel bar and games room to play table tennis with the youngest children, before sending them upstairs to bed. Carrie and her mother, an elegant woman who didn't care for cards, joined them and they sat around, chatting to Molly who was working behind the bar that evening.

The poker players assembled in the sitting room, and the game got underway.

278

There were five round the table, their faces illuminated by a hanging light positioned overhead, their modest sums of betting money in front of them on the wooden surface. The brothers, Godfrey and Vivian, were alike to look at, plump cheeked, bright eyes and thinning grey hair, but very different in personality. Whilst Vivian was a gregarious, smiling optimist, his brother was more pensive and pessimistic. They both enjoyed a game of poker and played well, one always expecting to win, whilst the other felt he would probably lose.

The two boys, proud to be playing their first game of adult poker, behaved very differently: Chris leaning forward, jumpy, excited, his eyes darting around, whilst Geoff sat upright, holding his cards carefully and playing with watchful care. Jean, her glasses on the end of her large nose, cigarette holder in hand, played her cards coolly and decisively. Freddie, on his feet, keen to learn more about the game so that he might be permitted to join the following year, lurked behind the sitting players, forbidden to comment on anyone's hand. In his mind, he dubbed Jean a hard Diamond, whilst dogged Godfrey was a probably a Spade.

'Raise the stakes'

An hour and a half later, the game was still progressing. Maureen and Molly had returned to the room, and Maureen was trying to signal to her brothers that the boys were tired and that the game should be coming to an end. Vivian and Jean were clearly winning, Godfrey was nearly out of money though his son Geoff had been lucky and still had plenty to play with. Chris was obviously losing, an intense and desperate look on his face. He had just lost to Jean, his Two Pairs no match for her Straight.

"Always see but never raise a one-card buy," admonished Vivian. "I've told you that before." Chris nodded jerkily, irritated with himself, but still fascinated by the game. He could cope with bad luck, but his mistakes made him feel bitter.

Three hands later Chris, after drawing three cards to his

pair of queens, saw with glee that he had a Full House with three queens and two eights. Geoff and Jean were not playing the hand, having thrown in after the draw. The betting started. Chris was trying ineffectually to conceal his excitement. Vivian was playing with an air of confidence, and in the next round of betting Godfrey dropped out. Chris was almost out of money but knew he had a winning hand. Vivian, with an amused, slightly wicked glint in his eyes, kept raising, and the bets got higher and the pot got bigger. Chris, determined to win more off his wily old uncle, pulled the birthday tenner out of his pocket and slapped it down in front of him.

Geoff gasped, and Maureen sighed. Jean was imperturbable but Freddie could hardly contain himself. His brother was going to fleece his uncle!

"I'll raise you," he said fiercely and recklessly, instead of matching Vivian's stake and saying, "I'll see you."

The older man smiled and, slowly opening his wallet, he drew out a twenty pound note. Looking into Chris's flushed face, he said quietly, "I'll see your ten and raise you another ten."

'Throw your hand in'

Chris looked stunned, as he realised he had less than a pound in front of him

And the house rules meant that no one could lend him any more.

"You can't do this to me," he pleaded.

"Oh yes I can," his uncle, with a serious but sympathetic look on his face.

Chris lost it. With a snarl, he slammed his cards down on the table face up to show to everyone his beautiful Full House.

Quietly his uncle, closed the cards in his hand, put them face down on the table, and leant forward scooping up the stake money, including his nephew's birthday ten pound note. Godfrey closed his eyes, as if sharing his nephew's pain.

"I know I've lost," moaned Chris. "What did you have then?"

"You weren't able to see me, so that's my affair," replied his uncle.

"You were bluffing. I know you were bluffing," agonised Chris.

Freddie, having watched this drama, was furious. He ran round the table, and stood accusingly over Uncle Vivian. "That's mean and horrible. I thought you had a heart, that you were a Heart. But I'm wrong. You're really a nasty Joker!" He ran out of the room, banging the door behind him.

The game was over. Geoff felt awkward, concerned for his cousin, who was sitting with his head theatrically in his hands, whilst the others softly cleared the cards off the table.

Maureen walked over to the mantelpiece, and leant against it. "Time for bed, boys." Jean lit up another cigarette and adjusted in its black holder. Godfrey polished his glasses and gave a melancholy sigh.

Chris slowly raised his head, and stared vengefully at his uncle. He had to get his own back. He needed to strike out and hurt the older man. He suddenly recalled a moment he had witnessed the evening after they had arrived at the hotel, a snapshot glimpse of Vivian and Molly embracing in the dim corridor between the pantry and the back service stairs. It had been a fleeting embarrassment but now it was a weapon.

'He's had his chips'

"You're a cheat," Chris spat out the dirty word. "You cheat at cards, and you cheat on your wife. I've seen you and Molly – kissing." He looked round desperately, to see the effect of his accusation, his revelation, his bad manners.

Jean stared at him, drew on her cigarette in its holder and blew out smoke unconcernedly. Molly, standing behind Chris where she had been watching the final hand, grinned and cuffed him over the head, Godfrey took off his glasses and started to clean them intently, and Uncle Vivian roared with laughter and said, "I never cheat. But I do break the rules – I'm lucky in cards and lucky in love!" He reached over and took Jean's hand, smiling across at Molly.

Chris, blinking back tears of rage, disappointment and loss, muttered something inarticulate and rushed from the room. There was a moment's silence.

"How about a glass of port, old man?" said Vivian to his younger brother.

Godfrey said quietly, "That, Vivian, was a bit cruel. It was the kid's birthday. I think you ought to return the tenner."

"Certainly not," said Vivian. "It's a part of my grand scheme to put them all off gambling forever."

"Some of your schemes," interposed Jean dryly, "Are doomed to failure. Such as your campaign to make me give up smoking."

"You really should stop, my dear. It's very character building."

"Don't be ridiculous, Vivian. My character's already cast in stone." And Jean leant back and blew a perfect smoke ring, which drifted upwards whilst her husband and his brother drank their port, and Molly cleared the table, her mascara smudged with tears.

* * * * *

'Winner of the pot'

But the "Fells Gang" had short memories and they came back for more in subsequent years, when Freddie and Carrie were allowed to join in. The young people often lost their money but not their taste for the game. The pride of being treated as an adult and being allowed to gamble and lose their money (and not get given it back) was slightly greater than the pain of losing. Vivian's crushing defeat of Chris was counterproductive as it only sharpened the boy's desire to beat his uncle at cards. And from time to time, when luck favoured him, he did win, though he never really managed to play his cards close to his chest! Freddie learnt how to assume a neutral face and became quietly adept at bluffing, whilst Geoff played a safe game, and Carrie didn't care whether she won or lost – it was all light-hearted fun.

And so cousins learned to play better poker, to cope with setbacks, flout rules, and claw their way out of difficult situations. On their visits north, they still ran wild, but stayed up later, moved on from games of "Sardines" to "Murder in the Dark", had forbidden drink and parties in their hotel rooms, and indulged in lengthy discussions about life. They grew up and spread their wings, their paths taking diverging directions. In different ways they became risk-takers, exhilarated and motivated by chance and danger.

Chris became a gambler, won and lost fortunes, but though often in debt, lived his life on the edge, and enjoyed a freedom from convention and responsibilities that others often envied. His brother, Freddie, moving on from his early interest in psychology, ended up working for a hedge fund dealing in futures, whilst his sister, Ella became an archaeologist and delved into the past, both occupations involving speculation and uncertainty. Carrie after her dancing career, led a happy hand-to-mouth life running a bar on a Greek island, whilst Dan, surprisingly, became mountain climber and guide, but also indulged in extreme sports, such as kite boarding and off-piste skiing. Geoff, his doubts and soul-searching transformed into faith at an Alpha course, trained as a teacher and went off to work at a mission school in Africa to risk all serving his God.

Their uncle Vivian grew older, running his hotel, pleasing his guests, and mildly addicted to his lottery tickets, Saturday racing and football pools, not to mention enjoying the occasional game of poker. A sentimental man, he missed round his table the young faces of those he loved, though he never said so. They rarely, if ever, came to visit him, having moved on or far away. He had meant to give them fun whilst teaching them caution, but they learnt instead that life was a gamble and that if they plunged into it with enthusiasm, it would never be dull.

WET FLOOR

Wet Floor

My mind wanders and recalls a child's computer game that my son used to enjoy.

It was called Theme Hospital and the player had to design and construct a hospital, plan budgets, install equipment and insert staff. Computerised puppet people dressed as nurses, doctors and porters tripped busily to and fro in an ordered and antiseptic world of medical fantasy. At odd moments, a toneless voice would make brief announcements such as "Doctor wanted in Casualty" or "Nurse to the Treatment Room."

Tonight I am in a real hospital that is a distorted echo of that distant virtual world. I have been lying on a trolley bed in Treatment Room Number 309 for some hours, having been smoothly delivered here on silent rubber wheels. I lie below a bright fluorescent light and beneath a white cover. I am a little worried but not as frightened as I was earlier on.

It's a January evening and I was taken ill whilst attending a performance of "The Mikado" in the local town. After the embarrassment of locating a "doctor in the house", and the discomfort of being removed on a stretcher, I surrendered myself to that old familiar pain. During my half-hour journey in the ambulance, a paramedic who said his name was Steve told me he has seen the "Phantom of the Opera" nine times. He used to work in the Sheffield ambulance service for seventeen years before coming south. He prefers it here because people talk to him instead of grunting. I tried to respond but he swept on to tell me that he had worked on New Year's Eve and picked up an eighteen year old boy with a crushed head who later died. He paused with a baffled look before leaning over to check that I was alright. Then he said that his wife was expecting again – in May. He was obviously a kind man but his non-sequiturs were confusing. Or perhaps I missed

287

the bits in between which would have made sense of it all. My hearing seemed to have diminished, and I felt unwell and disorientated.

"You alright, mate?" Steve's face hovered over mine.

I tried to nod but it hurt my head, so I whispered, "Yes." This was plainly silly, because I am clearly not at all right. Or else I wouldn't have been there hurtling through the dark countryside in a white rectangle on wheels. But his concern was comforting and he gave me a pat on the arm before telling me that he went to the Costa del Sol on holiday last year. I gave up – we were clearly not on the same wavelength.

I drifted off but jerked awake when the vehicle came to a sharp halt. Cold air and consciousness rushed in when the driver opened the rear doors. With care and diligence I was smoothly extricated and propelled towards the entrance of Accident and Emergency. As I passed through big doors, I felt as if they were sliding me into a warm oven, rather than a hospital. I managed to murmur my thanks. Just before I was trundled off squeakily down a long bright corridor, Steve said, "See yer, mate." Which is unlikely. But he might, I suppose.

Time passes. I close my eyes – it's rather bright in here. A nurse came by shortly after they shunted me into this siding and jabbed a needle in my arm, saying something about a blood test to which I did not manage a reply. She also gave me a couple of tablets. I no longer feel nauseous. I'm in a vacuum, lulled by the hum and clatter outside my door. All is pale and immovable here. I don't really mind waiting. The pain seems to have subsided a little.

Later on I watch those who pass outside my door, walking up and down. Occasionally they glance at me, furtively – hoping I will not catch their eye and summon them. I'm aware of my habit of averting my eyes to avoid involvement, so I feel a distant affinity with these figures and ponder the unlikely possibility that we might have something in common. But of course they see me as different and damaged – a sick prone middle-aged man with his knees drawn up to lessen a pain in the gut. And this is what I am. I have not had an accident. I am bowed but unbloody.

At length, after many footsteps, glasses of water and promises from various nursing staff, I see one of the medics. A small neat Indian doctor steps in to my room. He speaks to me. *They* are sorry that I have been kept waiting. I'm not sure who he is, and in answer to my request for his name, he tells me he is from Hyderabad and seems surprised when I tell him I have heard of it.

Examination over, he says *they* are waiting for some results and gives me something to sleep. Upon enquiry some time later, I am told *they* are trying to find me a bed in a ward. Who is this amorphous *'they'*, I wonder. My headache seems to be receding, and medication has taken the sharp edge off my pain. Thankfully.

A student nurse befriends me, and confides that this is her first night shift. Her plump face is alight with goodwill and curiosity. She tucks in the blanket needlessly. I am far too hot. But I don't protest – it is, after all, her first night. Feeling a little more communicative, I tell her that I am surprised to find the hospital so comparatively silent.

"It's a far cry," I say, "From the frenetic, hectic, TV drama 'Casualty'...... where it's all noise and confusion. Here everything seems ..... calm and efficient. Except for the delay...... in finding me a bed. And that doesn't really matter ...... because I have all night." Why do I sound so jerky when I feel quite calm?

She shows her teeth and says brightly, "I'm sure it won't be long now." I smile back to reassure her that her crumb of comfort has not gone unappreciated. She is a pretty little person. And I am a male patient. I rarely make a fuss. I am a patient man. I am faintly amused at my own pun.

Some hours pass. There is no natural light here so I don't know if dawn has come. The overhead light remains constant. Someone must have removed my watch. I feel stiff. The doctor, looking tired, returns. He has the results of my blood test. I am slightly disappointed to discover that the bacteria, which have caused my high fever, are commonplace and not rare or special. But *they* are nasty and vicious. That's why I feel so ill, he tells me. Soon I will be moved. *They* have found me a space.

I am finally transported to a ward and a bed – of rest, I hope. But this is not to be. A male nurse asks me dozens of questions and I get a bit irritable as all I want to do is sleep. Yes, I have had my appendix out. No, I do not have a wife. Next of kin? None. Or the whole world.

I now feel worse. My wrist has been connected up to some plastic tubes and a hanging bag of fluid. I am given some tablets "to make me feel more comfortable." The bed seems almost as hard as the trolley. At last I am allowed to close my eyes and try to ignore the pain that has crept up on me unawares. I feel as if I am sliding sideways – out of my own vision.

I hear a voice, and cautiously open one eye. I am lying down and I can see the white pillow rearing up on the right hand side of my face, and the white sheet rising up over my arm on my left. Both are blurred. I feel as if I am in a crevasse, and can see only a small 'V' of the outside picture. There is a shiny clean surface, and a notice propped up on it, on which, if I screw up my eyes, I can see the word: "Floor". That's good to know. I'd probably have guessed anyhow, as I can also see a pair of shoes on it and two feet standing in them. Why would they want to label something so obvious? Am I in some sort of asylum where inmates are so deranged they need a notice saying "Window" sitting on the window sill, or a placard announcing "Ceiling" hanging from the ceiling? My brain hurts with the effort of trying to work this out. I have no inclination to move my head but merely contemplate this curious oblique slice of vision.

After a while I close my eyes. A few minutes – or hours – later I hear a voice saying, "Just doin' under your bed." I cautiously open my eyes and focus on a small woman in a blue overall thrusting a long pole around underneath me. She straightens up, pulling her mop back into view, and sees me watching her. "Awake then, are we?"

She recedes and I widen my vista by moving my arm to open up the gap between my pillow and my bedclothes. I see the woman push her mop into a plastic pail a few feet further away. Amid the squishing sounds, she tells me, "I'm Ada." When I don't respond with a chummy greeting, she realises that there's little chance of a chat with me. So she bustles with her mop across the ward and interrupts a man sitting up in bed reading a newspaper. "How's it going' then?"

"Much better, Ada," he says without looking up. He is clearly trying to avoid lengthy communication.

"Goin' 'ome soon, then?" she enquires.

"That's right. This afternoon, after the doctors have been round and confirmed my discharge." He still hasn't looked at her, and she's hopping and mopping up and down in front of him.

"Well, that's done for today. See yer all tomorrer." She drags her pail and mop out of view, and then comes back and picks up the notice with its superfluous information. I see it is actually a cone and reads "Wet Floor". With a clatter and a large sniff she is gone.

Time passes.

I wake up when a nurse wheels in a metal stand and connects me to another sachet of fluid which will drip into my vein. She plumps up my pillows, and asks me if I would like to have supper. So it's the afternoon. What happened to the morning? I wonder. Feeling somewhat better, I sit up and look around. This is a side ward containing four beds. Only three are occupied. The man who was reading the paper has now gone, and his bed is empty. There are clearly other parts of the ward as there are a lot of voices, bleeps and background noise in the general vicinity. Nurses in a variety of different uniforms move around. One of them comes in to take my temperature, pulse and blood pressure, and says she is Debbie. She is gentle and smiles encouragingly at me. Shortly afterwards, a young man in green cotton pyjamas comes in to plonk a tray on a trolley table, which he slides across my lap.

I look around. Opposite me under a humped white sheet is an old man who is clearly agitated. I have been aware for some time of whimpering noises and restless movements from across the ward. Bars on each side of his bed have been raised to prevent his falling out. He has been turned over, washed, propped up, lain down, and soothed, poor indignity. Though clearly very frail he is trying to get out – it seems he wants to go for a pee. Debbie gently and with infinite patience reassures him that he has a catheter and does not need to exert himself and get up. There is pallid bafflement on his face as he struggles with his covers and croaks, "Let me out."

A few minutes pass, Debbie reappears. "Lie down, Gordon. Lie down." The poor man rattles the bars of his cage and thumps his mattress in his distress. The nurse repeats with calm patience, "Lie down." He sags back dwarfed by his pile of pillows. Later on, when a sandwich arrives for his supper two other nurses decide to sit him up. The old man is roused by this and leans forward trying to rise.

"Sit up. Lean back. Sit up and lean back," the green dressed nursing duo chant. The repetition seems to lull Gordon, and having given up any attempt to eat his sad little sandwich, he sinks into listless acceptance, making small sighs and grunts.

I have been watching this spectacle with growing horror. If we live too long, do we all come to this? A voice on my left cuts into my sombre thoughts and asks me if I am feeling better. I turn to see a man – probably in his early forties – with a bandage around his head and right eye. I respond to this friendly enquiry, and we have a brief exchange about why we are both in here. It seems that my neighbour is recovering from an operation two days ago, and he is waiting for inflammation to reduce before he can leave hospital. His one visible eye is very red.

I pick at my meal, and later on after the regular monitoring checks carried out by Debbie, who then puts up another sachet of antibiotics to drip down the tube into my arm, I slide down and try to sleep. Unlike A & E downstairs, in this ward the night is punctuated by low conversation, harsh croaks, chinking teacups, sonorous bells, footsteps, buzzing telephones and voices, voices, voices. At some point a newcomer is wheeled in and deposited in the bed next to Gordon. The figure is comatose and snoring quite loudly. The night nurses bend over him, solicitously talk in low voices, and then leave. Amazingly, I manage to sleep.

The next morning, the horrid choking and retching sound of someone vomiting wakes me. It is the latest arrival, and a nurse is beside his hunched figure, holding the bowl and murmuring soothingly. With a gasp the patient sits up and wipes his mouth with a tissue the nurse hands to him. He is a young man with a pallid spotty complexion; his skin looks waxy and he is shaking. He is clearly in an ill humour because, instead of thanking the nurse, he glares at her and tells her to leave him alone. She quietly withdraws carrying the bowl and a towel, and he sits there staring straight ahead, looking bloated, bleary and belligerent. Later on, I discover that he has taken an overdose of some drug. This evokes general disapproval and, as he is in no mood to communicate and mention any mitigating reasons, he is forfeiting any chance of eliciting sympathy.

The next episode in the daily saga of hospital life is the re-appearance of the pert and chatty little cleaner who was here yesterday. "Hello boys. 'Ow are we all today?" She plonks her bucket with its mop on the floor and then proceeds to wash the ward floor with brisk and efficient strokes. She pauses when half way across and leans on her mop. She catches my eye – I can see she is aching for a natter. Today I am happy to oblige. "'Ow long've you bin in 'ere?" she asks.

I pause to work it out. "Well, it must be about a day and a half including a longish spell in A & E." She nods, and wrings out the mop.

"So, are you goin' ter ask me how long I've bin 'ere?" she says. What does she mean? I wonder if she starts very early in the morning or if her working hours are too long. She chortles on, "I've bin here for twenty-nine years. And there ain't a single ward in this place that I 'aven't cleaned a thousand times." She fixes me with a triumphant look as if to say, "Cap that one!"

I murmur, "That's amazing." Which it is, totally.

"The name's Ada," she reminds me. Within minutes I have her life history. Widowed at the age of thirty-one with four children, she started work cleaning in a pie factory and then came to work at this hospital. She is 64, rides a bike to work and retires next year. She has seven grandchildren one of whom is a physiotherapist. She rents a small flat from the council. "I don't 'ave many things. I came with nuffing and I'll go aht with nuffing."

"Red Eye" next door has clearly been deluged with the same information when he was well enough, and he is carefully keeping his eye averted. Now it's my turn.

"People are wot's important," Ada announces. "Family and friends." And everyone in this hospital is her friend, she claims. The place is her second home. She gives me a detailed description of all the wards and rooms she "does" and has "done" for nearly three decades. She is worn down to the end of her mop, she says, dramatically shaking it. This reminds her that the current task is unfinished and she continues washing the rest of the floor area, humming tunelessly. With frizzy hair, varicose veins and a big heart, the woman is a saint.

She gives me a cheeky grin, and marches off with pail and mop, only to return seconds later with her cone and its warning: "Wet Floor", which she plops in the centre of her shiny floor. "See yer tomorrer," she says in a singsong tone and exits stage left, without a bow and determined to ignore any request for a curtain call.

I lie there stunned by the diminutive dynamo and her cheerful pride in a dreary repetitive daily task that she has been doing for nearly half her life. I vaguely recall a hymn that I used to know which mentions a servant who "makes drudgery divine," sweeping a room as if it's for God and his law. I decide to ask her tomorrow whether she is a "Believer". That should bring an interesting response.

Afternoon has come round again, and Debbie, blonde and busy, though not beautiful, is back on the ward with her kind smile, her plump legs and an update on last night's soap. My neighbour, Red Eye, humours her by pretending interest. I discover his name is Malcolm when I hear her address him – no one in hospital uses surnames any more, it seems. She asks me how I am, and I say I am less tired today. She tells me cheerfully that she often feels tired as she's on her feet all day. Someone calls her, and off she goes, an overweight angel on castors.

Visiting time. Of course, I have no visitors because I've made it clear I don't want anyone to be informed. My sister Amy died last year, and my brother Tom lives in Singapore. I wouldn't want him contacted – we are as distant emotionally as we are physically. I am retired and therefore have no work colleagues who need to know my whereabouts. The few friends I used to know have faded away discouraged by my lack of communication. I choose to absent myself from places where conversation might be forced upon me. I prefer to keep people at arm's length.

Though I'm not sure that my arm – and perhaps the rest of me – isn't becoming attached not just to my drip, but also to the whole hospital experience. The novelty of having other people around me hasn't yet worn off. My stay here seems like a brief appearance on a public stage during a lifetime of private obscurity. It disturbs me that I find this untidy episode not uncongenial. Could this Theme Hospital be substantially authentic – the genuine article? And could it be that my habitual solitude is the retreat from reality?

This train of thought makes me uncomfortable. I don't want disorderly life to upset the even tenor of my quiet days alone. I don't want to contemplate the possibility that I might have got things wrong. That my withdrawal from the world – apart from the weekly shopping nightmare or the occasional pleasant evening at a concert when I can listen without conversing – might mean I'm missing out.

To put an end to these disquieting reflections, I look across at the old man who has three visitors, all of whom he is miserably unaware.

"Poor Dad, " I hear one of them say. "Poor old Dad." Perhaps the old boy has had a fall or has a terminal illness. Are his relative gathered for the end? They look awkward and sad. The bed's occupant stirs and groans, and opens his eyes for a few seconds, inducing nervous laughter on the part of those sitting beside him. Eventually one of them rises to her feet, and pats the cover, "Well, we must be off now, Dad." Pat, pat. They all prepare to depart, looking relieved at their imminent release. The other woman offers advice, "Take care of yourself, Gordon," whilst the man chimes in ludicrously with, "Keep smiling." It must be obvious to anyone that the invalid can do neither of these things. They leave.

"The Addict" in the corner, recovering from his overdose, glares across at "Red Eye" and me. With his pinched desperate face, he is surly with the nurses, rude to the doctor and angry at the world – as represented by the others in the ward. The nurses, usually so kind, are losing patience with his ill humour. During supper, he purposefully tips his bowl of soup, a bilious green colour, into his bed. The nurses mutter and glower in the doorway – this is the third time they will have to change his bed linen. One of them says to the other that he can lie in his own mess, as far as she is concerned. But they soon relent and clean him up – again.

I am surprised and touched by the tolerance and good-humoured care that most of the nursing staff display. This afternoon Debbie sat beside "Poor Dad" and stroked his arm for half an hour to calm him down. This croaking, demented specimen of aging humanity is not just an object of pity but a focus for her attention and tenderness. How do the nurses manage the daily repetition of tedious chores and menial labour? Yet for the most part they do – with chirpy good humour, quiet sympathy, or brusque efficiency. To do this job they must genuinely care about other human beings. Which I don't!

Am I that hard hearted? I feel the stirrings of an old internal debate that I long ago managed to suppress. "Play safe, beware, don't get involved," says a warning voice deep within. But a lighter voice chimes in that life without human contact is meaningless and bleak.

I wrench my mind into neutral, and listen to the cacophony of evening time in the ward. I grab a newspaper and furiously read my way through it. Without registering that this too is a record of the real life that I am trying to elude.

296

Two hours pass. Lights out. "The Addict" gets up and lurches to the toilet a couple of times, swearing under his breath as he collides with something he considers an obstruction. I manage to get some sleep during the night in spite of the constant background hum, restless slumber and patrolling staff. And yet the murmur of muted human voices and soft footsteps is somehow comforting.

Morning. I have been awake for some time – my mind has been in overdrive. My head feels clear and my thinking has been cruelly honest. Self-criticism is painful but necessary. I have been reviewing my life – my earlier mistakes, the idyll of my few years as a family man, my withdrawal from the human race following the terrible loss of my wife and son, my rejection of any redemptive rehabilitation, and my present solitary existence. I have realised that there has been a double tragedy – one caused by chance and the other self-inflicted. For years there was no meaning and nothing mattered.

My stay in this hospital could be seen as a tiny echo of my life – illness and the process of recovery. It is a pinprick of light, which has reminded me that I don't have to stay in the dark. My days lack colour, they lack people. They lack communication, connection. Those I have to come into contact with are given nicknames and put in pigeonholes in my head. They don't – or didn't – matter very much to me. I could change. I can try. I need the Adas and the Debbies of this world to pull me back.

I test the water by initiating a conversation with Malcolm (I consign the label "Red Eye" to the delete file my head), and we pass a convivial ten minutes discussing our political differences. I then ask Dan, which is "The Addict's" name, how he is today, and receive a watery wave of his hand, and a cough. But not a snarl, as before. Gordon – no longer "Poor Dad" – is again comatose, but after breakfast, while I have a short walk around the ward, I see him watching me with a puzzled expression on his crumpled features, and give him an encouraging smile. So far so good.

Then in comes Amazing Ada. Today, whilst whizzing round with her mop, she tells me that three years ago she re-married. "Just for company, mind you. I'm too old to want a bit of 'how's yer father'." After the wedding they went to Margate for three days – but it rained. Her husband is a retired postman, and they get on just fine because he's in the habit of waking up early too. He's got eight grandchildren, so that makes fifteen in all. It's hard remembering their birthdays.

I decide to put the big thorny question, "Do you believe in God?"

"Course I do." The reply is prompt and positive. "He's my Lord and always 'as been. I can't imagine me life without me faith. I've told 'im that when I gets to heaven, I'll do my bit by keeping the place clean an' cheerful." She cackles a laugh and flourishes her mop. Picking up the bucket in her other hand, she marches off, booting the "Wet Floor" plastic cone into position with a nifty backward kick that wouldn't be out of place in an Arsenal match. I sigh with admiration. Malcolm grins at me. She is almost the complete archetype of the charlady with a heart of gold, but that doesn't make her any less impressive.

Shortly afterwards the doctors come round, one shy with a freckly innocent face and a shiny new stethoscope hanging out of a pocket, but looking as if he should be still wearing a satchel, and the other in a crumpled suit, older and self important with a large nose and a stern expression. This is my consultant and during the three brief minutes he gives me, my problem and its treatment, I discover that tomorrow I will be discharged.

At last I can leave! Instinctively I feel that I simply cannot wait to get out, and that I can't put up with another twenty-four hours of this un-themed, unpredictable chaotic clutter of people, equipment, intrusive sounds and unvoiced pain. And then, almost immediately, I feel a spasm of anguish that soon I'll have to leave the hospital, its recovery programme and its liberating medicine! And go home. Alone.

Later that day I decide to discuss my dilemma (to re-join humanity or reject it) with Malcolm. After listening to my

298

agonising attempts to explain what I mean, he clearly thinks me mad. Blokes just don't go around baring their souls in public. This is something I obviously need to learn! Embarrassing one's friends won't do. How do I extricate myself?

I grin and tell him that I need a drink and clearly have too much blood in my alcohol stream. He looks relieved that I've returned to normal, and agrees that he too would like to nip out to the pub. We decide to meet up for a drink after we've both left the hospital. That'll be something different – I haven't been to a pub for a long while. (We probably won't do this but it's a nice idea.)

At visiting time that evening, Malcolm's wife comes in, carrying a box of chocolates. I barely noticed her the last time, but now I study her face as she talks animatedly with her husband and tells him her news. She has a kind expression but though she is clearly trying to be calm and cheerful, she is tired and has an undercurrent of worry just below the surface. Her husband introduces me and we exchange a few words about where I live. She digests the fact that I'm a widower (I can't think why I told them that), she says we both look much better (I'm not sure that he does), and she smiles warmly and encouragingly at us both. After she's left, he shares the chocolates and a joke with me.

After supper Dan tentatively approaches me – I am sitting in my chair – to ask if he can borrow the newspaper. I smile and hand it over, with some inane question to him like, "How's it going then?"

He stares at me, shrugs and turning to go back to his own bed mutters, "O.K. Thanks," over his shoulder. He has even further to go to claw his way back than I do!

Gordon, poor fellow, is lying on his back with his mouth open and his eyes closed. He's too far down the track to make any sense of the world any more. But that doesn't mean to say he hasn't had a full and productive life. Now, nearing the end, it is the acceptance and consideration of those who care for him that lends him some dignity.

After listening to some music through my headphones, I settle down to sleep. Tomorrow morning I shall be disconnected

299

from my tube – and from the hospital. I might see Ada again, if I'm lucky, but sadly not Debbie.

The night nurse puts out the lights, and the ward becomes dim as we all move obediently into night mode. In a few hours I shall be gone from here, returned to home and health. When I turn my back and walk away, I may have taken a step in the right direction. And one step leads to another. I shall tread hopefully and carefully – I don't want to slip.